One Great Lie

ALSO BY DEB CALETTI

The Queen of Everything

Honey, Baby, Sweetheart

Wild Roses

The Nature of Jade

The Fortunes of Indigo Skye

The Secret Life of Prince Charming

The Six Rules of Maybe

Stay

The Story of Us

The Last Forever

Essential Maps for the Lost

A Heart in a Body in the World

Girl, Unframed

AND DON'T MISS

He's Gone

The Secrets She Keeps

What's Become of Her

DEB CALETTI

NEW YORK LONDON TORONTO SYDNEY NEW DELHI

An imprint of Simon & Schuster Children's Publishing Division
1230 Avenue of the Americas, New York, New York 10020

Jacket photograph of dress by ariwasabi/iStock, of clothesline
by Brad and Jen Butcher/Stocksy, and of Venice canal by Joanna Nixon/Stocksy
Author photograph by Susan Doupé

Interior design by Tom Daly
The text for this book was set in Adobe Caslon Pro.
Manufactured in the United States of America
First Edition
2 4 6 8 10 9 7 5 3 1
Library of Congress Cataloging-in-Publication Data
Names: Caletti, Deb, author.
Title: One great lie / Deb Caletti.
Description: First edition. | New York : Atheneum, [2021] | Summary: Charlotte's dream of a summer writing workshop in Venice with her favorite author brings the chance to investigate the mysterious poet in her family's past, meet fascinating new people, and learn truths about her idol.
Identifiers: LCCN 2020037539 (print) | LCCN 2020037540 (ebook) | ISBN 9781534463172 (hardcover) | ISBN 9781534463196 (ebook)
Subjects: CYAC: Foreign study—Fiction. | Authors—Fiction. | Betrayal—Fiction. | Sexism—Fiction. | Venice (Italy)—Fiction. | Italy—Fiction. | Mystery and detective stories.
Classification: LCC PZ7.C127437 One 2021 (print) | LCC PZ7.C127437 (ebook) | DDC [Fic]—dc23
LC record available at https://lccn.loc.gov/2020037539
LC ebook record available at https://lccn.loc.gov/2020037540

For Charlie Zephyr

Chapter One

Lucchesia Sbarra, poet.

Published Rime, *and possibly another volume, both lost.*
(1576–unknown)

Picture it—the exact coordinates where Charlotte's life will change and never change back: a table in the Seattle Public Library. On it—the book *Biographical Encyclopedia of Literature: Sixteenth Century.* Above—an angled ceiling of enormous glass panes, which makes the library feel like a space colony of the future. Just ahead—yellow escalators and green elevators, shades of disco-era neon that sometimes give Charlotte a migraine.

Now picture Charlotte herself—her long dark braid is over one shoulder. She's wearing a sweatshirt, zipped all the way up, which looks kind of goofy, but who cares—she's always cold. She's trying to write a report on a long-ago female Renaissance poet Isabella di Angelo but can only find information about the guy everyone already knows about, Antonio Tasso. There's tons and tons of stuff about Tasso and his poetry. But all she's been able to unearth about Isabella di Angelo is this one fact, repeated again and again. Charlotte's brown eyes stare down at it: *Tasso's longtime paramour. Paramour*: old-fashioned word for someone Tasso had sex with.

Charlotte's good friend Yasmin is across from her, studying for her macroeconomics test and sucking on sour apple Jolly Ranchers. Yas loves those. Whenever she leans over to talk to Charlotte, her breath is a great burst of fake-apple sweet. Charlotte's boyfriend, Adam, is there too. He sits to her right, his knees touching hers under the table, the sleeves of his hoodie pushed up to his elbows. He's always touching her like this, like she's his lucky rock, or like he's worried she'll run off if he doesn't hang on.

Nate sprawls in the chair next to Yasmin. They've been together since sophomore year, and Nate has stopped working out, and he has a little splootch of belly over his stomach, and he's on his third day in that Kurt Cobain T-shirt, and this bothers Yasmin because he doesn't seem to be trying anymore. Also, his pits have a slightly tangy odor, which is a constant problem for Yas. It's the end of spring quarter, right before break, and Charlotte and Yasmin have serious stuff to do, because they're perpetual overachievers with lots of AP classes, and graduation is coming. Charlotte's got this term paper, which is going nowhere, and Yasmin's final is going to be brutal.

Adam and Nate are just fucking around, though. Nate made a triangle football out of a note card, and Adam has his hands up like goalposts, and they're flicking it back and forth and making whoops of victory and *Aw!*s of defeat, and they're basically being way too loud for a library. A guy with a big beard and a backpack scowls at them. A little kid stares, wide-eyed, like they're a riveting puppet show, maybe wishing he could get away with stuff like that.

"Guys, *stop*," Yasmin says. "Show some *maturity*." She sounds like her mother right then, Charlotte thinks. Yasmin's mom is very serious, and always on her case about her grades even though she gets straight As. But Charlotte wants them to knock it off too. She and Yas are both the polite, anxious sort of people who worry about getting in trouble. She wishes she weren't, but she can't help it.

Nate tries to grab Yasmin's butt, and she pulls away, annoyed. Charlotte looks up to see if the librarian is watching.

And that's when it happens: Charlotte's eyes scoot in a fateful arc, from Nate's hand on Yasmin's butt, across the space of the library, stopping just short of the librarian's desk, because there it is, that flyer. It's posted on a noticeboard hanging on the wall by the bank of escalators. She's not sure why she didn't see it before, because the words practically call out to her now, which is a cliché, but true.

Anything about writing calls out to her, though. Short-story contests, ads in the *Stranger* for writing classes, articles online. New notebooks, packages of pens, fat blocks of printer paper. Anything that has to do with writing has drawn her since she wrote her first story, "The Land of the Mixed-Up

Animals," when she was seven. Wait, no. Anything about writing has pulled her in probably since she was five and read this line in *Where the Wild Things Are*: *That very night in Max's room a forest grew*. Is that beautiful or what? Words were forests to explore in your very own room, warm tents to hide in, and magic cloaks that transformed you. *I'LL EAT YOU UP!* Max shouts to his mother, so words also let you be what you wished you could be—impolite and bold, someone who could talk back and get into trouble and not care.

After that book, even when she was that little, Charlotte would run to her room to madly scratch out some idea, and since then, piles of *stories* grew, her own forest where she could be wild. Her mind started to be a writer's mind, with ideas constantly falling forward like an annoying wisp of hair you have to keep pushing aside. She stumbled on a secret: writing was a place she could be honest in ways she couldn't in real life. And after that incredible discovery, all the sentences were roads leading to something *meant*, and all the ideas she'd urriedly scratch down were doorways to her future. She never wanted to be a veterinarian, then an astronaut, then a scientist, like most kids. Only a writer. And that report she's working on, about that poet from way back in the 1500s? Isabella di Angelo was a great-great-great-(too many greats to count)-grandmother on her mother's side, so, see? Isabella's existence is *proof* that writing is in Charlotte's *blood*.

A lot of people (okay, her father) don't take her and her writing seriously. He acts like she's making pictures with macaroni and glitter. But she has the will and intention of an artist already, even if she's young and has a lot to learn. She's making art *right now*, like you do when you're an apprentice, and so is her friend Rebecca (photography), and Dara (painting), and if you don't think so, you're wrong, Charlotte's sure. Her biggest dream: to say something that *says something*. How great would it be, to be one of those young writers you hear about, published ridiculously young? Her own photo in an artistic black-and-white on a jacket flap—can you even imagine it? She can. She does. She believes it can happen. She *wants* it. She can feel that want like a fire inside. No, that's a cliché, too, and you're supposed to avoid those, if you're a writer. But the point is, it burns like a passion does.

Charlotte rises from her chair. "Hey," Adam says. He reaches out to tug the tail of her sweatshirt to bring her back to him. He thinks she's mad at him for being obnoxious in the library. But she just wants to see that flyer. From there, she can only read the words *Aspiring Writers.*

Up close now . . . Wow. It's advertising a new summer study abroad program, one you have to apply for. It looks expensive. Very. So, no way. It's in Italy, on a private island, La Calamita, across the water from Venice. She's never even heard of that island, and Italy feels like a planet in another cosmos. There's a photo of a villa. Her family could never afford that.

But wait.

In smaller print: *Scholarships Available.*

Her heart actually speeds up with thrill-fear. But then,

she sees another daunting phrase: *College Students*. She isn't one now, but she will be in the fall. Does that even count? She'll be enrolled. Technically, she'll be one, right? There's nothing about age, but, God, she'd probably be the youngest one there. This gives her an anxious whoosh of intimidation. She spins the rings on her fingers like she does when she gets nervous.

There's also a romantic, grainy photo of a Venetian canal, with a gondolier guiding his boat under a bridge. It's a basic shout of *Venice*, but who cares. It's not corny or unoriginal to her. Not at all. It feels like fate. She's in that library right this minute studying Isabella di Angelo, and Isabella di Angelo lived and died in Venice way back in the 1500s. Her mother's side of the family was there for eons until her grandma moved to the US as a little girl. What are the odds? It feels like an offering, meant just for her.

Charlotte's never even been on an airplane. A place like Venice is so hard to imagine, it almost doesn't seem real—a postcard place. But now, look. She's actually touching the glossy paper.

She removes the pushpin and takes the pamphlet down to examine it more closely. And that's when something even more stunning and astonishing and terrifying and marvelous occurs, because inside the fold is Luca Bruni's photo. She knows this photo; of course she does. It's the one where he's straddling a chair, his thin shoulders leaning toward the camera, his long arms folded. His hair is kind of a mess, and his nose is a mountain on his narrow face, but his dark eyes look right at you, *into* you.

Luca Bruni! Holy shit, Luca Bruni has a summer abroad writing program in Venice!

It's incredible. God. God! He's one of her favorite writers ever. Just the thought of him gives Charlotte that very particular reader's pleasure, a sigh mixed with a thrill. Just the thought of him also gives her that particular *writer's* pleasure, a sigh mixed with awe. Under his image, there's a small paragraph with his bio, but who needs it? Who doesn't know him? He's known all over the world, a celebrity, the way only the tiniest handful of authors are.

As she stands in the library holding the pamphlet, Charlotte's heart begins to thump in double-espresso time. Above her is the futuristic ceiling, and all around her are words, old words, new words, words from when Isabella di Angelo walked the stone streets of Venice in 1573. But more importantly, Luca Bruni stares up at her from that pamphlet, and two shelves over and four shelves up are some of the most beautiful words she's ever read. She can lead you right to it, Luca Bruni's shelf.

The words inside *A Mile of Faces* are so beautiful. The words inside *Under the Sudden Sky*, *The Tide of Years*, *The Forever King*, and *The Glass Ship* (oh, especially that one) are beautiful too. All of Luca Bruni's work is beautiful, and powerful, and meaningful, and raging, and funny, and soul-crushing, and life-changing, full of blood and bone shards and heartbeats. And in his interviews, Luca Bruni himself is powerful, and meaningful, and raging, and funny; arrogant, and tender, but sometimes cruel, too, full of blood and bone shards and heartbeats.

This is what she knows more than anything else as she stands there, clutching the pamphlet, her chest filling with hope. She knows this without a doubt: Luca Bruni's words—they will shatter you.

There's something she doesn't know, though. Not yet.

His words will shatter you, but so might he.

Chapter Two

Amedea Aleardi, poet.

Little is known of her life, and most of her work is lost.

(Dates unknown)

Charlotte feels some sort of determination, an iron core of it, rise in her body. A challenge, petrifying but exhilarating. This is what a dream feels like. An engine cranking up, a sky that stretches on and on. She replaces the pushpin, but not the pamphlet. It's wrong to take it; she should just write down the information, but she's already feeling proprietary and competitive. The fewer people that apply, the better.

Yasmin raises one eyebrow. They stare at each other, a meaningful stare full of paragraphs. Charlotte has looked into Yasmin's eyes since they sat next to each other in that horrible algebra class in the ninth grade, when Mr. Shattuck would scream and throw the whiteboard eraser at anyone who talked. Charlotte would get bad, bad stomachaches in that class because she can't stand it when anyone yells. It scares her, when you're as good as you can be but still get screamed at. After that, she and Yas were forever friends, same as two soldiers in a trench.

Charlotte flashes Yas the pamphlet before tucking it into her backpack and zipping it up tight. Yasmin gives a slow nod of acknowledgment and grins. They know each other so well. Besides, Yas understands going for the impossible. She's trying for a summer internship at NASA.

"Totally," Yasmin says. It's an entire pep talk in a single word. Sometimes all you need is just one other person to believe along with you.

"Score!" Nate shouts, and pounds the table with his fists.

It's the kind of beautiful Seattle day that makes people wear shorts and take the tops down on their convertibles even though it's too cold, if anyone's honest. Which also means it's a day where everyone in the city heads to Green Lake. After they leave the library, Charlotte sits on a blanket with Adam at their favorite spot on the grass, near the boat rentals. Yasmin and Nate run across the street to Starbucks. She and Adam are alone, aside from a million people at the park, so they kiss, and Adam sneaks his hand up her shirt.

They've been together since the fall when Adam and his dad moved here from Portland. Right away, she was drawn to the moody, brooding loner-ness about him, like she was light and he was dark, so together they were a full rotation of the Earth. He was so different from Owen Burke, her boyfriend during sophomore year, student body treasurer, tennis team captain, someone who would never step on a crack, just in case. Nope, Adam had shadings of her first serious crush, Jake Kerchek, eighth grade—the same piercing eyes and mop of hair, only Jake was slightly cruel (he made fun of her for being in orchestra) and mostly ignored her, except for when they were lab partners, where she did most of the work.

Charlotte probably has some messed-up draw to darkness, who knows, but Adam plays the guitar and he's really good, and she loves that. He has that curly brown hair, and he's thin, and she likes that, too, or rather, she likes the way his jeans just lay on his hips as if they're balanced on a hanger. She was attracted to Adam in ways she was never attracted to Owen Burke, and when she had sex for the first time in Adam's bed when his dad wasn't home, she didn't feel like she'd lost her virginity or anything else. She felt like she'd gained something: a secret, like the hidden, zippered compartment of a suitcase that makes it larger.

Now Adam's tongue is slipping into the corners of her mouth, and his fingers are wriggling under the elastic of her bra. Usually, Charlotte loves kissing him, loves her skin on his skin, but she's distracted. She's thinking about what story she should write to submit with that application. Something strong, something Luca Bruni will relate to. Most people probably know him from that TV series they did of his book *One Great Lie*, but then again, *A Mile of Faces* is the one everyone studies in high school or college, the one that his fans always name as their favorite. It isn't Charlotte's favorite, though. It's great, but

The Glass Ship is *hers*. She feels ownership about it like that. Same as you do when you love a song from a band that no one's really heard of yet.

She's pretty sure *The Glass Ship* is Luca Bruni's most personal and biographical book too. It's just a guess, but a lot of details match the ones from his childhood—a sad, silent mother; an abusive, absent father who left them alone and poor in the village of Arquà Petrarca to go work in the US. Luca Bruni's depression and mood swings, present forever after that.

Charlotte has the (ridiculous, childish, okay, but so what) feeling that if he knows *The Glass Ship* is her favorite, he'll be pleased with her, like she can see something about him that other people don't usually see. Maybe she should write about her own loneliness, since the ache of it drips off the pages in *The Glass Ship*, or about her silent, absent father and angry mother. He'll feel a connection to her maybe, like she feels to him.

"Char?" Adam pulls away and looks at her. Ugh! This sounds awful, since his hands were up her shirt, but she sort of forgot he was there, and now he's noticed. That pamphlet in her bag is what she feels desire for right then, not Adam. She just wants to get home and get started.

"Yas and Nate are coming." It's true, thank goodness—Nate's holding the cardboard tray, and Yas pretends to stick a finger down her throat from seeing them make out. It's a good excuse—Charlotte doesn't want Adam to see the secret plan in her eyes. He's always worried she's about to break up with him. It's like she's his whole world, and she doesn't want to *be* a world. She wants to be *in* a world. She wants to tromp around in it, explore it, own it. Plus, darkness is tiring sometimes. In her mind, her life has already changed, gone beyond Adam; she's somewhere in another country, and the sun is hot, and boats slide through the waters of a canal, and words are everywhere. Written, spoken, taught; genius words, beautiful words, hanging like ripe lemons from a tree.

That night before dinner, Charlotte has her laptop open. She should be working on her report, but she isn't. One: That report is becoming impossible and frustrating beyond belief, because Isabella di Angelo seems to be forgotten by everyone but her mother's family. Two: Well, on one tab, there's the website for Luca Bruni's program. A hundred times already, she's looked at the images of his villa on La Calamita, the words *La Calamita* a lyric in her head. On another tab, there's the application for the scholarship, and on another, the blank page of a new document. It's utterly empty except for her name and address in the upper left corner, and a blinking cursor.

That cursor insists. *Hurry up, hurry up. I'm waiting,* it says, again and again, and Charlotte kind of hates that cursor, but she kind of loves it too. It has the tick of a clock. Clocks are pressure, but they also say, *You better get going and make the most of life.*

A warm and buttery smell comes upstairs from the kitchen. Her mother, Adele, is back from work at Dr. Denton, DDS's, where she scrapes and sprays and peers into the dark caverns of mouths, handing tools to Dr. Denton before he asks, anticipating his every fucking need. Those are Adele's words. *All the dirty work of the dentist for a fraction of the pay!* Downstairs, she bangs pans around. The pans sound mad. Adele sounds mad a lot, even when she's not talking. Charlotte feels guilty at that sound, really guilty. She's gotten so good at guilt that she feels it whenever *anyone* is displeased or upset, or when she's been a disappointment, or hasn't given someone what they want. She should go down and help, but mad isn't exactly inviting.

In the room next door, Charlotte's little sister, Ella, plays some boy-band music. Adele yells for Ella to turn it down. This same scene has occurred at least twelve million times over the course of Charlotte's life already. Marvin, their Jack Russell terrier, lies on Charlotte's bed, snoring and farting as he sleeps.

"Oh, Marv," she says, and waves her hand.

It's silly to even start on a story. Dinner will be ready any minute. Still, Charlotte's dying to get to it. Instead, she fills in the easy parts of the application, the basic name-and-address stuff. Suddenly, Marv shoots off the bed, a dog rocket, barking his head off, racing downstairs as the front door opens.

"Hey, guys!" her father yells.

Charlotte hears him trudge up the stairs. *Trudge*—it's the exact right word, her writer-mind says. Her father has been gone for a week, but aside from Marv, no one dashes over to greet him because this is usual life. He's a traveling salesman, though Charlotte only sees the traveling part. The sales part is a bit of a mystery. She's not even exactly sure what he sells. Something to do with cellular technology. The wireless something-something that connects to the other something.

"Hey, Dad," she calls.

Through her half-open door, she can see him in her parents' bedroom. He loosens his tie. He heaves his suitcase onto a chair and unzips it, retrieving his toiletry kit. Most of the time, he keeps his suitcase packed. Now, he disappears into their bathroom, and Charlotte hears a flood of peeing and then the opening and shutting of drawers, as if he can't find things. When he returns after a trip, he seems weary and distracted and uncomfortable—lost, even. Their house is the hotel in a foreign city, and his real life is elsewhere. He spends a lot of time reading things on his tablet and makes very little conversation, like he's waiting at the airport and they're strangers he doesn't want to make eye contact with, in case they start asking him where he's from.

When Luca Bruni writes of loneliness, when he says his heart has a hole that the wind whistles through, she knows just what he means.

At the dinner table, the pan of mac and cheese is passed around, but the tension is the actual main course. You can stick a fork in it and eat it. Ella taps her foot to Charlotte's. She catches Charlotte's eyes. She makes an *uh-oh* face, her eyes big with alarm. Charlotte and Ella have a whole silent language of leg pinches and hand squeezes and glances. Mostly, those things just say *watch out*.

"This is good, hon. Thanks," Charlotte's dad says.

"Well, we're glad you could join us."

Adele's sarcasm . . . How would Charlotte write this? It's the pointed end of a shovel scraping around Charlotte's insides. And, you know, Charlotte gets it, she does—her mom is lonely too, same as Charlotte is, and mad, and left behind. Maybe Charlotte is also mad, but it's hard to hear her own feelings when Adele's are so loud. Adele's feelings are a giant, fierce animal that takes up the whole room. Adele is also smart and funny, and loves them fiercely, but she also hates fiercely and is impatient fiercely and critical fiercely. *Fiercely* is a land you must tiptoe across so you don't get blown up by a hidden mine. *Fiercely* has you cringing and waiting for something awful, pretty much on a permanent basis. *I'LL EAT YOU UP!* Max shouts at his mother, but Charlotte would never dare do that.

"How's school been, Char?" her dad asks.

How? Twenty million things happen in one day alone. Her dad doesn't really know her. Then again, sometimes it feels like *no one* really knows her. Not even Yasmin, or Adam, or her second closest friend, Carly. Charlotte has secret spaces, and private thoughts, and unspeakable wishes, and, God, wouldn't it be great to have just one right person you could show your true, unhidden self to?

"Good," she says.

"How're things with you, Ella?"

"Good," Ella says. Another kick under the table.

"Wow. This conversation is riveting." Adele clanks her fork down. "Charlotte's doing a huge research project. Ella's making a to-scale model of the Parthenon that's already required three separate trips to Michaels, if you want to know what's going on."

Ella pushes her plate away. She rolls the corner of her paper napkin into something that looks like what Luke James and his friends smoke out by the shop building at school.

"Mom . . . ," Charlotte pleads, because, ugh! Can't Adele just be pleasant for once? Can't she *try*? The vicious circle is clear as day. Her mother is mad because her father keeps leaving, and her father keeps leaving because her mother is mad.

"What?"

"He's been gone for a whole . . ." This isn't a good idea. She shuts up. The *he* moves his macaroni around his plate.

"You always have to take his side, don't you?"

They sit in silence. Charlotte can actually hear her sister swallow her milk. Her mother, with her short dark hair starting to get tinsels of gray, stares out the window at a different life. Now the horrible tornado of guilt starts in Charlotte's stomach and spirals up. It's hard to explain why she feels guilty all the time; she just does. A silence like this could have been used as a medieval torture device. Her whole life is devouring her, slow second by slow second. She loves her family, really, a lot. It just seems like maybe love would feel different than this.

She's got to get out of there. Do you see how badly she needs that writing program? A trip that takes her away? She wants to go to her room, to at least disappear inside of a book, because books let you go somewhere else while staying exactly where you are. She weighs the pros and cons of saying *excuse me* and leaving. *Fiercely* also could mean rages. Adele's loving breath had been on Charlotte's cheek, but her furious breath had too. These silences are almost worse, though. They could eat through metal, like the nitric acid from AP Chemistry, and all Charlotte has is her skin to protect her.

She stays put. After dinner, Charlotte and Ella clear the dishes. Upstairs, there's the sound of muffled, intense voices. A fight. The macaroni and cheese has lost its shine and has settled into a congealed clump of defeat. Even though there's only a little left, Charlotte sticks it in the fridge so they don't have to wash the pan. She lets the fridge door smack shut. This is all the revolt and rebellion she can manage.

"Want to come to my room?" Charlotte asks. Ella's only twelve, but she has really bad anxiety, and fighting always makes it worse.

"Nah, I'm okay," Ella says.

Charlotte kisses the top of her sister's head. It smelled like Suave, version strawberry. In her room, Charlotte puts her headphones on. She can't hear the argument, but she can still feel the tension. Tension is in her bones. She has tension for bone marrow, and stress deep down in her DNA.

Any thoughts of working on the application are gone. She can't do creative and hopeful things when a big mattress of sad-guilt-gross lies on her. Maybe this is what it feels like to be depressed. She always thought depressed meant crying all the time, but maybe not.

Charlotte takes off her clothes and gets into bed. She opens *The Glass Ship* to where the bookmark is. She never bends back the pages in Bruni's books. It's a sign of respect, his place in the hierarchy of beloved authors. It's okay to be careless with some books—you can fold the pages, crinkle the cover, let the bathwater ripple the paper. But not Bruni's. She treats them like something sacred.

This is her third time reading *The Glass Ship*, even though she never usually reads a book more than once. Tonight, she plans to travel very carefully through it, to study it, before she works on her story.

Before long, the studying vanishes. She's lost in the novel. She *lets* herself get lost. The words surround her, hug her, protect her. The glass ship isn't an actual ship. It's a small toy Bruni's character Nino finds in the dirt behind his family home in the poor village in Italy. It's a metaphor for the fictional-but-not family in the book—fragile, lost, buried in the earth, the last place a ship belongs.

She reads and reads. It gets really late. The fighting has stopped. The moon has lifted up into her window. Her guilt and sadness have also lifted. The thing is, Bruni shows how he is broken, and she is broken, too, and maybe they are broken in some of the same ways. It's so comforting. Someone *understands*. He sees her already in the way she's longed for, just through his words. She isn't as alone as she feels, because look—someone else has felt this exact same way.

She imagines him standing around at some literary party, or drinking a glass of wine by a fireplace, or doing whatever great thing he's doing right then. And this is hard to explain, but he, at the literary party or wherever, once felt the same way as she does now, in her twin bed with her old *Finding Nemo* sheets, her long black hair stuck up in a messy bun, her toe polish chipped. They are together somehow in the hard world, and if he could survive and be as magnificent as he is, you know, maybe there's hope for her. This is weird to think; he's old, older, too much older, and she doesn't mean it how it sounds, but they are in that bed together too. She holds his words right there in that bed. They are a beautiful wave inside of her.

To connect to people like that—it's magic. It's intimate. Nothing is more intimate than someone who knows your heart. Nothing is more dangerous than someone who knows your heart. Holding someone's heart like that is power.

Chapter Three

Girolama Castagna, poet.

Nothing is known about her, except her married name, Malatesta, listed with her one surviving poem.

(1600 or so)

Charlotte has to sit through AP Chemistry and AP Lit and AP Calculus, and then lunch, and then AP US Government and then Beginning Judo (the only elective available, ugh), and then orchestra practice after school, and then a fight with Adam in the car on the way home, because he thought she was flirting with Ben Silver (bass) because she looks right over at him from the viola section. Carly says Adam is showing Red Flags, but Charlotte is sure that he just needs extra reassurance because his mom left the family. She feels sorry for him, and she's seen him cry, which breaks her heart. *Feels sorry for* and *love* are easy to get mixed up. Plus, that guitar, and those jeans. They're the kind with buttons, and buttons are really great to unbutton. Damage and sexiness are easy to get mixed up too.

She can't wait to get out of Adam's car, though, and get home to her story. Right at the lyrical finale of Symphony no. 3 in F Major, she got the idea of what to write. She argues with more energy than she even feels, just to hurry up and leave. She slams the door. Within minutes of going upstairs, Adam starts calling and texting, and she turns her phone off.

The story is called "The Blue Night," and it's about a sad and lonely girl who takes a rowboat out onto Green Lake and almost drowns but doesn't. The boat is buried under the water, same as the one in *The Glass Ship* is buried under the ground, but she doesn't even really realize this until later. She sits at her desk and pours her heart out on the laptop she bought with the money from her summer job at Java Jive. She gets right in there and feels every word and gives them to the page as if she's offering her tender, vital heart.

It comes out with such passion that she thinks it might be pretty good. It's the kind of passion when, God, you need something *so bad*. She should wait until morning to look at it again before she sends it. Luca Bruni is also an adjunct professor at Boston University, teaching in one of the oldest creative writing programs there is, so this is no time for punctuation mistakes or amateur sloppiness. But she doesn't wait. She reads it after dinner and makes a few changes and finishes filling out that application online.

She attaches "The Blue Night" and presses send. *Send* is one of the scariest words there is. Her heart thuds like a fist on a door. The fist says, *Open up*. She has no idea if the door will actually open or if it will stay shut. It's such a large dream against such impossible odds that she tries to make herself forget what she's just done.

Of course, she can't sleep.

The moon shines a bright beam into her room. From where she lies, she can see that laptop. It's open a little, so there's a narrow wedge of blue. There's the old, old, ancient moon glow, and the new-today glow of technology, but they're both light.

Charlotte kicks off the covers. She gets out of bed. She quietly takes the stairs to their rec room. The house was built in 1906, but its basement was decorated in 1998. There's a stenciled border of ivy around the ceiling, and a pine computer desk from IKEA, with built-in slots for CDs that no longer exist. There's a floral couch that's seen better days, the cushions sunken and soft from years of tired bodies plunking down, and an answering machine from when there were answering machines.

Lots of time periods are smushing together, because right then, she tips the spine of a certain book. She has to stand on her toes in order to reach it. Oh, man, she has to be careful; that book is so, so old, a treasure, valuable, maybe the most cherished thing their family owns, and that's why it's in the highest, farthest spot.

The Verses by Isabella di Angelo. It's so old that when Charlotte brings it down, an ancient smell comes with it. The mustiness and history of five hundred years, the brittleness, too. This book was written in a place where water surrounded it, and it smells like water. Deep, old water, like it had been drowned for centuries and then brought up dripping.

The Verses is almost five hundred years old, but it still always opens up to the same page—the poem called "In Guerra," or, in English, "At War." Charlotte shouldn't even be touching this small book with its vellum cover, which resembles a coat she once had, made of ivory pleather. Of course, the book's not made of ivory pleather, but calfskin, silky yet hardened, and the pages are crispy from age and easily damaged. The paper is crackly and as yellowed as an old blister.

It opens to that particular poem because there's a slip of paper inside the book, a translation of "At War," written down by her grandmother.

Even in English, the poem is hard to understand, and it makes your head hurt when you try: *With capes of panther and crescent shields, each soldier carries a quiver of arrows and a well try'd Spear. The troops in Burnisht Silver, the troops in Burnisht Gold, gaze upon each other, their Foes.*

The poem is about Alexander the Great meeting a bunch of soldiers, Mr. Olivera told the class in AP World History and Lit last year. Because, of course, everyone knows this poem, the very same one: "In Guerra (At War)." Only, it's written by Antonio Tasso, the most widely read poet and novelist of the Renaissance, the guy who inspired composers, artists, and writers for generations, the ancient dude who tormented every student required to analyze that poem. Two years ago, there was that hit Broadway rock opera based on his most famous novel, *La Campagna*. Everyone started wearing his image on T-shirts.

The words in Isabella di Angelo's poem are right in Charlotte's room, too. She can find them in *Contemporary Literature* by A. A. Rawlins, next to Tasso's bio. They're also in *Anthology of Stories, Poems, Plays, and Essays*. Tasso again. She never even told Mr. Olivera about Isabella and *The Verses*, because it sounds so outrageous. But many times, Charlotte has oh-so-carefully opened *The Verses* to the title page to see the date it was published: MDLXXIII. 1573. And she has looked up the date of Antonio Tasso's "In Guerra": 1573.

She's not the only person in their family who's wanted the answer about who really wrote that poem, or why it was there in *The Verses* under Isabella's name. Adele has tried to find out more, with no luck. Their Aunt Tony has. A few years ago, she even tried to contact a few professors who studied Tasso's work, but no one even returned her calls or emails. Their grandmother, who wrote out this poem on the airmail sheet, had wanted to know too, and so had her mother before that. Whisper to whisper to whisper, woman to woman to woman, year to year to year, sits the rumor no one else cared about: that those words were really Isabella's, not Antonio Tasso's. Stolen by him.

Maybe this was just one of those extravagant yearnings people have, like when they want to believe they were an Egyptian queen in a past life. But maybe it wasn't. No one in the family knew very much about Isabella di Angelo. Only a few facts had lasted through the centuries, and they were probably lucky to have those: She was a noblewoman of some kind. She'd maybe been in a convent, San Zaccaria, in Venice. She'd written a second book, but no one knew anything about it. She'd been Tasso's lover, one of many, from the sound of it, though how this *and* the convent thing could both be true was a mystery.

Aside from that book on their shelf, *this* was the only true proof of her existence: her connection to him. Charlotte can still recite the one line about Isabella that she's been able to find in all those days of trying to do that research report: *For many years, Tasso stayed in Florence to be near both his wife and children and his many concubines, including his longtime paramour Isabella di Angelo.*

But Charlotte understands something else: Isabella di Angelo was a real woman, who had her own heart and her own struggles and her own desire to write. Charlotte sees it in these italic swirls.

Living there in Venice during the Renaissance, well, Charlotte can't even imagine, but Isabella di Angelo *was* there, on those streets, surrounded by water-filled canals. She was real, and she had her own dream. The same dream Charlotte has. Isabella di Angelo has been forgotten, but still. Her words are in those covers, and her blood is in Charlotte, and that means Charlotte's own dream is possible.

She brings the book upstairs. The moon has been there

longer than five hundred years. It knows more than the sorry humans it shines its light on. Charlotte doesn't know why she does it, but she lifts the ancient volume up toward the moonlight. It's one of those crazy, inexplicable things you do but don't exactly know why. For good luck maybe. For a change in fortune.

Of course, when you're so full of hope and need, it's hard to remember something else about that magical, romantic moon: for eons, forever, it's been the witness to all the bad shit people do to each other.

Chapter Four

Nina Siciliana, first-known female Italian poet.

Her existence was discovered in 1780, hundreds of years after her death. Male poets claimed she was imaginary.

(Dates unknown)

The next day at school, Adam is an anxious wreck. When he sees Charlotte, he rushes to her and holds her tight like she's returned from another era in a time-travel movie. She's the star in the film of his life, a story which has little to do with the real her. She could probably do anything she wanted and he'd still love her, which feels both great and awful. His utter devotion is bringing out her worst, most uncaring parts. A tear rolls down his nose, and he wipes it with his sleeve, and his eyes are sunken as if he hasn't slept, and she lets him shove her up against her locker, because she caused him all this agony. Plus, when their clothes are off and they're under some blanket, his skin on her skin is like water against water.

Kissing is also a distraction from thoughts of foreign travel and students from around the world and a summer at Luca

Bruni's villa. She has no idea, really, how to envision it—it's all just a pile of amazing in her brain. What's a villa even, anyway? Start right there. When any of this pops into her head, she shoves it out. She refocuses on Mr. Miata discussing the impact of media on public opinion in AP US Government and forces herself to concentrate on Adam's mouth on hers, or on Carly and Jade arguing about the ending of *The Last Jedi*.

And this is basically what happens every day for the next few weeks after she presses send. She gets home from school and checks the mail that's fallen on the floor through the slot in the door, gathering up the pieces that Marvin has chewed and flung to the far corners of the room, the only exciting moment of his day. She forces herself to be casual as she looks through roof cleaning coupons and electrical bills for any response from the writing program. Nothing, nothing, and more nothing.

Dreams can be rough on you. Dreams can put you through hell until they maybe finally come true.

Things start to suck, bad. Her father leaves on another trip. Adele finds Charlotte's birth control pills tucked back in her bathroom drawer. She's in such a fury that she grabs a chunk of Charlotte's hair and yanks her head back, the little pink packet of pills looking innocent but shockingly exposed on the bathroom counter. If this were a book, it might be the whole book, girl has sex for the first time, even though this is barely the whole of her, or anyone else.

And not only is there that ugly fight, but Ella has such a

bad anxiety attack at school that she has to go to the nurse's office because she can't breathe and Charlotte has to bring her home. Charlotte's migraines start up, a machine in a factory in her head, a machine that cuts through steel, and she wants to get out of there (her house, her head), but her big dream of *out plus more* is looking stupider by the day. There's been no word, none at all, from the writing program.

Charlotte slips into a bad mood, the way a crocodile slips into a swamp, with only his eyes left above the water. Her mother flings hate-arrows at her for a week, until her anger downgrades into scowling at Charlotte's every move and saying, *Watch your tone, miss*, when Charlotte speaks. The world is suddenly full of assholes riding Charlotte's bumper when she drives herself and Ella to school, and she and Adam get in another fight because he parked far away and it was raining when they went to see a movie and he didn't care if her hair got wrecked. He never cares, he never sees, she says, but that's not really true. She's maybe trying to be awful so he'll break up with her. She decides to hate big dreams and hope both, because they can be shiny and awesome, but also stingy and downright mean.

She puts Isabella di Angelo's book back up on the shelf. The moon-prayer she made to her that night was a bust.

Charlotte shoves *The Glass Ship* under her bed, where it lies with a dusty flip-flop, some old term papers, and a pair of sunglasses she thought she'd lost. Then she brings the book back out again in case this is bad luck. It's hard to tell what's bad luck.

She tells herself to be positive. To envision the outcome she desires. To believe in herself and in fate, et cetera, et cetera.

She tells herself to stop being positive. To forget about it and be realistic. That it will only happen if it's not so important to her, et cetera, et cetera.

She's being an idiot, to feel so much about someone like Luca Bruni, who's a stranger. She doesn't know him. She should never give her heart and hope to him because of his words.

And yet, a small part of her feels sorry for anyone who's never felt that way about someone—a writer or an artist, or a singer who makes you believe that the world is a beautiful, complicated, but *meant* place, a place that's yours, to harm you and love you and lift you and open its arms to you. A writer, or an artist, or a singer, who makes you *feel*.

It's raining. Pouring. Rain drips down the windows, and whooshes through the drainpipes, and pummels the roof. The gutters pour a river. The air smells like morning: toast, and the browned-butter scent that means Adele cooked an egg.

"Dork!" Charlotte calls to Ella, who's in her room with the door shut. No answer. She knocks and then peeks in. Ella's sitting on the floor, drawing an elaborate tree in her art pad. It's Charlotte's job to make sure she and Ella don't burn the house down during spring break. "Wanna go to the library with me?"

She's still got to finish that report. She's made zero progress. If she doesn't find something about Isabella di Angelo and fast, she's going to have to go to plan B and restart the biggest project of the semester in less than ten days.

"Sure." Ella retrieves her library card from the fancy, velvet-lined jewelry box they both have, gifts from their dad. When she lifts the lid, a ballerina dances in a circle inside. It seems like their dad wants them to be like that—pretty, and only seen when they're let out of a box. He's always praising their cousin Andrea, who's fragile and soft-spoken, *a beautiful young lady*. To be honest, they kind of hate Cousin Andrea, who gives half-cruel compliments like, *Oh. Interesting shirt. I like it.*

A jewelry box is a great spot to keep a library card, though, Charlotte thinks. The place where you store valuable things.

"Someday, I won't need you to drive me anymore."

"True."

"Maybe we should practice," Ella says.

"Nice try." Charlotte turns the key to their old, ailing Honda. She looks over at her sister with her dark hair tucked over each ear and her serious brown eyes, and her skinny legs, getting longer by the day. She thinks about all the things she knows that Ella doesn't know yet, and she feels a rush of love for her, which disappears in a second, because Ella starts messing around with the radio, just to be annoying.

The Seattle library is a strange place to try to go backward in time, because it's so space-age. Ella heads off, her backpack over one shoulder. Charlotte hunts through *Biographical Encyclopedia of Literature: Sixteenth Century* and *The Oxford Companion to Italian*

Literature. No Isabella. Good luck with *Annali d'Italianistica* or *Forum Italicum*—she'd need a translator for those. She goes back to the enormous *Italian Literature and Its Times* and *Tasso's Men and the Literate Republic*, in-library use only.

An hour later, she only has more and more information about Tasso and his life in Venice—his background, his work, his legacy. Accolades upon accolades. *Genius, master.* Blah, blah, and more blah, about him, him, him.

It's not going to happen. Isabella is an unknown woman, who lived a million years ago, in a foreign country. Even that call to Aunt Tony, Ancestry.com fanatic and collector of Precious Moments figurines, did nothing to help. *There's got to be more information somewhere,* Aunt Tony said. Charlotte knows exactly where that *somewhere* is, but she's given up hope about that.

Tasso is in those books, big as life, though. If he was the subject of Charlotte's report, no problem. He's got *volumes* written about him. But Isabella is gone, lost to history except for the fact that she had sex with the guy.

The migraine is back, and so is Charlotte's irritation. It's been weeks, and she hasn't heard from Luca Bruni's writing program, either. Time to face reality: Isabella di Angelo doesn't matter. No one cares.

Ella has more books than she can hold. They should've remembered the bags they bring to Trader Joe's. When they go to the library, it's always like they're hauling food home, food if you were pioneers about to get snowed in for the long winter.

The rain has stopped, and the sun has come out, and everything looks like it's just been born, so Charlotte drives them over to the 7-Eleven on Aurora to get a Slurpee. She gets lucky and finds a parking spot at Green Lake, next to a big RV with the license plate CAPTAIN ED. They sit on the grass and play their favorite game, The Next Dog That Passes Is Yours.

Ella is deftly using her straw-spoon, angling it up and down with the speed and agility of a kayaker. Charlotte gets stuck with a corgi, which is hilarious, because it looks like a sourdough loaf with legs. Ella laughs so hard that Charlotte can see her grape-purple tongue. Bikes whiz past, skateboarders. She tells herself all the stuff disappointed people say. Snap out of it! Look here, at this day. Her stupid sister she loves like crazy. Dogs. Sun. The general goodness of people. Friends and a guy who's devoted to her. She has so much. She should be grateful. This is the truth.

When they get back home, she gathers up the QFC Coupon Saver, the cable bill, and the Venus swimsuit catalog (Gross, why do they even get this?) from the floor. Marv has terrorized a postcard for a two-for-one dinner at Homeport, and now it's in the living room, sticking out from under the couch.

She kneels, and reaches. And then she sees it.

An envelope.

Her stomach drops. Her blood stops whooshing. She can barely breathe.

Calamita & Co.

A fat envelope. Too fat to just be the word *no.*

Her heart pounds. Hey, it's a miracle, because her fingers still work. They're trembling hard, but she manages to tear the flap open. She sees the first few words. *We are happy to . . .*

"EL!" she screams. "El, El, EL!"

Ella flies down the stairs, her hand to her chest like an old lady. "What? You almost gave me heart attack!"

"God, Marv! It could have been lost under there forever!" Charlotte picks up Marv and gives him a big darn kiss on his black lips.

"HGTV Dream Home?" Ella breathes.

"Better, El. Way better. Not just a dream home. A dream *everything.*"

Chapter Five

Issicratea Monte, poet.

At age fourteen and seventeen, she achieved fame by reading her poetry at state occasions, after studying with the famous poet Luigi Groto. She died when she was twenty.

(1564–1584)

Adele also screams when she hears the news. She screams and grabs Charlotte and practically lifts her off her feet. Any anger about birth control pills is gone, any tension is gone, there's just joy and celebration. One big truth: Adele has believed in her all along. She's praised and supported every story Charlotte's written, every bad piece of poetry. Believed without a doubt. *In your blood,* she said and said again.

"Why didn't you tell me you applied?" Adele's eyes show a flash of hurt, but then she waves her hand. "Oh, never mind. This is wonderful. This is so exciting." Adele loves Luca Bruni too. She was honestly sad when the TV series *One Great Lie* got canceled, even though it was kind of lame. She read Charlotte's copy of *The Forever King* and shushed Ella when she interrupted her during the last pages. She once looked at Luca Bruni's author photo and wiggled her eyebrows up and down and said, *I mean, wow, right? What is it about him?* but Charlotte ignored her. That's surface-level love, anyway, when hers is deep and real.

She calls her dad with the news. He's in Sitka, Alaska, and it's hard to hear him. He's in a busy restaurant or a bar with lots of people having fun. He's excited and proud, but as soon as he hears *Venice*, Charlotte can tell he's slowly freaking out, asking her about hidden costs and surprise expenditures and expressing concern about her traveling to a foreign country alone. Her, a young woman. *What do we even know about this guy?* he asks. Her dad's not a reader. He doesn't get it. The only author he knows is John Grisham, so Adele gets on the phone and says excited and reassuring things, even though they don't really have all the information yet.

Charlotte calls Yas and Carly and Jade. Marv hops around on Charlotte's legs since her voice is all jazzed up. She doesn't tell Adam yet, because he'll just get all insecure and wreck the mood. Charlotte swears, not ten minutes after they hang up, Yasmin and Carly appear, ringing the doorbell like crazy. Yasmin somehow has streamers, and Carly has a heart balloon, probably from her birthday last week. Yas wraps the streamers right around Charlotte herself. Ella doesn't want to be left out and sticks a dusty plastic flower from the arrangement on the dining room table into Charlotte's hair, and Carly keeps saying "*Arrivederci, Roma!*" because it's the only Italian she knows.

Adele orders pizza, even though it's a splurge. Yasmin and Carly join them, and they eat in the living room on paper plates.

It's the best day of her life, at least so far.

Which will make that moment, right there, one of the hardest to look back at later.

In the morning, at school, she tells Adam the news before Nate or someone else tells him first.

"Why didn't you say anything about applying?" he asks. He keeps zipping the zipper of his hoodie up and down and up and down.

She shrugs. "It seemed like such a long shot."

"I'm so proud of you." He kisses her cheek. He looks really happy for her. "You know what would be great? I could come. I've got all that money saved from Mr. Tel Tech." Mr. Tel Tech is his father's company, and he's worked there every summer since he was thirteen.

"I think it's just, you know, for the people in the program."

"I don't mean stay *there*. Somewhere near there. We could hang out in your free time." He takes her hands. Her cheeks flush. She's not sure what the flush is. Embarrassment, maybe, or maybe anger, or maybe the rush of feeling that's like she's shoving him without actually shoving him. Darkness isn't just tiring. It's tiring plus tiring equals exhausted.

"Yeah, we'll see," she says.

It goes better, way better, with Ms. Perlman and Mr.

McNulty, AP Lit teacher and creative writing teacher during junior year. Ms. Perlman has taught *A Mile of Faces* in her class ever since it came out, and Mr. McNulty had them write a piece of flash fiction based on Bruni's *New Yorker* piece, "The Robbery." Mr. McNulty always talked about the time he once rode a subway with Luca Bruni in Boston but was too nervous to speak to him. Mr. McNulty also read two of Charlotte's stories aloud in class because he thought they were so good.

Mrs. Chirron at the front office lets Charlotte go back to the faculty lunchroom. When she tells her teachers the news, Ms. Perlman lets out a little cry, and her eyes get watery. Mr. McNulty stands and pumps Charlotte's hand as if she's just been promoted to company VP. "I knew it," he says. "I knew it! I know talent when I see it."

Ms. Perlman has her fingers pressed to her cheeks. "Oh my God," she says.

Charlotte has found the golden ticket in the chocolate bar, and now she gets to be one of the few to go into the incredible factory. She gets to see how the magic is made.

An email from Luca Bruni's personal assistant, Bethany Sparrow, arrives. She's handling all the program details. Her name seems so sophisticated. Charlotte looks her up. Bethany Sparrow is beautiful. The blond, twisty hair on her head is beautiful, and so are her eyes, blue like the water under a thick sheet of Antarctic ice. And she's so young, only twenty-three, but already published. Three years ago, she was a student of

Luca Bruni's, and he believed in her talent so much that he introduced her to his agent, and a book of her stories came out last year. This is what she says, anyway, in an article in *Poets & Writers* magazine titled "Mentors Matter." "Sparrow is a blazing talent. The voice of her generation," Luca Bruni said about her. Those are the words that were on the cover of her book. Wow. Wow, wow, wow. To be chosen like that—Charlotte can't even imagine how Bruni must have changed Bethany Sparrow's life. But, see? These are the things that can happen.

Whenever Charlotte spots Bethany Sparrow's email address in her inbox, she gets goose bumps and huge nerves, and rewrites her replies a million times to make sure she doesn't sound silly or immature. Sometimes she has a rush of *oh my God, what did I get myself into?* because maybe the story he liked was just a lucky fluke. There are forms to fill out. Information sheets. Edited information sheets, since this is a new program, and they're still working stuff out. Questions about flights. Ticket information. Only she and one other girl, Shaye Rivers, have scholarships, so Bethany Sparrow is arranging their travel.

There's a lot of anxious stuff to manage. Charlotte looks up Shaye Rivers, she looks up airplane safety, she looks up the city of Venice, and everything she can find on La Calamita, and the villa itself. This doesn't help. Shaye looks intimidating and airplanes crash and the city of Venice is sinking. And, oh my God, they quarantined sufferers of the plague on that island, and then it held a crumbling mental hospital, until Luca Bruni bought it for next to nothing at an auction, transforming the place. It's all pretty eerie. She can feel the eeriness in her whole body. Still, what piece of land there *wouldn't* be heavy with history? And wow, that villa. It's beautiful. She can hardly believe she'll be *sleeping under the same roof* as Luca Bruni.

Charlotte had been very close to Luca Bruni once before, closer than Mr. McNulty was that time. Close enough to actually smell his cologne over the table. She and Carly went to hear him speak at Elliott Bay Book Company when he came to Seattle on tour for *The Tide of Years*. He was one of Carly's favorites too, though when it comes to books, everyone is her favorite. The place was so packed, every chair was taken, and people were jammed in the stairwell and up through the store itself, a few actually lingering in the street. Even though she and Carly could only see him if they stood on their toes, and even though a woman's purse was smashing into Charlotte's side, and even though a lot of the people were probably there because *One Great Lie* was on TV, once he started talking, all that disappeared. He spoke so powerfully and movingly that the purse woman started to cry, and Carly (strong enough to throw a javelin 148 feet) had tears in her eyes, and Charlotte herself felt like her heart had been crushed by his voice. He's brilliant, that's all there is to it.

Afterward, they waited in line to get their books signed. And he stayed and stayed, you know, for every single one of them. He made sure every person who wanted his signature had it, and when it was their turn, Charlotte froze and couldn't even speak. She slid her book across to him and only could manage a *thank you*. Carly, though, told him how amazing *A Mile of Faces* was. How incredible. She was able to actually chatter and tell him what it meant to her, while Charlotte could only look at how his shirt cuffs met his wrists, real human wrists, and notice how long his fingers were, and how he was even taller than he looked on his book jacket. With his narrow face and large nose and wiry hair, and his lanky, almost awkward body, he wasn't what you'd usually think of as handsome, but magnetic energy rays shot from him in all directions. She could smell that cologne, something heavy but somehow clean, and she just stood there, stunned by his realness. His leather bag sat beside him, and it was so weird, because that bag came from his real house in Boston, and stayed in his real hotel room, and was carried over his real shoulder, when he was wearing that real leather jacket hanging over the chair.

Outside, in the cold burger-and-cigarette-smoke air of a Capitol Hill night, they opened their books and compared inscriptions.

To Carly, with the beautiful eyes. L. B. Carly smiled up at Charlotte, pleased. So pleased. But shyly, you know, because she knew she'd won something. Of course he noticed her eyes—everyone did, and her face and her body, because Carly was gorgeous. Also, smart and funny and sarcastic and athletic, but gorgeous was what they saw first. Still, seeing that inscription, Charlotte felt a gut punch of disappointment. She felt like the ignored sidekick. Inside Charlotte's book, though, there was a quickly drawn image of a ship beside his signature. And it was like—she didn't know. Just, maybe that he silently recognized her, too.

A few days later, when they all hung out at Carly's, Yasmin saw the inscription in Carly's book and said, *That's kind of pervy*, but they ignored her. Only they understood how that night felt.

Charlotte had stood across a table from Luca Bruni, but she hadn't been this close, and neither had Carly. Not personal-assistant close. Not *summer abroad writing program* close.

Her father may have been right about extra expenses, although she doesn't want to admit it, because Luca Bruni's company is covering her flights and lodging and program fee, but she has to cover other stuff. They do. She and her family. First of all, this means clothes, and a laptop bag, and an international cell phone plan, and a passport. The passport is expensive right there, and she uses some of her own money from her savings account, because every time Adele has to take out her credit card again, Charlotte can see the muscle in her cheek, pulsing like one of those little bulbs that take blood pressure.

Graduation is coming too. They have to rent the cap and gown, and they order the least expensive choice of announcements. "I already have a dress I can wear," Charlotte says. "The one we got for Dad's work thing last year." She decides to skip the class party, because it costs as much as the passport. Her birthday arrives on top of that. There's the ritual dinner splurge at Olive Garden, *and* a new roller bag.

Adele has to take a day off work to go with Charlotte to the passport office. They bring her birth certificate and a tiny photo of her, and fill out a bunch of papers.

"I hope this is all worth it," Adele says, buckling her seat belt back up. She's been saying stuff like that lately too. Not just *This is so damn exciting!* and *I wish your grandma could see you!* But things like *Wow, look at you, Miss Fancy* at Charlotte's new suitcase, or *This all looks very . . . complicated* at the travel itinerary that arrives from Bethany Sparrow.

Once again, the guilt seeps inside Charlotte like she's got a permanent leaky faucet in her body. She wishes her mother was happier and had a happier life. She wishes her father—who knows, whatever. Still, when that passport comes in the mail, it's so beautiful. It's more important than any class party or new dress or anything else. The blue cover feels as soft as leather, and she traces her finger on the gold seal, and inside, there's a map, and there's her photo. There are all those blank pages and their possibilities.

"Let me see it," Ella says.

It's one of those things that's hard to hand over, even if you want to be nice. She lets her sister hold it for a second and then snatches it back. Charlotte believes that every book is like an open door. She's believed that since *Where the Wild Things Are* and *The Hobbit* and *The Lion, the Witch, and the Wardrobe*, and, and, and . . . Books hold spells and amulets and foreign lands.

They keep you safely hidden, *and* show you the world. And this little book is no different. It doesn't have any words, only blank pages. But it's an open door to foreign lands, for sure.

She slides it under her pillow. *That very night in Charlotte's room a forest grew.* She'd never admit this to anyone, because it is silly and unsophisticated, and whatever else, but she sleeps with it there. She sneaks her fingers underneath to feel the blue edges of it.

It's hard to sleep, though. There are no amulets in the real world, and a part of her feels uneasy. She keeps thinking about those plague victims. So many people died on that island, one article said, that the earth on La Calamita was 50 percent ash. She has to shake away the thought—that it's strange, you know, to build your beautiful home on the bones of other people.

Chapter Six

Catella Marchesi, poet.

Studied with the then-famous poet Giacomo Bratteolo. He helped her get published for the first time by including seven sonnets she wrote in a volume he put together when she was only twelve.

(1585–sometime after 1623)

Charlotte finally finishes that stupid paper so she can pass AP Lit. She does a quick (well, as quick as fifteen assigned pages can be) analysis of T. S. Eliot's poetry, because there's tons and tons of information on him. Three-quarters of the way through, Charlotte discovers he's pretty sexist and racist, but whatever, because she's got to get the thing done. Finals week is intense. For prom, Charlotte wears the dress they bought for her cousin Andrea's wedding a few weeks before. Prom night, Nate drinks too much and pukes out the window of Carly's dad's car. Yasmin ditches him and stomps off into the dark carrying her shoes. Adam sings softly in Charlotte's ear as they dance, and then they make out like crazy in his car at Green Lake, because his parents are home and there's nowhere to be alone.

Charlotte gets accepted to UW and Seattle U, a Jesuit school, where she decides to go. They're giving her a big scholarship, even though she's only Catholic because of old relatives. She graduates with honors. Her dad takes lots of pictures, and Ella tries to get in them, and caps and gowns are so weird when you think about it. Principal Harvey's speech was pretty much the same as last year's, but she still feels all passage-of-time emotional and also excited, because she'll be leaving for Italy in *four days*.

It's hard to concentrate on anything. She wakes up at night with nerves. Besides Luca Bruni, besides a foreign country, besides a villa, there'll be kids she's never met before. Not kids—college students. Talented ones. Rich ones. She wrote a little story. Mr. McNulty read a few of hers in class, but that's all the evidence she has of her talent. She's gone to school with the same people practically all her life. She can't imagine a *villa*, even with the photos. That part jams in her mind every time. They stayed at a Red Lion Inn for Andrea's wedding, and it was so exciting that Ella jumped around on the bed, even though the pool was closed. A night out at Olive Garden is a big deal to them. They only go when it's someone's birthday.

And the earth is made of ash, don't forget, her stupid mind nags.

Carly's mom and dad have a graduation party at their house. Everyone's there, Carly and Yasmin and Charlotte. Adam and Nate and Jade, and some of their friends from band and orchestra, like Raymond and Zoe, who usually stick together. It's in the Hardwicks' backyard, which seems fancy to Charlotte because it has a hot tub, and on the far corner of the grass, one of those little greenhouses she's seen at Home Depot. Carly's quiet little grandma, Baba, who lives with them, is there too, sitting in a lawn chair and wearing a sweater even though it's hot out. It's probably the nicest house Charlotte's ever been in. On the front porch, there are terra-cotta pots with junipers bent into spirals.

"This is the next phase of your journey!" Nate says, standing at the corner of the patio next to another large ceramic pot spilling blue and yellow flowers. He lifts his hand in the air to orate. He has a nice shirt on—a dress shirt with short sleeves that he maybe took from his dad's closet.

"It is the first day of the rest of your life! The future is yours!" Yasmin shouts, and they both crack up. This is when they're really good together, the way they joke around, which probably means they're mostly just friends. Anyway, the prom puking has been forgotten, or at least forgiven.

"It wasn't so bad," Carly's mom says, setting out a bowl of pasta salad on a picnic table draped in a CONGRATULATIONS, GRADUATE tablecloth. They're all making fun of poor Principal Harvey's speech, which he probably gave every year, his armpits soaked with sweat. Carly's mom always saw the bright side. She saw the bright side so often that Carly's brother stole from her purse and got addicted to drugs and now has the opportunity to turn his life around at one of those schools where kids have to hike in the mountains and build a shelter in the woods.

"Be the change you want to see in the world!" Nate says.

Adam nuzzles Charlotte's neck. "Mmm. You smell so good," he says.

Carly's dad grills burgers, and then gives a real speech, about how proud he is of Carly and all of them. How she's the daughter of his dreams, and how Yasmin going to NASA inspires him, and how going to Venice will be a life-changing experience for Charlotte. Baba grips Charlotte's hand and holds her eyes, as if trying to reveal everything she needs to know. They eat, and everyone talks about the camping trip to Deception Pass that they're going to go on, and that Charlotte and Yasmin will miss. Jade pleads with Adam to get his guitar, and so he does. He sits on top of the picnic table and plays and sings, and Charlotte thinks for the millionth time that his voice sounds like that guy from the band Uncut, only better. It makes her think of how she likes to be with him in the small bed of his room, lying naked against his thin body, and how his eyes are so sincere, and how he's really sweet to her, and how it's going to be really, really hard to break up with him.

"Call me, text me, send photos," Yas says as she hugs Charlotte goodbye at the end of the night. They won't see each other again until summer is over.

"You too. Sneak your phone into that antigravity thing so I can see you float in midair." She hugs Yas hard.

"Be careful, okay?"

"Of course."

"No, I mean *really*."

"What?" Charlotte's tone is semi-annoyed. It's gotten dark, and there's only the flicker of the tiki torches in the Hardwicks' backyard, and the yellow of the porch light with a circle of bugs zipping around. Well, there's enough light that Charlotte can see Yasmin make that expression that says *You know what.*

Charlotte makes a face.

"You remember what I told you, don't you?"

"Yes, Yas," she says, as if she's being reminded to look both ways before she crosses a street.

What Yasmin told her was that she'd heard from somebody's somebody that whatever, whatever, it doesn't really matter. Luca Bruni flirted or something with one of his students, or a couple of them, or who knows what, but Charlotte can hardly see the importance of this. Honestly, if you look him up online, all you'll see is buckets and boatloads and pages and pages of honors and praise and stars and quotes and fawning and love and admiration. Deserved, all of it. Read just one, just *one*, of his stories, and you'll know it's deserved. Plus, he's married! He's always talking about how devoted he is to his wife, Althea. He mentions her in every speech she's watched online. So what if he's a little flirtatious. Think of all of the important men in history who were kind of like that. JFK, et cetera, et cetera—hundreds of et ceteras. She doesn't really stop to think that *kind of like that* is pretty pathetic, as far as excuses go.

"I'm serious."

"Okay, okay."

There's stuff Yasmin has no clue about. Like how Luca

Bruni is a feminist, unlike T. S. Eliot. "'Sexism and racism are my biggest concerns as a writer. I support women. I identify with women,'" he said in one interview she read. He says that stuff *all the time*. "'The average male thinks he's pro-woman because he thinks he's a good guy and people tell him he's a good guy, but it's not the truth. I'm interested in a rebuke of that kind of bullshit. To show my privilege as a male without being preachy.'" She's been reading everything about him that she can get her hands on. Yas doesn't know Luca Bruni like she does. Charlotte doesn't want to fight, though. She just folds her arms and plants her feet, and lifts her eyebrows in defense.

"Char . . ."

"I hear you, Mom! Stop worrying." Charlotte's own mom hasn't given her advice like that. The opposite. Adele's been rewatching all the *One Great Lie* episodes, and Charlotte can hear her up late at night, laughing sometimes, the glow of the TV still visible through the bottom crack of her bedroom door. It's a nice sound, a wonderful sound, instead of the arguing she normally hears. She caught her mom looking at Luca Bruni's photo again too, on the back of *The Forever King*, one eyebrow up, the same way she does when she spots a particularly nice pair of heels. Like there's a dream in those heels. Too expensive for her, hard to walk in, but still.

"Hug me," Yasmin commands, and Charlotte does.

She doesn't expect to do it right then. She really wanted one more afternoon with him in his double bed, the poster of Jimi

Hendrix over them, Jimi with rainbows of color around him like he's the center of heat in an infrared map. Charlotte's going to miss his sweet eyes staring down at her (Adam's, not Jimi's), and Adam's fingers making their way down her skin, and the way that their bodies feel together, like two smooth, cool dominoes. But there he is, leaning against his car, and they're standing in a circle of lamppost light, and suddenly the timing is right. Right timing can be like an unexpected break in the clouds out of nowhere.

"I've been looking at flights, you know. I can maybe come over in late July. Dad says I can use some of his air miles. . . ." He takes her fingers. God, he's cute, and the way he just played that guitar hits the center of her, but she knows she has to do this. It's like he's standing in the middle of a country road, getting smaller in the distance, which is the way she'd describe it if she were writing it.

"Adam," she says.

"No." He shakes his head. He looks over at the neighbor's tree. He's felt this coming, like you do, only you don't want to admit it.

"You know I love you, but . . ." She's already pleading.

"*But* should never be bigger than *I love you*, Char. Never."

"I just think . . . we're going different places, you know. I'm going to be gone a whole summer. You shouldn't be tied. . . . And it wouldn't be right for you to come. You'll always be so special to me. You deserve better." Her speech is as full of clichés as Principal Harvey's. Her words are dirty little pebbles in her mouth, but the truth is harder to convey, that you can't have the past and the future at the same time.

"This sucks, you know. Really sucks."

"Adam! I'm sorry."

"Now? *Here?* Waiting until two days before you're going to leave. Okay, bye. Send a postcard."

He tosses his keys in the air, catches them, but she sees he's about to cry.

"Don't go like this!"

"*Me* don't go like this? Whatever. I gave you what I have, and if that's not enough, that's not enough."

He walks around the car and gets in. He slams the door. But he seems kind of determined, too. He reverses with a screech, and then, as he drives off, she hears his stereo go on. No, she *feels* his stereo go on, the heroic and thumping beat of fuck you, and the resolve to move on. She thought there'd be some sobbing or clinging or begging, but no. His self-respect is a relief, but it hurts a little too. It gives her immediate second thoughts. It's too easy to let good stuff slip through your hands while you're busy grasping at big, impossible dreams that might wreck you.

Adele's words pop in cruelly, as Adele's words often do. *I hope this is all worth it.* Standing in Carly's driveway that night, her trip and her writing and Luca Bruni and his villa are all hazy unknowns. Her knowns are being popped one by one, like she's throwing darts at balloons. Adam is gone. She sees his love for her disappear down that dark street. Her friends are planning a summer minus her. Her family has laid their belief and their money on this unreliable dream. Like a gambler, Charlotte has dipped to the bottom of her own savings. Right then, it's like all her eggs are in one basket. Like there's a lot at stake if this goes wrong.

Chapter Seven

Lucia Albani, poet.

Acclaimed from the age of fifteen, little is known of her own work. She's remembered now only as a woman who was praised by ladies' man Torquato Tasso, had a sonnet written to her by Giovanni Bressani, and was the subject of a painting by Giovanni Battista Moroni. She had to flee her home when her brother murdered a member of a rival family, and she died shortly after.

(1534–1568)

The last thing Charlotte does before zipping up her new suitcase is bad, a terrible idea. Dangerous. Stupid. She takes that old book, that old, fragile, valuable book, and she wraps it in the softest thing she has, the white nightgown they got from Target that almost looks expensive. She tucks it into the plastic compartment in her bag, away from any possible damp or damage. She shouldn't do this. If her mom notices that she's taken *The Verses* with her to Venice, she'll freak. But it's a silent vow. To learn more about Isabella, to maybe even find out the truth about that poem. If a small, forgotten piece of her lives somewhere, it's there. They'll make the trip together, and they'll have their chance together. *I promise you,* Charlotte says to her.

Charlotte's dad gets off work early, because he and Ella are taking her to the airport. Adele stays behind, because she *can't take it*, she says. Going to the airport and seeing Charlotte walk away *will just do me in*. Every time there's any mention of Charlotte leaving, Adele gets all wavery-voiced, and worry has also been added to the excitement/resentment mix.

"Remember Amanda Knox," her mom says, before kissing Charlotte and hugging her so hard she can barely breathe.

"I'll make sure not to be unjustly imprisoned," Charlotte says.

"How could I fly over to get you? How could we afford a team of lawyers?" Adele's joking but not. Anxiety is etched around her eyes. Charlotte might as well be blasting off into space.

Her dad checks the time on his phone. "We need to get on the road." Lately, he's been full of energy and information, describing how to go through security, telling her that she'll have to remove her shoes and her jacket, giving her small bottles to put any liquids in, advising on the best way to line up before boarding. It's like discovering he has a whole secret talent, and he keeps making an excited face and squeezing her arms, the way she and Carly do when one of them hands over a great book the other hasn't read yet.

"Love you. Love you, love you, love you," Adele says. She's smushing the breath out of her.

"Love you too, Mom," Charlotte says, and means it.

Ella kicks the back of her seat the whole way, acting like she's seven, rolling her window up and down to be irritating. Her father remarks on how traffic is slightly lighter than usual, and how the security line looks slightly longer. Charlotte checks a million times to make sure she still has her passport.

Ella makes big eyes at the sign that says not to joke about bombs and pretends to throw a bomb. They hug right next to the serious people in uniforms checking IDs and boarding passes.

"Have a brilliant adventure," her father says. She's never ever heard him use the word *brilliant* or *adventure*.

"Try not to cry every day I'm gone," she says to Ella, and then regrets it, because her sister's eyes are filling with tears.

"Oh, Peanut," she says.

Charlotte puts her arms around her sister. The leaky faucet of guilt overflows in Charlotte's body. She's abandoning her, and Ella will have to deal with all that shit on her own—the tense dinners and the phone fighting and the chance you might say the wrong thing at the wrong time. But it's weird, too, how the moment she can't see them waving goodbye anymore, old Charlotte Hodges waves goodbye too. Old Charlotte Hodges seems to be left behind with them.

There are lots of alarming noises in a plane—grindings and whines, stuff that makes you realize you're in a flying machine, and she has to look around to make sure no one else is panicking. No one is. A flight attendant rolls a cart down the aisle, and she's still smiling, even though her lipstick looks tired. Charlotte tries to forget the demonstration of oxygen masks popping down from above, and the plastic card with the cartoon people whooshing down an inflated slide, and that alarming tilt as they lifted off. She settles in to the miracle of clouds. The big sky makes her think about all the things she wants to write. How she wants to capture all the large feelings of life and the universe and the nameless lifts she sometimes feels in her heart, and the despairing drops. God, if she could capture all of that somehow, it would be so magnificent.

She's brought a notepad, of course. She always has one with her, even if she sometimes has no idea what she was trying to say when she reads back whatever she wrote down. She removes it from the seat pocket in front of her. A pen is stuck into the spiral, and she takes it out. Terror does its jab-jab-jab, because, shit, look what she's gotten herself into. She's going to actually have to write and share in front of people who have real talent and not Roosevelt High/Mr. McNulty/proud mom talent. From what her packet says, they'll be doing daily writing prompts in various locations, which they'll share with the group for critique, while also working on a longer piece to submit for publication. *Critique* sends serrated fear right through her. It makes her twist the rings on her fingers. It felt so brave to send in that application, but that was nothing. That was private, in-her-own-room bravery, which is totally stupid compared to out-in-the-real-world bravery.

There are lots and lots of hours on this plane, so it might be a good idea to start something here, where no one's looking. She bites the end of her pen. What's important? What does she really feel? Just frozen, right now. Like a fake. A frozen fake full of terror, yikes. She's floating in the sky for the first time ever, and a flight attendant is asking what she wants to drink, and hey, a little table folds down for a tray of dinner, and so, forget writing anything.

She gets nonchalant about the plane pretty fast, after the thrill and intense fascination of peeing in a cubicle thirty-eight thousand feet above the earth. The jumbo jet doesn't feel very jumbo. You can't just decide to get out of there. She gets bored and uncomfortable and watches two movies and misses home suddenly, bad, like she's left forever. Her neck aches. There are many hours of this on repeat, plus a few exciting little trolleys of food and beverages going past, and the lights going up and down at odd times, plus feeling strangely connected to the people near her, a man who works on his laptop for hours, a woman in headphones who sleeps. The clock on Charlotte's phone appears extraordinarily confused.

Night, day, night. And then some magic words. The pilot says they're starting their descent into Venice Marco Polo Airport. Charlotte's head has felt weird and tired and full of static fuzz, but it clears suddenly, and she's zapped full of energy and nerves and leans over to look out the window, but all she can see is darkness and sprinkles of lights, like she's looking at the starry sky upside down.

They hit the runway with a *bam*, and the tires screech, and she swears she feels the tail of the plane swivel. It doesn't explode or burst into flames, so she's made it. She's too nervous and excited to text her mom that she landed. She just gets her stuff and follows everyone out because Venice Marco Polo is a swirl of confusion. Her instructions from Bethany Sparrow say to go through customs and then meet at the vaporetto dock for their driver. She looked all this up, how to go through customs, what a vaporetto even is. (A water-bus, cool. Even the word *vaporetto* is cool.) All of that zaps from her brain, though, because around her is the bright white of the airport against the dark night in the windows, and a concerto of language, foreign words on signs, and people rushing around with bags. The realization that she's in a foreign country tumbles her like a sock in a dryer.

She follows the swarm, a jet-lagged baby lamb. She does whatever the people in front of her do, and before she knows it, she's filling out a form and handing it over, and getting her passport stamped. She spots her luggage from the spinning carousel with the thrill of seeing an old friend again, and she hopes that if she follows every rule and is as nice as possible, she won't get Amanda Knoxed.

She's outside. It's around ten p.m. here. *You are breathing Italian air,* she tells herself. Already, it even smells different. Salty, briny, a back note of fish; gasoline from boats, night, a deep smell she finds delicious. It's crazy, but right outside the airport, right out the doors, there's water, shimmering in moonlight. There are boats in the water too, and a wide, open-air one that must be the water-bus. People are getting on, filling its benches, heaping their luggage into a pile. It's hard to feel like she's in her own body. She looks all around to see what to do next, when she spots a man holding a sign.

HODGES.

Her name! How crazy to see her name here. She was expecting Bethany Sparrow, but this is a short old man in a rumply green sweater and trousers, with a serious look on his face. Serious, as in irritated. Displeased with her already.

"That's me!" she says to him, and his expression doesn't change. She gets her first sinking realization that friendliness might not work here like it does at home, although, truthfully, that gross feeling that she's made him mad is as familiar as her own pillow.

"*Benvenuta*, Hodges. Aldo." Aldo flings her bags into a boat made of highly polished wood, which glows in the moonlight. It's beautiful and long, open in the front, a covered area with benches and little windows in the center. It's like a boat in a James Bond film or one of those movies where they rob an art museum and go on a high-speed chase. She's not nearly glamorous enough. She needs to brush her teeth and take a shower.

He hops in. Holds out a hand to her. She takes it, a warm old hand, and gets in. He stands behind the wheel. She doesn't know what to do, so she wobbles unsteadily to one of the padded seats in the front. She feels uncomfortable with the gruff old man, just the two of them. Her fingers do that nervous thing—her rings, the spinning. The boat sloshes, and then he turns the key, and the engine sputters to life.

The water is choppy, and the boat picks up speed. She has to grip the edge of the boat to hold on. He's going fast, even in the dark of night, and she's been here all of an hour, and already it's uncomfortable and dangerous and thrilling. Behind them, on the back of the boat, a flag flaps hard in the wind. She doesn't know if she should make conversation, because the man only grunts every now and then as he drives, taking an occasional hit out of a thermos. The wind whips loose bits of hair from her ponytail around her face, and whatever is in that thermos doesn't smell like coffee, and the boat *bamps* when it hits a wave.

Around her, even this late, there are boats with little green lights glowing at their bows, zipping through the dark canal, passing them with great speed. The water is purple-black, the waves tipped in silver by the moon, a triangle froth of white in their wake. Aldo turns on some music. Opera, how perfect. It's dramatic and surreal against the boats and the water rushing beside her.

"Vivaldi?" he asks. Charlotte only knows *The Four Seasons* from orchestra, but she nods.

He turns it up. *"Orlando finto pazzo,"* he shouts. She has no idea what he's trying to tell her, but then he says, "He wrote it for Anna Giro," and she realizes *Orlando finto pazzo* is the name of the opera. Charlotte nods again and smiles, like she knows what he's talking about. God, there's so much she doesn't understand about this place, let alone the world, and all the people she's about to meet probably *do*.

And then she spots it up ahead—the city of Venice, the leaning, tipping, glowing buildings all squished together, the white dome of Saint Mark's; all of it so unbelievably old and weird and tattered and remarkable, like some strange stage set. When Aldo drives closer, she doesn't see the city so much as feel it, though this music is contributing, the way it all goes together, the trembling voice, the shimmering structures with their iron balconies. Her heart is overflowing with emotion, as if it's filling with water, and she can't begin to imagine how to ever explain this surreal, intensely magical place to her family. As Aldo slows, she can hear the sound of waves, the way they slosh up the sides of the buildings, and she can see the old archways, the shades of orange and yellow and dim white that she can glimpse even in this light. Shades that seem soaked and submerged for hundreds of years so that their color seems to both fade but also glow with history.

"Yes?" Aldo asks. He lifts his eyebrows in a question.

"Yes," she says, and then he accelerates and arcs away. It's hard to leave, to go farther from the city of Venice instead of closer, but she understands that Aldo did this just for her, giving her that brief view. Now, they head across the lagoon.

She can see it, La Calamita. As they get closer, Aldo turns the music down. It's a much smaller island than Venice straight across the water. From this distance, Charlotte can spot the bell tower, with its red pointed top, all that's left of the church that was once there. And she can see the huge villa with its high, curved windows, mostly dark. She can't wait to get there, but honestly, it looks so isolated, too. She feels very far from home. At this late hour, the boat puttering toward the island, it's not hard to imagine what that building had been for centuries—the fortress where plague victims were quarantined, and after that, an asylum, and after that, an abandoned structure of crumbling half-walls and decrepit rooms, until Luca Bruni came along to transform it.

"La Calamita," Aldo says. It's strange, but he sounds disgusted.

That place. From this distance, it looks haunted.

Chapter Eight

Lucia Bertani dell'Oro, poet.

Though not much is known about her own work, her sonnet praising two female poets (Veronica Gambara and Vittoria Colonna) was one of the earliest examples of a woman claiming she was inspired by other women and not by a man.

(1521–1567)

Aldo expertly steers the boat into a narrow canal next to the bank. They glide toward a small landing where Aldo hops out and ties up the boat before retrieving Charlotte's suitcase and helping her to the dock with an outstretched hand. As they walk toward the villa, it seems less eerie, maybe because Charlotte starts to recognize stuff from the articles she read about the renovation. First, they pass a long, redbrick building with white arched windows and a curved tower, which she knows is a library now, and then a large open area where part of the old crumbling hospital has been torn down to create a beautiful brick patio with a pool and an outdoor dining space, empty at this hour but strung with lights and surrounded by bougainvillea. Before he bought the entire island for seven hundred thousand dollars, the place was a ruin of collapsed beams and rubble heaps of brick and who knows what else. A jungle of vines climbed into broken windows and up iron stairwells, into old hallways open from where the roof had caved in, or edging through decrepit shutters. The rooms were still littered with abandoned objects: metal bed frames, old shoes, bathtubs, and the iron bars that used to imprison people inside. Now it looks like a luxury hotel, not that Charlotte has ever been in one of those before.

Aldo wheels her bag over the cobblestones. It's the only sound except for the waves hitting the bulkhead of the island. Then Aldo huffs and grunts as he hauls the bag up the set of white stone stairs at the front of the villa and across an elaborate white balcony surrounded with pillared arches.

Inside the doors, Charlotte gasps. "Wow," she whispers. There are only a few lamps on, turned low, but she can see the enormous living area, surrounded by more arched windows that reach all the way up to the beams above. The draperies go from ceiling to floor, and the walls are a golden yellow except for the farthest wall, which is covered with a huge mural of a ship. A glass ship, rising on a dramatic wave.

"This is incredible," she breathes. "How did he *do* all this?"

Aldo snorts. "How? Mrs. Bruni with all the . . ." He rubs his fingertips together to indicate money.

She follows Aldo up a stairwell, stepping as quietly as possible through the hallway that comes next. Outside of a door, he hands her a key. It's an iron key, a large one, the kind she's only seen in movies with castle doors, a hefty key.

"Thank you," Charlotte says.

"Why do you all have to arrive here in the middle of the night?" Aldo grumbles.

Charlotte turns the knob as silently as she can. She knows from the packet of information she got from Bethany Sparrow that she'll be rooming with Shaye, the other scholarship recipient, who's a sophomore at City College, part of CUNY, the City University of New York. After much online stalking, Charlotte also knows that Shaye graduated with honors from Bryant High in Queens, and has a grandmother who just died and a cat and a fondness for Mexican food and beer. She did a lot of campaigning for a progressive senator, too. This is both awesome and intimidating when Charlotte's been old enough to vote for, like, *weeks*.

The room is dark, and it has high, high ceilings and long blue draperies hanging from decorative iron rods, and two beds, and it's *huge*, and there's a shiny, hard floor underfoot, and thick, wide moldings, and a door that leads to a bathroom. Overhead, there are rough-hewn beams across the ceiling, same as in the enormous room downstairs. The lump in one of the beds is Shaye Rivers, but she doesn't wake up. Charlotte can see a head of spiky brown hair and an arm hanging down, sporting the black swirls of a tattoo.

Charlotte uses the bathroom as quietly as she can and gets

into the empty bed. She peeks through the tall, tall window next to it. She can see the little green lights of Aldo's boat zipping away, maybe toward a home in Venice, not here. She sees the lights of that city far off too. All the little pinpricks of life in this foreign place. It's surreal. She's exhausted, and she's just catapulted through space, so her head spins. How do you wake up in one world on one day, and another the next?

She's so overtired it's hard to sleep, and a stranger is breathing quietly near her, and the sheets are so, so soft and smell like lavender, and opera music plays in her thoughts. She holds her phone under the sheet so the light won't wake her roommate. Bethany Sparrow said there'd be Wi-Fi, and sure enough, it pops right up. *Calaorg.*

She texts her mom that she got in, and then her mom texts back, asking a hundred questions, until Charlotte finally lies and says she has to sleep. She messes around on social media and texts Yas a photo from the plane, but everything from home seems so far away. She's still wide awake. She looks up *Orlando finto pazzo.* She doesn't even really care what it is, but 95 percent of the stuff you look up is pointless, urgent and then forgotten. It means "Orlando, the fake madman," and it's an opera Vivaldi wrote for his student Anna Giro when she was sixteen and he was forty-eight. He liked her maybe too much, plus he also taught hundreds of young girls, only girls, who lived in the Venetian orphanage Ospedale della Pietà.

Oo-kay. Got it. She shuts off her phone. She lies there

and looks at the high, high ceiling, and the green shutters of the high, high windows. The thought of sixteen-year-old Anna Giro and that old guy gives her the creeps, but those kinds of things happened back then.

She feels the pulse of anxiety. She's trying not to think about everything that happened on this island, too. It's hard not to imagine people in torment lying in the exact spot she is now. Before, all the facts she read about this place seemed deliciously eerie: the shipwrecks that littered the waters out there from way, way, way back during the Napoleonic Wars, when French soldiers were brought ashore here and buried alive. The thousands and thousands of people with the plague, stuck here, doomed. Those asylum doctors, who did whatever they wanted to their patients, because no one was looking and no one cared.

Back home, that history was stuff from long ago, stuff that didn't matter anymore, stories, interesting and cool, but not really relevant. In the middle of this night, though, actually *here*, history seems suddenly closer than she ever imagined it would. It's up and around and below her actual body. It's giving her the serious creeps.

And then, all at once, she feels a nugget of *real* panic. *The Verses*! She has to make sure it made it here. She gets out of bed, unzips the suitcase inch by jagged inch. She wriggles her fingers around. Where is it? Okay. All right. There it is. It's sitting body to body against her copy of *The Glass Ship*, a book that's soft and foldable from so much reading. Her heart slows.

She vowed to be Isabella di Angelo's champion and protector, but maybe it's the other way around. It's hard to tell. But it's comforting, you know, to think that someone else has been here before her.

Chapter Nine

Maddalena Campiglia, poet.

While the famous Torquato Tasso was praising and flattering her, and Muzio Manfredi (who called himself a "celebrant of women") was writing her flirtatious letters, she was busy challenging traditional female roles, and expanding the subjects women addressed in their work. She wrote non-religious poetry, as well as sonnets about female desire, love between women, and female solidarity. She also expressed public outrage at a misogynistic poem of Manfredi's.

(1553–1595)

"Seattle seems cool," Shaye says. Charlotte can see her arm tattoo now—it's an anchor, with the words *I refuse to sink* scrolled underneath. She has another one, right on the lowest part of her back just above her bikini bottoms: *Facta non verba*. No idea. Another thing to look up.

Charlotte and Shaye are stretched out on towels on lounge chairs by the pool. Katerina Chandler sits at the pool's edge with her feet in. Katerina is from Minnesota—*but not* that *part of Minnesota*, she said, and rolled her eyes, meaning who knows what. *And not really even from Minnesota, since I was adopted from Russia back when people could still do that,* she explained. It was hard to know what to say to that, so no one said anything. Katerina wears a one piece she keeps pulling up and pulling down self-consciously. She's nice, though. The nervous-nice where you apologize a lot and laugh at things that aren't that funny and give a lot of compliments, which means maybe she and Charlotte could be friends.

"*New York* seems cool," Charlotte says to Shaye.

That first day, the schedule is free so they can hang out and shake off their jet lag, but tonight, they're having a dressy meet and greet with Luca Bruni. God, Charlotte's nervous. She can't believe she's going to meet him, that they're all going to *be at a party* with him.

"Am I blocking your sun?" Katerina says. She tilts her head to one side.

"It's fine," Shaye says. She means the sun, not New York. "I've never been anywhere else, until now."

"Really?" Whew—what a relief. "Same." Charlotte hears her own voice. It's way too eager, and she hates herself for a second. Ugh—she's ass-kissing her heart out, which is a mixed metaphor, but whatever. Shaye isn't the type to be too eager. She let someone draw an anchor on her body with needles, plus Latin.

"It's my first time here," Katerina says. "I haven't been to very many countries."

"They put us scholarship people in the same room," Shaye

says to Charlotte, and scrunches up her face, like, *What did they do that for?* "Everyone else gets their own." It seems kind of ungrateful to Charlotte. That morning, she got a glimpse of the rest of the villa, aside from the far wing that belongs to Luca Bruni, which is off-limits. Each bedroom is incredible—painted in cloudy greens or blues or oranges, some with frescoes of columns and arches painted over the beds, all with those high windows and beamed ceilings, elaborate bed frames, and floors of deep brown wood or polished stone. If Charlotte hadn't been given a scholarship, she'd never be able to visit a place like this, let alone stay here.

At the other end of the pool, there's Avni Sharma from San Jose. She's a writing seminars major at Hopkins, she said. Charlotte has no idea what that even is, and besides, it's hard to concentrate on what she was saying, because Avni is so beautiful. More beautiful than Carly, even. Avni has this dark hair that could star in a movie by itself. She has stunning dark eyes, and this cool manner that tells you right away that she's probably brilliant, too. Avni's dad is a doctor, and her mom published a book of short stories, and she's mentioned this a couple of times already. It reminds her of Blake Trevor at home, who always drives his dad's BMW like he earned it himself.

Two other girls, Hailey Murphy and Ashley Chen, are splashing around and screeching in the pool. Avni and Hailey are the only ones who speak Italian. Hailey's been getting private lessons at her parents' house in Miami, and she keeps saying stuff to them they can't understand, with an overdone accent that sounds like an American in a pizza commercial, the kind who'd kiss his fingers dramatically and say, *Delizioso! Mwah!*

Avni and Hailey and Ashley *did not* get their bathing suits at Target, that's for sure. Hailey has long blond hair, split into two braids that day, and Ashley has this cute, short layered haircut that she sure didn't get at Supercuts. Charlotte has no idea how much sunglasses like that cost.

The only boy so far, Eliot Vankard, sits on a lounge chair and bites the edge of a cuticle. His legs and arms are arctic white, and he wears round glasses. It's hot, but you can tell there's no way he's taking his shirt off. He told them he's attending Kenyon. Charlotte knows it has one of the best writing programs in the country, but he jokes that he's majoring in cow-tipping. You can tell he jokes a lot, which is probably related to not taking his shirt off. Charlotte didn't even apply to Kenyon. She's not going to actually get a degree in creative writing, because her dad said it's too impractical. She'll major in English, and even that's a compromise from business, like her dad wanted.

Ashley splashes Eliot on purpose from the pool. "Hey," he says, and draws back, like the water might scorch him.

"Come on, get in here!" she calls.

"Play with us!" Hailey dances the ends of her two blond braids his direction. She and Ashley seem more fun than the usual people who want to be writers. Even in her high school, kids who liked to write mostly kept to themselves and didn't have a lot of friends and had a life no one knew about, haha. Except for Ben Fry, who thought everything he did was genius and started a literary magazine, mostly with his own poems about life in the gritty streets, when he lived in Wedgwood, where people walked their dogs and ate kale and locally sourced food.

The pool is so beautiful. As beautiful as it was in the shots in magazine articles Charlotte read. The white towels of the lounge chairs look astonishing against the blue of the pool, and that looks astonishing against the orange of the villa, and that looks astonishing against the slate green–gray of the canal, and the wide lagoon beyond.

Charlotte wants to take pictures of everything. *Everything.* She's trying to hold back, but it's all photo-worthy. She's used the word *beautiful* a hundred times in her head already. That morning, there was a buffet breakfast with breads and cheeses and fruits, and she waited until no one was looking so she could snap that, too. Even the fruit was beautiful. She never cared about oranges before, but these were so inviting, and they tasted like summer.

There's been no sign of Luca Bruni. One more student is arriving later, and then they'll have that party tonight, where they'll meet Luca for the first time. Her stomach flips again at the thought. He's old, but she kind of wishes she had a body like Avni's, or eyes like Carly's, because she still remembers what he wrote in Carly's book.

At breakfast, they met Bethany Sparrow for the first time too. It was funny to meet the actual her after all those emails. Charlotte got her book of stories from the library but stopped reading halfway through because they were about the revolution in Chile. Who is she to judge, but it was hard to trust those stories when Bethany Sparrow was from Virginia. Bethany's hair was pulled up in a messy bun, and her blue eyes flickered like a faulty cable connection. She talked so fast you had to listen hard, and her phone kept ringing, and she'd look down at it, and then back up, so she probably wasn't really listening to anything they said. When Charlotte saw her again later, on the brick patio with overhanging lights and lemon trees, Bethany was on the phone, her shoulders bent down around it like a secret.

In addition to Bethany, there's also the gray-haired woman who moves in and out with the food, maybe a chef, who sighs a lot and brushes crumbs from the table with her hand as she gathers up the pastries. She also spots flashes of Althea Whitaker-Bruni, Luca's wife. At least, Charlotte's pretty sure it's her. In the photos of her online—the red carpet shots for the *One Big Lie* premiere, an article about the villa restoration, a gala for the Boston Children's Museum—her blond hair was long, but now it's cut to her chin in a way that's almost severe, and her face has the stern, businesslike expression of a news anchor. Aldo is everywhere too, zipping around in the boat, but also walking with a bunch of guys on the little stretch of seawall in front of the island, looking concerned.

"Where do you go again?" Katerina asks Shaye.

"City College. Part of CUNY."

Beautiful Avni has been listening in. Her gold jewelry glints as she applies her suntan lotion. "CUNY? Where's that? Never heard of it."

"It's in Harlem."

"So, it's a *community college*?"

"You say it like, 'So, it's an STD?'"

"Hey, I didn't mean anything." Avni puts both hands up, like *back off*. Her nail polish is the same color as Blake Trevor's dad's BMW, too.

"C-U-N-Y. Good thing that last letter isn't different." Katerina laughs.

"Yeah, good one. No one's ever made that joke before," Shaye snaps.

Katerina catches Charlotte's eye and makes an *uh-oh* face, and she makes a *yikes* one in return. It reminds her of her and Ella when their mom's in a bad mood.

"If no one's getting in the pool, I'm getting out." Ashley's layered hair is still dry except for the ends. "Where are the margaritas?" she jokes. She's mentioned alcohol maybe three times already, so maybe she's a partyer.

"Same," Hailey says, and lifts herself out of the pool.

The two of them are toweling off when Charlotte's sure she hears a motor. She realizes she hasn't seen Aldo in a while. Ashley hears it too. She finger-combs her hair, then looks down the path toward the canal. "You guys! Maybe it's Leo."

He's the only one not there yet, according to Bethany Sparrow. The motor cuts out. A few moments later, Aldo appears on the curved path to the villa, rolling a suitcase, a guy following him. They pass the pool and head toward the villa doors, and the guy raises one hand in a wave. Everyone goes silent at the sight of him. Silent, because wow. *Wow.* He's that good-looking. Katerina makes her eyes wide, and Charlotte does the same in agreement. Eliot says *shit* under his breath, like he agrees too.

Black curls, olive skin, teeth as white as clean sheets—he walks loose and lanky, but confident. Charlotte immediately thinks of Adam, because imagine how insecure he'd be getting *now.* In romantic comedies, Leo would be the type to have mirrored sunglasses, and he'd be an asshole, but he actually looks *nice.* When they reach the stairs, he takes his suitcase back from Aldo, insisting. If she were writing this badly, a girl like her would have a surprising romance with a guy like him. If she were writing it honestly, he'd make her so uncomfortable, every word out of her mouth would be embarrassing beyond belief.

"Leo has *arrived,*" Avni says.

"Um, *hot,*" Hailey says, and Ashley pushes her back into the pool.

"We're all here," Charlotte says. She wishes she could stop sounding so perky. Perky and enthusiastic and overeager things just keep popping out. She spits cheery words like bullets of self-protection. Because, God. Everything is beautiful, and everyone is smart and talented, and most of them clearly have money, and her insecurity rises like water in a natural disaster.

There's not a lot to hold on to. Ass-kissing is the last resort of any anxious person who's in over their head.

Chapter Ten

Laura Terracina, bestselling Italian poet of the sixteenth century.

She wrote on feminist themes—describing powerful women from her time and from the past, urging women to go beyond their expected pursuits, silencing male poets who slandered women. She was most published Italian poet of the century, but has been nearly entirely forgotten after death.

(1519–1577)

The whole energy in the villa changes that night, because they're about to meet Luca Bruni. Charlotte can feel the electricity in the air. Cliché, but so what, it feels like that—a flashing static something. Everyone's dressed up. Shaye's wearing a bandeau dress and lots of bangles up her arm (Claire's—twelve for five bucks, she announced proudly), and Charlotte's got the sundress on that she wore for graduation. Leo's wearing pink pants and a white shirt, because he's gorgeous *and* stylish. He's chatting with Avni, in her shiny gold top and tiny white skirt and high wedge sandals with a hole cut out of the heels.

The party is in the main room, the one with the huge glass ship mural and the arched windows that reach to the ceiling. Outside, each of those windows is flanked by white Roman columns, and a balcony stretches out, shorter columns making an elaborate railing. Far off, over the water on the island of Venice, Charlotte thinks she can spot the dome of Saint Mark's Basilica, and the pointed tip of its bell tower.

Avni and Leo sit on a buttery soft couch, which is set across from buttery soft chairs. The same chairs are also set in conversational pairs, facing out at the view, perfect for reading, in Charlotte's opinion. The doors to the balcony are open. Glass tables along the back wall are filled with white dishes of appetizers and a tray of champagne flutes. Music plays, some kind of electronica, and Eliot bobs his head to the beat like a heron snagging fish. Ashley tips down a flute of champagne and reaches for another. Hailey picks up a tiny bread with stuff piled on it and then licks her thumb. There's playful shoving and joking. Loud voices, laughter, high spirits. Energy. It's so exciting, watching the doorway for Luca Bruni to appear. And it sinks in, really, how amazing all of this is, even though it's nerve-racking, too. *This*, all of them here together, wanting to write, wanting to do this same thing, make this art. Wanting to learn from a master, because they love *his* art in particular, and because learning from a master you deeply admire is what young artists have done for eons. And they did it here, in this country, going back to the Renaissance and before.

Bethany Sparrow walks around with her head bent, speaking into her phone, plugging one ear so she can hear. She does this a lot. More than anything else so far.

"I'm nervous to meet him," Charlotte admits to Katerina and Shaye. "I saw him at a book signing once, but this is totally different."

"Same. Wait right here," Katerina says. In a minute she's back with a flute of champagne. "You don't have one of these. Here. That'll help."

Of course, Charlotte has drank before at parties, and Nate brought all that beer to the hotel room Carly's parents rented for them after prom. But she doesn't drink much, and Yas just won't until she's twenty-one. If Charlotte's mom ever smelled it on her, she'd kill her. After Nate's beer, she practically ate a tin of Carly's Altoids before she went home. Now she takes a few sips. In seconds, her limbs feel loose and warm.

"Hey, look who's here," Shaye says.

Charlotte's heart skips, but Shaye is nodding toward Althea Whitaker-Bruni, with her sleek blond hair and tangerine shift dress, who just sat down with Avni and Leo.

"She looks so different from her photos," Charlotte says. Different—*older*. Harsh, even. She doesn't know what she was expecting. Maybe, after all the loving things he says about her publicly, someone who looked . . . *nicer*.

"Hide me. She's terrifying," Katerina says.

"What does she do? I see photos of galas and stuff, but it's hard to tell." Charlotte wants to know everything about them. It's all interesting. Each little fact and crumb of gossip makes her feel closer, let in.

"'Do'? She has money. That's what she does," Shaye says. "Or else *did*, before he bought this island and they built *this*. Plus, she manages *him*. Can you imagine how much this cost, even if you have money? I heard they're thinking about renting it out when they don't live here or have students. Like, an event venue or something. I mean, no wonder they have to take in rich-kid writer wannabes. Sorry," she says to Katerina.

"No worries," Katerina says. "I'm grateful he's doing it, for whatever reason."

"I saw him today." Eliot appears next to them. "He walked right past me, but he didn't say anything. Just went down the hall to their living area and shut the door. He's way taller than I thought."

"You look nice," Katerina tells Eliot. He's wearing tan pants and a white shirt and a tie, and his hair is combed like it's school picture day.

"I changed my clothes three times. I mean, *Luca Bruni*. Big Mike says, 'You only have one chance to make a first impression.'" He rolls his eyes. Big Mike, *the* Big Mike, former NFL player and owner of the Big Mike Gym chain, is—get ready for it—Eliot's *dad*. He told them earlier, and he seemed used to their shock. *Yeah, yeah. Go ahead and say it—I must take after my mom*. Poor Eliot.

Everyone ambles around, and the food thins out and then gets cold, though the music still thumps. Charlotte stares up at that huge mural of the glass ship. The waves look so real, they seem to come right at her. She remembers a passage from the book, about the way a ship can never be truly ready for the power of water.

"It's beautiful," Leo says, next to her. He's so good-looking, he's almost a living, breathing version of a statue you might see here. A whoosh of pre-humiliation fills her. If she were writing this, the girl would somehow find her voice.

"I love that book," she says.

"Same. My favorite of his. I cried." He shrugs and smiles. It's hard to imagine that someone like Leo would find it relatable. She feels a funny pang of jealousy, the proprietary feeling you can get with a book or a song you love, since that book is *hers*.

"I actually brought it," Charlotte confesses. Now *she* shrugs.

"Hey, I get that. Some books change your life. I wonder where he is? I'm so jet-lagged. It's getting late."

Really late. Hailey and Ashley have plunked down in the buttery yellow chairs. Shaye's bandeau dress seems finished for the night. Eliot has loosened his tie. Althea Whitaker-Bruni left a long time ago. The music keeps pumping, though.

Finally, Bethany Sparrow clinks a glass with a knife. It's really not necessary, since they're all just sitting around *waiting*.

"Hey, guys!" she says. "Hey, I'm so sorry, but Luca won't be able to make it tonight. He isn't feeling well."

Charlotte's stomach sinks.

"Oh, no," Katerina says.

"Is he okay?" Charlotte asks.

"I'm sure he'll be fine. He's only . . ." Bethany searches

around for words. "Unwell." Her face is tight. The muscle in her cheek clenches in and out. It must be hard to deliver such disappointing news.

Because, wow, they're all crushed. The mood in the room drops. He can't help it if he's sick, but they were so excited to meet him. Someone shuts off the music, and the lights go up, and now there's no party; there's just people in a room.

The gold of Avni's top looks tired in the bright light. Katerina's lipstick is worn off, and Shaye's bangles droop. Avni starts heading upstairs, carrying her heels.

In their room, undressing for bed, Shaye says, "He was going to speak at the City College graduation last year, but he canceled. Maybe it's a thing."

It seems cruel. The poor guy doesn't feel well, after all.

Charlotte spots the Latin tattoo on Shaye's lower back again. "I like your tattoo. What does it mean?"

"*Facta non verba.* Deeds not words." She sounds mad.

It's a strange motto for someone who wants to be a writer. But then again, maybe it's perfect—a warning for those who fall in love with language too easily. Who give love too much leeway.

They say the first meeting you have with someone will tell you everything you need to know about your future relationship. This *not meeting*—same. At least, this is how Charlotte will think about it later. The way they all brought everything they had—their shine and talent and adoration. The way they waited and waited. The way Luca Bruni got to decide whether or not they were worth the bother.

Chapter Eleven

Barbara Lotti, poet.

Wrote on erotic themes, but mostly kept the gender of her poetic voice unclear.

(1519–unknown)

"Every day for two years, over fifty people worked on this place. An icon, really, to Italy's golden creative ages," Bethany tells them. The group has already toured the original living quarters of the old hospital workers, and now the incredible brick library with its turret and views out to the canal, where Luca Bruni keeps his own desk. Now they're standing at the edge of La Calamita, looking across the entire property. The air smells like sun and salt water and some kind of warm fruit. It's already hot, and Charlotte feels the sting of a burn on her shoulders.

"The whole pool area was excavated, and the antique foundations had to be entirely restructured, and the old sea-wall had to be repaired, to protect La Calamita from flooding. Three cranes were mounted simultaneously to raise huge volumes of Italian marble, wood, plaster . . . And tons of artisans—decorators, glassblowers, painters, mill workers, upholsterers, and on and on, have been working in *a tempest* of building materials. . . ."

"A tempest?" Leo grins. He's right. It's kind of over the top.

"Luca's words." Bethany gives a little shrug and then it's back on script, stuff Charlotte pretty much read already in *Design Magazine*. Still, it's exciting to hear about it while she's right on the island. "Stuccos, Venetian 'marmorino,' Italian marble, Venetian glass and fabrics. They wanted to meld the oldest and world-famous Venetian traditions with every contemporary amenity."

"*Marmor-rino,*" Hailey says with her usual exaggerated Italian accent, and Ashley gives her a little shove. Already, those two are joined at the hip, and sharing clothes. Hailey's wearing the sun hat Ashley brought to the pool.

"Over this way." Bethany begins to walk again.

Behind the buildings, they walk on one of the clearer paths through shrubs and trees, heading toward the bell tower. On the way, they pass a small abandoned building, mostly boarded up, aside from a green door hanging open from its hinge. Shaye trots over to peek inside.

"Don't go in there, you guys!" Bethany yells over her shoulder. "It's not safe."

Eliot is peeking inside too, but then he lets out a shriek and runs to catch back up with them.

"Brr." Shaye shivers.

"What was in there?" Charlotte makes a *yikes* face. It looked creepy.

"Ugh. Disturbing cement floor. An old toilet. Hooks on the wall, like for coats. Ghosts," Shaye says.

"I see dead people!" Eliot cries.

They step over and around ruins of brick and crumbled plaster and make their way down the path until they're through the brush and out on the far side of the island. Up ahead is the bell tower and the small building attached to it. The whole structure is covered in iron scaffolding, still under renovation, and dripping with vines and brambles.

"Wow," Hailey says.

"Oh, scary," Ashley says. "After what happened up there."

"What happened up there?" Eliot asks. Charlotte has no clue either.

Ashley only grimaces in answer. "You don't want to know."

Avni looks up, peering through another pair of expensive sunglasses. "I wouldn't want to go up there."

"This gives you some idea of what a disaster the whole place was." Bethany waves one arm around, indicating the scaffolding and mess. "They're still working on this building. The views are pretty amazing up there, if you're brave enough to climb the stairs."

"I'm brave enough," Shaye says.

Bethany shakes her head. "Liability," she says, and then goes back to her tour guide script. "Next year people might be able to. But, before the Brunis, no one would touch this place, with its haunted history. No one would even *step foot* on the island."

"Except for the dude who painted *that*," Hailey says, pointing to some graffiti under the scaffolding. Ashley laughs way harder than it deserves.

Bethany ignores them. "Over the centuries, one hundred thousand people died on La Calamita and were buried in the plague pits. They say this soil is made of ash from the dead. Venetians also said they could hear screams coming from this place."

"I heard a scream last night," Eliot says. He seems to mean it.

"That was Hailey. She was in my room and stepped on my wet towel in the dark," Ashley says. They both start to laugh.

"You *guys*," Avni says, like she's tired of them already.

"One evil doctor took patients to this building, to perform torturing experiments on them, until he himself became deranged. Pursued by island ghosts, some thought. He flung himself from this very tower," Bethany says.

They're all looking up, and, honestly, no one wants to joke now. History is only words, until it isn't. Until it's real stuff that happened to people.

"I told you that you didn't want to know," Ashley says, but it's not funny. They're all silent, staring toward the tiny balcony up there, and it's hot, and Charlotte's wishing she'd brought a water bottle, when suddenly, the green shuttered doors of that little building burst open. Ashley screams, and Charlotte jumps back, and Eliot shrieks and stumbles into Leo, who makes a face.

But it's him.

It's Luca Bruni. He's wearing shorts and a Clash T-shirt, and he doesn't look the least bit sick. He's taller than you'd think, and he looks handsome, really, in that odd, rumpled, almost geeky way, with his unruly hair and big nose and, somehow, the most magnetic smile you've ever seen in your life. He's laughing. He's laughing so hard about shocking them.

"Writers!" he shouts. The word, spoken by him, sends a deep blush through Charlotte's face. She's not sure he's serious, calling them that, because he's smirking, too. But he wouldn't have chosen them if he didn't believe in them, would he? "Look at us, here together in the birthplace of some of the most epic writers and artists in history! Virgil, and Dante, Tasso, Petrarch—the poets! Ovid and his *Metamorphoses*—the first work of the stream of consciousness genre. Julius Caesar—thank him for all these *memoirs* we see now!" He rolls his eyes, and they laugh. "Boccaccio's *Decameron*, first romance novel! And that's before we even get to opera and art and sculpture, architecture—Vivaldi, Michelangelo, Da Vinci . . . Are you *inspired*?"

So much so. So much so already. Hailey gives a little squeal. God, think of it. It all gives Charlotte goose bumps.

"Avni Sharma!" Luca barks, as if he's calling roll.

Avni raises her hand. She does it so coolly, though, with the kind of confidence Charlotte can't even imagine. She looks him straight in the eye, as if she's already decided she would meet him head-on.

"Saffron and sex," he says. "*Very* steamy, yet understated."

She raises her eyebrows, and her mouth drops a little, as if he's thrown her off her game already. Charlotte has no idea what the words mean, but Avni must. "That's me."

"Shaye Rivers," he says. And now Shaye gives a little wave. "Stained couch. Whiskey." He mimes putting a knife in his chest and pulling it out again. Their application stories, Charlotte realizes. That's what he's referring to.

"Yep." Shaye crosses her arms. She sounds defiant. But Charlotte sees that she's pleased, too.

"Katerina, Katerina. Katerina Chandler."

She smiles shyly.

"That mother, who leaves." He smacks his hand to his heart. "Fuck."

"Sorry," she pretend-apologizes.

"Do it again." He goes down the list. *Ashley Chen, the party of the century! Hailey Murphy—I laughed so hard at that old guy. Eliot Vankard. Fantasy's not usually my thing, but wow.* And then, Charlotte herself.

"Such a lonely girl," he says. His eyes lock on to hers. "Hidden for too long."

She blushes. Her whole body seems to. It was such a revealing thing to say, it's like he just removed her clothes. She feels the shock and embarrassment of that, but also the quiet, illicit thrill of it too. She's struck.

He moves on to Leo. "Leo Dimitri." He looks at Leo for a long time. "Ah, I got it now. Mr. Hot Shit, huh?"

Leo looks down at his white pants, rolled up at the cuff, and his blue T-shirt and sandals. "I—"

It seems kind of mean, and he's the only one who doesn't get addressed by something in his story. But Charlotte isn't paying much attention to it. It's hard to, with the large feeling in her chest. *Such a lonely girl. Hidden for too long.* It felt full of meaning, as if he understood her already. His words had undertones of a challenge, or maybe a promise. They were so personal that she wonders if anyone noticed.

She doesn't have much time to think about any of it, this weird electricity that she feels after he says that and looks at her like that. Because Luca Bruni suddenly claps his large hands together, and Bethany Sparrow is handing out notepads and pens.

"Okay!" Luca Bruni shouts. "Sit down somewhere. In this place of ghosts and ash, I want to know what haunts you."

Chapter Twelve

Battista Vernazza, writer.

Entered the convent at age thirteen and spent her life there. Four books and numerous poems were published only after her death.
(1497–1587)

What haunts them—this will be the theme of the larger story they'll be working on for the next ten weeks, Bethany announces. And what haunts Charlotte? Failure, right then, as the pens scritch and scratch around her, and the pages turn. She's thumped with a pang of missing home, because this all feels large. She tries to find a shady spot on the tower steps, but it's hot, and there's so much to distract her—seabirds squawking as they circle around the fishing boats out front; a choke hold of ivy climbing up the brick; the tilt of Avni's beautiful face, looking for inspiration in the azure sky; Luca Bruni (Do they call him *Luca* now?), sitting close enough that she can see the brown hair on his legs and arms, and his long fingers—the ones that typed *The Glass Ship*!—around a pen of his own. He must feel her stare, because he looks up, and they meet eyes, and she smiles, embarrassed, and pretends to write again. Oh, God, Carly would just die if she knew what was happening right now.

The electric feeling—it fills Charlotte again, and with it comes a zap of desire to expand her life to its outermost edges, to *do* this thing right here, and do it so well that Luca Bruni *sees*. So, okay. What haunts her? Her dad, leaving for the hundredth time, maybe lonely, in lonely hotels and lonely airports; her mother, with her frustration and rage that feels as if it's *pacing*, waiting for something, whatever, anything. Her sister, at home without her. Her own longing and uncertainty, and some big hole that feels like hunger.

Isabella di Angelo. Yes. The way she never got what she deserved. Maybe that's what haunts her: everyone in her life who doesn't get what they need most.

Throughout the day, she spots Eliot in one of the yellow chairs in the huge living room, bent over his pages, his white shoulders turning the color of a pomegranate from their morning in the sun. And she sees Hailey and Ashley, by the pool again, notebooks on knees. Leo is sitting on the edge of the canal, sandals off, his feet making italic swirls in the water. She also sees Luca Bruni and Avni, sitting across from each other at a table on the garden patio, Avni's head tilted, listening, as Luca Bruni leans back in his chair, one leg crossed, speaking in a way that looks commanding and satisfied. Can you imagine, being that relaxed and commanding at the same time? Charlotte can't. Of course, girls like Avni get all the attention too, Charlotte thinks, but then hates herself for it. He's a grown man. A grown and famous and married and, like, practically forty, man. Stop! She doesn't know what's wrong with her. That look he gave her, it just . . . Whatever. She's being stupid. What he said to her, the *way* he said it—it's taking up weird space in her head. He is. He's just so funny and full and magnetic.

Dinner is at eight. The patio is lit with those white bulbs strung overhead, and there's the sweetest smell of lemons on trees, but also the *I am suddenly STARVING* smell of food—garlic, tomatoes, seafood, who knows what, but wow. Platters are passed around. There's spaghetti with tomato sauce and a smoky cheese. Not the thick sauce that blops from a jar at home, but scant, barely-there tomatoes. And shrimp scampi, and these little dumplings that have a seafood sauce and are filled with . . .

"What's in these?" Charlotte whispers to Shaye.

"Bread and maybe prawns. *Canederli*, I heard someone say," Shaye answers as Charlotte scoops.

How far away are high school and her mom and dad and friends? Far, very far. Far enough to do stuff you wouldn't ordinarily. Far enough that you feel like a newborn person. The paper tablecloth that said CONGRATULATIONS, GRADUATE and the way she and Yas colored on the bottom of their shoes with ink pens was practically minutes ago, but it feels like years. Adam is a tiny, vanishing speck from the past. All of this says *amazing adult future life promise*, scary but awesome. There's wine, and Donata (the gray-haired woman, more the villa manager than chef, Charlotte has learned, since there are two of those, too) keeps bringing more. The warmth of it fills Charlotte from the center of her chest outward and makes her thoughts get pleasantly hazy.

Althea (who Luca Bruni introduces as *my beautiful wife, Althea Whitaker-Bruni*) sits on his left, and Avni sits on his right, and they're all straight across the table from Charlotte. Luca Bruni seems much less open than he was that afternoon. In spite of the beautiful night and food and wine and the glow that makes everything look magical, he sits straight and uncomfortable, and his speech is careful. The conversation around the table gets louder and louder, and Charlotte's doing that kind of rude thing where she's talking to Shaye about this guy Shaye just broke up with who drank too much, while at the same time trying to hear whatever Luca Bruni is saying.

Luca's wife barely eats, and she cuts her food into teeny pieces she just moves around her plate as she tells Leo about using a decorating firm in Boston, where they live, to get every Venetian detail right, searching for gilded mirrors and . . . It's hard to catch the rest. Althea's blond hair shines under the lights, and Charlotte can see the varying shades of color a hairstylist carefully put in. Althea's hands are manicured, flawless white-pink nails. Shaye must be doing the same thing as

Charlotte, though, because she interrupts herself and says, "Hey, Bruni, you must have sold a lot of books."

Wow, that's rude, especially after what Shaye told them at the party, how Althea was the one with the money. Althea's eyebrows turn downward, but Luca only laughs. A huge, delighted laugh. His laugh is so awesome.

"More than almost any living writer aside from that dude who writes *horror*, but nah. I only bought the piece-of-shit place no one else wanted. The brilliant Althea Whitaker-Bruni did the rest."

"It's amazing," Katerina ass-kisses.

"Immensely talented, *and* beautiful," he says.

A lemon mousse arrives. Shaye leans over and whispers, "Jesus, is he required to compliment her every time he opens his mouth?"

"Really," Charlotte says. It's one of those relationships you're sure you can understand in two seconds. You're probably wrong, though.

"Poor guy," Shaye says. No kidding. It's strange—Charlotte admires him so much, but seeing even that small glimpse into his homelife . . . She feels sorry for him too. Really sorry.

When Althea gets up to excuse herself for the night and then exits, everyone exhales. The mood lightens. It's like the recess teacher is gone. More wine is poured. The laughter gets louder. Luca—that *is* what they're calling him now—keeps setting his arm against Avni's, or maybe it's just Charlotte's imagination. Ashley says, "Oh my God, mmm, mmmm, I could eat this all day," and licks the lemon off her spoon like it's, um, not a spoon.

"Wow," Luca says, and chuckles. "You're good at that."

"Jeez, Ash," Hailey says.

Bruni leans on the table with both elbows and looks at them deeply. "So, who's ready to reveal their innermost secrets?"

"I told you guys to bring the stuff you wrote, right?" Bethany Sparrow says from the far end of the table, where she's spent a lot of the evening tapping on her phone. There's a boyfriend back home, someone said.

"Right. I'll go first." Avni stands. She probably always goes first, Charlotte thinks, then immediately regrets the thought. Avni is confident and smart and gorgeous, but she's also nice. Earlier, when she found out Charlotte just graduated, she offered all kinds of great advice about her first year of college. And when Avni reads her piece about how she's haunted by her own ambition and the shadow of her doctor father's success, Charlotte sees she's talented, too. Really talented. Like, from that very first sentence, she writes with authority, but you feel the honest pain there too. Her father sounds like an arrogant asshole, but she never says it like that. She just shows it in a scene with Avni's mom in the car. Avni is someone who could really make it as a writer, Charlotte realizes. She could make it right now.

"That was really amazing, Avni," Shaye says. "Wow."

"Beautiful," Luca Bruni says. "Beautiful. Haunted by *I won't ever be enoughs*. Yes."

"Next?" Bethany Sparrow says.

"I'll go." Katerina pulls her notebook out from her bag. "It's hard to read in this light."

"Here," Leo says. He shines his phone flashlight.

"Fuck, man, don't you know chivalry is an insult to female power?" Luca says, and Leo's face falls.

"I can see," Katerina says, and begins to read. God, it's sad. What haunts her is an orphanage, one she was actually in, in Russia, where she was born. Smells, the feel of a coat, her mother's coat, being left all alone—man. It's devastating. The table is quiet. There's only the *chirrup* sound of night insects and the far-off lap of waves against the seawall.

"Wow," Hailey says. She holds the ends of her two braids together. "I can't even imagine it."

"Hey. Mutual abandonment issues, you and me." Luca Bruni looks at Katerina across the table, until Eliot pipes in.

"Who even wants to follow *that*," he says, but then he does. It's a funny, funny piece about not fitting in. The kind of story that's sad but hilarious, where he's made fun of, and you laugh, but you see how the laughter is heartbreaking. Luca Bruni begins to talk about truth, how mining that shit is *power*. It's the second time he's used the word *power*, but when someone like him says it, it's like he's sharing his with you.

The laughing and the heartbreak, the amazing way Katerina described that coat, and the tender way Eliot described the kid who stole his journal, and the night and the stars coming out and the crickets and the lemon smell growing stronger as it gets later and later—it all makes Charlotte want to write *so hard*. It makes her want to create something wonderful and meaningful. It makes her believe she *can*.

"One more?" Bethany Sparrow lifts her index finger.

Charlotte spins her rings. But the wine also makes her feel braver than usual, and so does the far-from-home feeling. "I'll go."

Everyone quiets in order to listen. God, they're *so* quiet, just waiting. But here's her voice, on this island, in this incredible foreign country, surrounded by people who are becoming more familiar. Here are her secrets—the big hole, her father with the suitcase always packed, the slam of dishes and doors, the generations of needs, going back to the long-forgotten Isabella di Angelo, who was maybe the true creator of one of the most famous poems in history.

"Whoa, for real?" Hailey says. "You've got to find out if it's true."

"Antonio Tasso! Analyzing that stupid poem was the only paper I ever got a C on," Katerina says.

"Man." Eliot shakes his head. "I don't know. That's like saying your relative actually wrote Dante's *Inferno*."

"Patriarchal masculinity, the underbelly of civilization—you think it's impossible?" Luca Bruni says to Eliot. "Female artists were *a threat*. All of them. *Of course* their historical legacies were stolen or lost or 'forgotten.'"

Charlotte never thought of it that way, exactly, but she loves how Luca Bruni is a feminist. He shows it in a million ways. No, she loves everything about him.

"There's got to be someone here who could tell you more," Avni says. "If you could stick it to that guy, it'd be awesome. He's a total asshole." Charlotte's face scrunches in doubt. "You didn't know that?"

"I've read twelve million books about him, and they all say how amazing he was," Charlotte says.

"A book about him came out after *La Campagna*, when there was that Tasso craze. He supposedly had sex with everyone in sight. He was a tyrant, too. To his kids, his wife, students he taught. Tromped around like an egomaniac."

"Is that bad?" Eliot says, and they all laugh.

"If that poem wasn't his . . . that'd be so fucking great," Avni says.

"But you said she was in a *convent*? I don't get how she could be doing it with the guy. Tasso's just going to go waltz in there and have sex with a nun? It sounds a little far-fetched," Ashley says.

"I always wondered that too," Charlotte admits.

"Far-fetched? No way!" Luca Bruni says. "Those places were full of party girls. Are you kidding?"

"Wait," Leo says. "So, she lived in Venice, and her book was published in 1573? The *plague* struck in 1575. Maybe she was actually *here*. Like, *right* here, on this island."

"Maybe she still is," Luca Bruni says.

• • •

It's getting late. Everyone gets up to head back inside. There are calls of *Buonanotte! Buonanotte a tutti!* Good night! Good night, everyone! Charlotte says it too, even though she knows her accent is laughable. She's halfway to the villa when she realizes she forgot her phone. She returns to the table, snags it where it's half hidden under her napkin. Luca and Avni are still lingering, just the two of them under the little white lights. He keeps touching her arm as they talk, and then, as Charlotte nears, she hears him say, "Hey, you know, I'd love to read more of your stuff."

"You would, huh?" Avni tilts her head, pleased.

"I would, huh." His voice is teasing. "I'll give you my private email."

Charlotte edges past awkwardly. Inside the villa, she tries not to look at the huge painting of the glass ship, and as she climbs the stairs to her room, the feeling that she might create something wonderful slips. The warmth and bravery of alcohol is leaving her. She feels sober, in every definition of the word. She feels uncomfortable about the two of them back there, or maybe just competitive. Luca didn't say anything about her piece, not really. Neither did anyone else. He certainly didn't offer his email to her.

Nothing feels as important as pleasing him. He's so large and great and funny, and this is her big chance. She's going to have to do better.

Chapter Thirteen

Isabella Cervoni, poet.

Wrote her first important poem at age fifteen, and political poems from the age of fifteen to twenty-five, when any more information about her disappears.

(1575–1600)

"Stern, huh? Wow, you don't picture him with someone like that. I wonder why they never had kids."

"No idea."

It's morning on La Calamita, but getting late at home. Ella's over at her friend Aanya's house for a sleepover, so they don't get to talk. Earlier, though, Charlotte caught Yas right before she boarded her flight to Maryland, for her NASA internship at Goddard Space Flight Center, and she finally answered all those texts from Carly, too, about the party Nate gave, where only four people plus Adam showed up. It's weird, but that gossip feels too distant to be relevant. Like a NASA rocket, the boosters that propelled Charlotte skyward have detached and are falling away.

Now Adele wants to know everything: what Luca Bruni's like, and how he dresses, and what sort of person his wife is. Charlotte walks the outer edges of the villa, away from everyone else, as she answers her mother's questions. She almost doesn't *want* to share. She wants all of it—the behind-the-scenes stuff, the private moments, the whole experience—to be *hers*. The ground is rocky, and she has to step carefully over it as brushy stuff rubs against her ankles. She avoids the patches of overgrown foliage, trying to stay on the path.

"Well, call again soon so Ella can talk, and keep posting those photos. Wow, they're amazing. I want to see *everything*. Aunt Tony keeps texting every time she sees one, like she just can't believe you're there."

Charlotte spots an unusual rock and bends down to pick it up. It's yellowed and old, and has a strange, spongy appearance, and a deep hole, and—oh, God, oh, shit! She flings it away, and the only reason she doesn't scream is that her mother is on the other end of the line. Oh, jeez. She knows what that was. She's seen bones before. Only when they've given them to Marv, but still.

"Oh, Char, I'm glad this experience is everything you dreamed it would be," her mom says.

A bone. An actual *bone*.

It's hard not to think about what Luca Bruni said last night. How maybe Isabella is still here, actually and truly, on this island, amid that earth and ash. It's hard not to think about who else might be too.

• • •

Now they're riding away from La Calamita in two boats, one driven by Aldo, and one driven by Aldo's son, Marc. Apparently, she's not the only one who finds the island eerie—the water taxi drivers refuse to go out there, Bethany tells them, not just because it's too far, but because they think it's haunted, and they're superstitious. Charlotte is stuck with Aldo again, and his booze breath and opera on loud, the bow of the boat high as they speed through the water.

"Vivaldi," Eliot shouts. "We're going to be walking on the same streets he walked on! The same streets as Michelangelo, and Marco Polo, and Antonio Tasso. Sorry," he says to Charlotte.

"It's fine." She shrugs.

"Classical music sucks," Shaye says as Hailey applies sun lotion to her fair skin, and as Ashley holds her hat on her head with one hand so it doesn't blow away. Charlotte's own dark hair is pulled back into a long ponytail. She sits on the hem of her sundress so it doesn't blow around.

Luca Bruni is on the other boat with Avni, Katerina, Leo, and Bethany Sparrow. Charlotte really doesn't mind which boat she's on, though—it just feels so good to be off La Calamita and heading into Venice for the first time. It's crazy, because . . . well, there's an incredible villa, and that pool, and the lemon trees, and the food, and every corner of the place is worthy to share on social media. But it's spooky, she thinks, the way La Calamita closes in on you. Maybe any small island would make you feel like that, but out here, on this boat, she can breathe. She's getting farther away from that piece of bone in her hand, and all those ghosts, and the image of Luca's hand touching Avni's arm *stroking, that's what he was doing, admit it* that night at dinner.

The boat cuts and bumps through the choppy waves, until Venice all at once reveals itself in a broad panorama of interconnected islands, and bridges, and tilting palaces, and lacy buildings. Aldo slows, and then arcs inward, entering the Grand Canal, the wide waterway that curves through the center of the main island. There's so much to take in—the motorboats zipping, the gondolas (real gondolas!) bobbing at their red-and-white-striped mooring poles and gliding through the waters, the large Rialto Bridge ahead.

The boats dock, and they all climb out onto the landing. Everyone's talking at once, though Avni looks cool and unimpressed, reminding them with her offhand posture and aloof gaze that she's been here before.

"No cars," Charlotte says. Of course, this is obvious, but it's suddenly weirdly noticeable. A city with no cars, just boats, and as they begin to walk, she can already see hidden alleyways of water everywhere, the tucked-away canals of mirror-like green. Also: sounds. Shouts in Italian, one gondolier to another; a waiter outside a restaurant, urging tourists inside; overheard bits of dialogue in other languages too, French, and maybe German, because the street is busy with tourists.

"This way," Bethany Sparrow says. The schedule lists

Walking tour of Venice and *Saint Mark's Basilica*, though the daily writing prompts are always a surprise. The group follows Bethany down one stairwell and up another, past shops with gold jewelry or glass or handbags in the windows, past groupings of tables with white tablecloths in outdoor restaurants, and rows upon rows of gondolas alongside flat, old fishing boats. Bethany turns into an alley, where there's the sound of glasses clinking in a restaurant, and above her, Charlotte sees shutters and more shutters. The alley opens onto a street with other shops—clothing, violins!—where everyone seems to be hurrying somewhere. Rushing past her: old ladies with shopping bags, and people on their phones, and two nuns, even.

"Bruni!" a guy calls from a balcony, and waves. Further on, a trio of teens shout his name, and everyone has to stop so they can get his autograph. Wow, they love him here, she sees. Maybe even more than in the US. He's a *celebrity* who actually lives here part of the time, so it's probably like spotting Hunter Eden or someone from Armor Class Zero in Seattle. And he's so great with them! He's speaking in Italian and obviously cracking jokes, because they're laughing, and he takes the time for a photo with each of them, leaning his long frame down, smiling so wide. He's got that big, awesome laugh that's like a prize you earned when he does it. He's *full*—of energy and joy, like they just poured it into him.

But *those* kids . . . *They* have to walk away, content with a photo they can post. They don't get to spend the summer with Luca. They're not his very own students, living under his roof.

He's *theirs*, you know. He's special, so they are too. It feels good. It feels like a balloon in your chest.

Now they cross a piazza with a fountain in the center, and go up and over more canals, past tiny markets with fruits and vegetables outside, and mysterious doors painted in all colors. It's a maze. Who knows where they are now, after twists and turns down the slender stone streets, where some buildings most definitely look like they're sinking, and others look like a Disney movie set, with patches of exposed brick and flower baskets under the windows. If she were writing it . . . Forget it. She just wants to remember it, all of it. The portly waiter sweeping, the bored shopkeeper having a smoke, an old man whistling as he strolls down an alley, tourists poring over maps and trying to figure out where they are.

And it's all so old. *So* old. Yeah, Vivaldi and Michelangelo and Tasso walked on these same streets, but so did Isabella di Angelo. Right here. Her heart beat in this same place. That ash, that bone, Charlotte's vow to *know* her, to know *what happened* to her—it feels more urgent. It's a nagging question.

Up ahead, behind Bethany Sparrow, Luca Bruni walks beside Avni, their sleeves touching, as the group proceeds down a cold passageway. Suddenly, they're standing in an enormous, sunny piazza, with a wide sky overhead, and what a shock, because there's Saint Mark's Basilica, in all its ancient, rising glory—gold archways and spires and towers.

"Wow," Shaye says, and Eliot has his camera out already, though Hailey and Ashley seem more interested in the hundreds of pigeons that fill the square. Ashley has both arms out, inviting them to land on her. Hailey takes a selfie, and Leo fishes a guidebook out of his back pocket to read more about the place.

Inside, Bethany leads them on a tour. Charlotte stares at immense ceilings of gold and mosaic floors of gold and cupolas of gold, and at the paintings of winged angels everywhere you look. Had Isabella ever looked up at those same painted clouds? Probably, right? Charlotte wants to *know*, though. At home, the mystery was intriguing, but here, it's just plain frustrating.

After they leave, back in the sun again, they scoot several tables together at an outdoor café and drink tiny cups of espresso. Luca Bruni talks about setting as character, as mood, as inspiration. He tells them about *The Tide of Years*, how the pink-colored sands of the island of Budelli became a metaphor. He makes them laugh so hard when he tells them about gathering tin cans on the road to sell for money as a kid, but it's sad, too.

"I want a multisensory experience of one location!" Luca Bruni booms as Bethany Sparrow hands out maps. Luca looks kind of tired, actually. "Your choice. Be back here by five."

If Charlotte's mother knew she was set free in a foreign city with only a map, she'd probably freak out. A part of *her* is freaking out, but the other part is jazzed on that tiny cup of adrenaline she just drank. She decides not to go very far so she won't get lost. She'll walk in one direction, but stay close to Saint Mark's. This is easier said than done. She steps up and over waterways, turns down narrow passageways, and almost immediately, she has no idea where she is.

Somehow, as if she's led—and later, she will believe this, that she was led—she finds herself at the opening of a short street with a tall brick building at the end. There's a table out front, stuffed with sheets of paper and tubs of photographs, and several spinning card racks. Also, a wheelbarrow. A wheelbarrow full of *books*.

A basket full of books hangs from a nearby tree too. Charlotte snaps some photos for Carly and Ella, because they would *love* this. As Charlotte stands in the doorway, a cat circles her legs.

Inside—wow. *Wow.* There's the most shocking, chaotic, magical bookstore she's ever seen. It's stuffed, jammed full. Books are towering and tipping like the city itself. Books are piled in old bathtubs, and more bathtubs, wooden boats, and barrels. Books are stacked and jumbled in a full-size gondola in the center of the room, and crammed into sinks, and waterproof bins. Charlotte winds her way under old chandeliers and around heaps of maps and manuscripts, marble busts, and antique paintings hanging high up on the walls. At the far end of the store, a set of green shuttered doors, painted with the words *Alta Acqua Libreria*, are propped open by an antique chair, revealing a canal.

Another iron gate leads to a patio, where she finds several green tables with chairs. Stacked against the patio wall, higher than you can reach, are old, worn books, warped by water and tattered by time, formed into a staircase. The painted sign on it reads: *Follow the Books. Steps. Climb. Go Up. Wonderful View.*

Of course, Charlotte does. At the top, over the wall, the view *is* wonderful—the canal, with tall, green shuttered houses, a string of laundry from one window to another.

Charlotte sits at one of the iron tables. It's the easiest writing assignment ever. She spills words until her hand cramps, describing the murky smell of the canal water, the tottering stacks, all those stories on the shelves and in boats. Voices—the woman behind the register, speaking to a young guy at the counter. She can only make out *Dante* and *biblioteca*—library.

It suddenly hits her: Isabella's second book of poetry could be here. She types *Alta Acqua Libreria* into her phone to find out more. Incredible—this place has over a hundred thousand volumes, and they're in those boats and bathtubs to protect them from the *acqua alta*, the seasonal flooding that happens on the island. *A hundred thousand volumes.* She only needs *one*.

As she heads toward the register, she spots a small book in English about the old Venice convents and brings it to the counter. "*Scusi,*" she says to the woman. She's about Charlotte's mom's age, with short wavy hair, a take-no-shit expression, and bold, chunky jewelry worn with her white shirt and jeans.

"Yes?"

"I'm looking for a book? By a Venetian poet from the 1500s? She's not very well known. She was a, um . . ." What would you even call it? Especially to this stranger, with her impatient eyes? “A friend of Antonio Tasso’s?” It all seems so silly when she says it aloud. *Of course* they won’t have it.

“Impossible!” the woman says. “How do we find her in all of *this*?” She sweeps one arm out.

“I’m sorry. *Grazie*,” Charlotte says. She slides her money across the counter. She’s embarrassed. Uncomfortable. She wishes she could just leave, but her politeness-guilt slinks in. “I love your store. I love books.”

God. She takes her bag and heads out of there. She’s nearly out the door when the woman calls to her.

“Wait. You said Antonio Tasso? You can see the poem, do you know? ‘In Guerra,’ at the Biblioteca Marciana. *He* you can find.”

“‘In Guerra’?” Sure, it’s his most famous poem, but this feels like *fate*. “I didn’t know. Thank you.”

“Ask for Dante Luchessi.” She’s writing the name on the back of the store’s card. “He can show it to you. Call him, if you need.”

“Dante?”

“Dante, my son.”

Chapter Fourteen

Margherita Sarrocchi, poet.

One of the first female poets to write an epic poem, to which she dedicated most of her life. In it, she featured female friendships, and rewrote the depictions of women by male poets, showing that their lives didn't revolve around men. Now, though, she's mostly known for her correspondence with Galileo.

(1560–1617)

Charlotte gets a little lost going back. She has a moment of panic when she doesn't see the group anywhere. She texts Bethany Sparrow.

Where are you guys?

A second later: *Ding.* Their location. The far southwest corner of the Doge's Palace, according to the map, right by the Bridge of Sighs. Charlotte just needs to head toward the lagoon from where she is in Saint Mark's Square. Okay, there they are, at the very edge of an outdoor corridor made of marble and arches. The edge of it drops straight into the Cannaregio Canal.

She's the last one to arrive. Everyone's huddled around

Katerina. Katerina is soaking wet. Her brown hair is sopping, and her mascara has smeared to two arcs under her eyes, and her skirt actually drips. She's lost a shoe. She's crying.

"Oh my God, is she okay?" Charlotte asks.

"She fell in." Shaye smirks. "She wanted Ashley to get the Bridge of Sighs behind her in a photo, and she stepped too far back. Good thing Ashley was using Katerina's phone, or it'd be gone."

"Wow," Charlotte says. She never even thought about the possibility—falling in, drowning.

"SIGH," Eliot says dramatically, and begins to laugh.

It's one of those things that's not funny but kind of funny, especially since Katerina's okay. Luca Bruni has his arm around her shoulder. Bethany's handing her a zippered sweatshirt from her bag. But when Eliot laughs, Luca's head snaps up. He stares right at Eliot, shooting him missiles of anger with his eyes.

"You think this is hilarious? You want to go in yourself and see how funny it is? I can make that happen, dude." Luca's voice drips fury, and he doesn't look lanky and awkward anymore. This change—it's shocking. It's something new about him Charlotte would never have expected. Sure, she's seen him rage at critics in articles and stuff, but those are *words*. Standing here, he looks ready to fight. He leans forward, and his long finger jabs the air, as if it's Eliot's chest.

Eliot blushes fiercely. He's so thin and pale, you can see his neck break out in blotches. Leo's face goes serious, and Shaye looks down. "I—hey, I'm sorry," Eliot says. "I'm sorry."

"Luca, it's fine," Bethany Sparrow says.

"Fuck, man. This isn't funny. She's scared to death."

Charlotte spins her rings on her fingers. Rage makes her anxious. Really, really anxious. She wishes she were back in that bookstore, or *anywhere*, but not here.

Bethany turns her attention back to Katerina. "You okay? Ready to head back?"

Katerina nods from the huddle of Bethany's sweatshirt. Luca Bruni squeezes her shoulder and then says, "Let's go."

On the way back, in their boat, Eliot is quiet. No one says anything about what happened. There's that awkwardness in the air, the kind that makes everyone speak more carefully, the kind that you can feel prickling underneath your skin.

That feeling lasts through dinner. At least it does for Charlotte, who's very familiar with the sort of intense outburst that makes you uneasy for hours afterward. It's so familiar, she's practically homesick, at least for the bedroom she usually hides in. She wants to kick Eliot under the table, same as Ella would, to make sure he's okay.

Maybe she's the only one feeling this way, though, because everyone else seems to be laughing and having fun. Katerina sits next to Luca, with Avni on his other side. His wife, Althea, has gone back to Boston, and Luca's returned to his pre-outburst self. He's joking and laughing, running his hand through his mess of curls and saying *Ah, shit!* when Shaye calls him out on something, his playful eyes glinting in the candlelight.

And, yes, there's all the stuff she read about his quick temper, his snappish answers to stupid questions at lectures, his cut-them-dead remarks to journalists who even slightly criticized him. There was that glimpse of rage lying just under the surface that she saw today. But what's hard to understand is the shift Charlotte feels right now, as he sits across from her. He used that rage to defend Katerina, and so while it scares her, it also makes Charlotte feel weirdly protected. She feels his . . . *power.* A knowing settles into her, that his temper or fury could keep someone, her, a young woman, safe. It's such an amazing, incredible, magical idea, that she can almost overlook how unsettling that sort of temper is too. You have to be careful with people like that, Charlotte knows. You don't want to ever upset them. You never know what they might do when they get mad.

"He's kind of an asshole," Shaye says that night. She's just taken a shower, so her usually spiky hair is damp and flat, and her arms are looped around her knees. "Have you noticed?"

Charlotte shrugs.

"Ugh. It's hard when assholes are charming. But when they're charming and brilliant and funny *and* write something like *A Mile of Faces* . . . forget it."

"Really," Charlotte says.

"You know what I hate, though?" Shaye doesn't wait for an

answer. "The way people *use* him. Those kids today, wanting his autograph. Everyone online posting those stupid selfies with him. Like meeting him for two seconds shows how great their own life is. Like he's not an actual *human being*."

"He seemed okay with it. He seemed to love it."

"I mean, he's not just *an object*. He's not just a Famous Person. I'd never do that. I'd never post a photo. I care about the actual *him*."

Charlotte wakes up in the middle of the night. Maybe from the sound of two people laughing loudly outside by the pool. Or maybe from the light of Shaye's laptop, her fingers tip-tapping on the keys.

Shaye's head is bent down, but Charlotte can still see her expression, lit by the dim blue glow. She can tell just how Shaye feels by looking at her. Charlotte has felt that way herself. Determined. Determined to write something really, really good. Maybe unforgettable. The desire to rise so high that maybe you finally prove something to a person that matters. The desire to be good enough to be *seen*.

Chapter Fifteen

Aurelia Petrucci, poet.

Daughter of an exiled ruler, she wrote political poetry but was known for her beauty and charm. While she was alive, she had many admiring male poets, who dedicated books to her and wrote her flirtatious, flattering letters. Her early death at age thirty-one sparked many gushing, lamenting poems, calling her an angel, praising her looks and her poetic talents. She was so exceptional, one of her most persistent admirers wrote that she "wasn't an imperfect female, but a perfect male, in a woman's body."

(1511–1542)

For the next few days, their schedule is so busy, there's no time for texts from friends, or social media, or calls to home, aside from the photo she sends Ella of a brown-and-white dog and a woman sitting at a café table across from each other like a married couple. Honestly, there probably *is* time for a call to Ella, but whenever she thinks of her anxious little sister, shivering at swimming lessons (she always gets so cold), or enduring those tense dinners with her parents, just the three of them,

Charlotte has to shake off the guilt. It's a relief to be away, yeah, but it's also so fun, a blast, piling into boats, and spilling out again into new locations.

Everywhere they go, Charlotte keeps that card close to her, the one from the woman at the bookstore. She moves it from pocket to backpack to purse. It's not about the boy's name on the card. In fact, she's sure she can find the poem on her own. It's just that the card is like holding a key to the tiniest open door of possibility, because she's going to get to see, actually *see* with her own eyes, *the* poem, "In Guerra," in real life. Maybe she'll notice something, some clue, or trace of evidence. Wouldn't that be incredible? Whatever happens, this is the closest to Isabella di Angelo she's likely to get. She can't wait.

But she has to wait. It's not time for Isabella yet, even if, of course, it's way, way past time for her.

They take a trip to the fishing village of Chioggia nearby, and they sit on a spectacular, rocky overlook as Luca speaks to them about truth and fiction. Afterward, they start work on the main project of the summer: using the emotional truth of their "haunting" piece in a fictional story, aimed at publication. The day after that, they visit Padua and sit in a beautiful blue chapel with medieval murals, after hearing Luca speak about symbolism. Then, there's a visit to a hidden corner of Venice, where they see Scala Contarini del Bovolo, an incredible spiral staircase made of arches that winds ninety feet up a palace tower, where Luca talks about structure. Everything has *meaning*, and Charlotte's swept up into Luca's humor and passion for words. It's more than exciting—it's *inspiring*. Luca is her own dream, in human form. He's a charismatic promise.

She's beginning to feel close to everyone, even Avni, even Leo, same as when she was a stagehand for *Our Town* in sophomore year, their small cast experiencing something that belonged only to them. They're all getting to know each other—Eliot's the funniest one, but people get annoyed with him after a while, and he doesn't notice. They've started to call Ashley and Hailey "the twins," even though Ashley's Chinese American and has short dark hair, while Hailey's blond and always seems to be channeling a Swiss girl in the Alps with those braids, and even though Ashley's always searching for shade and complaining about the heat, while Hailey, who's from Miami, doesn't mind if it's scorching. Shaye hates anything that seems fake or insincere, and she acts tough, but she's *very* sensitive to criticism, so you have to be careful when you say stuff about her work. Katerina is scared of everything—bugs, curvy mountain roads, anything sudden—and she cries easily. Leo's nice and smart, and everything he writes is crazily poetic and full of insight, but he pisses off Luca Bruni to no end. No one knows why he seems to hate the guy, but it's unnerving. *It's easy to have a voice when you come from money*, Luca says. Or, *You're not a writer just because the first time you put pen to paper, it's golden. You're not a writer because you have some talent. I worked my fucking ass off, man.*

In the evening, they gather for dinner. There's always wine flowing. Yas's and Charlotte's moms would totally disapprove, but they don't need to know. They are not her, and they are not *here*, in the enchanted place. When Charlotte holds the stem and tilts the glass for a sip, she can feel herself warmed by the alcohol, her knees a little wobbly, and under those strings of white lights, everything feels like something she might want. When Luca joins them, wearing a white linen shirt and Tuscan orange shorts, or something equally vivid and relaxed, their conversations get brighter and their laughter louder, and they share what they wrote that day, seeking Luca's laugh or nod or gleam of approval. Someone puts on a record, an actual record, and the night fills with music, music that can only be described as longing on a round black disc.

It's magic. Magic, even if when she goes up to her room, she has to force herself not to think about all the little touches and flirty stuff he does with Avni. She'd never tell Yas about *that*, either. It's just the way he is. He's got that something-energy. He's a fiery blaze that's so riveting, and so full of brightness and heat, that you can forget that fire burns and destroys, too.

When she gets into bed, she opens that book, the one about the old Venice convents. You'd think it'd be boring, but it's not. Right off, there's stuff about the convent Isabella was supposedly in—San Zaccaria. It's crazy fascinating, because, God, those poor women, *girls*, really. Rich and prominent families would stick their daughters there, to keep them out of trouble, to keep them *virginal.* Or, the girls would be shoved in those places so the parents would only have to pay a small amount of money for her upkeep, compared to the dowry they'd have to fork over if she married. A daughter was a father's property, and her virginity added to the value of that property. He could hand her over to whatever guy he chose, or imprison her forever, wow. One of those daughters might have been Isabella.

So, Charlotte tucks down into the covers, and reads as long as she wants, because Shaye stays up late downstairs or something. Charlotte tries to ignore the weird howl of wind at night on La Calamita, and the insistent bashing, bashing of waves, and the unnerving ashy earth underneath her, and she reads about girls as young as nine years old, three years younger than Ella, even. Girls locked away for the rest of their lives, betrayed by their families, miserable. Girls who decided to have fun anyway, with all-night parties and concerts and visitors, sneaking out to meet men, men coming inside to meet them. And girls who did something else in those convents, something that saved their lives and gave it meaning, something that proved that a voice has an unstoppable *will*: girls who made art.

Chapter Sixteen

Fiammetta Frescobaldi, writer.

Placed into a convent when she was thirteen, she decided to dedicate herself to writing. She compiled books on history, art and architecture, and the geography of places she'd never go. None of her work was published, but it survives, and her beautifully handwritten manuscripts mimic the fonts of print books and include title pages and a "publisher's" emblem, just like a real book would.

(1523–1586)

Something happens during their next outing. Something Charlotte doesn't even notice at the time, but will think and think about later, after. After her life feels wrecked.

It seems like a regular excursion at first. No one knows where they're headed. They board their usual private bus that waits for them on the mainland. As they drive, Charlotte tries to read the signs for clues. This is starting to feel different from their other trips, though. They're on the bus much longer, and when they turn off the main highway, they drive forever in a scruffy valley with only the occasional olive grove and the low-slung cement house.

And then Charlotte spots the blue arrow sign.

"Arquà Petrarca," she says to Shaye, who sits next to her.

"Oh my God," Shaye says.

They all know what that is—the village where Luca Bruni grew up, with his strong, silent mother and his cruel father who left them, poverty-stricken and alone, to go work in the US. It's the village he described in *The Glass Ship*, even if he used a fictional name, *Valanga*. Translation: avalanche. That glass ship that the child finds is buried in the dirt there.

"Arquà Petrarca!" Shaye shouts over the noise in the bus.

Luca Bruni rises and looks at Shaye. He has to hold on, because the road is rough. But he points his finger at her as if she's the winning contestant on the game show. She beams. Charlotte's pissed, because she's the one who spotted the sign. It's kind of irritating, how they all compete to get his attention. If she wasn't a part of it, she might think it was sort of gross, how desperate they seem and how all that fawning and admiration just make him even bigger and more important. But then again, come on. Say you want to be an artist, and Picasso is smiling at you across a table. Or say you want to be a basketball player, and there's Michael Jordan, complimenting your layup, or whatever—Charlotte doesn't know sports. The point is, your own personal human-God dream actually responding to regular little you.

Oh, man—that village. High on a hill, with narrow stone streets, and shabby stone buildings with red-tiled roofs. She can see it, the poverty—the small, leaning structures with few windows, and tiny dirt yards, or no yard at all. It's like a place that time forgot, a phrase she'd have to cut if she were writing this. There's, like, one grubby, ancient store and a beat-up restaurant and a church with a bell tower, but not much else. The girls have to pee, and the only bathroom is a gross hole in the ground in the restaurant, and Hailey runs out after, pretending to scream, until Ashley tells her not to be an ugly American. As they make their way through the village, Luca points out a building that he says was the school. A man passes and mutters "*Ciao,* Luca," and he nods in response. They know who he is here, too, but there's no large smile or lit-up face. No one seems that happy to see each other.

Now Luca leads them another direction. Charlotte is walking next to him. His head is down, and his steps feel heavy, and his mood so low she almost doesn't want to interrupt his thoughts. Then again, he's so unhappy, she wants to help him. The poor guy. She feels like she has to do *something.*

"What a hard place to grow up if you had big dreams," she says.

He slows, and he looks at her, the way he did that first day. As if he really *sees* her. All week, he hasn't seemed to notice her much, but now he does. "Exactly," he says. *"Exactly."* He has this way—well, it's hard to explain. When he stares in your eyes like that, he sees you, yes, but he also understands you and approves of you and maybe even wants and desires you. It's unnerving, but it's such a good feeling, she wants to make it happen again.

They arrive at a big stone house, unusual in this place, a beautiful house, with two large arches and an elaborate garden. They wait for the rest of the group to catch up. "Your childhood home, right?" Eliot cracks, and Shaye shoots him a glare.

"Petrarch's house," Bethany Sparrow says. "Writer, poet. One of the most famous figures in Italian literature. Considered to be the father of the Renaissance."

"Wow. Right next to your school," Ashley says.

"Yep. Everyone hated my father. When he was home, he was a tornado. We were always scared." Charlotte can relate. "And even when he wasn't home, we were still hiding from natural disasters. Picture a skinny, nerdy, frightened kid, a *poor* kid, passing this place twice a day."

"Nerdy? No way. That's hard to believe," Katerina ass-kisses.

"Oh, yeah," he says. "Girls never looked at me until *Under the Sudden Sky*."

"Everyone loves Big Mike, but I still always hid in the library," Eliot says.

"How do you ever get out of a place like this?" Luca sweeps one arm across the landscape. "*This* is how. Remembering that the most powerful man from the village I wanted to escape was *a poet*. Remembering, every fucking day, who came before me. Learning from them, honoring them. I made art because I saw what was possible *every day*. I made art because *he*"—here he points to the house—"showed me who I could be. Him and others like him. Let's get out of here."

• • •

The bus makes its way up a long dirt road, to a flat scenic lookout on the top of a hill. It's a large, natural terrace. "Il Pianoro," Bethany tells them. It means "the plateau," but it's also just the name of this place, this ridge of Mount Mottolone, with the sprawling view of the southern Euganean Hills. All at once, there's a picnic, spread out on checked cloths. Bethany and Luca remove meats and cheeses from a cooler, and wine, as always. Focaccia and olives from this very region. Luca holds out his cup for Bethany to fill, and the golden hills recline lazily around them, shrubby peaks with vineyards and olive groves, and wispy parfaits of clouds.

"What inspires you? *Who* inspires you? Who *exactly*? Tell me." Luca taps the toe of his sandal against Avni's. She rolls her eyes. He's flirting with her again. It's so annoying that even *she* seems irritated by it. Luca stuffs a thin slice of prosciutto into his mouth.

"Aren't you, like, fishing for compliments?" Leo says. It's direct, almost confrontational. Leo's maybe finished taking shit from him. It seems brave, but really stupid, too. Dangerous, even. He could finish Leo's career before it even starts.

"Dude, really," Luca says. "You lack imagination." He downs the last of his wine. "And, hey. While we're on the subject of inspiration and mentors! I had an idea last night."

"An idea?" Bethany Sparrow says with disapproval. Bethany's hard to figure out. She and Luca act like exes who decided to stay friends, Charlotte thinks. They have that vibe where they seem to know a lot about each other, *a lot*, but still pick fights. She's getting a book published, so why does she need to work for him? Maybe Charlotte's dad is right, that writing is impractical as an actual job.

"It's going to be great! Come onnn," he says to Bethany, as if she's just no fun. "I want to take you guys somewhere. One at a time. You and me. We'll get *inspired* somewhere special. Somewhere that *changes* the way you *think*. Work on the haunting piece, no distractions."

"Luca." Bethany looks pissed. This is clearly messing with her careful schedule.

"We want them to have their best shot at getting published, don't we?" he says.

"That would be incredible," Hailey says.

"Well, you know, maybe I know some people." Luca laughs.

"We'll discuss this and let you know more after." Bethany starts packing stuff up, crumpling packages, shoving garbage in a bag.

"Nothing to discuss. Eight students. Nine weeks. Plenty of time. Just a few hours, one day of the week! Cool," he says.

"Cool," Shaye says.

"Really cool," Katerina says.

"We'll start tomorrow. You first, Avni."

Of course she's first. Maybe she's even *the reason* for this. Eliot makes a face.

Avni sighs. "It was supposed to be a free day," she says, and then gets up to take a photo of the hills in the yellow glow of afternoon.

It's funny, but right then, Luca Bruni looks like a rejected child. His face kind of falls. When beautiful Avni just gets up and walks away, Charlotte *does* see the nerdy kid the girls never noticed. It's strange, you know, how you can feel sorry for someone so powerful, even when he's a married old guy flirting with one of his students. She notices his sandals, how his toenails need cutting, how the underneath part of his neck is starting to get the soft, rooster-y thing that old guys have.

She suddenly feels extremely uncomfortable. The mood is weird. She's maybe getting a headache. *One at a time. You and me.*

"He just wants to fuck her," Eliot mumbles on the way back to the bus.

"Don't be such an idiot," Shaye says. "For God's sake."

Chapter Seventeen

Vincenza Armani,
poet, composer, actor, sculptor, director.

As a female artist, she led a life outside traditional boundaries. She wrote in a wide range of genres, and her heroines were nuanced people. She was poisoned by her jealous lover.

(1530–1569)

Early the next morning, Charlotte watches the boat speed away from La Calamita, with Luca driving and Avni standing up, wearing all white, looking like a movie star. She looks so confi-dent, but Charlotte will never forget that piece she wrote, about how she has to succeed in order to get her father's approval. You can't look at beauty and think it solves everything.

"I wonder where they're going?" Charlotte says.

"Whatever," Shaye says.

"Dai dai! Andiamo!" Aldo shouts. "We stay or we go."

Go—at least Charlotte, Shaye, Katerina, and Eliot are. When the boat accelerates and the bow tips up with speed, and they're zipping away from La Calamita, Charlotte feels it again—that sense of relief, an exhale. But something else, too, this morning: excitement. Giddy glee. She gets to go see Tasso's actual poem, finally. When she woke up, she sent a text to her mom and Ella, even though they were still likely sleeping: Today, the Tasso poem! and then she added tons of exclamation points and a few dancing emojis. It's stupid to have some Dan Brown, Da Vinci Code dream of some great discovery, she tells herself. But still. It's the closest she might get to Isabella.

"See you guys," she says when they reach the dock. It's hard not to run.

This library—it's like a palace. More museum than library, like those photos Charlotte's seen of the Louvre or the Vatican or something—the long hallways with elaborate paintings, the high domed ceilings, and gold everywhere. Angels and more angels, scholars, and battle scenes. Titians and Tintorettos. Artifacts under glass. She reaches a dead end—a room of marble statues—and has to backtrack. Compared to the Seattle Public Library, this is pretty much mind-blowing.

So far, though, she hasn't seen any actual *books*, no shelves, or rows, or anything resembling a library. She hoped she'd just see the poem displayed here somewhere, but this place is enormous.

By sheer luck she finds a giant center court, grandly rising upward on all four sides, each floor rimmed with archways, until they hit a glass ceiling. And there *are* actual books in here, not as many as you'd expect, but still. If you ran your hand along those spines, centuries of history would rush across your fingertips. Kings and wars and wisdom and madness, art and disease and stories, stories, stories. There are long wooden tables for reading here too, and, thank God, a desk with a librarian sitting behind it.

"*Scusi?*" Charlotte asks.

"Yes?"

"I was looking for the Antonio Tasso poem 'In Guerra'? I was told you have it here."

The librarian tip-taps on her computer. "It is not here, in the Monumental Rooms. It is in the main collection. In the Zecca." She gestures to her left. "Do you have a card?"

"A library card?"

"*Sì, sì!* A library card," she says, as if this is a stupid question, which it maybe is. It didn't even occur to Charlotte that she'd need one. She just expected that the poem would be under glass here somewhere for everyone to see. A whoosh of disappointment hits. This stupid hunt seems over before it even starts. But then, wait. That *other* card. Maybe this is why the bookstore woman gave her his name. She fishes it from her bag. It's worth a try.

"Is there a Dante Luchessi here I can speak with? His mother, from the . . . ?"

The woman snickers. "The bookstore? He is in Conservation and Restoration. You cannot go there."

"Oh. I'm sorry. She said I should call him, if I needed."

The woman sighs dramatically. "And you said you wanted to see the Tasso poem? Not the Rialto Bridge or the campanile?"

"The Rialto Bridge? No, no. I was just hoping to see the document."

"Pfft! All right. Follow me."

It's awful. The woman's heels make huffy *clip-clips* of inconvenience. Charlotte's apologies tumble out—*I don't want to be a bother, I really appreciate your time, I didn't mean for you to walk all this way*—but the librarian is going so fast, she's probably not even listening. Charlotte almost wishes she never asked. Now they seem to have crossed into another building, and Charlotte sees where all the books were hiding, because there are arched stone corridors of books, and golden hallways with books, and many different reading rooms and offices, like the secret, modern workings of the ancient place they just left.

The woman stops at two glass doors. CONSERVAZIONE E RESTAURO, the sign reads. The librarian pushes the doors open, and Charlotte shyly follows her in.

"Dante Luchessi," the librarian says to another woman behind a desk. She rolls her eyes dramatically.

"Maria?"

"Sì, certo."

"Pazza! Prego." She waves them through, but it's almost as if she's clearing the air of an unpleasant smell. Asking for Dante Luchessi was a mistake, that's for sure.

They zigzag through the shelves, which hold antiquarian books, and *brr*, it's cold in there. Freezers line the walls—at least, that's what they look like, and there's a separate glassed-in cubicle where books sit upright on racks. At one table, a woman peers at a document under a magnifier. At another, a guy whisks a small brush on a yellowed paper.

"Dan-te," the librarian sings. *"Guarda! Una bella ragazza!"* The guy looks up. He's close to Charlotte's age, with a swoop of dark hair and stylish round glasses and a shy smile. The woman with the magnifier snickers. All the eye-rolling and scoffing—it's making Charlotte so self-conscious, she blushes. The librarian clip-clips back through the shelves.

"Can I help you?" he asks. Oh, man—Charlotte will never get tired of the Italian accent. For a brief second, she flashes to Adam. She's barely even thought about him since she arrived. But now she remembers how she liked to unbutton those buttons on his jeans. Dante has got that same narrow Adam build that Charlotte used to love.

"I'm looking for 'In Guerra' by Antonio Tasso? The original poem? I guess I can't see it without a library card. Your mother said you might show it to me."

Now the woman with the magnifier actually snorts. Charlotte has no idea what's going on. She's beginning to regret coming. But then Dante says, "Of course I can show you," and he smiles, and Charlotte could maybe not care less about snorts and snickers.

He has to look it up. He moves to a desktop computer and types. "A million books here." He shrugs. "Thirteen thousand manuscripts. Going back to the fourteenth century."

"Wow." Imagine having so much stuff, you don't even know where a really famous poem is. It gives her hope, because *a million books*—things could get overlooked or forgotten. One woman's poetry could.

"Okay. *Prego.*" He gestures for Charlotte to follow. Outside the Conservation and Restoration rooms again, there are more hallways and salonlike rooms. You could get lost in that place and never be seen again.

"I'm Charlotte, by the way. And hey, thanks for helping me. This place is incredible. *Huge* and incredible."

"I am never tired of it."

"So you work here? Conservation and restoration. That seems like an amazing job." *For someone so young,* she doesn't say.

"I'm a student. At Ca' Foscari? University of Venice. Conservation science and technology for cultural heritage? I have two years of laboratory studies. Classes again in the fall."

"Conservation science and technology for cultural . . ."

"Heritage," he says, and laughs.

"That seems like such an unusual thing to study."

"Not so unusual here? It's useful for jobs in the Ministry of Culture. Or a museum technician, or restorer . . . Lots of things."

"That's so cool. That it's not unusual, I mean. Where I'm from, everyone mostly studies, I don't know . . . *future* stuff. Like, computers or technology. Not past stuff."

"Oh, we do that, too, but I want to work for the Ministry of Culture. It's in my blood, I guess. My father was a . . . *storico?*"

"Hmm. Story?"

"*His*-storian. Right? And my mother with the bookstore, so . . ." He throws his hands up, like *What are you going to do?* He opens a door that leads to a wide marble staircase, and they walk up. "What about you? Do you study computers? Yet you want to see the Tasso poem."

"I'm here for a writing program. Just for the summer. Before I go on to a university where I live in Washington."

"Ah, writing!" He smiles, like he's surprised but pleased. "In the capital."

"No." She laughs. "Washington the state. What were you guys working on in there? It looks so interesting."

"Some papers, found in the flood? Every year, the *acqua alta*, the *water* rises. . . ."

"I heard about that."

"There is always damage. More to restore—books, manuscripts, art. But last year—ugh. It was very bad. Mosaics in Saint Mark's. Vivaldi scores . . . The entire Fondazione Giorgio Cini library on San Giorgio Maggiore! San Zaccaria, it flooded too. The carabinieri barracks to the right, the walled-off convent to the left . . . *Che casino!* The old barricade was wrecked, and boom! Three hundred years of books and records, floating in dirty water. Bones, too. The convent cemetery was . . ." He scoops with his palm, indicating under the building. "This floor," he says, opening another door.

"Bones, oh my God. But all those books and records, wow."

"Every year, it happens," he says. "Something! The books—they've been in the freezer for six months, in a special chamber, so the ink is preserved and the papers don't . . ." He smashes his hands together. "Now they air-dry. We check for mold. We clean. Every week, more documents arrive. This is all so interesting." He rolls his eyes.

"It *is*." She can't imagine anyone doing anything like this at home. Adam wasn't much of a reader, let alone caring about the book itself. He cared about his guitar and messing around online. "You said San Zaccaria? I might have had a long-ago relative that was at that convent. She was from a noble family, but that's about all we know."

"Yes? *Un Veneziana*, huh?" He smiles. "My father traced a relative to Santa Maria delle Vergini, another convent in the city. Here we are."

This room is full of manuscripts mostly, upright in glass stands, and also lying flat in cases that circle the perimeter. Dante speaks to the librarian, an older man with white hair and tired eyes.

"Okay! Over here," Dante says. The poem sits in one of the double-sided upright cases, so that you can view the front and back of it. It's yellowed and fragile-looking, and yet the italic script looks strong and bold. Shivers prickle up Charlotte's arms. It's hard not to just press her forehead right up against the glass. Whether these were Tasso's words or Isabella's, it's astonishing to think that Tasso once held this very paper in his hands almost five hundred years ago. Dante is silent next to her. Seeing it feels so monumental that she almost doesn't want to speak.

"My whole life, I've lived here and never seen it," he says after they've gazed at it for a while.

"It looks like a letter," Charlotte says. She can't read it, of course, but there are a few words at the top, set apart from the rest of the text, before the poem begins.

"It does. It *is*." Dante leans toward the glass. "*Mio Phoebus*? I can't tell."

"What's that?"

"*Who* is that, maybe. *My Phoebus*."

"Look at the back. It's amazing. Look at the seal." It's a smudge of crimson wax, with an image pressed in its center.

"The wax stamp, yes. It was one way to lock the letter, before envelopes. You see the folds," he uses his hands to indicate the multiple tucks and pleats. "Into a little package, a small rectangle. And then the wax seal." He makes a circle on his finger where a ring would be. "A signet ring. Do you know them?" His eyes are so serious behind his glasses.

"I know of them, but not much about them."

"You had one if you were important. A high social standing. They were engraved with symbols. Initials, or coat of arms. Something to identify the wearer? Only the wearer. They were very personal. Like a signature."

When he says this, Charlotte feels an immense drop of disappointment. The image in the red wax—it's a *T*, with its long center and outstretched top, the sides filled in with light, decorative curves. "It's definitely a *T*," she says.

"Yes. And look at the red string. It must have wrapped around the letter. And then the wax on top. The thread would have to be cut to open it, but the seal is whole. I don't know much about this, but it is beautiful."

It is. But that *T* eliminates any doubt that the poem was Tasso's, or at least, that he sent it. "Oh, well." She sighs.

Dante looks at her, puzzled. "It's not what you expected?"

She doesn't even want to tell him. It sounds so ridiculous. But it doesn't really matter now. "It's crazy. Silly. But that relative in the convent? My family always said she was the one who actually wrote it, this poem. That Tasso stole it from her. They had a relationship. She's mentioned in his biographies." She studies Dante for any sign of a smirk or a laugh, but there isn't one. His eyes are sweet. "I was just hoping to see something. Discover some . . . clue, or whatever. About her or this." She gazes at "In Guerra." "Silly. I mean, it's only been five hundred years."

"Not silly. We find unknown things all the time. Just a few months ago, a researcher discovered the oldest drawing of Venezia! From the 1300s. He found it in a book in the Biblioteca Nazionale, and no one ever noticed it there before. Last year, my professor, Dr. Martina Ricci, found a poem from the 1500s by a woman she studied for years. Hidden, because no one ever looked for it! Our work—it's part restoration, part discovery, like a detective. Right in this room—look. There's so much we don't know."

She glances around at all the manuscripts, at the lines and words and scrolling italics, all the stories of people over the centuries. "That *T*, though," she says.

"Here's another Tasso." Dante has wandered over to an adjacent glass case. It's a poem too, but this one's written on a single sheet of yellowed parchment. "Tasso's 'Sonetto.' 'How can I bear to hear . . . ?' What? It's hard to read. 'The piteous sound of complaint.' Or something like this. Ugh! Hard to understand in all of the . . ."

"Frosting swirls," Charlotte says, and he laughs. "This one doesn't look like a letter. No ring stamp. And the writing is different." It's not true hope, though. In the red wax of "In Guerra," that *T is* a signature.

"The writing *does* look different," Dante agrees. "But it's years later? Maybe more . . ." He clutches up his fingers as if they're old and arthritic.

"Yeah, probably," she says. "And that wax seal just seems to decide things."

"Ah, sorry," he says.

"I was hoping for even a little window of possibility. I guess you can't expect to solve a five-hundred-year-old mystery in ten weeks anyway." She shrugs, but the disappointment—it's huge. Bigger than you'd think. It feels like something sinking. She doesn't even know why it's so big. She just wanted to rescue Isabella from Tasso's shadow, to bring her to light, to prove this thing that nags at her like truth does. It's unfair, because something happened, and Isabella just sits unseen and unknown, small and invisible. Voiceless. And after Charlotte read about the girls locked away in the convents, she wanted it even more. She must have wanted it very badly, because it actually hurts, that red wax *T*. It practically shouts. *I was here. I was the one. Me, me, me.*

Chapter Eighteen

Tullia d'Aragona, writer.

Considered to be one of the best writers, poets, and philosophers of her time, she wrote strongly about feminist subjects. She was also a famous courtesan in Venice, her mother initiating her into that life when Tullia was only eighteen. Though illustrious men of letters (including famed poets Bernardo Tasso, father of Torquato; Ercole Bentivoglio; Pietro Bembo; and Muzio Manfredi) were her courtiers and wrote sonnets to her, they also later derided her and her work. Poet Pietro Aretino condemned her, likely jealous of her success, calling her presumptuous and greedy.

(1510–1556)

"I should get back," Dante says in the sun of Saint Mark's Square after walking Charlotte out of the big doors of the Biblioteca Marciana. "The Dottoressa Martina Ricci . . ." He slashes a finger across his throat. "She oversees our work here. She is what you call a slave rider."

Charlotte smiles. God, he's adorable. "I really appreciate you showing me around. Thanks so much."

"Well, *in bocca al lupo*."

Charlotte scrunches her face in apology. "I'm sorry. I feel so rude coming to your country without knowing your language."

"In the wolf's mouth," he translates. "It means 'good luck.' You answer, '*Crepi*.' May the wolf die."

"*Crepi*." She grins.

"Maybe you'll still find your relative here somewhere." He smiles, pushing his hair from his forehead.

And then, because she just *has* to know, she suddenly asks, "The librarians. They were acting so funny about me seeing you. How come?"

"Ah! Um . . ." He grimaces. Then, he gives a *what the hell* shrug. "My mother," he admits.

"Your mother?"

"Ugh! She thinks I spend too much time at the library! She sends the girls over. From the store. *Che cavolo!* They want to know where the Rialto Bridge is, she sends them. The Guggenheim museum, she sends them."

"Oh, whoa. I'm sorry. Wow, embarrassing!" She puts her face in her hands in a pretend-hide.

"Well, I don't mind today." He gives a shy smile. "This is the first time anyone has wanted to see *a poem*. I can maybe show you around more, if you like? I'm an expert at the Rialto Bridge."

"Yikes, I bet."

"Or, if you want to see San Zaccaria, where your relative was?"

It's so funny, Dante, with his sweet eyes and serious glasses, offering to show her a convent. Adam or Nate—no way, this would never happen. When she wanted to go to the Seattle Art Museum once, Adam dragged around like a toddler, and Nate's favorite thing to do is play Fortnite. It's crazy but interesting that history is an everyday thing to Dante, *usual*, in the city all around him.

She laughs. Strangely, she feels more relaxed than she has the whole time since she's been here. She feels more like herself. "I'd really appreciate that," she says.

They exchange numbers, and Dante returns to his world of ancient books and drowned words. So what, she maybe watches him walk back, because he's adorable from behind. Those jeans, cute, cute, cute. She ducks into a shop and buys two rings made of Murano glass for her mom and sister, then sends them a follow-up text about seeing the poem: Pretty uneventful. She add a a few sad face emojis. It's kind of a lie. It was disappointing, but not uneventful, because she's walking around with a new bright slice of who-knows-what-might-happen.

Charlotte meets up with Katerina, Eliot, Shaye, and Leo for pizza. Katerina and Shaye and Eliot want gelato after, but Charlotte is stuffed, and Leo wants to take some photos, because it's another hobby he's probably amazing at. Charlotte wanders off to FaceTime Yasmin. It's morning where Yas is, right after breakfast. They've texted a few times since they both left, but it's hard to talk with the time difference, and Yas is as busy at Goddard Space Flight Center as Charlotte is here. Now Yas shrieks when she answers. It's so good to see her face, her familiar self.

Yas is excited, telling her all about the project she gets to work on, *Life detection in icy planetary environments.* God, Yas loves that stuff. They catch up on news from home—Nate broke his arm, Yas says, and Carly got a job at Elliott Bay Book Company. Carly and Yas had a stupid fight about veganism since Carly is trying it out, but Yas thinks it's just an excuse for Carly not to eat, and, oh, Adam has a new girlfriend.

"She's from the Eastside. I didn't know whether to tell you or not, but I didn't want you to just see it on social media."

"It's fine. That's great," Charlotte says. It *is* fine, and she's glad he's happy, and she doesn't want to be with him anymore, and she feels like a totally different person already from the one who used to be with him, but it still makes her feel weird. Like, who cares, but that was fast.

"So?" Yas asks. "Is it all still incredible? Is he everything you thought? Luca Bruni?"

Well, he is, but it's complicated. She can't exactly tell Yas the truth. Plus, this is a *private* experience. They're in his *inner circle*. When you get to be in a famous person's inner circle, you don't just go blab stuff about them. You don't tell all of the human parts that you now know. She feels protective of him. He seems to *need* protection. "He's *a real person*, Yas." It sounds sort of know-it-all.

"Does that mean he's hooking up with all the girls?" She laughs. She's just joking, but it kind of stings. Especially because he's out all day with Avni today, doing who knows what. She'd never tell Yas that, not in a million years.

"No, Yas. Not *at all.* He's not like that."

"I'm sorry! I was just kidding," Yasmin says. "Don't be mad! I miss you."

"I miss you, too. I miss everyone. But, yeah, it's a once-in-a-lifetime experience here. It's so amazing. *He* is. *Everything* is."

After she hangs up, Charlotte feels a gross disloyalty. But it's hard to tell who she's been disloyal *to*, Yas or Luca Bruni. No idea, but she just feels bad after all Luca Bruni's done for her. She decides to post a photo of her and Luca, one that Katerina took last week at dinner. Luca was messing around and put his head on her shoulder after making a joke. She writes one of those long, sentimental posts she usually stops reading halfway through when other people do it. She writes about what an incredible experience she's having with her literary hero, and how she's grown to admire him even more, and how astonishing it is to begin to call him a friend. Maybe she also does it so Adam will see. The minute it appears, she almost deletes it. It's just bragging, and kind of obnoxious, and in a way, she's using him too, like Shaye was saying. Shaye's right, people do just treat him like he's a Famous Person, not a human being, and she regrets it. But then the likes and hearts and comments start pouring in. Maybe it doesn't sound as awful as it feels.

That night, back at La Calamita, the mood is strange. Avni and Luca are still gone. Hailey and Ashley are fighting. There were sandwiches for dinner, and everyone just took their food somewhere else. Bethany Sparrow is nowhere to be seen. Leo and Shaye are having some long conversation by the pool, but Charlotte can hear Shaye getting annoyed. Eliot makes some stupid joke and hurts Katerina's feelings, and she cries and then goes upstairs.

Charlotte takes some dessert, a few cookies wrapped in a napkin, out to the library. She wants to be alone, plus that turret library has an awesome view. It's nothing like the library she was in today—everything smells new, but it has warm, comforting volumes and the light is low, and it sits at the very end of La Calamita, so she can see the silver glowing tips of the waves. She can see the whole lagoon, empty of boats anywhere near here. There is no tiny green light on a bow, heading back to the villa. It's just dark out there, moonlight shimmers and gray-purple clouds.

Charlotte opens her laptop. She types *Tasso, Phoebus, In Guerra*. She reads the Wikipedia entry, one she read before, when she was trying to do that report, but now she reads it again more carefully. It talks about the original document, discovered in Tasso's belongings after his death at age eighty-three, a document now in Biblioteca Marciana. When he first wrote it, it says, Tasso sent the poem in a letter to his father's elder cousin Febo di Goldini, it was believed, and it was returned to Tasso after Goldini's death. Goldini was the director of Venice's most distinguished opera house, and he was Tasso's only living relative, one who would certainly understand what a masterpiece it was. When she clicks on the link for that guy, she finds an oil painting of a very old man, upright at a desk.

It's a boring conclusion to the mystery.

She types in *San Zaccaria convent, girls.* She reads about two nuns who worked for more than a month to make a hole in the outer wall so that men could bring their boats up to visit in secret. It is so amazing, thrilling, how they kept fighting for themselves. She reads about it like it's a novel. Her cookies are gone. It's getting late, but now the Council of Ten, the feared enforcers who served the city leader, the doge, are coming to spy on the girls. The Ten are installing iron grilles and gates so no one can come in, and so they can't get out. The nuns are pelting stones at them and forcing them away.

She's so immersed that when her phone rings, she's startled. She looks up and is almost surprised to see herself in this newly rebuilt room in an old hospital building instead of a cold stone monastery. But she's really surprised when she sees who's calling.

"Charlotte?" Dante says. *Char-lot-ta.* Her name never sounded so nice.

"Well, hi," she says.

"A five-hundred-year-old question to answer in ten weeks! I asked Dottoressa Ricci about the threads. The ones that wrapped around the letter? I never saw that before. She said that men and women both *might* write this letter, but a woman would be the one to wrap it with the silk thread."

"Really?"

"If you got a letter like this, you would know before you opened it that is was affectionate. Even secret. It folds into a little package, like a gift between two people, more private than usual correspondence. Words of love, maybe?"

"That's weird, because I just looked up the Phoebus person, and he'd have been a really old guy. Tasso's uncle. I mean, *words of love*?"

"This is exactly what my professor said when she looked up the poem. 'An old uncle? This doesn't seem right.' She is interested in your forgotten poet. I told you she just published a book about Veronica Franco? Her own forgotten poet? *Veronica Franco e i Sei Tratti*."

"I'm so sorry. I don't know what that is. Or *who* that is."

"*Veronica Franco and the Six Traits*. She was the most famous *cortigiana onesta* of the Renaissance. Honored courtesan? Prostitute. But a poet. This is Dottoressa Ricci's area of passion. She wants to know more. You never said the name of your relative? You could talk to her. This is maybe your little window?"

The thought of talking to Dante's professor seems suddenly terrifying. She's real, a real researcher, an author, and the Isabella and Tasso thing isn't real, not really. It's a rumor, a wish. And what if they find that there's absolutely nothing to it, zero, zilch? What if *she* took *his* poem and put it in her book? Charlotte feels panic at this possibility. Sometimes it's more important to have the dream than the truth.

"I'm sure people would have known before now. You know, if there was really something to it. I'd hate to waste her time when it's probably just an old story my female relatives loved to whisper to each other forever."

"Don't be so sure. Whispers hold secrets. Secrets hold truth! And you don't have a lot of time."

"I saw that *T*."

"I have never sent a special message to *my* uncle," he says. *"Tutto fa brodo."*

"Argh. I don't what it means."

"Everything makes soup."

Charlotte leaves Luca's library and heads back to the villa. It's starting to rain. She feels the drip-drop on her skin. She thinks about all the souls here, sick and abandoned, in all kinds of weather, hot sun, fog, rain. Now it starts to pour. So hard that she suddenly understands how the *acqua alta* could flood churches, and cause bones and old papers to float to the surface. Avni and Luca Bruni are still not back. It's very late, but there's a restlessness in the house. She can feel it like that weird energy before it thunders. Shaye's actually smoking a cigarette out on the terrace, the orange tip glowing in the dark. Ashley passes Charlotte in the hall but doesn't speak. Charlotte hears Leo cough behind his door. She keeps looking out the window by her bed. She keeps listening for the sound of a boat, but all she can hear is wind and rain and the crash of waves. Maybe this is what parents feel when they wait and wait for you to get home. When it gets later and later and later, and you're still not there. Worry, turning to fear, mixed with the deep hope that the person you love won't disappoint you.

Chapter Nineteen

Leonora Benardi, poet, playwright.

Little was known of her or her work until a play of hers was discovered in 2010. She was one of the many women Curzio Gonzaga wrote poems of praise for in his book Rime. *Sonnets by male poets praising female poets were pretty common, though the praise was often used to demonstrate their own chivalry, proof to the world that they were male feminists.*

(1559–1616)

The next day, Luca, Bethany, and all the students take the water-bus, the *vaporetto*, to Burano—a small island in the Venetian lagoon—with its little bright houses in a row, painted in vivid shades of blue and pink and yellow and orange. Oh man, it's charming, totally different from the main island. Charlotte can't stop taking photos.

And then it's on to Murano, known for centuries as the island of glassmakers. Bethany Sparrow gives a tour. All the glassmakers were forced to move there in 1291, to prevent fires in the city itself, she says, but also to keep control of the artists.

The secrets of their craft were so precious, they were threatened with death should they leave, and also so precious that they were passed only from father to son. The privileges of being a glassmaker went to men alone, and as of today, there are still no women who hold the great honor of being a glassmaster, Bethany tells them. Female writers, too, had to be ushered into public acceptance by the praise of a male writer, she says. Bethany seems pissed. About art and who gets the honors of it, maybe, but probably more than that. The little muscle in her cheek is going in and out, and her voice is tight, and she looks away from Luca whenever he speaks, mad.

Charlotte feels different about those rings of Murano glass she bought. They're still beautiful, but she has new information about them. She realizes how wrong she was, back at that first party, when she was thinking so romantically about how young artists learned from masters for eons. That was men. Men learning, men teaching, men making art, allowing or not allowing women to do the same. Men's history, just like at home, in the library, when she searched volume upon volume for three words: *Isabella di Angelo.*

Storia, history. History—*his* story.

Charlotte is also watching every glance and moment between everyone, because something's going on. It's just like at home, with her mom and dad, when there's tension in the air. She wishes she could concentrate on the glass shops, and the ornate, elaborate Palazza del Mula they pass, but Ashley and Hailey aren't talking, and Avni walks by herself.

Now they all sit on the steps that circle around the bottom of the Murano Lighthouse. The sea is in front of them, and the snug little village behind. Eliot is flicking his pen open and closed, open and closed, and it's driving her nuts.

"You've got to figure out a character's relationship to the story when you think about voice," Luca says as he paces. "The attitude, the vulnerabilities. Their motivation—what are they getting out of telling their story? What are they hiding? How do they speak to different people?" He's wearing shorts, his long legs gangly. He's going back and forth, and then, shit, his toe catches. He almost trips, then scowls at the ground, like it did it to him on purpose. "In *A Mile of Faces*, Andre isn't the same dude talking to his boss as he is talking to Mia. Listen to how his voice changes. With Mia, he's a big shot, a hero. She's more consistent throughout. It tells you something about her. And about how they're in conflict as people. She only wants to be vulnerable, real. He's vulnerable as a strategy, when—"

"She doesn't seem real," Avni interrupts. Her voice is quiet and firm, but when she tucks her hair behind her ear, Charlotte can see that her hand is shaking.

He stops.

Oh, God. His face. The way it looks suddenly pissed—what is Avni *doing*?

"What'd you say?"

"I said, she doesn't seem real. Neither does Aurora, the wife. Tits and ass. Paper cutouts. One-dimensional." Avni's cheeks flush.

There are tourists all around, and the sounds of boats, and the clatter from the restaurant behind them, but Charlotte swears you could hear a pin drop. Cliché, but whatever. Eliot suddenly stops the annoying thing with the pen. He actually sucks in his breath.

"You don't know what you're talking about. You have *no idea* how to read critically. And you know what else? You lack imagination." Luca's dark eyes shoot missiles.

"'Her ass was subpar, and her breasts slouched, but the legs were long,'" Avni quotes. Charlotte can't tell if Avni is furious or about to cry, maybe both. "They're objects. And they're always gorgeous and sweet and yet they fall in love with that obnoxious dweeb, Andre."

"Avni," Katerina says, like she's correcting a toddler. "It's a *deconstruction* of misogyny. That's *the point*. An insightful and ironic portrayal of how a guy like that sounds."

"'Her tits could shake the earth, make a guy rethink the meaning of life in the universe.' It doesn't sound insightful. It sounds like something you believe. Like what you believe is *all right there*." Avni's voice catches, but her eyes flash. "Andre should have taken Mia's tits on that trip. *She* could have stayed at home."

"You know what?" Luca says. "It's amateur hour, confusing the author with the character." God, he's pissed. It's all making Charlotte anxious, very anxious. Her head throbs, like a migraine is about to start. She spins her rings on her fingers. It's the kind of how-dare-you-criticize-me fury Charlotte recognizes from her mom. But it's more than that. It's the kind of anger when you're rejected, maybe.

"*We* see the objectification through *his* objectification. It's genius, Avni," Ashley says. "It's intentional. He *meant* to do that. That's part of why it's so good. This was *written* by a *feminist*."

"Maybe everyone has a good point," Charlotte says. Ugh! Her nerves make her such a ridiculous people pleaser, an impossible task right now anyway.

"And you have to understand where Andre came from. All those Italian men, treating women like Madonnas or saints for generations," Katerina says.

"Blame his heritage, got it. Sorry. But it sure sounds misogynistic to me. And what about when the women don't want to have sex with Andre? He has no use for them." Avni shakes her head, as if she's had enough.

"It's *on purpose*, Avni." Now Katerina is getting pissed.

"A lot of dudes. A LOT of dudes have to wrestle with—" Luca says.

"Wrestle with *what*?" Avni interrupts, and now her voice shakes too, as she looks him straight in the eyes. "The word *no*?"

"Jesus, what happened last night?" Leo whispers to Charlotte.

She makes her eyes large and pretend-horrified in response, but she *is* horrified. Her head is killing her.

"She looks like she's going to *cry*," Leo says. She does. It's awful.

"Hey," Bethany breaks in. "Let's wrestle with something

else, okay? Rein it in, people. Today's prompt. Take a short scene from your work in progress, and write it from three different points of view."

Luca removes his phone from his pocket, looks at the time. And then he does something strange. He just walks away, lifting his hands behind him in a wave.

"You ditching us?" Shaye calls out after him.

"It's noon. I have an interview for the book," he yells over his shoulder. "NPR."

Just like that, all at once, it seems crazy and rude that Avni was arguing with someone like him. Someone who is now walking away to do a phone interview with NPR. They should be grateful for every second they have with an author who's that prestigious. NPR! NPR and its whole audience want to hear what he has to say, and he's just spent the morning with them and their little projects. You could forget how important he was when you were just hanging around with the real him, and now he's spent his morning being cut down by Avni, a student. Charlotte feels bad for what Avni just did. Embarrassed and ashamed on their behalf. Luca keeps walking. His back is a giant wall between him and them. What fucking idiots, his shoulders seem to say.

"Salute!" Luca Bruni says that night, raising his glass. He seems back to his old self. He's telling them about that essay he wrote for *Rolling Stone* magazine, the weekend he spent hanging out with all these famous musicians, like Jass Bassy and Armor

Class Zero, who let him play guitar during a concert. Then he starts telling them all this delicious insider-gossip stuff, like how Hal Vinnie of *Late Night Tonight* is really an ass, and how Naomi Meadows, from that show *New School*, once hit on him. Being on the set of *One Great Lie* was actually crazy hard work, because the director was always begging him for help, since Luca has such vision about everything. But there was *lots* of after-hours partying.

Avni is quiet. Eliot is so rapt at the fame gossip that, for once, he doesn't interrupt with jokes. Bethany Sparrow didn't show up for dinner. It's getting late, and no one's read any of their work yet. Charlotte hopes they'll get to. Hopes *she* gets to. Every time she writes, she gives it everything she's got. Even after the stressful day today, she does. It's like she's writing for one set of eyes—his. His approval of her writing would mean everything. If a genius says you have talent, then you do. And like he said the other day, he knows people. All the right people. *He* is people. There's no telling what might happen if she can finally prove herself.

Finally, Katerina offers to read. Honestly, Luca seems kind of disappointed that they're changing the subject, and sure, famous-people gossip *is* more fun. When Katerina reads, though, Charlotte can hear in the words how Katerina feels the same thing Charlotte does—a need to please, to get his attention, to be *good*. The scene where the mother gives up the child is from three viewpoints, like they were assigned: the mother, the child, the orphanage worker. But it's way more flowery than Katerina usually writes. She's trying to sound like him, Charlotte thinks. Katerina slurs her words a little. She's kind of drunk.

After she finishes, everyone gives a little round of applause. Charlotte jumps in to read before anyone else can. The "haunted" story she's working on for publication is turning out to be her own experience, hidden by "fiction," pretty much like everyone else's. The story is about a lonely girl who tries to find a forgotten Renaissance poet to fill the hole in the lives of everyone around her. She has no idea what the end will be, so she just keeps going from one part to the next, whereas Leo seems to have the whole thing outlined. Anyway, the girl goes to the Biblioteca Marciana, and in the scene, she finds an important letter from the poet, even though that's not what happened in real life. Charlotte's in the middle of reading the second viewpoint—the male librarian—when Donata interrupts, arriving with another round of dessert. The plates of *frittole*—little fried donuts filled with cream or rum-soaked raisins—are passed, and everyone's attention is on those now. Charlotte just stops reading and sits down.

"Biblioteca Marciana," Luca says, refilling his tiny glass with Sgroppino, a lemony after-dinner drink. "Did you know that Petrarch—*my* Petrarch"—he taps his chest—"donated all his books and manuscripts for what was supposed to be the first public library ever? Right here in Venice. When he left to go live in our little village, it never happened. His books were pretty much forgotten. Crumbled to *powder.* Stuck together in blobs from dampness. Poor dude died in his library at Arquà Petrarca but most of his great collection turned to *dust*. Fuck. *Chi s'è visto s'è visto.*"

"'Who has seen himself has seen himself,'" Hailey translates for them.

"In other words, that was that," Luca says.

For the first time all night, Avni speaks. "Petrarch was a stalker," she says softly.

Luca groans dramatically. "Come on, honestly? *Far ridere i polli*. Translate *that*."

"To make the chickens laugh?" Hailey guesses.

"It means *ridiculous*!" A few crumbs of *frittole* actually fly out of Luca's mouth when he spits the word.

"He's supposedly a genius for his romantic poetry, for those 'Laura' poems." Avni looks so beautiful tonight. She always does, but right then, her hair is up in a swoop, and her eyes look even darker with the evening sky behind her, and her white dress glows like the moon. Her voice is defiant, but it sounds . . . How would Charlotte write it? *Bruised.* Her voice sounds bruised. "I read about her when we got back that day. He sees her and falls in love. But she won't have anything to do with him. He's all full of desperate longing for *eighteen years*. For someone he speaks to, like, *once*, for two seconds! He doesn't even know her. But, hey, he'll tell you all about her hands and eyes and how he follows her all around. How he's pissed and simmers because he's *ignored*. One of the forefathers of Italian language, wow. I'm sure she and her husband appreciated his *genius*."

Oh my God. The table goes silent. That awful anxiety crawls up Charlotte's backbone, sinks its nails in. She doesn't even want to *look* at Luca.

"You have to take it in *context*, Avni," Katerina says finally.

"And you know what? You're really becoming a downer. *Guastafeste*," Luca says. Charlotte does look at him now. He's grinning, but his eyes aren't smiling. They've gone blank with dismissal. He folds his long fingers together. "The rest of us are trying to have fun here."

It's so tense, it's awful. Charlotte wishes Avni would just *stop*.

But she doesn't.

"Well, I think it's pretty weird, you know, how it's all right there, in his work. He tells you who he is, but you just can't see it, because you're blinded by the beauty of the *words*." Avni is staring Luca down. But Charlotte hears it—the tiniest crack in Avni's voice when she says *blinded*.

Luca fake-yawns. "Okay, kids. It's been a long day. Let's call it a night. It's been fun." Now he points both his forefingers in Avni's direction like pistols.

"They had sex," Eliot whispers to Charlotte. "Or they didn't have sex."

Charlotte kicks him. "Stop."

"*Something* happened," he says.

Everyone gets up to leave. Avni stalks off, her sandals clicking as she disappears like a white ghost through the garden. Ashley snags another *frittole.* "These are awesome," she says to Hailey. Apparently, they're friends again. "Want one?" Hailey shakes her head.

Charlotte is stuffing her piece back into her bag when she sees Luca grab Katerina's sleeve. The large moon in the purple sky catches the glint of his ring and his watch.

"I'd love to read more of your stuff," he says to Katerina. "It's good."

Katerina's eyes go from wine-hazy to bright. "Really?"

"Yeah. Let me give you my email. You can send it to me."

As Charlotte climbs the villa's stairwell, she looks at that beautiful glass ship painted on the wall. It looks so real. She has no idea how the artist did it. Glass ships don't even exist, but this makes you believe they do. It's magic, because up close, there are only all those little brushstrokes and bits of paint.

Inside her room, Charlotte pulls her dark hair up into a messy bun, tosses off her sundress, and puts on her comfy old T-shirt from home. She needs the comfort, because she has this sense of unease, the anxious feeling that something bad is going to happen. She takes her copy of the book from her pack. *The* book. *The Glass Ship.* Charlotte has the room to herself—she has no idea where Shaye is. She reads Luca Bruni's words. God, they're so beautiful and true that she remembers who he is, who he really is. Who he *most* is. The words are larger than any of the weird stuff that's going on now, aren't they? What those words do, how they affect people, they're worth more than how he might affect real people in real life, right?

On a night like this, with her tangle of anxiety, she wishes she weren't on this island, with all its dusty remains of sickness and history. It was a lot of years ago, and it doesn't really have anything to do with what's happening to her right this minute, she tells herself. But she just wishes the ground wasn't made of skeletons.

Chapter Twenty

Veronica Gambara, poet.

From a distinguished family, she received a prestigious education. When she was seventeen, she began sending poems to the famous poet Pietro Bembo, then thirty-two, who became her mentor. Little of her poetry was published during her lifetime, but she would correspond with many famous poets, including Bernardo Tasso and Pietro Aretino, who would later slander her, calling her a "laureated harlot," essentially an educated slut.

(1485–1550)

In the morning, at breakfast, Avni doesn't show up.

"Maybe someone should check on her," Shaye says. She never seemed to like Avni, but she looks worried.

"I will," Ashley says. "Be right back."

Eliot and Leo are at the food table, piling up their plates. Hailey sips her coffee. "Does anyone know what she and Luca even did that day? She barely said anything about it."

"Hot springs," Katerina says. "Near Luca's old village."

"Tergesteo, or something? That's what I heard her say," Charlotte says.

"Testosterone?" Hailey cracks, and they all laugh.

"I think it was near his old village," Katerina says. "I got the idea that it was fancy. Like, here's the positive thing about ambition haunting you. The before and after. His village to some upscale spa place, I don't know."

Ashley is jogging back toward them. "She's gone," she says. Her cheeks are flushed. It's already warm out this morning, and the air smells like lemons and seawater, sunny and beautiful smells, but Charlotte feels a sudden darkness. *Dread* is the word for it, even if she pushes that word away.

"What do you mean 'gone'?" Hailey says. "Like, out for breakfast somewhere?"

"*Gone*, gone. As in, there's nothing in the room. No bags. Her bathroom is clean. No makeup, no shampoo, nothing. She left."

"Why in the world would she *leave*?" Katerina says.

Eliot and Leo are back. "Cheese is the only food that matters," Eliot says, and plunks down his plate.

"What's wrong, you guys?" Leo asks. Leo's like this. He notices things. It's what makes him a great writer, Charlotte's sure. He looks worried.

"Avni left," Ashley says.

"*No way,*" Eliot says. And then to Charlotte, "I told you, they had sex or they didn't."

"God, Eliot," Hailey says. "Stop it."

"It's not true anyway," Shaye says.

"How do you know?" Eliot sticks a roll in his mouth.

"I know, okay? They didn't. He wouldn't. I just know. Jesus."

"Jesus didn't have anything to do with it," Eliot says. "He wasn't even here."

"She was *really* confrontational with him yesterday. Maybe Luca kicked her out," Katerina says. "I almost couldn't blame him if he did. It was so disrespectful."

"I'm going to call her. We need to find out what happened." Ashley takes her phone from her pocket and tries right then, as they all wait. "No answer. One ring, like it's turned off."

"Way to leave without saying goodbye," Hailey says.

It turns out Luca Bruni is gone too. At least for two days. He has to appear at a publishing event in New York, so Bethany Sparrow has arranged for a virtual visit with Ursula Sorrow, who happens to be a good friend of Luca Bruni's. No one can believe their luck. Her, like, *twelfth* book just won another medal. She's a little wacky, honestly. When she talks to them, she veers off in a hundred directions, and during the call, her face keeps freezing in weird expressions that make Eliot snicker. They all get the giggles like they're in elementary school, even though Ursula Sorrow herself is talking to them, calling Luca *Lulu* and stuff like that.

Later, at the pool, Shaye swims laps, and Leo's reading his third book on Italian history.

"I didn't learn anything about writing, but hey. Now we know Lulu once pretended a banana was a penis at a fancy awards dinner," Eliot says. His pink skin is actually getting brown, and he's trying to grow a mustache, which they all make fun of.

"That was hilarious!" Hailey says.

Ashley was up in her room, but now there's the sound of flip-flops approaching, and here she is, a towel around her shoulders. "Mystery solved," Ashley announces. "I got a hold of Avni. Her mother got sick, she said. She had to catch the first plane out."

"Oh, *sad*!" Katerina says.

"I didn't really believe her at first, but she just said, 'No! No, *really*. My father told me I had to come back.'"

It's a relief. And it's a double relief when Bethany Sparrow says that Eliot will be going on the next one-on-one trip, as soon as Luca returns. Charlotte was worried he'd pick Katerina, but she was wrong. Charlotte's so glad she was wrong.

That night, though, she looks up the village of Tergesteo. She remembers the name thanks to *Tergesteo/testosterone*. But it's not a village. Not at all. Her unease cranks up a notch.

"Shaye," she says.

"What." Shaye's so irritable. She's hard to be around, honestly.

"Tergesteo—where Luca and Avni went. It's actually Esplanade Tergesteo. It's a *hotel*."

"So?"

"Don't you think that's weird?"

"Not really. It's a spa. They didn't *stay*."

"It just doesn't feel right."

"He didn't do anything with her like you think."

"How do *you* know?"

"He told me. I asked."

"When? I mean, *why*?"

"Are you always so annoying? Dear God, how am I the only one with a roommate?" Shaye snaps.

Charlotte closes out the images of those glossy floors and curved glass walls and shining blue swimming pools with white chaises all around. She can't imagine ever staying in a place like that, let alone with Luca Bruni. It looks incredible and expensive, like a dream, but she'd better just shut up.

Chapter Twenty-One

Compiuta Donzalla (likely a pen name), one of the earliest Ialian female poets.

Three sonnets survive, and they discuss the only two life paths for a female besides becoming a courtesan: forced marriage, or a life of seclusion in a convent. Her talent was considered unnatural, miraculous, beyond the norm for her sex, so much so that for a while, even her actual existence was questioned, same as Nina Siciliana.

(Early thirteenth century)

"This was where all the papers—" Dante lifts both hands to indicate a rising. He and Charlotte stand in front of an open doorway, cordoned off. It's part of a long white building, with curved arches and green shuttered windows. Charlotte cranes her neck to look inside. Picture a damp, musty cellar, and the smell of it too. She sees a pile of rubble—old brick, crumbled between two dark hovels. Also, the half-hearted signs of cleanup—a wheelbarrow full of debris, various tools tossed about, big bags of who-knows-what, no workers in sight. "This doorway . . ." Dante taps on the frame. "Was an iron grate? With holes. And so, the water . . . Whoosh! The old walls couldn't take it this time. And when they fell, there was this . . . *bella tesoro*."

"Beautiful something . . . ," Charlotte says.

"Treasure. Beautiful treasure." Dante smiles. He combs his hair from his face with his fingers.

She was so happy when Dante called yesterday. *Are you* sure *you want to spend your free day doing this? Showing me a* convent? *My guy friends at home would have to be bribed with food*, Charlotte had said, when he'd suggested they meet at San Zaccaria. *They are too busy playing American football and video games?* he'd joked. Then he'd explained that his interest was natural, part of their culture. When students chose which kind of upper secondary school they wanted to attend—classics, science, fine arts, tech—*liceo classico*, literature and philosophy and history, was the oldest and the most demanding of all, not a place for sports teams. He thinks *this* is funny, that Americans have sports at school.

"Beautiful treasure, but bones, too." Charlotte makes a face. She hasn't forgotten that part. It's eerie to think of that old cemetery, drowned by floodwaters.

"Yes, but the treasure! Even a record of dowry payments from the sixteenth century, when your relative was here. Isabella—I am forgetting. Your eyes are too pretty."

It sounds like a line, but he seems to mean it. He pushes his glass up shyly. She smiles. "Di Angelo. Isabella di Angelo."

"Of angels, of angels." He taps his forehead, as if to set the name permanently in his brain. "Dottoressa Ricci keeps asking and asking, so I need to remember. This is how she is. She has the nail stuck on her head!"

He says it like it's a compliment, but it's hard to tell. "The dowry payments they'd make—I read about those."

"A convent was much cheaper than if a daughter married. We see it on the list. Only hundreds of ducats, compared to thousands for marriage. More, if they were rich."

"What would that be today?"

"Hmm. Impossible to say. A ducat was a gold coin. A piece of gold."

"The convent was *right here*? It's crazy to think of it. I have to take a picture so my family can see." She fishes her phone out of her bag.

"Of course. It was over there, too, and gardens." He points to the other side of the San Zaccaria church, with its flat white front that looks like a smashed wedding cake. "Let's go in. There's a surprise. *Dai*."

They step through the doors of San Zaccaria, away from the July sun, and inside, the church is cool, deliciously cool. There's a wax-and-wood-and-old-prayers smell, and above and all around, huge paintings and columns that rise to the high ceilings.

"Behind these paintings?" Dante whispers. "There are still the old grilles, where the nuns could listen to the service from inside the convent walls."

"Man. They weren't even let out to go to church? Wasn't that the point of being in a convent?"

He makes a face. "Many of them were not even religious. Some tried to *escape*."

"It's so awful. Is this the surprise? The hidden grilles?"

"You'll see."

They walk down the aisle, then turn to view the huge paintings and altarpieces on either side of the church. "Who knows?" Dante says. "Your Isabella's face could be right here somewhere in these paintings." His eyes are so serious again behind his glasses that he seems to mean this, too.

"Wait. What do you mean? Really?"

"The nuns here? They were very important to art of the time. They *hired* these artists." He nods toward the painting they stand in front of. "Commissioned them through the grilles of the convent! They approved the sketches, made the decisions. Financed it, even, through rich relatives. We study this in History of the Arts, three years." He smiles.

"That's *a lot* of art history in high school."

"Is it?" he asks, and shrugs. "But the girls. They were artists themselves, too, you see? The nuns? And they put *themselves* in the art, their actual faces and figures. Set inside the paintings or sculptures. Images of their rings, their family coat of arms. Their own inscriptions on tombs. *Signatures.* To say, *You will see me. Even though you have locked me away, I am here.*"

"No way. I love that," Charlotte says.

"Sometimes they painted their image in a place of honor.

On the right side of Mary, or as large as a male saint." Dante laughs.

"That's amazing." Charlotte's beginning to love those nuns.

"They chose the artists. They decided the art. It was *theirs*. The art was *the power*."

It gives her shivers, especially when she remembers how young they were. She wishes she *was* here, Isabella di Angelo, her face hidden in one of these paintings. She could be looking right at her and not even know it.

They've made a full circle, and now they're at the front of the church again. "Over here," he says. To the right, there's a plain door marked with the words PLEASE CLOSE DOOR BEHIND YOU.

"Okay, *this* is the surprise, right?" she asks.

Dante just lifts his eyebrows mischievously. His dark eyes shine. He and Charlotte step down into a stone stairwell. A cool, damp mustiness circles around her. Dante takes Charlotte's hand, leading her lower and lower underground. She likes the feel of his hand. She likes the look of the back of him, his curly hair, his jeans and T-shirt, hanging just-right loose and stylish on him. She likes the way he glances back over his shoulder at her and smiles again. Her heart trips with the adventure of it, and the giddy spookiness, too, because the stone walls close up in vaulted arcs overhead as they descend. Finally, here at the bottom of this subterranean place, the light is dim, except for a white beam shining on a large stone tomb.

It's a crypt.

"Careful," Dante says. They step onto a raised brick walkway, and as her eyes adjust to the light, she sees the most eerily beautiful sight. The crypt is flooded. Water surrounds them, covering the entire floor of the cavern. It's a pool of mirrors, reflecting ancient stone columns, which appear to both rise from the water and descend into it, reflecting the tomb and the arches of the brick ceiling. The only sound is the *drip, drip* of water hitting water somewhere inside, an echoey, eternal sound. Shivers prickle up Charlotte's arms, because it feels both sacred and strange. She sees the arched niches set into the walls too. Vaults with bones likely crumbled to dust by now.

"Who's buried here?" Charlotte whispers, even though they're the only ones down there. It's the kind of place where a loud voice would be disrespectful and shattering.

"A few old doges. From the time the church was built? And rebuilt again in the 1500s."

"Doges. They were the leaders of the city, right?" She read about them in her book.

"*Duca*? Duke, you say? Chosen from a powerful family."

They walk along the brick path, passing slowly in front of each vault, dimly illuminated from above. They stop at the large upright tomb sitting at the center. The water shimmers. There's a statue of a woman on the stone box. She wears Roman robes and a necklace, and she looks pleadingly toward heaven, with one arm outstretched and the other lifting her skirts from the floor. She's so dramatic and unsettling and romantic that

Charlotte feels her strength and her pain. Her image reflects in the water too. She appears to descend and to rise.

"Beautiful, yes?"

"Yes, very." Charlotte wishes she could cross through the several inches of water along the floor and walk right up to her, but they stay on the path and look at her from a distance.

"Is it always flooded like this?"

"During the *acqua alta*, much worse." With his hand, he shows her how high the water gets. Nearly to his waist.

"Yikes."

"You see why Venezia does not have many crypts, yes?"

"Definitely."

"We should get back to life," he says.

Maria Luchessi, Dante's mother, with her short, crimped hair and bold jewelry and piercing eyes, stares across the table at Charlotte. Charlotte was shocked when Dante asked her to come to dinner at their house above the bookstore. It was weeks before Charlotte met Adam's dad, Don, and even then, it was, like, for two seconds passing him in the kitchen. And it doesn't seem to have great meaning, either, the way meeting a parent might at home. It seems usual. A regular night. They're sitting in the Luchessis' small dining room, framed with tall, green shuttered windows and surrounded by the charming spillover from the *Alta Acqua Libreria*: a Roman bust on the sill, a wall jammed full of oil paintings in various sizes. A bookshelf holds hardbacks and paperbacks of all sizes and ages, but also a bronze horse, and an elaborate candlestick, and a beautiful framed drawing of an elephant. The tilting chandelier gives the room a warm glow, and the windows are open, and every now and then there's the putter of a boat outside, or the sluicing sound of a gondola passing.

After getting a tour of the house, Charlotte now knows that there's a tiny bathroom and three small bedrooms up that narrow, narrow stairwell—Maria's, Dante's, and the snug, book-filled alcove that used to belong to Dante's sister, Bria, before she *went away to university* (as Dante says it) in Rome. Around the corner from the dining room and kitchen, there's also a living room with an old red velvet couch, and carved wood end tables, and two green velvet chairs made soft and worn over the years.

That evening, dinner (*bigoli in salsa*—a thick noodle with a sauce, though Charlotte can't quite tell what it is) is delicious, and she feels like she's in a cozy hideaway with those wood beamed ceilings. Even though Maria's tone is abrupt, and her laugh is sort of cynical, she seems to know something about everything, and her eyes warm with devotion every time she tells another story about Dante. She's obviously really proud of him, and from the amount of times Maria mentions *liceo classico*, Charlotte understands that it's the most prestigious program.

Dante is so much more relaxed at home, louder, less shy, and he leans back in his chair, and pokes his fork in the air for emphasis. They've asked Charlotte lots of questions about her life in America—about her parents, her sister, her plans for university, her city. And Charlotte's learned so much about Dante tonight—how he loved his old dog, Luigi, now gone, and how he broke his arm the first time he played rugby, and how his father, who lives on the mainland, is a historian, and how his parents divorced when he was eight. How, God, he's cute in that light, and maybe all lights, and how great it feels when she says something that makes him laugh. It's like she's won a million dollars when he laughs like that.

But now, when the conversation turns to Charlotte's writing program, Maria makes a scoffing sound in the back of her throat. "Oh. Luca Bruni, hmm?"

"He's a great teacher. I've already learned so much." Charlotte's polite ass-kissing skills are in overdrive, but she feels it again—the urge to protect Luca, now that he's let them into his inner circle. She'd never tell the bad parts, or the complicated parts. The things she knows, about who he really is.

"Pffft." Maria waves her hand, like the idea of him is a bad smell.

Charlotte blushes. "You don't like him, or his books?"

"Eh. There are lots of books. The man—he always . . . *pavoneggiarsi*."

"Peacocks himself," Dante explains. He pretends to strut.

"Maybe a little." And maybe he deserves to. Charlotte doesn't say this, though.

"I don't like it." Maria sits back in her chair.

"I'm really grateful for the opportunity, though. I could never have come here on my own," Charlotte says.

"Building that place on *the dead*." Maria shakes her head.

"It was very controversial here," Dante says. "Buying that island. That villa. Like, putting it on a *cimitero*."

"I can see how that would be upsetting."

"I've heard the stories about him." Maria narrows her eyes and adjusts her necklace.

"Stories?" Charlotte's not sure she wants to know. Actually, she doesn't. "In the United States people think very highly of him. They teach his work in schools and universities. He's very popular. People *love* him."

Maria shrugs. "Well, *you*—how do you say, *avere gli occhi foderati di prosciutto*?"

"You have ham over the eyes," Dante translates. "Covered with ham. Not seeing."

Charlotte flushes with embarrassment. "Maybe."

Maria's disapproval sits like another guest at the table. That's how it feels to Charlotte, though maybe it's not as big a deal as it is at her house, because Dante cheerfully says, "I showed Charlotta the crypt at Chiesa di San Zaccaria." *Charlotta.* God, she loves the way he says her name.

Maria smiles, all disapproval vanishing. "A pool of mirrors, yes?"

"It was beautiful," Charlotte says.

"Charlotta's poet, Isabella di Angelo, was likely in the convent there," he tells Maria.

"The one who knew Antonio Tasso, I remember," Maria says. "Did you locate her book?"

"Book?" Dante asks.

"The one you asked for at the store," Maria says.

"A *second* book," Charlotte says. "We have a copy of her first one. *The Verses.* It's from 1573. They—my family—always thought there was another, but no one can find out anything about it."

"What?" Dante slams both palms on the table. "You have her book? The female poet? Dottoressa Ricci will be so happy. You can get it? *Mi raccomondo*?" He puts his hands together, pretend-pleading. "Let me write down the name." He takes out his phone.

"The Verses," she tells him. "And I don't have to *get* it. I have it."

"You have it? Here?"

"On La Calamita, in my room."

"You *brought* it in your suitcase from America? Oh, Charlotta . . ." He makes a cringing face.

"I know, I know. Don't say it. It was dangerous and stupid. I just brought her home for a visit, Dante."

"All right, I understand." He smiles. "And if she has to travel, it is better than coming in the mail! But it's here? You have to show Dottoressa Ricci. And you are looking for a second book? Why didn't you say? Next time, we will go see Dottore Paolo Berti. He oversees many, many *cinquecintene.* Twenty-five thousand or so."

"Chinkwa . . . ?"

He laughs. "The books of the sixteenth century? If your book exists in the original, it will maybe be there, in his collection."

"This is an island," Maria says. "There is nowhere for your poet to go. She is in Venezia somewhere."

"I hope so," Charlotte says. And right then, sitting with them at that table, in the warm, gold light of that room, she badly hopes so. The more she sees of that city, the more connected to Isabella she feels.

"Those nuns," Maria says. "They were so young! Imprisoned by their families. Their fathers. Because they were *girls*."

It gets late. Since the water taxis don't go to La Calamita, Aldo is scheduled to pick up Charlotte and Katerina, who's out with a friend visiting from the US. Aldo gets grumpier than usual on their free days, shuttling everyone around, so she doesn't want to keep him waiting. Charlotte thanks Maria at the door, and to Charlotte's surprise, Maria kisses both her cheeks and urges her to visit again.

Dante walks Charlotte back to the dock near Saint Mark's. It's such a beautiful night, and the waters of the canals twinkle, a different set of mirrors from the ones in the crypt, mirrors that are filled with the flickers and shine of life. Before they reach the busy harbor, along a street beside a narrow canal, Dante takes Charlotte's elbow, and they stop and kiss. His hands are in her hair, and it's a sweet and delicious kiss that stops time for one great moment and makes her wish she didn't have to return just yet.

"Wow," she says.

"Wow, Charlotta," he agrees.

They reach the dock. Aldo is there with the boat, and Katerina is already on board.

"Good night, Dante."

"Buonanotte," he says, and squeezes her hand.

"Thank you for today and tonight," Charlotte says. "It was so great. I'm . . . peacocking myself." He laughs, and her heart pours coins like a winning slot machine.

Aldo starts the motor. Charlotte feels a little twinge of loss and longing and she steps away from Dante and onto the boat. He stays on the dock until the boat pulls away from the city. When he's too small to see anymore, Katerina says, "Who was *that*?"

"New friend."

"Yeah, *friend*. I can tell."

Now Aldo turns up the music. Opera. Vivaldi. The city gets smaller too, and the boat *ba-bamp*s along the waves. Katerina stands, looking out at the beauty, her hair whipping in her face. Charlotte stands beside her. The ancient island with its tilting buildings glitters, as if lit by hundreds of flickering candles. The purple-black waves catch diamond glints of the moon. It's so beautiful, Charlotte is overcome. She has to swallow back tears.

"Look at this," Katerina says, meaning *everything*.

There is so much everything. The nuns of that convent and the flooded crypt and Vivaldi and books and history and power and love. So much history. History can feel so distant sometimes, and other times, close enough that you can feel it right inside of you, close enough that you can see it moving away from you and toward you at the same time.

"I know," Charlotte says. "I know."

She smiles at Katerina and Katerina smiles back, and Charlotte is filled with a feeling that's hard to explain, but that she'll never forget. Tonight, it's the two of them who are here together, sharing this experience, while Luca Bruni is somewhere else. Tonight, they are the similar and equal ones, and he is apart. They are the music students, and he is Vivaldi. They are the young sisters in the convent, painting themselves next to the saint.

Chapter Twenty-Two

Diodata Malvasia, writer.

Entered the convent of San Mattia at age seventeen. It was long thought that she only wrote one book, until a second was recently discovered.

(1532–unknown)

Luca Bruni sits at the edge of one of the high, rocky cliffs of Due Sorelle, a beach at the edge of the Adriatic Sea. They've visited other beaches, but none like this. All around are the clear green-blue-aqua (there's no real word for the shade—emerald, maybe?) waters of the sea, dipping into curved coves where it changes to an even more vibrant green. More dramatic than the white beaches and the stunning colors, though, are the jagged white pinnacles, sculpted by corrosive winds that rise from the water.

Even with his thin, awkward frame and hair gone wild in the wind, Luca Bruni looks majestic sitting there. It's that unnameable something, plus his crooked nose and long legs crossed at the ankles. The crazy thing is, Charlotte isn't even distracted by the scenery. No one is, because Luca's reading a piece from the new book he's working on. *His new book!*

Right now, the title is *Moment before the Fall*, which could be better, he admits. But what he's reading now . . . Oh, God—how can she describe it, other than to say she gets goose bumps? No one moves as they listen to him read. And then they all burst out laughing at one moment, because he can do that—he can write with so much *feeling*, the *all-of-life* feeling you never even knew *had* words, but then, he turns right around and cracks you up.

When he's done reading, he sets the pages down on his knee and waits a moment before looking up at all of them, seated at his feet. No one speaks for a while. Hailey just says "whew" under her breath. This is the power of words coming from someone like that, someone with his, let's just say it—genius. Brilliance. It blows Charlotte away every time she remembers that there are just twenty-six little characters in their alphabet, the same twenty-six characters every person using the English language has to use, and some do *this* with it. There's the handful of people who wield that alphabet in ways that affect you and change you and forever alter the way you see yourself and the world around you, so, damn.

In a moment like that, well, who cares about any . . . indiscretions on his part. (It's such a polite and forgiving word, *indiscretions*. It sounds as blameless as a napkin that slips from your lap.) All the weirdness with Avni, et cetera, has faded anyway, and he and Bethany Sparrow seem to be okay again. Last week, he took Eliot to see the statue of Madonna dell'Orto, since Eliot's haunting piece is about the rejection he's felt all his life. Apparently, the statue *itself* was rejected by the priest of the church it was meant to go in, so the artist stuck it in his own garden, where it began to glow, a miracle that became a place of worship. Eliot was practically high when he came back, telling them about it. He was talking a million miles an hour.

When Hailey got back yesterday, same. She was all, *You guys, you guys!* And they gathered around her like she was the sole voyager to a new land. Her piece is about a young woman haunted by the fear of making mistakes, since her entrepreneurial father almost lost the family fortune a jillion times. Luca took Hailey to the Scuola Grande di San Marco, a medical museum with strange, scary, outdated medical equipment—*hundreds of years of the failures that led to societal progress*! Hailey told them. That night, she called her dad, and they were on the phone so long, she almost missed dinner.

The thought creeps in: *Luca's on his best behavior*, but Charlotte shoves it out. Because, well, look at him. He smiles and shakes his head in almost-shy happiness that they liked what he just read. He folds his long fingers around one of his knees and leans back. And it's amazing, you know, incredible, that they get to be his first audience for this book. *No one* has heard this before. Just the eight of them, including Bethany, who's also beaming at him, like he's being very, very good at last.

"We all know my ego is outsize already, and you aren't helping," he says, and they all laugh. It's another great thing, how he admits to his dark pieces. Really, his flawed human self is right out there, and that takes guts. Charlotte loves him, you know? She loved him before, but now she really does.

"Question!" Ashley pops her hand up. "What you just read, it's on *paper*. Actual paper. Longhand, right?"

He holds the pages up and out to them so they can see that she's correct. His spidery loops and letters are there, handwritten.

"Don't you worry about losing them?" Ashley continues. "I mean right now, what if a big wind blew them right off this cliff? I mean, you type them into your laptop, too, right?"

"Well, after the book is done, *someone* does. But I like the immediacy of it, hand on the page. The *intimacy* of it."

"Nooo!" Eliot says. "If you lost what you just read . . ."

"This whole business is risk!" he says. "Writing is *dangerous*. More precious and powerful *because* it's dangerous." His eyes dance. "Am I right? Danger makes you feel less . . . *dead*. And lonely." It's hard to imagine him feeling dead and lonely. With such a fabulous life, how could he? But then again, his childhood was sad, so sad. That he even used the word *lonely*—it makes her feel awful for him.

"Okay, we talked about setting here, in one of the most beautiful places I've ever seen," he says. "In the next twenty minutes, I want a paragraph of this!" He sweeps his hand around those green waters. Shoot, Charlotte has to think of something better than *green*, and fast. "Winner, I'll take to dinner. And later, work on a scene from your haunting piece that gives me some fucking glorious setting that I can *feel*."

Ugh—Charlotte hates these fast-write assignments. She sucks at spilling stuff under pressure, so she just gets down what she can. She uses *emerald* and *sapphire*, jewel tones, but it's lame. When they read aloud, Leo clearly wins. He's so good-looking, and his skin is getting darker as the weeks go on, and set against the white shirt and pastel orange shorts he's wearing, wow. And he doesn't use something lame like *emerald* to describe the water. He compares the color to looking into the eyes of someone he once loved. When he finishes, there's a moment where no one speaks.

"How do you *do* that?" Charlotte says. "That was *amazing*."

"Hey, you're all winners," Luca says. "Okay? All of you. I'm taking you to Cantina Do Mori tonight. Oldest *bacaro* here. Like, 1462 or something."

"Ba*cah*ro . . . ," Eliot says with an exaggerated accent.

Luca Bruni grins. "Sounds a lot better than 'tavern,' huh?"

Shaye's taking forever in the bathroom. Charlotte sits at the edge of her bed, yellow skirt and white T-shirt on, flip-flops, too, her black hair loose and shiny. She just needs to pee, and swipe on some lip gloss. She looks at the clock on her phone for the jillionth time, and as she does, it rings.

"Charlotta!" Dante says.

Oh, his voice. Twelve hundred smiling emojis. Since they

had dinner at his house, she and Dante talk at least once a day. Charlotte finds private corners of La Calamita, like the poolside at night, or the scrubby paths in the back of the villa that lead to the tower, though she avoids the abandoned buildings of the old hospital. It's corny, but whenever she sees his name on her phone, her heart actually flutters. How would she describe it if she were writing it? Not like a butterfly, because it's way stronger. More like a pterodactyl, but that's not exactly romantic.

She's also been able to see Dante again, twice. Enough to know that there's a pull between them. It's different from Adam, where the intensity came from Adam's insecurity and moods. With Dante, they're *both* in that amazing place where you want to hear all the stories of another person, and be with that person more, more, more. Last Sunday, she met some of his friends, too. They drank espresso at an outdoor café, and Nicco, and Raffaele, and Raffaele's girlfriend, Gaia, were friendly and laid-back. Stylish and sophisticated, but easy with it, like it was part of them instead of an effort they were making.

And she saw him just yesterday, when the Biblioteca Marciana was open, and Dante had a lunch break. Charlotte was free, since Luca was with Hailey.

"Dottore Berti will find the book if it exists," Dante said when they headed into that majestic library. He was walking so fast, she could barely keep up. He always praises his professors' passion and determination, but he has it too. The Isabella and Tasso story—he loves it. It's like a mystery that gnaws at him. They'll be talking about other stuff—Raffaele's girlfriend, for example, how she's a huge reader and would get along so great with Carly—and then out of the blue, he'll say something like, *We need to trace the di Angelo name, that's what we should do.* He's going to be so good at his job.

When they neared the small library-within-a-library overseen by Dottore Paolo Berti, Charlotte felt so hopeful. The *cinquecintene* collection has nearly twenty-five thousand original books from Isabella's time alone, Dante had told her. But when they walked in, it wasn't what she'd expected, not at all. There were hardly any volumes on display, and no one was even behind the reference desk until Dante dinged and dinged and dinged the little bell on the counter.

Finally, Dr. Berti walked out from the back. He had black hair mixed with gray and wore large, artistic, black-framed glasses and a stylish, expensive-looking suit and tie. Charlotte wanted to catch Dante's eye and peacock-strut, but didn't. Dr. Berti was definitely *pavon*-something, whatever Maria had said. Right away, Dante and Dr. Berti started talking in rapid Italian, Dante huffing with exasperation.

Finally, Dr. Berti slid a pen and a little piece of paper across the counter.

"Your phone number," Dante said to Charlotte. He made a face like he wanted to roll his eyes but couldn't.

"I will look. I will let you know. I will call you if I find anything," Dr. Berti said to Charlotte in English.

Her hope crashed. She wrote down her number and thanked him, but she had no real belief she'd ever hear from him. She saw it here before—promises, but no follow-through. Situations like that half-fixed wall and the abandoned wheelbarrow in the convent building, or the guys just standing around day after day on the damaged floodwall in front of La Calamita. Bummer, too, because she told her mom that morning that they were about to find the book.

Now, on the phone, as she sits at the edge of her bed, Dante asks, "Have you heard from Berti?" He's been demoted from *Dottore Paolo Berti* to *Berti*, she notices.

"Not yet."

"Cazzo."

"What does *cazzo*—"

"Don't ask. Ugh, I wish Dottoressa Ricci wasn't gone. And she said to only call for emergencies."

"This is definitely not an emergency. We haven't known anything about Isabella for hundreds of years."

"But you are only here for a few weeks," he says. "So, it is *urgent.*"

"Don't say it, don't say it." She's begun to realize the trouble she's gotten into. She's going to have to go home, and it's already awful to think about.

"You will break my heart."

"Dante, God, stop being so adorable and amazing," she says. Because, ugh, he is. He's beginning to feel so familiar, too, even after this short time. Of course, that can happen when someone shoves you up against a building and you kiss like crazy, and your hands are all over each other, like after they saw Dr. Berti.

"No, you—"

"Oh, wait. I've got to go."

Shaye's just stepped out of the bathroom, and *whoa*. She's got a short black dress on, and her spiky hair is gelled up, and she's wearing *makeup*.

"Baciami," Dante says, and makes a kiss sound into the phone. He's a goof like that, and she loves it.

"I will not," Charlotte says, and laughs. She watches Shaye wobble as she straps on some high heels. "I'll call you later."

"What are you staring at?" Shaye snaps.

"Just, *wow*," Charlotte says. It's weird, you know. Shaye caring like this. Shaye wearing *lipstick*.

Shaye stands, tugs at the hem of her dress. "Really? Do I look okay?" she asks.

Chapter Twenty-Three

Veneranda Bragadin, poet.

When she wrote a sonnet in objection to Giovanni Battista Barbo's misogynistic poem, she sparked a vicious feud with him. He fought back with hostility, impugning her honor, but she didn't back down. She accused him of being senile and told everyone that he visited prostitutes, since he had no other options.

(Dates unknown, likely 1613 or so)

Cantina Do Mori is tucked away in an alley behind a set of wooden doors. Bethany isn't feeling well, so it's just the seven of them and Luca, and he's in a grand mood. His strides are large and jovial, and he keeps shouting stuff over his shoulder at them as they walk. People turn around to look. Now he stops at the doors.

"One of two entrances." He taps a long finger on the door. "Which I'm sure Casanova appreciated. Did I tell you he used to come here? He could slip out the back, so he didn't get caught by some husband-dude." He winks and then goes in.

"Casanova?" Ashley asks.

"You don't know who he is? Are you kidding?" Hailey says. "How'd you get to college without knowing that? He's, like, the most famous bad boy in history. Like, a really famous seducer of lots of women."

"Can you two stop fighting for five seconds?" Shaye says. Even dressed up, she's in her usual mood: semi–pissed off.

"Come on! Go in, you guys!" Katerina says.

It's a small and wonderful place. Warm, charming, busy. Copper pots hang from the ceiling, and you're immediately hit with the smell of salami and cheese, and it's dimly lit, with no tables, only a long wooden bar. They all take seats. Soon, glasses of a cold, fizzy red wine appear in front of them, which Shaye downs in, like, a minute. Charlotte worries about her, a lot, because her dad's an alcoholic, and she seems to drink two of anything before Charlotte's practically touched hers, even if Ashley's also like that. Charlotte's a nervous Goody Two-shoes about alcohol, though, she knows. Her mom's always warning her when they talk on the phone not to drink a lot, and to be careful, and to remember that she's nowhere near the legal drinking age at home.

Whatever. The fizzy wine is refreshing, since it's warm in the little *bacaro*. It tastes way better than that gross *limoncello* they sometimes have after dinner too, which looks and tastes like Pine-Sol. Eliot is on one side of Charlotte, and Luca Bruni is on the other, and they're all sitting so close, she can practically feel the heat coming off Luca's skin. Now there's plate after plate of *cicchetti*—finger food. Dishes of everything from *tramezzini*—crustless sandwiches stuffed with meat and cheese—to fried artichoke hearts, to those sardines that are everywhere, which she's finally starting to like.

"Setting!" Luca shouts, and at first, Charlotte thinks he means this place, but then realizes he wants someone to read.

"I didn't even bring anything," Eliot says.

"Too loud in here! Forget it," Shaye shouts.

Who cares if it's loud, if it's what he wants? Besides, Luca's sitting right beside her, and he's the only one who needs to hear. And *of course* she has the pages they print in the library, just in case. Usually, no one gives her all that much attention or a very hard critique when she reads. She's the youngest, and they treat her like that. But she killed it this time. She's sure of it. In her piece, her character visits the flooded crypt at San Zaccaria, just like she did. She knows he'll *feel* it, just like he wanted, because that setting *lives* in her—in her DNA of eons ago, and now as a memory she'll never forget. So she reads about the mirrored pools and the columns, and the tomb in the center of the vault, and it feels like truth. She reads until Hailey shouts, "We can't hear you," and then Charlotte just sits down, and everyone starts talking on their own again, over the clank of plates and people going in and out.

You really can't hear anything in there. There's no way anyone can critique. But Luca heard. He finally hears, after all the weeks where she's felt pretty much invisible. His eyes were on her the whole time she read. Now he leans over and says "really good" in her ear. His breath is hot, and it actually makes her blush.

"Honestly?" She practically has to shout, even with him right there, since it's gotten so loud.

He's leaning toward her, close enough that she smells the wine on his breath. "Yes," he says. And that magic word, *yes*, fills her with warmth, a warmth that flows from her cheeks all through her body, as if she's just swallowed those first sips of wine. It's triumph, but not just that. She's pleased him. Finally. He keeps looking at her like she's brand-new.

The joy of pleasing him carries all the way through dinner, and outside again, as they walk back to the boats waiting for them near Saint Mark's. Everyone's in a good mood. They're talking loudly, jostling each other, and laughing. Leo and Shaye are both a bit drunk. Charlotte feels like she's in college, the way she imagines a college night out might be, since she hasn't had one yet. Except, there's this amazing genius writer walking next to her. Honestly, look at him right now, grinning, walking all casual with his hands in his pockets. She just loves him. This experience has changed her life.

Now he bumps into her as they walk. He's so much taller than she is, but she bumps him back. That's the kind of night it is. But he's walking so close to her that their arms practically touch. When he looks over at her, it's like . . . a force of energy. The same one she felt that first time he stared in her eyes back at the tower on La Calamita, the tower from where the evil doctor jumped. It's the kind of energy that makes you want things. Him, even, or maybe just to give him things. You, but not your body exactly. Just the truth of you. Like you could hand over your whole, full self, and he would *know* you.

He's holding her eyes, you know, a little too long, but she doesn't look away. It feels . . . large. She feels the intense focus of it, a hot beam of sun through a magnifying glass. He's making a statement, or it's a dare, or an invitation.

"Hey," he finally says. "*I* described the sea like that. Like the eyes of a woman I loved. In one of the first pieces I published in *The Atlantic*."

Charlotte doesn't know what he means at first. It takes her a second. The sea, the eyes of a woman? But then she realizes—he's talking about that piece Leo wrote today. The one she praised.

Luca leans in really close, like he's telling her an important secret. "He's not *that* amazing," he says.

She doesn't know what to say. And that look, the way he was staring in her eyes—she wants to say it's confusing, but maybe it isn't. It's like they're both her age, or both his age, or like they're both famous authors or both students, even if they're not. They are definitely, definitely not.

When they get in the boat, on the whole ride back, she *feels* that look. She feels it through her whole body. It bashes against the *really good* that he whispered in her ear. Because he meant it, right? That it was good? It seemed good. Both things feel true—the look he gave her, *and* the words about her writing. The look doesn't have to mean anything or go anywhere. It just says that maybe he's attracted to her and she has talent.

He's so awesome and so important that she trusts him not to lie about either of these things.

That night, as she lies in bed, she keeps replaying the scene, his eyes on her, the whisper, the way he bumped into her as they walked. His eyes on her, the whisper, the way he bumped into her as they walked, again and again, same as she replayed that first kiss with Dante, same as she did her first moments with Adam, when he slipped a note into her hand as they passed in the hallway at school. She realizes she forgot to call Dante back, and now it's too late.

Something wakes her up. She has no idea what. Maybe some spirit from the plague haunting. Maybe Isabella's *The Verses*, whispering under her mattress. Maybe just wind or waves or water rising. But she sees that Shaye isn't there. Charlotte's worried about her. Shaye has a lot that haunts her. The piece she's been working on is about her dad's alcoholism, but there are hints of other things too, a sexual assault from a guy in high school, her own depression. Charlotte gets up and walks down the stairs in the dark, past that huge glass ship painted on the wall, into the living room with the tall windows. Shaye isn't there, either. Charlotte steps outside, but she can't see her anywhere. She hopes Shaye is all right.

Chapter Twenty-Four

Barbara Strozzi, Venetian noblewoman and composer.

One of the first female composers to publish under her own name, she has more music in print than any other composer of this era, including Vivaldi. There are claims that she was a courtesan, but she was likely just accused of this since she was a musician, and because her work could be risqué in the extreme. She wrote often on themes of gender, tucking hidden messages into her pieces. Single mother of four, she was raped by the father of her first child.

(1619–1677)

Today, Luca is taking Katerina out, but he won't say where. What haunts Kat is that orphanage, and whenever she reads any part of her story aloud, it makes you want to cry. Even though her life sounds pretty good since she's been adopted, that orphanage never seems to leave her. Charlotte wonders if everyone who wants to write is haunted. *They* all are, that's for sure. She wonders if Luca Bruni knew this all along about them. That's why he chose this assignment. What haunts you is powerful. It's the truth of you, and truth speaks. Look at his own work, right?

But, also—she doesn't want to even think this, so why does it flash through her mind—knowing what haunts someone gives you powerful information about that person, doesn't it? You could use it, if you wanted. It would let you inside of them, like a secret pass code. Who would do that, though? It's a paranoid thought about Luca, with his big nose and long legs and loud laugh.

Katerina is excited but nervous. Luca plans these things, chooses particular places for a meaningful moment, a lesson, a message he wants to convey to them. Charlotte's anxiety amps up when she thinks about her turn. Just the two of them alone for the day—it's exciting and she can't wait, but also, she has a weird, nervous dread about it that makes her head hurt.

Aldo takes Charlotte and the guys and Hailey and Ashley into Venice for the day. Shaye was in her bed that morning when Charlotte woke up, but Shaye just wanted to stay on La Calamita and hang out. Maybe she was hungover.

Dante's mother, Maria, was right—he's always at the library, especially as more and more material from the flood comes in from the facility where it's being freeze-dried. He has to work today, but she got to see a lot of him last weekend. They even went back to Dante's house and saw his mom again. She can count on both hands the number of times she and Adam ever hung out with her parents or his dad, but it's different here. They also FaceTimed with Dante's sister, Bria, so she and

Charlotte could meet, and then Dante insisted they do the same with Adele and Ella. It was Sunday morning, and Adele was in her robe, and she had a pinched expression, impatient, irritated, and you could see all the breakfast dishes and the mail stacked on the counter, and it was embarrassing and awkward until Ella lifted up Marvin so Dante could meet him, too. His black nose looked giant, and the two black caves of his nostrils filled the screen, and it was so funny, thankfully. What was THAT? I hope you're being careful, Adele texted afterward.

Well, no, she isn't being careful, honestly. Not with her heart. Charlotte's got a big problem, and it's only going to get worse. She's going to have to go home, and he's going to be here, and she won't be able to come back again, at least not for a long, long time. And she likes him. *A lot.* He's so funny and sweet, and he's the kind of person who's so curious that his mind goes a hundred miles an hour, to the point that he trips on curbs and almost runs into lampposts. She finds this hot. *Really* hot—attractive and adorable beyond belief. And he's a good person. He loves his sister, and he stays late at the library because he's fascinated by his work, and he really respects his professor, and he's sometimes rumpled in that way that's so sexy. And you know another thing? He's not always looking at his phone. Adam looked at his phone every two seconds. *Everyone* looks at their phone every two seconds, but Dante is *there* with her. Ugh. Leaving him will be brutal.

Charlotte texts him when she's outside the Conservation and Restoration doors as they planned, but instead of him hurrying outside so they could go somewhere private to kiss awhile before he has to return to work, he texts back and tells her to come in.

When he sees her, he waves her over.

"Your professor is still gone, right?" She doesn't want to get him in trouble.

"A few more days. The conference is finished, but she is staying to visit family. Have you heard from Dottore Berti yet?"

"Nope."

"*Uffa!* This is what happens here, you see? They take their time, and do it when they want."

"Yeah. I noticed. You should have heard Aldo this morning, cursing at the guys doing nothing about the seawall. Italian Swearing Lesson, number fifty."

"Dottoressa Ricci won't stand for it, just wait," Dante says. "*Va bene*, my day is better. Come here. Look at this."

A beautiful document, a fragile piece of paper with scrolling words in Italian script, sits on Dante's workstation. "A letter to the abbess of San Zaccaria, in September of 1575," he explains.

"What does it say?"

"'It has come to our ears that four servants of your convent are very bad characters, namely bawds.'" Dante looks up at Charlotte and makes his eyes wide with pretend shock. "'Two of these are now pregnant.' Here there is something about receiving this news from others, but it's not clear." He gestures to an area on the letter. "And then there's more. 'You have not done your duty by warning us of this, for we wish to cleanse your convent of this disease. We charge and command you to conduct prudent inquiries about said sisters. One, Antonia, belonging to the noble house of Da Mula, daughter of Ser Nicolo, not a handsome woman, her age twenty-two or so . . .'"

"Ooh, mean. What else?"

"That's it."

"Nooo," Charlotte groans. "That's it? What happened to poor Antonia?"

"We may never know, or perhaps something else will appear."

"Wait—who wrote this?"

"Likely the Council of Ten. You know the Council of Ten?"

"I read about them."

"Or perhaps the *Patriarca*? The bishop, you say. Of the Archdiocese of Venezia. Dottoressa Ricci said that the convents are often in the Council of Ten documents. They were trying to control the disorder there, like nuns having sex and getting pregnant."

"Ugh! I want to know about Antonia! This is so interesting."

"I am only cleaning dirt from it."

"That's not true."

He smiles shyly at her compliment. "*Baciami*," he says.

"Here?"

"*Chissenefrega*." He waves his hand, doesn't matter, and so they quickly kiss. "Call me?"

"Dante!" she pretends to call. It's the stupidest joke ever, but he still laughs, and she loves it times a million.

She wants to see the church again, and maybe explore what used to be the convent courtyard that they missed last time. Charlotte *really* wants to walk on the same ground Isabella di Angelo did. Charlotte feels her here. And this may be the closest she ever gets to her or the truth about the Tasso poem, at the rate they're going. But still. Even this, that she was *here*, right with that pregnant sister Antonia, probably—wow. She can't even imagine it. What a story.

Charlotte walks up the stairs to the church doors, but just as she's about to step through, something alarming happens. The guard begins to shout at her.

"No entry! *Indossare abbigliamento adeguato! Indossare abbigliamento adeguato!*"

He yells with such force and venom that she stops in her tracks. Oh my God, she has no idea what she's done wrong, and she's horrified and a little scared. But he's gesturing to her chest. In her sundress, her arms are bare, and the slightest dip between her breasts is showing. He's patting his chest as if hers is a disgusting sight. And now he's shoving something at her. She remembers, too late, how Bethany Sparrow warned them to dress modestly when they first visited Saint Mark's, and how Avni had kept a shawl in her purse to drape over her bare shoulders.

The guard forces a blue paper poncho into her hands. It's

the pale, sickly shade of the crinkly gowns at the doctor's office. When she puts her head through the hole, the drape goes all the way down to her shins, covering her knees, too. She's humiliated. A curl of shame rises up, but she steps inside the church anyway. The poncho rustles as she moves, and the whole time that she's there, wearing it, she feels bad. That poncho isn't protecting *her*; it's protecting everyone (and God, too, she guesses) *from* her. That long blue poncho tells everyone she's immodest. That something about her body is wrong enough that it shouldn't be seen.

She doesn't stay in the church for long. And it's stupid, but when she's back outside, she doesn't take that poncho off until she's out of sight of that guard. She doesn't want him to yell at her again. She wants him to think she's good, and that she follows the rules. But the second he's far enough away, she rips it off her head and rolls it into a ball and shoves it into her handbag.

Right here on the grounds of San Zaccaria, Charlotte wonders if Isabella, and Sister Antonia, and the other girls too, felt this same bad feeling, this gross shame prickling up their backs. It reminds her that maybe she shouldn't get all romantic about things that happened in the past. She shouldn't make it into something it wasn't, just because it seems like a great story. You could forget that history was something that happened to real people.

Chapter Twenty-Five

Gaspara Stampa, poet.

Considered to be the greatest female poet of the Renaissance, most of the 311 poems she wrote were dedicated to Count Collaltino di Collalto, a man she loved but who left her. She poured out her sorrow in her work, using her pain to inspire her, and this eventually led to her survival and triumph. Her cause of death at age thirty-one in Venice is listed as "a sickness of the sea."

(1523–1554)

"Shaye, you coming?"

"I, just—" Shaye lifts a finger, then keeps typing. She's been working on a story of her own, separate from their assignments, one that's getting longer and longer. Charlotte sees the title, *Don't Be Going*, when Shaye has her laptop open. Every now and then, Charlotte sneaks a look when Shaye gets up to go to the bathroom or to talk on the phone. It seems really personal. *The way you laid on me was like a memory.* Stuff like that. A couple of times, when Shaye's been away, she says she's been out at the tower, writing. The tower! God, Charlotte can't understand how she'd want to go out to that place alone. Shaye doesn't talk about the story much, but she bragged that she showed Luca, and how he kept going on and on about it. And, sometimes . . . sometimes she slams her laptop shut when Charlotte comes near. It's not the story she's hiding, though. Charlotte saw emails. Emails she was reading, emails she was writing. To who? Someone at home, someone she met here? No idea.

"You don't want to miss out!"

"One sec, *Jesus*."

"Okay! Do what you want! See you down there, then."

Charlotte's been excited for this night since they arrived. They all have. Whenever Dante's talked about it too, it's only made her want to experience it more. Even Maria described it as *magic*. Festa del Redentore. The Redeemer Festival—a celebration of the end of the plague in 1576, when the doge of the time promised God a church if he'd end the suffering. When the church was built on the island of Guidecca in the Venetian Lagoon, a new tradition started—a once-a-year pilgrimage across a temporary bridge from Venice to the church doors, the only time the two islands are connected. Now, it's a weekend event that's a huge party for the city. Dante said there'd be so many people, he doubted he'd even be able to find her tonight, when all the boats gathered to watch the fireworks, or even tomorrow, when everyone made the pilgrimage across the bridge. But he'd be out on the water too, with his friends, on Raffaele's boat.

Ever since that night at Cantina Do Mori a week and a half or so ago, Charlotte has felt a super-awareness between her and Luca. Sometimes when he says something really funny or meaningful, he looks at her for her reaction. And sometimes when he hands a plate across a table, she swears he brushes his hand across hers on purpose. She catalogs these things in her head, but they're so subtle, it's hard to tell if she's just making up some big story.

There was that time, though, where she was sure she wasn't making it up. The day after she wore the poncho at San Zaccaria, she went to the La Calamita library to work on an assignment, since it was so blisteringly hot out. He was there, writing at his desk with the view of the water.

She didn't want to bother him and turned to leave. But he said, *Hey, come over here*, and when she did, he handed her a page filled with his loopy script, and she got to read something no one else had ever seen. Think about *that*. She was the first. It was only a few paragraphs, a dreamlike scene on a stairwell. He actually had a grammar mistake or two in there, like anyone else would.

It was so amazing, and she couldn't help thinking how far she'd come from back at home, when she'd read his book in bed and imagined him at a fancy literary party or something. Now here she was, with the real him, a him she *knows*, and he was showing her his new work. Something that would go in a book and maybe win awards and who knows what else. It was hard to follow, actually, but she told him how magnificent it was, and he seemed pleased. He stood very close to her.

You like what you see? he said, lifting his eyebrow in a flirty double meaning. It was a joke but maybe not a joke. And instead of feeling that great energy . . . she felt uncomfortable. He was standing so close that when he grinned, she saw that he had something in his teeth. And this is hard to explain, but the way he looked right then—sort of awkwardly bent down toward her—she could see the dweeby guy he was when he was younger, the one who girls never looked twice at. He seemed . . . needy? Sad? She made a joke back to him and got out of there.

That night, Charlotte called Carly. She didn't call Yas, because Yas would be judgmental. Charlotte was kind of rude, because she didn't even ask about Carly's new job at Elliott Bay; she just launched in, like you do when a crisis is simmering. She told Carly she was confused about what was going on between her and Luca Bruni, but she wasn't really confused. Carly wasn't confused either. And she was way more judgmental than Charlotte thought she'd be. *Be careful,* Carly said. *I don't like this.*

It doesn't mean anything! He's only flirting. Shit! She never should have told anyone, not even Carly. She just needed someone to *talk* to. *You make it sound like he's doing something to me, like I'm a victim or something, when I'm not. I don't even mind it.*

He's old, and famous, and he's, like, your teacher, Carly said. *You're . . . you. From Roosevelt High, who wants to be a writer someday. It's wrong.*

God! Carly doesn't get it. Luca Bruni doesn't see her as Charlotte from Roosevelt High who wants to be a writer someday! He sees her as herself, someone he maybe desires, and it's kind of thrilling that he's attracted to her. Come on, Carly pretty much loved that inscription he wrote to her! Charlotte doesn't know what she even wanted from Carly, maybe just for her to say everything was okay. She decides to keep her mouth shut from here on out. And she'll be careful to keep *it*—the thing between her and Luca—where it is. She'll manage it, same as she used to manage Adam and his insecurities.

Right now, though—it's an exciting night. The uncomfortable moment in the library when he had stuff in his teeth has faded away, and when she sees Luca already down at the dock, handing stuff to Aldo in the big open skiff they're taking to the festival, she's just happy. Leo's trotting toward them from the villa, and Katerina appears with a sweater tied around her shoulders, and Luca is laughing and boisterous, wearing a stylish white hat with a blue brim. In the golden late-afternoon light, he looks like the magic famous writer, the romantic talent she wants him to be. He looks handsome and charismatic, with his long limbs and mop of hair and crooked nose, and she can't wait to get in that boat. If he shines his light on her tonight—good.

Aldo has attached several poles to the front and back of the boat, and now, before they leave, they string white lights back and forth between them and hang paper lanterns of all colors and shapes between the lights. Two tables are set up in the center of the boat, covered in white tablecloths. When they all finally get in and motor toward the Bacino di San Marco, the basin of water in front of Saint Mark's, Charlotte can see boats of all kinds and sizes streaming in too. Small motorboats, sailboats, and sleek wooden cruisers, decorated with garlands and flowers and flags and lights, all putter into place beside them. There are little white lights strung along the shore as well, and people are already gathering there. Instead of the usual few tables outside the restaurants, lots have been smashed close together. The water is sloshy and jubilant from so many boats, and there's waving and shouting from one to the next as neighbors and friends spot each other. And it's clear, you know, that this is a celebration that really belongs to the people of Venice, not to outsiders.

Aldo guides the boat, gesturing his hand forcefully to other captains to hurry them along. He jets in and out among them until he maneuvers right up to the newly set-up bridge, which links the island of Venice to the island of Guidecca and leads to the doorway of the Redentore church, with its beautiful white face and huge white dome and spires.

"For hundreds of years, it was a bridge of wooden barges, but now, pontoons," Bethany Sparrow says loudly over the sound of the motor. Gas fumes sputter upward, merging with the smell of the sea.

"Enough with the history. Let's find a spot and open the wine!" Luca says jovially.

Aldo veers the boat in an arc. He speeds away, heading to the spot where most of the boats are gathering and angling for the best view of the fireworks, tying up to one another in a huge flotilla. Aldo slows, and the motor putters as he glides up to a speedboat already in the middle of a lively party. Aldo throws a rope, and the man misses.

"Coglione!" Aldo says.

"Testicle," Hailey translates, and they all laugh as Aldo tries it again. The man ties them up, and soon enough, another boat is heading toward them to do the same.

"Vacci piano!" Aldo yells.

"Slow down," Hailey translates again, and they laugh again. Now the driver is throwing a rope to Aldo, amidst shouts of *Attento!* and *Fermare, fermare!*

"Wait, stop, stop," Eliot translates, and Hailey punches him. "Hey, only *I* get to do it!"

It's all chaos, but happy chaos. Luca is hunting around in the storage areas of the boat, and Shaye keeps switching seats for a better view, and Katerina and Charlotte are helping take the food out, unwrapping plate upon plate of meats and cheeses and breads and figs and tomatoes and olives and fried sardines and melon and, and, and. Luca sets glass candles on the tables and then lights them, because the sun is beginning to set. Eliot folds a slice of prosciutto into his mouth, and Ashley says, "Stop! Wait for everyone else." Luca is pouring drinks—a splash from one bottle and a splash from another, passing around the sparkling orange mix. Leo stands to reach for his glass and bumps Luca's hand, spilling orange on Luca's white shorts.

"Che due palle!" Luca spits.

"What two balls!" Hailey translates, but no one laughs. They all hold their breath, because she should have kept her mouth shut. Leo can never do anything right in Luca's eyes. He seems to hate the guy. *Hate.* If the rest of them accidentally do anything to embarrass or insult Luca, he'll get pissed, but if Leo's knee is going up and down when Luca's talking, or if he has an opinion, or, honestly, *blinks* wrong, Luca's on his case. Leo just takes it—makes his face very neutral, though Charlotte has sometimes seen his eye get a nervous tic. He's gotten quiet, hangs out around their edges, mostly with Katerina, who's also been more subdued lately, who knows why.

Now Luca blots the liquid with a napkin, but then he laughs, and so they all do too, in relief. Nothing will spoil this night. The hot day is cooling, and the sunset is the same shade of the orange drink in their glasses. Food gets passed around, and as they eat, there's jovial shouting and the lilt of Italian accents all around them, and then comes the sound of people playing mandolins. Luca tells the story of the time his cousin tried to teach him guitar, and Ashley tells a story about when her mother's *guzheng*, an enormous Chinese zither, got stuck in her Mini Cooper, and Eliot tells a story about bringing one of those huge party sandwiches from Subway home in his convertible, and how he had to ride with one leg over it, which leads to a bunch of suggestive jokes, plus more stories. That orange drink is strong, and Charlotte tries to sip, but it's delicious, too. Everything softens quickly, and she feels so happy and lucky as the boats rock and slosh. Luca opens some wine, and bottles seem to be emptying fast, and the entire city is a glittering party on the water, until it's finally ten o'clock.

Luca sits next to Charlotte. Their arms aren't quite touching, but it's as if they are. The space is so small, she can feel the heat from his skin. All night, he's caught her eyes and stared a moment too long, and she hasn't exactly minded. They're *all* here, and he's choosing her, and the night is just fun and high spirits. And it's not like she's been innocent, either, whatever that means. She's tugged on his sleeve, or touched his arm when he's said something funny. It's like—it's hard to explain. It's happening in a different universe than her life with Adam, or Owen Burke, boyfriends from, you know, *high school.* And it's a separate world from her relationship with Dante, too. Luca Bruni is so much older than she is, and he's experienced so much more, but that's part of what makes this flirty whatever so large and important, because his approval, his wanting her, is bigger than all the approval she's ever wanted from anyone, combined. Her dad, never home. Her mom, never happy. Any guy who never paid attention to her is now only a meaningless boy in comparison. Any girl who was ever cruel is small and unimportant, because when he looks at her like that, it's like a huge *See? Fuck you.*

The party has gotten louder all around them, but finally, the crowd lets out a collective gasp as the fireworks begin.

Charlotte has seen tons of fireworks, great ones, over Lake Union on the Fourth of July, but they were not *these*. This is sky art, set against the huge dome of that church. Explosions of red and green and pink, then all colors at once, and then a row of colored sprays, looking like fountains along the bank. And since it all reflects in the water, in that boat, they are *surrounded* by fireworks, shimmers and glimmers and glints, up and around and down, and Maria was absolutely right, because *magic* is the only word. Luca leans toward her.

"Your eyes are shining," he says in her ear.

No matter what happens after this, and a lot will happen after this, very bad and unforgettable things, it's a moment she won't forget. Stories are always more than one thing, and so are the people in them. There was the plague, and then there was a bridge between two islands. Suffering, and fireworks.

Chapter Twenty-Six

Semidea Poggi, poet.

From an aristocratic family, as a young nun, she was involved in several scandals. She was so good at charming men into visiting the convent that she was accused of using "love magic." Equally shocking, she not only sang but also played the trumpet and the trombone. Later, she wrote nonreligious poetry. Her convent appears to have been complicit in helping to get both her and her work outside its walls.

(1551 or so–1637)

When the last shimmers of sparks blow out, leaving a dark sky, they gather the dishes and crumple up the napkins and throw away the plastic cups. All the boats untie and drive away in different directions, their bow lights exploding outward in another kind of firework.

"Go to Lido," Luca Bruno tells Aldo, who groans.

"It's late," Aldo says. "Too late."

"They have to see it."

"I'm too old for that," Bethany Sparrow says, even though she's not much older than they are.

"Lido," Luca commands.

Lido is a nearby beach, where the party continues. Luca hands a few blankets to Leo, and Luca himself has wine bottles tucked under his arms. Aldo drops anchor near shore, and they all plop overboard into the shallow water and run to the sandbar, which is quickly covering with people.

"I have to pee so bad!" Shaye says.

"Same," Charlotte says.

"We'll be here!" Luca sets the bottles onto the blankets on the sand.

Bethany Sparrow comes with them, leading the way, though they couldn't miss the long line into the cement structure of the restroom. Shaye has her arms folded as they wait. Is she mad? She seems mad. She's barely speaking to Charlotte. On the way back, Shaye walks ahead. Charlotte tries to catch up. "Hey, what's wrong?" she asks.

"You're such a child," Shaye snaps.

"What?" Charlotte snaps back.

"Do you think he really *likes* you?"

"God, Shaye, what is your *problem*?" Really, it's so irritating, the way Shaye always acts like the ultimate authority on Luca, like she's the only one who really *knows* him, who's honest enough to confront him, the only one who cares about the *actual* him, good and bad. Like she's put a fence of ownership around him, even if she sometimes thinks he's an asshole. But maybe they've just reached that point when too much drinking goes from fun to fighting. Yasmin's boyfriend, Nate, would get like that if they went to a party, though he was the only one who drank a lot when they went anywhere. Ashley and Hailey and Leo are still having a great time, though, and they get up to join some other people from one of the boats that they were tied to in the flotilla.

"If you're not back here in a half hour, you have to find your own way home," Luca calls, and they wave to him over their shoulders. "Old man Aldo has to go to bed."

"You mean *you* do," Shaye says, and Luca scowls at her. "What?"

And then Eliot starts nagging Katerina again about where she and Luca went last week. It's become an exasperating game. She refuses to tell them anything. "Is it a public building?" Eliot asks, though they've tried all this before.

Katerina shakes her head in irritation.

"A museum, a villa, another city?" He cracks all his knuckles one by one, an annoying habit of his.

"Eliot, *stop*." It's hard to know if Katerina means the questions or the knuckle-popping.

"Our secret, huh, Kat?" Luca says. On the blanket, he tips his toes to hers, but she only shrugs, and Leo looks off toward the water.

"Time to go yet?" Shaye says.

It's definitely getting to that point where the fun is turning to something else. Or maybe Shaye's mood is just ruining everything. Luca blows a whistle with two fingers and motions to Ashley and Hailey and Leo, who wave, indicating that they should go on without them. During the boat ride back, everyone's quiet. The moon is out, and the water looks spooky, and when they reach La Calamita, the villa looms up in the darkness.

Shaye gets out, stalks up to the villa. No thank-you, no anything. Charlotte thinks Shaye's acting ungrateful. Eliot and Katerina and Bethany Sparrow straggle up, hauling drooping blankets and bags of garbage. Charlotte's carrying a sweatshirt that Hailey left behind, and Ashley's jacket. This incredible night—Charlotte hopes it doesn't end like this.

It doesn't.

Inside the villa now, next to the huge mural of the glass ship, Luca takes a pinch of her top to slow her. "Hey."

"Hey," she says.

"You know, if you ever want to send me something you've written, feel free," he says. "Let me give you my private email. Give me yours, too."

The next morning, only Katerina and Charlotte and Eliot head out to the second day of the festival. Ashley and Hailey and Leo aren't back home yet, and Luca and Shaye and Bethany are sleeping in. Aldo's son, Marc, is there to drive them, in one of the usual boats.

Before they even dock, it's a magnificent sight. From the boat, they can see it, the bridge, full of people. Everyone who isn't too exhausted from the night before—which means quite a few families with children and old ladies and old men—

walk along the pontoons to the church, and now Charlotte and Kat and Eliot join them. They flow into this river of individuals all making the same pilgrimage. The three of them can't even squeeze into the church for mass, so they stand outside and listen.

"I don't understand a word they're saying," Eliot says.

"Me neither," Charlotte says.

"They're just praying for their relatives who were too hungover to show up," Katerina says.

But as Charlotte listens, packed in with this crowd of people who are all experiencing the same moment, this acknowledgment of suffering that happened nearly five hundred years ago feels strange and moving. When it's over, the crowd flows like a river out again and then disperses. Charlotte, Katerina, and Eliot head toward the water to watch the gondola regatta. The gondoliers, in their white pants and black-and-white shirts, dig hard with their oars as they race, the pink and red and yellow and blue boats sluicing through the water as the onlookers cheer.

For a few minutes, Charlotte even forgets about Luca last night—those long looks, but even more, the exchange of email addresses. Of course, she remembers witnessing that same moment with Avni and Katerina. But *when* she remembers—well, right then, his flirting feels forgivable, understandable. The chanting and rituals and songs she heard this morning have urged forgiveness, softened her heart for it. And now a new group of gondoliers fly past them, and an old man is hopping up and down and yelling, and the water twinkles, and the sun is warm, and it's all so wonderful, and her heart feels *so full* that she wants more, more, more. She feels a deep, intense longing for everything she's ever experienced in the past, and everything she has yet to experience. Maybe Luca just has that hunger too, for all of life, for every experience, the way she feels right this minute. There's so much to desire and want in life, it's hard not to want it all.

"Charlotta!"

No way!

No way! Really? She can't believe it! It's Dante, with Raffaele and Gaia. He's shoving past people to get to her, and when he does, he practically lifts her off her feet.

"Did you see it? Did you see it all?" he asks.

"You were right. Your mom was right. It was *magic*," she says, kissing him.

"I can't believe I found you," he says.

She is so, so happy to see him. It's so normal. He is, they are. It's such a relief.

Chapter Twenty-Seven

Vittoria Colonna, poet, writer.

From a powerful family, she became one of the most successful female poets of her time, but today she's mostly known for her friendships with famous male poets and artists, including Michelangelo. Engaged at age three, married at seventeen, widowed at thirty, she was only eighteen when her poetry first became known. There's evidence that her own work was among the prohibited and unsanctioned books that convent nuns secretly bought with their own money and kept hidden with their private possessions.

(1492–1547)

They have today free after the busy weekend, and Charlotte wants to sleep in. Her alarm is off, and so at first, she's confused at the *buzz, buzz, buzz* of her phone. She tries to hit snooze.

But it's not the alarm. Her phone's ringing. Vibrating on silent. When she rouses, she sees that Shaye is gone. Her bed is rumpled, but then again, her bed is always empty and rumpled lately, as if she couldn't sleep and went elsewhere.

There's the single buzz of a message now. It's a man, speaking Italian, and it's hard to understand at first. She has to play it twice before she even realizes who it is.

Dr. Paolo Berti. Oh my God, it's Dr. Berti, and he's found something. She has to play the message again and again for the exact words. Her heart is beating fast. *I have* Fa Rima dalla Casa di Dio *by Isabella di Matteo di Nicolo Zorzi Angelo. I am here until four o'clock.*

She calls Dante. She's so excited, it's hard to even tap his name in her phone. "Dante?"

"Are you all right, Charlotta?"

"Dr. Berti called."

"What, what?"

"He found a second book. At least, I think so. It was hard to tell. The name sounded different. He's there until four."

"Come! Come now! I will meet you."

She showers in two seconds. Throws on some clothes. Outside on the patio, Eliot is the only one up. He's wearing a bathrobe, and he's drinking coffee. "God. Where are you going so early? No one's even awake."

"The library. You won't believe it."

"No. No *way*," he says. They all know the story; they all know Charlotte has been looking for more about Isabella. They all know everything about each other's stories, at least they think they do. "Don't even say it. You fucking found the poet."

• • •

Dr. Berti instructs Charlotte and Dante to wash their hands in a sink down the hall from his office in the collections room. Charlotte can tell that he's excited too. His movements are quick, and he keeps adjusting his stylish glasses impatiently. Finally, when Charlotte and Dante are done, he sets the book on a soft velvet cloth, which lies on a pad. The gentle handling makes Charlotte think of the way she wrapped *The Verses* in a nightgown and stuffed it in her bag, and how it's still underneath her mattress. But the book in front of her, a second one by Isabella—it gives her chills. This is not some abstract concept. Isabella was here. She was as real and as human as Charlotte is right now. She was a heart-beating, blood-whooshing individual.

This book is a little larger than *The Verses*, but it has that same yellowed leather cover, with only the title on the front. *Vellum*, Dr. Berti tells her, when she remarks on this. *The skin of a calf.* Yikes.

"What does the title say?" she asks.

"Fa Rima dalla Casa di Dio." Dr. Berti smiles smugly down at the book.

"Rhymes from the House of God," Dante translates. "You've always said she was in a convent, Charlotta."

Charlotte is awestruck. Her face flushes. "I can't believe this." It's almost hard to breathe. She wishes her mom and her aunt and her grandmother and her grandmother's grandmother could see this.

"All right?" Dr. Berti says, as if preparing them for a secret.

And then he opens it, at the slightest angle, and when he does, she also recognizes the same insignia that's on the first page of *The Verses*: two lions holding a ribbon, which loops through the branches of a tree.

"My book has that too," she says. "The lions."

"This is the printer's mark, you see?" Dr. Berti explains. "The publisher, *F. de Giunta*. Both the same, then. And the date, 1575, two years after your book."

But now she also sees the name, extending across the paper.

Isabella di Matteo di Nicolo Zorzi Angelo.

It's wrong. It isn't hers. Sure, there's an "Isabella," and sure, there's an "Angelo," but that's it. She doesn't even want to say it. She feels that crack of sadness that comes before full-on disappointment.

"Di Nicolo Zorzi Angelo?" Dante's voice is an awed whisper. He doesn't seem disappointed, not at all. His eyes are wide.

"It's maybe not the same person," Charlotte says. "*The Verses* only says 'Isabella di Angelo.'"

"*Di Nicolo Zorzi Angelo*, could this be?" Dante asks Dr. Berti. "A granddaughter?"

Dr. Berti shrugs. But he also leans back on his heels with such clear pleasure that Charlotte has no idea what's going on.

"What, what?" she pleads. "I don't understand."

"Nicolo Zorzi Angelo—" Dante's eyes are *glittering*. "Charlotta, he was *a doge*. A doge, Charlotta! Believe me, I know. We memorize them for history. Your Isabella was the granddaughter of *Nicolo Zorzi Angelo*. Let me look." He is already searching on his phone. "From 1568 until his death in 1577."

"How did we not know before? How come she never showed up anywhere?"

"All we had was the name 'Isabella di Angelo,'" Dante says. "The names were different then, yes? And they varied—daughters used the father's surname sometimes, or more often, his *first* name. 'Isabella di Angelo' means she is Isabella, daughter of Angelo, maybe first name, maybe last. To find anything . . . There are *hundreds* of possibilities! Hundreds of Angelos! But, *Di Matteo di Nicolo Zorzi Angelo*—this means *daughter of* Matteo, who is *the son of* Nicolo Zorzi Angelo. And there is only *one* of *him*. You see?"

"I think I see," Charlotte says. Her head spins.

"When I go to look for a *poet* called Isabella di Angelo in this collection, *my* collection," Dr. Berti says, "there is only *one* book." He taps the cover gently.

"But why wouldn't she use the same name on both?" Charlotte asks. It still seems impossible.

"The first book—perhaps she did not want to be very clear about who she was," Dr. Berti says. "But the second book? She wants everyone to *know* she was the granddaughter of a doge."

Dr. Berti wraps the book in the velvet cloth again and tucks it away on a shelf under the counter. "I've already made certain," he says. He ushers them to his computer where he *tip, tip, tips*. "Dogaressas of Venice. Wives of doges. The wife of Nicolo Zorzi Angelo, the doge, is Maria Cappello. And there's just one son. One, yes. Matteo." Dr. Berti adjusts the shoulders of his beautiful jacket, as if all of this is his doing. "I don't see any other children. Of the doge, or Matteo. So she is likely the only grandchild. But we will check the *Libro d'Oro*."

Charlotte shakes her head. She has no idea what that is.

"The *Libro d'Oro*, the gold book," Dr. Berti explains. "The names of all the *nobile*. The *Libro d'Argento* is the silver list. Ordinary citizens. There was also a catalog of *meretrice*."

"*Meretrice*—prostitutes," Dante says.

"Could you tell what the poems were about?" Charlotte wishes he'd bring the book back. He took it away so fast, she wonders if they'll ever see it again.

"Ah, a beautiful poem about Venice. 'Built upon the waters so the sea returns, thus sending its furious waves to purge the noble city . . .'" He strokes his chin, as if he's remembering someone he once loved.

"We can borrow the book, *sì*?" Dante asks.

"No, no, no," Dr. Berti says.

"So that we can learn what else is inside?"

"No, no, no. Impossible. Impossible."

"Even briefly? Dottoressa Ricci is interested. She will want to see. This is her area of study, you know. Her book, about Veronica Franco—"

"Impossible. *Col cavolo che lo faccio*." Charlotte's lost. She was sure *cavolo* meant cabbage.

Dr. Berti and Dante switch from English to Italian. The words are like beautiful galloping horses, speeding so quickly past that they become a single blur. She hears *Antonio Tasso,* though, and *Nicolo Zorzi Angelo.* She hears *Ricci.* There is more head shaking. The rare book will not leave this room.

"He got possessive pretty quickly," Charlotte says to Dante as they leave Sixteenth Century Collections.

"Ugh! *Stronzo!* He said he will look through the *Libro d'Oro* for her name, but the document is handwritten, and this will take time. He is not even interested if she was the true author of the Tasso poem. He sees no way of finding proof. *Girare a vuoto,* he says." Dante whirls his finger in a circle. "He's sure it will go nowhere. *She* took it from him, likely. That's what Berti says."

"I feel like that book just disappeared forever."

"Don't worry, Charlotta. We will find a way. Dottoressa Ricci returned home yesterday, for the festival. It is all *capitare a puntino*! Happening at the little dot!"

"Happening at the little dot?"

"What do you say? All happening together. In a right place at a right time. Yes? I can *feel* it."

Chapter Twenty-Eight

Dianora Sanseverino, poet and writer, noblewoman.

Though she was the granddaughter of both a prince and a pope, very little of her work survives.

(1524–1581)

Down the hall from Conservation and Restoration, Charlotte and Dante kiss goodbye. He has to work. It's a long kiss, but not long enough.

Charlotte sits on a stone bench outside the Biblioteca Marciana. She tries to look stuff up on her phone with the new details she has. She still can't find Isabella, even with her longer name. Before, there was only information about Tasso, and now she can only find Nicolo Zorzi Angelo, though not much about him, either. She sees his portrait. He has a beard like a hipster and grandpa eyebrows and a comical gnome hat. She sees a paragraph about him becoming a doge—who elected him, what the votes were. That's it. His name appears in a few other places, but the sites are all in Italian.

It's a beautiful day outside. She stretches her shoulders after being curved around her phone, tilts her chin to the sky. In her hand, her phone vibrates. She has a new email. And no one her own age sends those, right? No one, and so her stomach drops with some gross combo of alarm and marvel, because it's him, she just knows it. She barely *ever* gets email. And she's right. Oh, God, there's his name, in bold, unread black. She's almost afraid to do it, but she clicks.

Hey, whatcha doing?

That's it.

That's all. But it feels strangely personal, like a text Adam or Dante might send her, not a grown man–famous author like Luca Bruni. Mostly, it feels like something no one should know about. A secret. Charlotte looks at those words forever. She types, deletes, types, deletes again.

Not much, you?

She presses send, in that fast, eye-squinched way so you don't change your mind. Ugh! What a stupid reply. She's such an idiot! But once it's done, it's like she's stepped off a ledge. Off that scary tower, maybe, only she's the patient. The doctor, the one who did the experiments—he's still up there, watching her fall.

When she looks up again from the drama and misery of her phone, she's staring straight at the Doge's Palace. It's directly in front of Biblioteca Marciana. Like, a few steps away. Katerina fell into the water under one of its archways. It didn't even occur to her—he *lived* there. Right there. And something else suddenly occurs to her too—that she's related to *him*, as well, the doge, not just to Isabella. She's awestruck.

It's incredible. The Doge's Palace is an enormous, lacy white building, one of the main landmarks in Venice, full of masters' paintings and elaborate rooms, and some guy with her DNA lived here once. It's hard to believe. History always feels so unrelated to your own life.

It's five thirty in the morning at home, but she can't wait to tell them. This news is huge, and it belongs to her and her mom and her sister and her aunt Tony, and all the women of their family who kept the question of Isabella and that poem alive. She FaceTimes Adele, who picks right up. Adele's expression is all panicky because of the early hour, and she's wearing her favorite summer nightgown, white with blue flowers, the one that she's had for so long, they don't even see it anymore.

"Char! Is everything okay?"

"It's fine, everything is fine."

"For God's sake, where have you been? You practically disappeared. Why don't you ever call me back?"

Why? Because after that call with Dante, Charlotte's mom has sent a jillion texts, wanting to know everything. As if it's her *right* to know everything, and those messages just press at Charlotte's walls. But also . . . since Luca Bruni has been so . . . whatever, Charlotte's been afraid her mom will hear what's going on in her voice. Her mom has a way of doing that, knowing when something's off, same as a shark zeroes in on the smallest drop of blood. "I've texted you back! I've been busy."

"Ella, come here! Wake up!" Adele yells. "It's Charlotte!" In a moment, her sister's sleepy face is there too.

"Why are you calling so early? Are you in lo-oove?" Ella teases.

"You guys! Stop about Dante, okay? This is not about him! I've got to show you something. It's important. See this huge white building?"

"Wow," Ella says.

"It's gorgeous!" Adele says. "I still can't believe you're actually in Italy."

"That's the Doge's Palace."

Ella snorts. "Is that 'dog' in Italian?"

"Doges were the main leaders of the city, and they were, like, chosen from the ruling families." Charlotte doesn't have all the facts herself, honestly. "And are you ready for this? Isabella di Angelo—"

"Oh my God! Oh my God!" Adele squeals.

"Her grandfather was a *doge*."

"You're kidding. No way. *No way*."

"Well, we think so. We're pretty sure. We found the second book. *Fa Rima dalla Casa di Dio. Rhymes from the House of God.* We knew she was in a convent, right? And we knew noble, but not *that* noble."

"We?" Her mother's eyebrows fold down.

"I *told* you already, Dante's helping me. And a librarian, too.

Don't worry about it! The point is, he, the doge, probably lived *there*." She swings her phone around so they can see.

"That's incredible. That's just incredible. I can't believe this. Look at that place," Adele says.

"Mom! Move your head," Ella says.

"And *she* probably lived . . . Well, walk with me."

"You're not at the villa. Are you on Wi-Fi?" her mom asks. "I mean, roaming charges . . ."

"I know, I know. It's worth it, I promise. It'll take me, like, two minutes to get there."

She walks along the Grand Canal, holding her phone out, as Ella shouts out stuff like, *Haha! Those guys in the striped shirts look like mimes!* and as her mother asks questions, and oohs and ahhs. When she hits Campo San Zaccaria, she turns left.

"What is *that*?" Ella asks.

"A church. An amazing old church," her mother says.

"Yeah, a church, but look on each side." Charlotte slowly veers her phone to her left and then to her right. "Do you recognize it?"

"The church looks cooler," Ella says.

"Is that the convent you sent pictures of? *The one?*" Adele's voice is hushed.

"Pretty sure. The noble parents sent their daughters here."

"Wait, what?" Ella butts in.

"The men, like, you know, the fathers—they sent their daughters to the convents, pretty much so they wouldn't have sex and stuff. Or so they didn't have to pay for them to get married."

"OH MY GOD," Ella screeches. "That's NO FAIR. So, what, *they* lived in that PALACE, and she had to live HERE? For how long?"

"Well, sometimes from when they were maybe nine—"

"NINE?!" Ella shouts. Ella's twelve. "Until *when*?"

"Until . . . always."

Ella's face goes still. "That's awful. That's so sad."

She's right. She is so, so right. It's unbearably sad, and none of them speak for a moment. Charlotte's sundress looks too playful. Her fun tour for her mother and sister seems wrongly cheery. Suddenly, she wants to cry. Her chest hurts. It's heart-ache. And when she looks at that old convent, and when she sees her sister's face in the tiny square on her screen, she feels a swell of emotion, and her eyes fill with tears.

"Charlotte? Charlotte?" her mother asks.

"I'm okay." Her voice breaks. "I'm all right."

At their usual spot near Saint Mark's, Charlotte waits for Aldo. The boat is there, but he isn't. She watches all the commotion along the waterfront, fishing boats coming in, a couple having a fight. When her phone rings, she's so happy to see Dante's name.

"Charlotta!" Oh, man, she's in trouble. How's she going to leave him? How, how, how? "When can you come in? Dottoressa Ricci wants to meet you as soon as you can. Not tomorrow, because her child has gotten a *colpo d'aria*. Maybe on the airplane."

"Stomach problems?" She hears *d'aria* as *diarrhea*. "I didn't know your professor had a child. I don't know why, but that surprises me."

"*Colpo d'aria*, a hit of air! You know, like in your eye or your ear or your head!" She doesn't know. She has no idea what he means. "And, yes, a daughter, she is three. But let me tell you! Dottoressa Ricci doesn't like the way Berti acts like the big man! You don't make her mad, I warn you! In one hour, she looked through the *Libro d'Oro* and found her right away. The doge's son, Matteo, has a wife, Barbara di Donatello, and a child. A daughter, Isabella di Matteo di Nicolo Zorzi Angelo. One hour, like that! And then she headed right to Berti, tells him she needs the book for research. He handed it right over, like a bank robbery! She'll tell us more when we meet."

"Can we do it Thursday? Luca has some kind of copyediting deadline, so we've got the day free."

"Thursday! *Non vedo l'ora*."

"I can't wait either," she says.

"*Baciami*," he says, and makes a loud smooch into the phone. He thinks this is super funny.

"I won't do it, you dork," she says, and he cracks up.

Oh, God. What if she loves him?

Still no Aldo. She scans the crowd. Her eyes land on the library again, and the Doge's Palace straight across. She realizes something strange. The Alta Acqua Libreria, Dante's mother's bookstore, where she began her search, is, what, maybe half a mile to the Biblioteca Marciana? Which is only a few steps to the Doge's Palace. Which is less than another quarter of a mile or so to San Zaccaria, which is only the shortest distance back to Alta Acqua Libreria. Plotted on a map, they would make a tiny triangle in the city of Venice, and an even tinier triangle in the country, and a speck of a triangle in the world, and a nearly invisible pinprick of a triangle in the universe. And yet all of the answers she's been seeking, all of the places she's been tromping to in order to find those answers, every monumental piece of this particular puzzle, have been in this small, small area.

Capitare a puntino! Very literally. Happening at the little dot.

Chapter Twenty-Nine

Chiara Matraini, poet, writer.

Married at fifteen, widowed at twenty-seven, she began a scandalous affair with a married poet, Bartolomeo Graziani. They lived together openly and entertained intellectuals and writers at their home, until Graziani was murdered. Likely, Chiara's own family killed him, out of revenge for her sullied honor.

(1515–1604)

"And this candy-cane house, this Disneyland architectural baby of a Dutch Willy Wonka on mushrooms, and a haunted fun-house clown—"

They laugh.

It's a great description. A Luca Bruni description. But Ca' Zappa, the white-and-red gabled villa in front of them, sitting alone on its own island, is actually very beautiful, Charlotte thinks. It's hard to take it in, though, honestly, when her stomach is sick with upset and worry. She's been on edge all day. They've already visited three islands—La Certosa, San Francesco del Deserto, San Michele (the cemetery of

Venice)—and now they're all sitting on the brick wall in front of the isolated, fairy-tale-like Ca' Zappa. But Charlotte's mind is preoccupied, and she feels a strange separation from everyone else. It's been two days since she pressed send on her email back to Luca: *Not much, you?* and he hasn't written back. She keeps checking her email, but nothing. Silence. He's been avoiding her too—not meeting her eyes or trying to make her laugh. She fucked up. She feels embarrassed. He'd chosen her, and clearly, she wasn't worth it, or up to the job of being chosen. And the weirdest thing is? She felt uncomfortable and anxious when she got that email. She kind of wished he never sent it. But, man, now she wants another one so bad.

"In terms of mood—what a stark difference from La Certosa, with its pretty little marina full of yachts, or San Francesco del Deserto, with the monastery and cloisters, or San Michele," Luca says, crossing his long legs at the ankles.

"For the next few days, you'll write about one of the islands we've visited today, focusing on mood," Bethany Sparrow says. "We'll share at the end of the week."

"Don't forget, we also began today on Venice itself," Luca says. "Do you know what Petrarch called Venice? The *mundus alter*—another world."

Now Luca takes a few of his own pages from his bag. He begins to read. And that voice, that commanding voice, keeps all of them riveted in place, hardly breathing. No one shifts or moves. All eyes are on him, and only him. It's another piece from the book he's writing. His character Ricco is talking about Venice in the 1500s, at the height of its rule—how everyone saw it as a shimmering palace that seemed to float on the water, a magic act, a brilliant impossibility. How, when invaders came, trying to attack it, it was protected in that lagoon. Ships couldn't reach the shores in that shallow water, and the lagoon would fill with fog, smoke and mirrors, so thick that the armies would get confused. And if those soldiers somehow managed to get on land, the twisting streets, the trick dead ends, would make them lose their way. "'That floating, fantastical, unreal place was so powerful, it was *untouchable*,'" Luca reads, and then sets the pages down.

"Wow," Hailey says after a moment. She claps a hand to her heart. Charlotte feels that way too. God, she's messed up. She's messed up *so bad*.

"Ughhhh," Ashley says. "I hate trying to write anything after you read."

"Shit—it's beautiful, but it's so *sad*," Eliot says. "That Ricco feels that way about himself . . . I mean, it's awesome, but *lonely*."

"Mood is metaphor, mood is symbol, mood is backstory and pacing. Mood is . . . *manipulation of emotion*." Luca winks. His words are playful, but Eliot was right—the piece was beautiful, but sad.

"Mood is also the truth of a place at a given moment," Katerina says.

"Whatever that even means," Luca says.

Katerina's eyes shift ever so slightly. It's an expression

Charlotte's never seen her have before. Her face looks flat and hard, like a wall has gone up and will never come down again. Charlotte hopes she stays quiet and takes it. She often hopes this about her dad, when her mom is being nasty. But she also sometimes hopes he'll finally stand up to her too. With Luca, though—standing up just seems like a bad idea. They know he's easily tipped over into anger, or even fury. With his power, if he got *really* mad, what could he do? Way more than her mom could.

"Hey, are you ever going to announce the one-on-one this week?" Ashley crosses her fingers.

"Me me me," Hailey says, her hands together in pretend prayer.

Katerina whispers to Charlotte. "It's going to be you."

Charlotte scowls as an answer. She doubts it now.

"You're right. I haven't said." Luca wiggles his eyebrows up and down like he's about to reveal the surprise. Ashley leans forward. Leo sits very still. Shaye picks the edges of her fingernail.

"Charlotte, Charlotte," he says.

"Oh, wow," she says. Her chest fills—with anxiety and relief. Maybe she hadn't ruined everything.

"Friday?"

"Okay. Friday."

"Told you," Kat says under her breath.

"You know what?" Shaye says. Her face is flushed. She seems pissed, but what else is new? Charlotte waits for whatever is coming next, but nothing does. Shaye just shakes her head and looks off into the distance.

They stay on Ca' Zappa to begin the assignment, but Luca and Bethany talk over by the villa, a low, intense conversation involving lots of hand gestures on Bethany's part. When they're back at La Calamita, the sun is already beginning to dip. As they step off the boat onto land, and as Ashley and Hailey run off to get their swimsuits for a late-afternoon cooling off, Kat grabs Charlotte's arm as she heads in.

"Be careful," Kat says.

"What?"

"On Friday. Be careful."

Chapter Thirty

Giustina Niccolini, writer.

Placed in a convent in Florence at age eighteen, her chronicle of convent life was one of few that survive, though it was unpublished until 2011. In her pages, she mentions historical volumes that have gone missing, including "the first book of the chronicles," which she says was written on parchment but ruined by the waters of the flood. She writes how her own "obedience" was severely tested, and the personal aspects of her history are mainly concerned with how she managed to keep her virginity intact, in spite of many assaults on it.

(1558–1623)

Thursday. Mood: nervous. Is nervous a mood? Unsettled. Uneasy. For a few days, Charlotte's had a shadowy migraine, not the full-on pound, but the press and pressure that feel like her head is its own weather system, and a storm is coming. She and Dante are meeting with Dr. Ricci this afternoon, but what's even more stressful is her meeting with Luca Bruni is tomorrow.

She rides into Venice with Eliot and Leo in the early

morning, though, because it's too claustrophobic on La Calamita. On that boat, the bad feeling follows her. Eliot and Leo have discovered they're both fanatics about medieval warfare, of all things, and are blabbing on about it, but Aldo is quiet. He's not playing music. He just stares ahead as he drives, his face stony and preoccupied.

She's excited to see Dante and Dr. Ricci, but mostly, her head is filled with Luca, and more Luca. So much Luca that what seemed exciting and wonderful has tipped into an almost-sickening too-muchness. After he announced her day with him, she got an email. *Can't wait to see you alone.* The *alone* was anxious, thrilling, frightening, confusing. It also maybe meant nothing. She tried out fourteen thousand different replies and settled on *Me too.*

And then another email this morning: *Maybe we should go somewhere with a pool. You can bring your red bathing suit.*

Oh my God was her first gut reaction. This email meant he noticed her. Her body. In that red bathing suit she got when she went shopping at Target with her mom and Ella last year. It was on the clearance rack. Ella was so happy that day because Adele did something splurgy and fun and bought gummy worms. This memory makes her so homesick, she can barely stand it. She wants to be in her own room, with her own pillow and her own stuff, and she misses her family so bad that she even feels heartsick with longing for Marvin, lying on her bed and farting. She just wishes that she and

Ella were at Green Lake, playing The Next Dog That Passes Is Yours. The thought of it makes her want to cry.

Then again, maybe his message didn't mean that at all. For someone who works with words, his could be taken lots of different ways—innocent, not, somewhere in between. No matter how many times she tries, she still can't see them clearly. *Sounds great. Can't wait,* she answered.

Ugh! Should she have used an exclamation point? Did a period seem like too little? What should she give him? *A lot,* she guessed. He seemed to need a lot, and deserve a lot, and be used to a lot. And that was her place, to be the one who gave, since even the time and attention of someone like him meant she owed him something.

Honestly, she had no way of knowing what to do. Being with Adam or even Dante wasn't enough experience to prepare her. Owen Burke wasn't. Jake Kerchek, from middle school, sure wasn't.

And then, right before Charlotte steps off the boat, his name appears in her inbox again.

It might get hot.

The streets of the city have just been cleaned and are still wet. Everywhere she looks, Charlotte sees those caution signs, an image of a block figure falling backward. She grabs an espresso at Caffé Florian and tries to work on their last assignment. Writing tip number one: strong coffee. Of course, she chooses

San Francesco del Deserto for her island, since it still houses a convent. Double points: she fits the courtyard from there into her haunting story, too. Luca will like that. The mood of that courtyard . . . Well, she tries to put herself in Isabella's place. A woman with a heart and desires and dreams, set inside walls. The mood is . . . longing, loneliness, frustrated need, though maybe those are all the same thing.

Her head hurts, bad. The unanswered *It might get hot* feels like a ticking clock. What should she say to that? Still, though, when she puts the words on the page, she hopes Luca sees them. Same as they all do, same as they look at him first after they read, every time. Her writing still matters so much to her. And he's still the open door, an opportunity. He's put out his hand and made an offer. Anyone would die to be in her place right now.

Charlotte has caught a few glimpses of her before, but now Dr. Ricci is standing right next to her, with Dante on her other side. Dr. Ricci is younger than she seemed from a distance, with her hair pinned up in a serious way, matching her serious skirts and serious sheath dresses. Up close, Charlotte notices her manicured hands, and her height—she's much taller than Charlotte. The only jewelry she wears is a clip in her hair, a green, jeweled bird, and even that has an air of confidence and authority. Her dark eyes drill into Charlotte's as the three of them stand over Isabella's book on the desk in her office.

"Look what you have found, hmm?" She raises one eyebrow,

as if they're both in on a magnificent secret. "A doge's granddaughter, a poet we know nothing about. Lost to history! It's remarkable, yes?"

"Very," Charlotte says, and Dante catches her eye and smiles. He's so pleased, finally getting them together like this.

"*This* city, Venezia, was the center of women's writing at the time. But we are only finding their work now, because we *look*. And these poems . . ." She taps the desk with the edge of her nail. "Even more remarkable."

"Really?" Whew! Relief. Her nagging worry was that she was wasting everyone's time.

"Yes, yes, *yes*! It's a beautiful discovery. *Beautiful*. In this book, she is very outspoken. She is challenging the images of the women in Petrarch's and Tasso's poems. Their work told the world what a female should be. The *ideal* woman. The one who should be desired—she was silent, and unattainable, chaste, and modest. Sober and obedient, too. The six traits."

"Dottoressa wrote about this in her book, as it pertained to Veronica Franco—"

Dr. Ricci interrupts Dante. "Your Isabella is directly confronting the traits, as Veronica Franco did. And they were writing at the same time. Franco's *Capitoli in Terze Rime* was 1575. You can imagine my excitement."

"I'm so sorry. I've never heard of her."

"Few have, but we've all heard of Petrarch, haven't we?" She nods in sarcasm. "Veronica Franco was a courtesan. *Revered* by the public. For her creativity, her talent, for championing the causes of women, for trying to say that intelligence, not chastity, was the real female virtue."

"I had no idea women back then were talking about that stuff." It seems unbelievable. Who knew? She thought feminism was a recent thing.

"More than one did, and now you have brought me another."

"That must have been really brave of them, to write like that. I can't imagine."

"It wasn't an uncommon subject for females to write about, or talk about. But, yes, it was dangerous. At the point Veronica Franco became most successful . . ." Dr. Ricci exhales dramatically. "She was accused of magic. Her talent—magic. Her beautiful words—*magic*. She was brought to trial. At the Venetian Inquisition."

"Oh my God."

"Think of it—on trial for being a brilliant woman! Her sentence was suspended, but she never recovered. She lost everything—money, reputation. Gone! You know how it happened? Male poets. They brought charges against her. She was too successful. They said her sins brought on the plague."

"That's so awful."

"Now, think of *this*—your Isabella was the granddaughter of a *doge*. To speak out . . . These poems—" She taps the desktop again. "I am very interested in these. She is strong. She is *angry*. She challenges—no, *condemns*—the behavior of men who exile women to the convents, engage in sexual acts with them there, and then imprison them for their obscenity."

A shiver rises up Charlotte's neck. Dr. Ricci holds Charlotte's eyes with her intense ones, and Charlotte can feel Isabella, her courage, filling the space between them. Finally, Dr. Ricci speaks. "This bravery. Well . . . we don't know what happened to her, do we?"

All at once, to her surprise, Charlotte's eyes fill with tears. It's hard to even talk. Beside her, Dante clears his throat. He blinks, like he might cry too. "No," Charlotte whispers. "We don't."

"We must find out more. Your Isabella could have inspired Arcangela Tarabotti," Dr. Ricci says, as if Charlotte should know her, too.

"I'm sorry," Charlotte shrugs.

"*Sister* Arcangela Tarabotti," Dr. Ricci explains. "Another Venetian writer. From the early 1600s. In a convent from age eleven. She wrote about power, about the power structures, about forcing girls into the cloister and denying them an education, same as your Isabella did here, years before her. Her most known book, *Tirannia Paterna*."

"*Paternal Tyranny*," Dante translates.

"Dante says you have the other book?" Dr. Ricci asks. "With the Tasso poem?"

Charlotte nods. "*The Verses.* I should have brought it. I don't know what I was thinking."

"Something is not right. The strings around the letter to the uncle," Dr. Ricci says to Dante, circling her finger, as if wrapping the floss around the paper. "The Phoebus. No, no, no. It's not right."

"The red wax, it's a *T*," Dante says.

"I saw, I saw," she says impatiently. "She writes several poems to *Il Toro* in this book. Is there a connection? It will take months to transcribe all the poems. *Bene*, we can start there, yes? *Il Toro*?"

Dante's eyes gleam with excitement when he looks at her. Charlotte is lost, though. "What, what? I don't understand."

"Your Isabella addresses several poems to The Bull, *Il Toro*. Who is he? Your Tasso maybe? We can search this phrase in the *banca dati*. The data bank? We will see if we can find these words somewhere else. Another poem, a letter, anything. It's a little window," Dante explains.

"Can you bring the other book tomorrow?" Dr. Ricci asks her.

Tomorrow.

It might get hot.

The unanswered email on her phone ticks like a bomb in her pocket. "I'm so sorry. I can't. Maybe this weekend? Or next week? I study writing, and I am meeting all day with Luca Bruni tomorrow."

"Who?" Dr. Ricci says. "I have never heard of him."

"It's so strange," Charlotte says to Dante when he walks her outside. "I still can't believe how history is so *present* here. Like, all of these buildings around us are from five hundred years ago. And you have festivals to celebrate the end of plagues. And even you, so interested in books and manuscripts from generations ago."

"You are from a young country," he says. But he's not really listening. He's kissing her neck. "And also, my father is a historian, and my mother owns a bookstore, and a job in the Ministry of Culture is good. Come here. Let's take a picture so I don't miss you."

They put their faces together, and he takes a photo with his phone. "Look." He shows her. "*Siamo carini*, eh? We are cute?"

"We are cute," she says.

On the boat late that afternoon with Leo and Eliot, as Aldo drives away from the ancient floating palace of Venice, Charlotte's mind stays with Veronica Franco and Isabella di Angelo and Arcangela Tarabotti. She thinks about that book, *Paternal Tyranny*. It could be a title on the shelf today. It's crazy, Charlotte thinks. It's really, really crazy that we're still talking about the same things that women were talking about five hundred years ago. Maybe history is *always* present, and never truly past.

Chapter Thirty-One

Arcangela Tarabotti writer, feminist, political activist.

Forced into the convent at age eleven, she spent her life in strict enclosure, writing radical, subversive books about the subjugation of women and patriarchal power structures. She was rebellious is other ways too—she cut off her hair and wore her habit in a "worldly fashion." Her writing was also her own: blending fiction with autobiography with political manifesto.

(1604–1652)

Charlotte tries to answer that email—*It might get hot*—a hundred times before finally sending another humiliating *Can't wait*. Now, on the morning when they're about to meet, she gets another one: *Come hungry*.

She arrives at the dock at noon, their appointed time. So many different feelings are bashing together that they all just become one blop of anxiety. Her hands actually shake. She's nervous to be by herself with him that long, first of all. She can manage not sounding stupid for short periods of time when lots of other people are around, but this is a whole day with him, so there's that, let alone the rest. Let alone the feeling that she's walking very carefully while holding a grenade. She has no idea what they're going to be doing, either. The outings are supposedly carefully matched to their haunting projects, but was he serious about the red bathing suit? She stuffed it into her bag but took it back out again after Shaye gave her a nasty look.

Aldo starts the engine. The boat putters, and smoke pours out as Charlotte gets in. Aldo barely acknowledges her, and then Luca is there, and he's wearing white pants and a rose-colored linen shirt, and expensive-looking white tennis shoes. He has a deep tan now, and he smells like cologne. He doesn't usually wear it, and now she remembers that cologne, drifting over the table at the book signing she and Carly went to. They're speeding away, away from La Calamita, away from the other students, away from Isabella's book tucked under her mattress.

"Fuckers haven't done a thing for weeks," Luca Bruni says.

She has no idea what he's talking about, but then she realizes he means those guys working on the seawall. He's right—there they are again, hanging out and smoking. They're either doing that, or no one's there at all.

"What's wrong with it?" Charlotte asks.

"The fucking thing is *crumbling*. They're supposed to be reinforcing it, rebuilding that whole area over there." He points to the far end. "We've had divers out here, because the thing's ancient. We're going to be fucking underwater if they don't get a move on."

"Oh, jeez," Charlotte says. "Yikes."

"Hey, you ready?" He tugs on her sundress playfully.

"I'm excited," she says. Brilliant things are coming out of her mouth right and left, wow. All of her self-talk about how she knows him, how they've already spent lots of time together, how the emails mean nothing, because he always jokes around like that . . . It disappears. His tall, genius man-self is right there, and it's just the two of them. Aldo, too, sure, but he's driving, making himself a blank object in the background, like she once saw waiters do at a fancy party for her dad's work.

Luca stands very close to her. He looks directly in her eyes. "I've got plans for you," he says.

And right then, for a moment, she feels a tilt. A tip into a direction she never wanted, even if whatever-this-is was sometimes a fantasy. That he would look at her and want her like that—it was an exciting idea that would never be real. That's why it *could* be fun and thrilling and interesting, because it *wouldn't* happen. But this is something actual. Not walking a line, but over it.

But then he steps back and grins. "Hey. What'd you think I was going to do? Did you think I was going to kiss you or something?"

It's stunning, the word *kiss* right there. It's so weird, because she was a girl who sat in her bed with his book, who dreamed about what he might be like, as she stared at his photo on the cover, as her sister played her music too loud in the other room. But now another shocking thing happens, and not even on purpose. "Ha. Don't flatter yourself," she says. It pops right out. And it sounds strong and confident, the kind of jokey, confrontational teasing that Shaye's always doing with him. It sounds flirtatious, like they're still just playing the game. But she has no idea where these words came from. It's not the real her, not the eighteen-year-old riding on a boat with an author she idolizes. Not the real her who's used to boys like Adam and Dante, Adam with his old soccer trophies still on his shelf. Dante, who still gets nervous around Dr. Ricci.

But he loves it. Luca Bruni laughs, a big loud laugh, right into the wind rushing at them, which messes up his hair as the boat picks up speed to cross the channel. He grins at her like she's the best thing ever. And then he pats his pocket for his sunglasses and puts them on.

"When I was starting out, Theresa Mayle took me out to lunch one day. You know Theresa Mayle?"

Of course she knows Theresa Mayle. God, who doesn't? Everyone had to read *The Lee Shore* in high school. Well, they all hated it and complained about it because it was boring, but still. She's one of the few authors famous enough that people know what she looks like. Those oversize glasses, that blunt gray hair cut severely to her chin. But the way he says it, it's like he's asking if she *knows*-knows her. Like he forgot maybe she and Theresa Mayle aren't hanging out at literary events together. Like Luca forgot she and he aren't equals, and in a way, this feels amazing, as if he thinks they *are* equals. Not someday in the future, but right now. Or maybe it's her that's forgetting. It's hard to tell who is.

"Only from her books," Charlotte says.

"We're sitting there, right? She pulls out the first story I ever published in *The Atlantic*. Tosses it on the table. Reads the part to me where Beto Baptisto and his girlfriend, Kiersten, are having a very heady argument about great literature. And then she leans back. 'Listen. Listen to what's around you,' she says. And we hear this couple next to us, right? The guy's saying, 'I got this bump on my neck. Do you think this is weird? Feel this.' And she says, 'I don't want to feel your bump. That's disgusting.' And Theresa Mayle sits back and says, '*That's* what a couple sounds like.'"

Charlotte laughs, even though it sounds like a story he's told a million times. Actually, come to think of it, she's sure she read something like that in an online interview of his, but she's positive the couple was talking about something else, like picking up after a dog or something.

"So, that's what we're going to do first, yeah? Lunch. A few years from now, you'll be telling this story to someone else." Now he lowers his voice so Aldo can't hear. "I told you to come hungry, didn't I?"

It sounds like he's teasing, but she can't see his eyes to know for sure. He's got his sunglasses on. All she can see is herself, reflected in the lenses.

In the restaurant, they sit side by side in a narrow booth. Her story is on the table. So is food, so is wine. Wine at lunch, two bottles, and one part of her feels like a stupid kid for even noticing, like Ella, when she used to get all shocked and mad at her parents when they swore. Another part of her doesn't want to seem like the stupid kid, so she drinks when he fills her glass.

He's pointing out lines he likes in her story. He makes some comment like *Is this your pent-up sexual frustration showing?* and laughs. See? This is just how he is. The flirty double meanings, the sexual jokes. The little touches on the arm. The puppy-dog fawning, like he's the geeky kid and she's the popular girl. She saw it with Avni and Katerina, and, heck, he probably did it with Bethany Sparrow and a million other people. So what? One thing that's kind of nice—it makes her feel like the popular girl, when she never really was the popular girl. She was the girl who had a small circle of friends, the girl who was always writing stuff, and trying to get good grades. She was the girl trying not to make her mother mad, because her mother could go from zero to furious in minutes, and the one with a father who preferred life on an airplane, away from them. The girl with the devoted but suffocating boyfriend. She kind of wishes she could take a picture of just the two of them here, so she could post it, and everyone could see this whole other side to her.

But now, after all the compliments about her piece, he critiques it. He tells her it needs more layers. She could do better. Way better. Is she really even trying? Well, not hard enough. *How much do you want this?* he asks. *There's the stuff that haunts you, but* why *does it haunt you? The layers are in the* why. *What is darkest here? No one can hear Isabella's voice, right? Her voice has been stolen by someone else. Like you. Like yours.*

He's harsh, and she feels crushed, but he's right, and this is another thing, a very true thing, a thing that will always remain true: he's brilliant. He does see the layers—the humor in the dark, the dark in the humor, the meaning in the moments, the weight and the why. *An angry, scary parent—you can't speak. You can't speak to power, and neither can your character. An absent parent, the father on the plane—no one is there to* listen. *No one listens to Isabella, either. Neither of you have ever been* seen. *And both of you are scared. You want things. You have layers.*

God, when he talks like this, she feels understood in some deep way she didn't even know was possible. He knows all of this about her, and he's maybe known it all along, since he read her first story for the application. This is why his work touches people.

And then Luca says, *I get it, okay? I relate.* It's like she's been forgiven for any of her failed writing, because they're *the same.* He tells her stuff about his own angry father. His hand across Luca's child face. He was scared too. His father told him he was nothing, and worth nothing. There was screaming and violence, as his mother cowered. He says it like she'll understand, even though it's all so much worse than she's *ever* experienced. And . . . he *survived* it. She's in awe. He's incredible. As he sits there talking, *his* past seems so present too. She can feel all of it, and she can even see him as this little child, and it makes her feel so sad. And so protective of him. Has he ever been truly loved and understood? It sure doesn't seem like it.

"You're amazing," she says. He shrugs. "No, you *are*."

"I'm a cold, arrogant bastard."

"No, you're not. You're sweet. You're a big softy." They've seen it lots of times. His eyes fill up with tears when they read something sad or heartbreaking, or when he sees a child begging on the street, or a three-legged dog, or, or, or . . .

"We're not too different, are we?" he says. "We could be twins. We're both so fucking lonely. It's more than I can take sometimes."

It's crazy, but it also makes him so attractive—his damage does. Even with his big nose and wild hair and thin, awkward limbs, his damage is a magnet. His damage makes him so vulnerable and open. Maybe it's her messed-up draw to darkness again, times a million. And why wouldn't she be drawn? Darkness is familiar. It's her twisted hearth, her home, her open door with the welcome mat, ugh.

Whatever, because it's still so wrong, what happened to him—he's worth *so* much, that she really wishes she could show him how loved he is, even though thousands and thousands of people have already told him that. Thousands and thousands of people have already told him that, and it's not enough, and how sad is that? He deserves better.

"You have so many people who love you," she says.

"Hey. You won't tell anyone this stuff, huh? Everything I just said? It's between us, right?"

"Of course."

The waiter arrives. He sets the bill on the table. "For you and your *piccola*," the waiter says, and turns away.

In an instant, Charlotte feels the shift in Luca's body. The little boy vanishes. All at once, a man, a furious man, sits suddenly in his place. "Oh, for *fuck's sake*," Luca says. He's *pissed*. She doesn't know what happened, but it's awful, and awkward, and she just wishes she could disappear. He reaches into his pocket, jams a wad of euros on the table. "Let's get out of here."

Charlotte feels so bad. Humiliated, even if she doesn't know why. Luca's fuming. She worries what *piccola* means.

"What did he say?"

"Little one! Your little one! He thought you were my *daughter*. God, what an asshole."

They walk. She feels that shame throughout her whole body. The big event of the day is still coming, though, Charlotte knows. Lunch was just the beforehand thing. But going back now would be fine, honestly. Beside her, Luca seems like he's been jabbed with a dagger. Little dribbles of hurt pride keep pouring out. "Come on, man. Do I look old enough to be your father?" he says again. She wishes he'd stop bringing it up.

It is so easy to get lost here. They make one turn and then another, cross a bridge, make another turn over a canal. She really has no idea where they are.

"Come on, give me a clue," she says. She tries to be super happy and playful so he'll get out of his mood. She doesn't want the day to be ruined.

"Almost there," he says.

And now they stop at a beautiful four-storied building, with arches and small balconies and green shuttered windows.

Wait.

She knows where she is. When she looks across the bridge in front of them now, she realizes she can see the back of Alta Acqua Libreria, the bookstore. She's so close to it. Once again, she's at the dot—steps away from San Zaccaria and the Doge's Palace and the Biblioteca Marciana.

"Do you know what this is?" Luca nods his chin at the building. She's glad to see that he's smiling again. What a relief, they're back on track.

"No idea."

"Look there." He points. It's a cross. A cross? It can't be a church. . . . "Still no idea?"

"I'm getting nervous," she says.

"Layers," he winks.

They walk into a high-ceilinged drawing room, with elaborate white ceilings and ornate walls, and a red-and-white diamond-patterned floor. There's a desk. And behind it—oh my God, she knows now. She knows.

It's a convent. They're in a convent.

Two sisters in traditional black-and-white habits talk quietly behind the counter, and when Luca walks up, the three of them speak to each other in Italian, and there is much fussing over Luca, and patting his hand, and beaming toward Charlotte, and she has no idea what they're saying. One of the sisters checks a large open book, a registry, maybe, and then she gives him a key. They wave their hands, ushering him on, a signal that he is free to go wherever he wants. When he rejoins her, he dangles the key like a prize.

"A convent?" Charlotte says.

"Foresteria Valdese Venezia. A convent *and* a hotel."

Something about the words *a hotel* makes her feel deeply uneasy. The unease whooshes in like water. She remembers Avni, and Esplanade Tergesteo. A couple descends the large staircase, carrying their roller bags by their handles until they reach the red-and-white floor. No one else is here, though. The place is very quiet. Empty, really.

"Let's look around," he says. Luca's all cheery again, playful, like they're having an adventure. They peek into a dining hall, with long wooden tables and beamed ceilings, and the hovering smell of cooked meat and vegetables. They peek into a narrow chapel, with two rows of wooden pews.

"Do you want to stay for the rest for your life?" he whispers.

"I don't think so." Charlotte wants to leave, actually. It's all too quiet. She feels the sense of rules all around, restrictions, constraints, but she also feels Luca's presence next to her, almost pressing in the silence.

"Casanova used to go to the convent, did you know? San Zaccaria. A regular visitor."

"That must have been fun," she says, but she doesn't mean it. She's trying to go along, but it's hard to know what to say. She feels so stupid. She feels out of her depth, like those times you're in an ocean, and you suddenly step off into a place where the bottom has vanished.

Now they're in a hallway. He uses the key to open a door. The room is small, and nearly empty. There's only a bed covered with a thin blue bedspread, and a desk, and plain curtains. There's nothing on the walls but a crucifix hanging over the bed.

Luca shuts the door behind them. Through the windows, Charlotte can see the light outside, turning the yellow-gold of early evening. How did it get so late? The space feels very small all of a sudden, and Luca seems so tall, like the grown man that he is, and he's wearing a wristwatch, she notices, and no one her age wears one of those, and his forehead is sweaty. He's gotten a splotch of something on his white pants. They're close enough that she can smell him. His fading aftershave mixed with sweat mixed with alcohol. He doesn't smell like the guys she knows—Adam or Dante. He smells his age. He smells like a man.

He drops his bag to the floor. "Are you going to just stand there, clutching your purse?" he asks, and grins.

"I—" She's starting to get a bad feeling, a panicky feeling, there with the door closed. It feels like wings flapping inside of her, hundreds of birds, like the ones in Saint Mark's Square.

"Can you imagine all the pent-up desire in a place like this?" he says.

He's standing very close to her. He sets his hands on her arms and is looking, or trying to look, intensely into her eyes, but she keeps glancing away. She wants out of that room. She can smell their lunch on his breath. Garlic. Wine. The sour scent of cheese. She's in way over her head. Panic is just . . . It's filling her, flooding her system. She has definitely not kept this situation where she thought she had. He is definitely forgetting again that they aren't the same. He leans down toward her.

"Wait," she says. "Wait. What are we doing?"

"You know what we're doing."

"Wait. Wait," she says. She puts her hand on his chest. But his face is in hers, and then his mouth is on hers, and his tongue shoves in her mouth, and it feels big and gross, and he's moving it around. It's not in her mouth long, but maybe long enough to remember forever.

She pushes him back. "Wait," she says. Shit. Shit! She came to this place with him, walked right here beside him. Shit, she flirted, and complimented him, and, God, she doesn't want to make him mad. She's seen him get mad. He's just . . . important, and—he's getting mad right now, she sees it in his face.

"What'd you *think* we were going to do?"

His tone has shifted again. He's pissed. She's disappointed him. The game isn't anything like she imagined. The one he was playing and the one she was playing were two entirely different games.

"No, no. I don't know. I thought—"

"You're acting like you're still in high school, *Jesus*. We're all just trying to have fun here."

"I'm sorry," she says. "I'm really, really sorry."

"I'm not going to *force* you! Fuck! Go. Go, then."

"I'm sorry," she says. "I'm so sorry." She feels a rush of shame and regret. God, she's such an idiot, and she feels such embarrassment and horror for how she's ruined everything. For how she's misread everything. She *is* sorry, for all of it.

She's got to get out of there. She wants out of that room. She wants out of everything. She grabs her purse. She flings open the door and hurries down the hall. She rushes down that stairwell, past the desk with the nuns, out the door, into the streets of that old, old city.

She doesn't know what to do. She can't go back. God, what is he going to say about her? Think of all the people he might tell. Not only everyone at the villa, but *everyone*. *You know what we're doing,* he'd said, his sweaty face near hers, and she did know, kind of, and what did he mean by *We're all just trying to have fun here*? Is this what *everyone's* been doing, aside from maybe Katerina, who told her to be careful? Hailey, Ashley, stuff like this, and she's been an idiot?

Oh my God, oh my God! She *did* act like a child. Like a naive girl. So what, he tried to kiss her, and why is she surprised, after every red flag? She's ruined everything—this whole experience, her trip, her big chance. Should she have just done it? She could almost gag, that memory of his big tongue in her mouth. She feels such shame and humiliation, and if these are part of the *layers* of truth, she doesn't want them. She doesn't want layers like that, layers of shame, and likely neither did Isabella di Angelo, or Veronica Franco, or Arcangela Tarabotti, but they were theirs anyway.

Chapter Thirty-Two

Fiammetta Soderini, poet.

Engaged at age eleven, married at fourteen. Little is known of her own work, but we do know she was surrounded by famous men: her uncle ran the Florentine government, her husband was a prominent banker, and her son became an archbishop. She was also one of the many, many female poets, artists, and writers to receive numerous flirtatious letters from prolific poet Muzio Manfredi, whose first volume of poetry began with an open letter "to the ladies."

(1497–unknown)

Charlotte texts Dante, but there's no answer. She calls, but she only gets his voice mail. She goes to the bookstore, but it's closed.

"Maria?" Charlotte shouts upward to the open windows with their green shutters. "Maria? Maria, are you there?"

"Basta!" an old man shouts back. A cat winds around Charlotte's legs. She doesn't know what to do. She can't go back. Not to La Calamita, that's for sure.

But now, there she is. Maria. She steps out onto the small

balcony. She wraps her robe tighter around herself. She looks down at Charlotte. They're replaying a twisted version of *Romeo and Juliet*. One woman calling to another.

"Charlotta?" Maria says.

"It's me. Can I come in?"

Now that Charlotte's inside Maria and Dante's snug home, with the open windows and books all around, with Maria apologizing for her robe *so early in the evening, you know, all I want to do is take the bra off*, explaining that Dante is *out with friends, some noisy taverna, no wonder he can't hear his phone*, everything releases inside of her. She begins to cry. It's a messy sobbing, the kind where you're sure everything is ruined and wrecked.

"Oh, *patatina* . . . What? What? Sit down." Maria's stern face goes soft and caring. Behind her air of disapproval, there's a tenderness that's so much a part of Dante. "Tell me. What happened? It is fine. It is okay."

Her arm is around Charlotte's shoulders, and now Charlotte feels embarrassed all over again, because nothing happened, not really. She's not some victim of something awful. She went right there with him. He tried to kiss her, so what. It's not a big, giant thing. But when she tells Maria, Maria acts like it is.

"Stai scherzando!" she says angrily. *"Stronzo! Bastardo! Pezzo di merda!"*

"He didn't hurt me or anything. I mean, I'm fine! I should have known! Honestly, how stupid could I be? Everyone said he was like this! I knew! I should have stopped any . . . *whatever*, from the beginning."

"Should, should, should! He is the big man with the ego, taking anything he wants. Let me get you something to drink."

Charlotte can hear Maria on the phone in the kitchen. And then she comes back with a small glass of brown liquid. "Here. Chee-nar," she says. "*Digestivo.*"

"Chee-nar?"

"No, no, no! *Chee*-nar! C-Y-N-A-R. Drink. Dante is on his way."

"I'm so sorry to ruin your evening."

"No, no. *Figurati!*"

"I can't go back there." Even this feels too dramatic, because maybe she should just face him and ignore it. *Deal* with it. But she feels repulsed. That tongue shoved in her mouth, God.

"Of course you can't." Maria shakes her head, as if it's decided.

None of it matters—her clothes, her stuff. Even her laptop. She doesn't even want to see it. She doesn't care what happens to it. Someone will ship it to her, maybe. If not, so what. It all feels different now. Especially every word she's written on that laptop. It all seems silly and childish. It was probably never any good. She had started to believe it—that she actually might have talent, that she might become this thing that seemed bigger and better and more meaningful to her than any other thing, a writer. But it all feels like a lie now. Not just her talent, not just her dream, but *all* of it. A writer was not someone who could do something bigger and better and more meaningful. A writer was not some kind of god or hero. It was crushing.

"I just want to go home," Charlotte says.

Charlotte calls her mom. She feels sick delivering this news. What a waste, of money and energy and love, even. It's nine hours behind in Seattle, one in the afternoon, and Adele is in Safeway with Ella, buying dog food. "Oh, honey. Oh, honey," her mom keeps saying. Within hours, her dad sends her the booking information for a flight home late the next day. No one even mentions how expensive that is. It *all* feels so expensive. The cost is enormous.

She spends the night in the small alcove bedroom that belongs to Dante's sister, Bria. It's the most magical book lover's dream spot, sleeping in this cozy, charming curve of books, with this enchanted city just outside, but she can't take in any of that now. She's going home tomorrow. She and Dante are sitting on the bed. He's near tears, and she has to keep wiping her eyes and blowing her nose.

"You can't leave!" he keeps saying.

"I can't go back there."

"You can stay here! We're not through yet. You and me."

She knows he's right, but some stories end sooner than they should. "I'm sorry. I'm so sorry."

"And we are so close to your Isabella! Dottoressa Ricci has a nail on the head. When she gets this way about something . . ."

"I really appreciate it, but I can't be here."

"We are so close to the mystery! What if we find more about the poem of Tasso?"

"I just want to see my family."

"I will never see *you* again," he says. "You will never come back here."

Her heart clutches up. He takes her in his arms, and they hold each other so tight, she can feel his heartbeat against her. But she doesn't answer. There's nothing to say. She knows he's right.

Chapter Thirty-Three

Laudomia Forteguerri, poet.

An accomplished writer, she's considered to be Italy's first known lesbian writer. During her time, she was known for her beauty, wit, and intelligence and was pursued by many famous men, particularly philosopher Alessandro Piccolomini, who was infatuated with her but later turned on her. In 1553 she led a group of women in the construction of a fortified wall to protect her city from invasion.

(1515–1555)

It's not until morning that Charlotte realizes it.

The book.

Isabella's book. *The Verses.*

Under her mattress.

Oh, shit. *Shit!*

She has to go back. She can leave everything else, but she can't leave that.

Oh, God. God! She tells Maria and Dante that she has to return to La Calamita. She'll just go get the book, and shove some things in her bag, and get the hell out of there. She'll hope like crazy that she doesn't see Luca Bruni. They need a boat, though, since those taxis won't drive out there. Dante tries to call Raffaele, but no answer.

"Sleeping in," Dante says. "After a late Friday night. I'm sorry."

"I will fix it," Maria says. And she does. She knows Aldo. Everyone knows everyone here, it seems. She phones him right up. "He'll be at the San Marco dock in an hour," she says.

These goodbyes, even the one with Maria—they feel impossible. And now, standing at the dock with Dante as Aldo waits with the motor of the boat running—Charlotte's heart is breaking.

"I can come to the airport, at least. On the boat with you, to that place."

"No, Dante. No." It's too gut-wrenching. This is so, so much harder than her breakup with Adam. Dante is right—this isn't finished. They're stopping in the middle of the story, but there's no other choice. It's painful to be in that city now. She just wants to go home.

They kiss for a long time, and when they separate, Dante's shoulders heave in a sob, and it's awful. He has to take his glasses off to wipe his eyes, and she is crying too.

"Goodbye, *dolcezza*. Goodbye, Charlotta."

She gets into the boat. She can't bear to look at him, standing there in his T-shirt and jeans, waving. Her chest aches and aches. There's the hole of loss there already, even though she can still see him. He gets smaller and smaller, as Aldo picks up speed.

"Bruni! Stronzo. Bastardo. Pezzo di merda," Aldo grumbles.

When she steps onto the ground of La Calamita, she remembers that the earth is half ash, made of the remains of the thousands upon thousands of souls who died here. She remembers the plague, and the doctor in his tower, and the way sickness and cruelty have been in our world forever and will always be in our world. The ashy ground feels soft under her feet, even though this is her imagination. It feels like every step makes an imprint, that every impression you make lasts and lasts even if you can't see it.

The pool sparkles wrongly. It's a beautiful day. A gorgeous day. The air smells like lemon blossoms. No one's around. It's Saturday morning. People are maybe sleeping in, or else they've already left. More and more, they've been going to the main island, meeting new friends, staying out late, making the city their own. She sees a few dirty dishes, crumpled napkins, half-drunk coffee in cups on the table from breakfast. Mess left behind for others to clean up.

She hurries. She's that deeply unsettled kind of nervous that sits close to dread. She feels like a spy, or an intruder. *Please don't see him, please,* she begs whoever might be listening. She opens the doors to the villa. She heads up the stairs, passing the mural of the big glass ship. She doesn't stop to look at it. She doesn't stop to admire how real it looks.

The hallway is empty, thank goodness. She rushes to her room and hurries inside. But in all that rushing and hurrying, she doesn't hear the sounds behind her door. She doesn't hear murmurs and rustling, so when she opens it—

"Oh my God," she says. "Oh, God." Her eyes go wide, and she can't move. It's Shaye and Luca Bruni, and Shaye's legs are wrapped around Luca's waist, and Charlotte can see his bare ass, skinny and wrinkled and weird, white compared to the rest of his tan skin, and then Shaye lets out a little shriek, and Luca Bruni drops her. Drops her just like that, enough that she makes a little thump and even stumbles.

"Oh my God," Charlotte says again. It's like she's in a dream. Her own self in her own body is somewhere else, and another girl is hurrying into that awful room and shoving things into her bag.

"What the fuck?" Shaye says. "What the actual fuck?"

"This is nothing," Luca Bruni says. "This is nothing." His words burble and echo as if they're submerged. He's trying to pull on his pants, hopping on one foot. And, oh, oh, she understands now, where Shaye had been all those nights, why Shaye wanted to believe that she was the only one who really knew him. Poor Shaye, for all her toughness and bravado, she thought this was *real*. She thought it *meant something*.

Charlotte reaches under the mattress. There it is, thank God. She grabs *The Verses* and sets it in her bag and zips it up. She snags her laptop, too, and then she's out of there. She has rescued Isabella di Angelo, that's what it feels like.

• • •

Down the stairs now, struggling with her bag, she nearly collides with Katerina on the front steps of the villa.

"Are you *leaving*?" Kat asks. But then she sees Charlotte's face and doesn't need an answer. "Wait. Wait, I'm coming too. Don't go without me."

Katerina rushes upstairs. Charlotte leaves that magnificent villa, walks past the perfect, glittering pool, and the gorgeous garden, and the incredible library, all of it.

She gets into the boat.

"Ready?" Aldo says.

"Not yet. One more."

"Bastardo! Farfallone," Aldo fumes.

She wishes Kat would hurry. *Please, please hurry!* she thinks. She wants to get out of there so bad. Luca might come out. Or try to talk to her. She doesn't ever want to see him again. Aldo starts the motor, and it sputters to life. *Hurry, Katerina!*

Okay. There she is. Thank goodness. She's rushing, one bag slung over her arm, her roller bag following behind her, veering and bumping like a reluctant child.

But now she stops. What, why? Come *on*! What is she *doing*?

Katerina drops her bag outside of the library, that beautiful turret. Whatever she's doing—there's no time for it. *Ugh!* In a moment, though, she's out again. She picks up the handle of her suitcase and hurries toward them.

"Sorry," Katerina says as Aldo heaves her bag into the boat. "Let's get out of here."

The boat engine roars. The smell of gasoline kicks up. That eerie, doomed island falls away behind them. What haunts you? This, now.

"Are you okay?" Charlotte asks, because Kat just has this *look*. The look on her face . . . What is it? If Charlotte were writing it . . . No. Forget it. She doesn't even want to do that anymore. That dream feels like 50 percent ash. Katerina's face is distant. Angry, maybe. Maybe full of sorrow, maybe all of it.

"He took me to Ospedale della Pietà that day, in Venice. Do you know what that is?" Katerina says as the boat picks up speed. "It was *an orphanage*. Hundreds of years ago. You had two choices if you were an unwed mother then, he told me. You could drop your baby in the canal, or slip it in the infant-size hole in the wall of that place. But orphans could thrive there, because it was a music school, too, where Vivaldi taught. Only the girls, though. Only if they were good enough."

La Calamita is getting smaller in the distance, but Katerina's eyes are still fixed on it as she speaks. "He took me to *an orphanage*, Charlotte. And then he shoved his face into mine, stuck his hand up my shirt, and kissed me, and I let him, and then *I apologized*. I told him I had a boyfriend so he'd leave me alone."

"I'm so sorry." Charlotte almost has to shout, because they're going fast now. The wind presses and whirls around them.

Katerina reaches into her bag. She's holding a stack of papers.

"What's that?" Charlotte's hair is whipping in her face. The bow of the boat smacks against the waves. "What is—" No, she knows.

Katerina moves to the back of the boat. She faces the white wake spreading out in front of her. And then she opens her hands. She opens them, and the pages fly out like doves. Like the doves on those church ceilings, the ones flying around the angels. Art with hidden symbols, with images of women, and names and signatures.

The pages, Luca Bruni's pages, they fly up and out and away. They flutter.

Aldo looks over his shoulder and sees what's happening. And he turns up the opera then. He turns up that horrible Vivaldi, with his school of orphan girls.

"Vivaldi. The great artists! Pieces of shit!" he calls. "This is for Anna Giro! And the *figlie*! The *nipoti*! The daughters and the granddaughters, *sì*?"

"Sì," Charlotte says. *Sì, sì, sì!* And then he guns the engine. He's going so fast that the pages fly out in all directions. They fly up and out, spiraling in midair before drifting down to the water, where they float and bob. They'll float until they soak and drown, but now they're like little paper boats. Not glass ships. Just little paper boats.

They speed past the city, the beautiful island of Venice. And of course, Charlotte thinks about what's on those pages, the pages he read to them at Ca' Zappa, drenched and riding the waves around them. And she thinks about Luca Bruni himself. His talent and his power and his charisma—*he* is a shimmering palace that seems to float on the water, a magic act, an impossibility. *He* is smoke and mirrors, an island of twisting streets and dead ends that would make anyone lose their way. Fantastical, unreal. Untouchable. Impenetrable by the enemy. So enchanted that he could rule for hundreds of years, smug in his position of command.

Chapter Thirty-Four

Lucrezia Marinella,
author, poet, women's rights activist.

Wrote a treatise directly challenging poet Giuseppe Passi's piece "The Defects of Women." She also criticized the work of many dead misogynistic writers, such as Aristotle.

(1571–1653)

"What is going on? What's wrong with you guys?" Eliot asks when he calls. He's not joking around now. His voice is serious, and maybe even a little worried, but it's hard to tell if he's worried for himself or for them. He's still in another country, but it doesn't feel like it right then. His voice is in Charlotte's ear, and all her hard work trying to shove the whole thing away is ruined. In the week since she's been back, she's tried not to notice how strange her own city looks, shady and weirdly new. It's odd not to hear the lilt of Italian, and the food is so different. But all of that is gone.

And when she and Dante talk *(I miss you, Charlotta. When are you coming back, Charlotta? Do you know what Dottoressa Ricci did today? She sent out an email to many colleagues, with the information about your Isabella, and the doge, and the books. She asked if anyone knew about an Il Toro. She is determined to find out who he is, Charlotta! The Bull!)*, he's far away too. Isabella is. Charlotte doesn't feel like doing anything, not writing, not even reading, not eating, even. She just feels the heaviness of loss.

She doesn't want to talk about it either. *It*—any of it, but especially those last few days. She told her mom what happened, and her dad knows too, and Ella has figured out most of it. But there's no way she wants her friends to find out, even Yas, who used to know everything about her.

The story is, she got sick. That she didn't want to come home but had to. It's pretty much true. If she tells the truth, it'll be like confessing. Because she flirted, and she knew what he was like, she did, but she went with him anyway. But worse—she was naive enough to think he really cared about her and her talent. She *believed*. She believed in him, she believed in herself. She believed she was more than something to fuck, and now she's embarrassed for thinking she was worth more than that. He probably never even really thought she had talent. Every word she put on paper was childish. A joke.

Yas has texted and tried to call. Are you feeling better? Call me anytime! I want to know you're okay. Sucks so bad you had to go home! Carly has reached out too. You still sick? Can I bring you anything? Did you ever find out what you had? Carly knows something else happened, Charlotte can tell. Charlotte called her that night in Venice to talk about

Luca Bruni, and now, whenever she lies to Carly, the word *sick* is something revolting and transparent between them. When she thinks about Yas and Carly coming over with the heart balloon and the streamers when she got the acceptance letter, or when she went to the faculty lunchroom to tell the news to Mr. McNulty, or Carly's dad saying how proud he was of her at the graduation party, or her mom rewatching all of *One Great Lie* with such excitement, everything hurts so much worse. She let them all down. It's not just her own hope that's been wrecked.

"I got sick," she tells Eliot now.

"Bullshit. You *both* got sick? Katerina won't answer her phone. Everyone here is furious that you're fucking this up for us. Shaye's ripping you guys a new one. Like, this doesn't make any of us look good, okay? The whole program. Three people leaving."

"We didn't exactly plan it, Eliot."

"Yeah, but a blogger from Pulp Media heard that three students just took off, and she called Ashley and asked her questions. I guess they went to the same high school in Arlington. They're wondering, you know? Hailey says it puts some black mark on everything we've done here."

"People get sick, Eliot."

"You guys are being selfish."

She doesn't reply.

"It's wild about Leo, though. That's one good thing," he says.

"What?"

"You didn't see it all over social media? He's getting a story published in the *New Yorker*. The *New Yorker*! Can you even believe it? He just turned *twenty* last week! *Of course*, it's someone like *him*. He's already got everything! That happens to exactly *no one*. People are saying it's because he put Luca's name all over the cover letter. It was the same piece he used for his application."

"Leo's so talented, I'm not surprised."

"Honestly, I always thought Shaye was *way* more talented."

Charlotte's shocked when he says this. But then again, you know, when she thinks about Shaye's writing, how she *shreds* you with her truth, maybe he's right. They'd all given it—*the best, the most, the number one spot*—straight to Leo. Charlotte herself had. He came with the honor the second he arrived on La Calamita, walking by that pool with his roller bag.

"Luca's treating him even worse now. He keeps slipping the word 'user' into every conversation. He looks at Leo like he *despises* the guy. If *Leo* left, I'd get it, you know."

"How is he?" When she thinks of Luca Bruni, all she sees is his skinny bare ass, Shaye's legs gripping his waist. She feels that tongue, a thick eel jamming in the cave of her mouth. But she wants to know what happened, you know, *after*. Maybe she just wants to hear how hurt he is that they're gone, or how upset he is about the missing pages. She's left that place, but this is far, far from over.

"He's thrilled! I mean, can you imagine? First shot at the *New Yorker* and getting in? His university is doing a story on him."

"No, I mean *Luca*."

"Oh, he's fine. His wife was here for a few days, and he was all formal, but after she left, we went to Cantina Do Mori after and had a blast. Some reporter from the *LA Times* is here today, following him all around for a photo spread, so we're free. He's pretending to be all shy and awkward, and the photographer is *eating it up*. All that pre-pub stuff for his new book, I guess."

Fine. Fine! Totally unaffected. "He didn't say anything about us going home?"

"Yeah, only like, 'I'm too nice, man. I'm too nice.'"

It's a gut punch. They were just characters in his story, easily edited, easily deleted. It hurts, but it's clear—the relationship she thought she had with him had taken place in only *her* mind. And it was *still* taking place in only her mind.

"Hey, Eliot, I've got to go."

"Yeah, sure. Maybe you guys could . . . I don't know. Make it clear on your social media or something that you were sick? I left Katerina a message asking her. It just doesn't look good, okay? Luca's all, 'Whatever, who cares? You can't cut it, then bye-bye.' *Ouch*, but you know how he is. Why should the whole program suffer, though?"

After Charlotte hangs up, she sits on the edge of her bed. Her old stories from Mr. McNulty's class are still in a folder on her dresser. Ella's playing her music too loud in her room. Her dad knocks on her shut door.

"Char? Heading out. Boston. See you next week."

"See you," she says.

Downstairs, she hears her mother say, "Why bother stopping

by, huh? Like we're the Ramada Inn? You should leave a tip for the maid."

Everything has changed, and nothing has changed.

And then something awful happens. Something worse. A series of things. The day after Eliot calls, she looks at Katerina's social media pages. She hasn't talked to Kat since they hugged goodbye and went their separate ways at the airport. She wonders if Katerina did what Eliot asked.

But no, no, she hasn't. Not at all. She's posted an image, though, with no caption. It's a photo of Luca's book, *One Great Lie*, the one from the TV series, sitting at the bottom of a garbage can.

The next day, Charlotte gets a call. She doesn't recognize the number, so she doesn't answer. She has a flash of fear that it's someone from Pulp Media, but it isn't. Maybe this is worse. It's Avni. She leaves a message: *Call me.*

When Charlotte finally does, her hands shake. It feels like things are overflowing, flooding, water rapidly seeping through old cracks. She doesn't want to hear what Avni has to say. Charlotte knows enough. It's plenty.

She forgot how strong and confident Avni can sound. Her voice is like coffee, rich and assertive. It shoots Charlotte back to that beautiful plateau overlooking the Euganean Hills, to *all* of the beautiful before the bad. The food, and those dinners under the white lights. The boat trips to incredible places, the pool, her gorgeous room in the villa.

But then Avni asks, "Why'd you guys leave?" Her voice is direct. "All I see is that post from Katerina. She won't answer my texts."

"I don't want to talk about it," Charlotte says.

"Then I have to tell you what happened at the Tergesteo hotel, in case you ever *do*."

Charlotte doesn't answer. She only exhales. She feels sick.

"What haunted me was . . . not measuring up to my father's expectations, right?" Avni says. "And so he brought me to this place. The Tergesteo hotel."

Charlotte groans.

"Are you okay for me to go on? Because I need to go on."

"I'm okay." Charlotte shuts her eyes.

"It was beautiful. The hotel. Really expensive. Right near Arquà Petrarca, where he grew up. We sat by this pool, and he talked and talked, about fear, and his own father's expectations, and how he fought through it, but now, look, he went from that to *this*. A place where he could have anything he wanted. Are you still there?"

"Yeah."

"On and on he went, and he kept saying, 'I could talk to you forever,' but I couldn't. It was too much. He was. He can be so overwhelming. You want him to *go away*, you know? At one point, this woman in a red dress walked past, and he said, 'I love girls in red dresses,' as if we were all interchangeable, and I started to feel this . . . *disgust*. And then he kept asking, 'Do you want a spa treatment? They have spa treatments.' I kept saying, 'No, no, that's okay,' and he was getting kind of pissed, and he said, 'Well, *Tiffany Morris* wanted one.' Basically saying, if a famous actress came here with him, what was wrong with me? But I kept thinking—if you could come here with a famous actress, why even *be* here with me? I mean, I watch Tiffany Morris on Netflix in my *dorm*."

"Right." The sick feeling in Charlotte's stomach has turned into a horrible knot of anxiety. She's scared to hear what's coming next.

"Finally, he stood up, and he took my hand and said, 'Come on!' Like we were having a fun time together. I was . . . I just wanted to get out of there. He led me back inside, past some ballrooms and stuff, and then down a hall, where the rooms were, and he stops in front of a door and swipes his key, and I'm like, 'This is good. Let's just go back.' And he's going, 'No, you gotta see this room. Look at this. You won't believe it.' And the second I went in . . ." Avni clears her throat. "I knew it was a mistake. He gave me a little push onto the bed and started kissing me, and his hands were all over me, and I finally shoved him off. He was like, 'Hey, hey, I'm sorry,' but it was the kind of sarcastic apology that's more like 'What's *your* problem?' He was pissed, but he looked like he might fall apart right there, too. Like he might lose it. He was a tsunami of emotions, God. 'We're only trying to have fun here,' he said. Who *we* was—no idea, because it wasn't me."

Charlotte's so nauseous, it's a sea inside of her. Her head starts to throb. *We're only trying to have fun here.* The beautiful stuff

Charlotte remembers is gone, gone, gone, and there's only the fat eel tongue in her mouth.

"Oh, Avni." Charlotte doesn't know what else to say.

"And you know what? The crazy thing? It's right there in his work, right on the page," Avni says. "Look at his characters! The women are *always* empty and adoring, or taking care of him like mothers. Having sex with them, and then tossing them away. Look at that creep K. K. Edwards, too. You heard what he did, right? It's all over his books. He says his books are *supposed* to be about sexism, sure. That he's *a feminist*. Just like Ashley and Katerina tried to say about Bruni that day on Murano."

"Yeah." Charlotte can't disagree, but it still hurts. She wishes she could form the hurt into a big intellectual ball like Avni is, but all she can feel is a sickening, edgy alarm.

"It goes on and on and on," Avni says. "You know what Norman Mailer said? 'A little bit of rape is good for a man's soul.' Do you know what *Hemingway* said? 'If you leave a woman, you probably ought to shoot her.' Hundreds of them! Going back to *forever*. Stupid fucking Petrarch. Once you start seeing it, you can't stop. Their books *tell you who they are*. Nothing's even hidden! And everyone loves those guys. They're *immortal*."

It was all over Antonio Tasso's work too. Not in "In Guerra," but definitely in that crazy popular musical based on *La Campagna*. All those women singing in the countryside, and Tasso's lines, spoken by the lead actor: *I can love her, and her, and you, and you.* And that other song that was supposed to be funny. "Hope Not for a Mind in a Woman." It was the first line of the book.

Avni's angry. But maybe it's not all intellectual. What will haunt Charlotte about this conversation later, when she's trying to sleep that night, is the way Avni's voice cracked when she said what happened in that hotel room.

And then Katerina calls. She's whispering. She's only told Charlotte and Leo what happened, not her parents, not her roommates. *What happened*—it sounds like an accidental force, not will and intent. Those passive, soft words are easier to say than *what he did*. Charlotte understands why Kat isn't telling anyone. Her admiration for Luca Bruni is evidence against her. It's like handing the gun to your murderer.

"*Bethany* called me," Katerina says. Bethany Sparrow is a whole other thing to wonder about. She brings up a web of questions. Did he do this with her, too? Or was she a willing partner? Or did he not even touch her, ever? If not, why not? How was the beautiful and talented Bethany spared? Which is only another way of asking the more nagging question: Why them?

"What did she say?"

"'I know *you* took those chapters. Charlotte's too nice. You're the angry, broken one,'" she says in a high-pitched Bethany Sparrow voice. "'Can you imagine what would happen if people knew what you did?' It was a threat, I know it. I'm supposed to keep my mouth shut and disappear. You don't have to tell me twice. What would my parents say? They'd disown me."

Charlotte doesn't say anything. A part of her . . . This is hard to admit, but she feels an awful knot of distress about those pages, his beautiful words, sinking into those ancient waters. She still wants to separate those words from the man, even though of course you can't. They don't just come from him—they *are* him.

Katerina hears what Charlotte isn't saying. "Don't worry about the pages," she says.

"What do you mean?" Charlotte bites the edge of her finger.

"Bethany made sure to tell me it had zero effect, taking the chapters. Totally meaningless. *Of course* he keeps a copy. If he writes anything longhand, she scans it, and someone types it up. They've got, like, three backup systems."

"So all that stuff about writing being a risk . . ."

"A lie. Another lie. What I did—it didn't hurt him. It didn't hurt him one bit."

After Katerina hangs up, a little curl of anger unfurls in Charlotte's chest. It's not only the lie, or the threat, or the *Charlotte's too nice*. No, the anger is a new, ugly wondering.

What haunted them . . . Is that why Luca Bruni *chose* them? Because they were already a little afraid, a little broken, in need of approval, or understanding, or acceptance? Because they were already drawn to darkness for their own reasons? No. *Vulnerable* to darkness. It was like he saw their damage, and showed them his, and then reached out his hand. The thing is, they thought it was the sort of strong, safe hand that might save you as you flailed in the water, and so they took it. But, instead, it was the kind of hand that would hold your head under until you drowned.

Chapter Thirty-Five

Franceschina Giustiniani, writer, memoirist.

Most likely she was the anonymous author of a chronicle about life in Le Vergini, a convent in Venice. The chronicle discusses the many young nuns who took male lovers willingly, and others who were forced to have sex by men who broke in. Many of their relationships were long-term ones, and many nuns had multiple partners, including Franceschina herself. The chronicle also discusses the numerous babies that were born, as did Franceschina's own child, as well as the nuns and men who were brought to trial for this behavior.

(Early 1500s)

Dante keeps calling. So consistently that Adele's distrust of him has faded, and she even chuckles fondly when she overhears his voice. Charlotte loves seeing Dante's face on the screen, even when it freezes in the middle of a weird expression. They screenshot these and send them to each other, and now she has a great collection of herself looking really, really awful. God, she likes him so much. More than *like*, definitely more, ugh. She tries not to think about the big hole of longing she feels when she hears him say *Charlotta!* It's impossible, *they* are, because she's never going back there.

August has turned to early September, and although Seattle University, where Charlotte's supposed to go, hasn't started classes yet, Dante is back at school, along with his work at Biblioteca Marciana. She tells him about Yasmin coming back home and breaking up with Nate finally, and about Ella's thirteenth birthday party, and he tells her about Raffaele moping around since Gaia went back to the University of Rome, and about his new classes, and a visit from his sister, and—

"Charlotta! I forgot to tell you. Do you remember Sister Antonia, the poor pregnant nun? You wanted so badly to know what happened, after we saw that letter?"

"Oh my God, yes!" It seems like a million years ago.

"We found another document. In the papers from the flood. A decree. From the Council of Ten to the abbess of San Zaccaria. November 1575. The pregnant noblewomen with 'weak and lustful natures' were to be jailed for being 'incorrigible and refusing to be chaste.' There are no names on the part of the existing document, but we're sure one of them is Sister Antonia."

"That's awful."

"Yes. Having sex with a nun was punishable by death, Dottoressa Ricci says. But the men were often found innocent. And then they would accuse the sister of being a prostitute and she'd be sent to prison. *Uffa*."

"Oh, no." It's crazy, but she wants to cry. Poor Antonia.

She was only a few years older than Charlotte herself.

"Will you come back and bring the book?"

"Nice try." Every time they talk, he begs and pleads. Dr. Ricci has also asked, in several serious and determined emails. She wants Charlotte to return with *The Verses*, packed into a special box and carefully cradled in her possession, since shipping is too risky. She's even offered to pay for the trip. Instead, Dr. Ricci has had to settle for the photos of the pages Charlotte's been sending. It's taking forever, though. She can only stand to do a chunk at a time. Those pages are so thin, and there are so many of them.

"Oh, fine. You don't come." On the screen, he runs one hand through his hair. "Some more photos, then? Dottoressa Ricci—*é pazza!* You are not fast enough! She is asking every day, on and on. She wants to see the whole. The first book—it is seeming nothing like the second."

"Really? Like how?"

"The first is poems about nature, history, religion. *Safe.* While the second is very outspoken. And so, what caused the change? She thinks something happened. Something big. Or else, the meanings in the first book are . . . *nascosta.*" He scoops two flat hands down, as if going down another layer.

"Like, hidden meanings?"

"Yes. She still cannot find *Il Toro*, though. It's making her crazy! She is sure he is important, whoever he is, but there is nothing in the *banca dati*. Only regular bulls, the animals, no nicknames, no men. No other mention of him in the pages you've sent. *Che palle!* You *could* be here to help."

He sounds a little annoyed. "I'm sorry. *I can't*, Dante."

He shakes his head.

"It'd be a miracle, though, right? To find him somewhere? The Bull?" Charlotte says. "What if he's Tasso? It all seems impossible."

"Yes, but it is bread for our teeth, huh?" Dante is grinning again at the thought. And then his face freezes, and he's still so adorable, even frozen, and God, if she could only kiss him again, right through that screen.

After dinner, Charlotte's lying on Ella's bed. Ella's giving a fashion show of the new school clothes she got at Target.

"This with this? Or—" Now Ella turns her back to Charlotte to take off her shirt. When she does, Charlotte looks toward the windows of their neighbors' house, and then gets up to make sure the blinds are shut tight. Dave and Diane Simmons are a perfect couple with the perfect yard with perfect flowers, only Dave sometimes peers at them when it's dark and their lights are on. Ella just turned thirteen, but she still has the body of an eleven-year-old, unlike Charlotte herself, who's always slouching to hide her boobs. Ella pops the second shirt over her narrow shoulder blades. "Or *this*?"

"I like them both. For the first day, though . . . maybe the second?"

Charlotte's phone rings. Ella groans. "You're *always* talking to him!"

"Shut up, it's not even Dante!"

It's Avni. For a second, Charlotte doesn't even want to answer. She's had a peaceful few days, not thinking about that bare ass and the eel tongue, and she'll be fine, you know, as long as the whole thing just disappears. Every now and then, she gets scared. Really scared. She knows something she's not supposed to, and he's powerful. At least, more powerful than she is, sitting here in Ella's room, with her old pony collection lined up on her shelf, above her soccer trophies. "One sec, El."

"Ugh!"

Charlotte leaves and then shuts her own door. She thinks of Katerina whispering into the phone. It's all such a secret. Her mother always said secrets are secrets for a reason, but it's more like a million reasons.

"Avni?"

"Hey. How are you?" But she doesn't really wait for an answer. "You're not going to believe this. No, wait, of course you are. There are more. Lots more."

"More of what?" She already knows, though. Suddenly, Charlotte's chest fills with a dark horror. She hopes Avni doesn't answer. She wants to hang up and never speak to Avni again.

"More of *us*."

That *us*—it turns Charlotte's stomach. It makes her into something insignificant—a number. It makes every good moment she had with Luca Bruni into something ugly and used.

"Lots more."

She feels nauseous.

"Are you there?" Avni asks.

"I'm here."

"I guess this blogger from Pulp Media started asking questions."

"Yeah. Eliot told me. A while back. I hadn't heard anything else, so I thought it was maybe over."

"No. Not over. It got too big. *Too big.* There were just too many people to contact and leads to follow up on. She called a friend for help, a reporter from the *Washington Post.*"

"Oh my God."

"They're all over the country. He traveled a lot, you know, tours. God, there's someone I *know*. From my writing program at Hopkins. This girl, Sarah. I talked to her. They met when he was giving a lecture, the year before I was there, when she was a sophomore. He offered to look at her writing. Gave her his personal email. Complimented her work after she sent it. He didn't promise anything outright, but he hinted around—that he might help, get her published, or make contacts, whatever. The things that mattered most to her. Sound familiar?"

"Yeah."

"They met up when he was in our city again. He wanted to meet at his hotel. She didn't really want to go, but she didn't want to cause a problem if she said no. He pressured her to have sex. He got pissed when she said she wanted to go home. She got worried about what he might say to people, how it would affect her whole life. She didn't tell anyone because she *went there*, she met him. It was her own fault, because she should have known. But she didn't know this was just *what he did*. It was his thing. Using his power and influence to get sex and feed his ego. I mean, the sheer numbers are crazy."

"Like what?" Charlotte's head pounds. She could throw up. If she were writing it—no. She doesn't want to write. She doesn't want to write anything ever again. It's like looking under a rock and seeing so many gross things. You want to slam the rock back down.

"Twenty, thirty? If that's the number of people who'll admit to it, imagine how many more there are. No one wants to say anything either, until they find out it happened to other people. Each time someone talks, they're like, 'Um, I think I might know someone else.' There's *a list*."

"I don't know what to say. I'm in shock."

"Rachel, the blogger, said it's, like, a known thing in the publishing world, him being like that. An open secret."

"It wasn't known to me. Not really."

"That's why we have to say something, Charlotte. People don't know. I talked to her. She wants to talk to you."

"Your friend Sarah?"

"The reporter from the *Washington Post*."

"No. I don't want to do that. I can't." The nauseous feeling gets worse. It mixes with a panicky alarm. "What happened to me wasn't that big a deal."

"'Not that big a deal' times thirty, or who knows how many, makes a big deal."

"Avni, no."

"Just *talk* to her."

After Charlotte hangs up, Ella shouts from her room. "Charlotte! Come *on*!"

But she can't come on. She can't move. She sits there feeling horrible and scared. Watching Ella try on her school clothes—it seems so innocent next to all the shame and badness she and all those girls feel about themselves now. And she realizes something else, too—how she was wrong that day when she was watching the gondola race, when she thought that Luca just had a hunger, for all of life, for every experience, the way she did at that moment. Because there was a difference between the yearning that comes from a hunger for life, and the kind of lonely, yawning emptiness that can never be filled. A difference between wanting, and taking and taking and taking.

Chapter Thirty-Six

Laura Cereta, writer and feminist.

One of the first writers to put women's issues at the center of her work, she spoke out about the "slavery" of women in marriage and fought for the right to higher education. Her critics claimed her father actually wrote her work, but she aggressively fought back those claims with words. She wrote with the intention of being famous, seeking immortality through her work, all of which was written between the ages of sixteen and eighteen.

(1469–1499)

The backlash is immediate after the article in the *Washington Post* comes out. Not against Luca Bruni. Nope. This is what happens to him: His agent will no longer represent him, but another one will. A few bookstores say they won't carry his books. An awards committee he's on says they'll conduct an investigation, and the university where he's an adjunct professor insists they're unaware of any allegations, and a handful of articles debate the issue of misogyny. Some readers are angry. Many professors and teachers refuse to change their syllabuses.

Do you know how many people love his work? they say. And then Luca Bruni himself crafts a beautiful piece about how the trauma of his brutal childhood affects his behavior today, writing that he never meant to hurt anyone, that he's learning from the experiences of females, an article which gains him heaps of praise and compassion.

No, the real backlash is against the young women who spoke out, and it's fierce. Brutal. Cruel.

What about Picasso? What about Polanski? What about all the brilliant artists going back to Shakespeare? He *abandoned his family—are we not going to read* Macbeth *because of that? You have to separate the art from the artist. No one is perfect. There's no proof! What did they think was gonna happen? You go out alone with a guy who's been hitting on you? This is censorship! You can't deprive people who need this work, this voice! Rock stars have been having sex with groupies for years, big deal. Are we banning books now? He didn't rape them. It would be different if he committed a crime. Innocent until proven guilty! If you want to exclude all the writers and artists guilty of lust and one-night stands and unwanted overtures, the shelves will be empty and the museum walls will be bare. He's the voice of a generation! History is full of power grabs and scandals and abuse. Denying the relevance of a bad man erases history! A person's art is totally separate from the person. They're taking this political correctness shit too far! Oh, we should* definitely *not teach him in the classroom so no little delicate flowers get "triggered"! Every last one of us is flawed! Every one! Should we not read the Constitution because our founding fathers owned slaves? He hasn't been convicted. Judge the works on their own merits! Since when is making a pass a crime?*

Charlotte has two quotes in the article. One in the second paragraph: *"He flirted with all the female students in the program. I just thought it was how he was," said Charlotte Hodges, from Seattle.* One in the second-to-last paragraph: *"He put his tongue in my mouth as soon as we were in the room," Hodges said of her encounter in August.* Avni has the most quotes, and then Sarah, and then a student in California, Maya, and then Katerina, and then Charlotte. The amount of times they're called *cunt* (and she hates that word, *hates*) in the comments also seems to follow this ratio. Avni—eighteen, Sarah—twelve, Maya—nine, Kat—seven, Charlotte—five. Charlotte writes the tally on a Post-it and crosses the number off when there are more, but then there are too many to count. Other comments repeat again and again in different ways. *They were just fucking him to get ahead. Cock tease.* I *would never have gone to a hotel room with the guy. She's trying to ruin him 'cause she's jealous. They* knew *he was married. They weren't thinking about his wife, were they?* All of these comments mean the same thing: she got what she deserved.

The comments and name-calling go up for Charlotte after someone finds the photo she posted that summer, of her with her head on Luca's shoulder when they were joking around. @Bookluvergirl tweets the photo with her quote from the article, and within minutes the comments begin rolling in. *HE flirted with all the students? Clearly, SHE was the flirt. Yeah, she doesn't look so innocent. Asking 4 it! I wouldn't want to stick my tongue in THAT. Tongue tart,* @Readermom476 says. *LOL!* replies @Literatee, with a GIF of a mouth opening and closing. *User.*

And you know, she *had* used him. Charlotte remembers how she felt when she posted that. She was proud. She wanted people to see it. It made her look important. But @Literatee and @Bookluvergirl and the hundreds of people who took photos with him used him too. *He* was also an object. A product. He was this thing: FAMOUS, and everyone wanted to be near that thing. It had nothing to do with who he really was. She wanted to be different from all those people who used him, but when she posted that photo, she wasn't. He also knew that, though, didn't he? Her adoration was useful to him. It meant she'd do almost anything for him. She knew how this felt, kind of. Adam used to do anything for her. He adored her like that, and sometimes, she was reckless with it. She and Luca Bruni *both* had ego, but only one had power.

"Stop reading the comments," her mother says. "Shut your laptop."

"Stop reading the comments," Yasmin tells her for the hundredth time. "Seriously, stop."

"Call me, Charlotta. I know, this is the drop that makes the vase overflow, but please! Don't disappear," Dante says.

"Jesus, Char. He's almost as old as I am," her father says.

It's one of those times when you hate your phone. How can one little rectangle be so loud? It's a million voices loud. Charlotte sometimes sticks it under her pillow or in a drawer, and it only comes out when her safe people call—Dante, Yas, Katerina, Avni. She's ignoring everyone else. Carly keeps calling and texting, but Carly makes Charlotte feel guilty. Carly knows Charlotte's wrongdoing. Adam texts too, just one, a thoughtful Hope you're okay, and it doesn't ask for anything, but it's embarrassing, because he knows. Everyone knows. She gets a text from a girl she sat by in orchestra, Reilly Rodriguez, saying thank you for speaking out, because her sister had something like that happen to her. She gets a note in the mail from her freshman-year biology teacher, Ms. Bricks, telling her it takes courage to speak up, sharing a story of her own from college, when she had to report a professor. It's signed *Susan*, not *Ms. Bricks*, and the kindness, the outreach, chokes Charlotte up. Her throat squeezes, and she puts both palms to her eyes after reading it. It means a lot. Mr. McNulty and Ms. Perlman—Charlotte can only wonder how they feel about this.

And then, a few days after the article comes out, the doorbell rings. Marvin starts barking his head off, and then Ella shouts, "Charlotte! Come dooooown!" She can hear Carly talking to her mom, since it's Adele's day off at Dr. Denton, DDS's.

Oh, God. Charlotte puts her head in her hands.

"CHAR-LOTTE," Ella yells.

When she goes downstairs, there is beautiful Carly, holding a card. Ella is sticking her nose down into a paper plate of cookies covered in Saran Wrap. Charlotte is sure she doesn't deserve the love of her friends, but she has it anyway.

"Chocolate chip. They're kinda hard. You know I suck at

baking," Carly says when Charlotte reaches the living room. She gives her the envelope. "Open."

The front of the card features a beautiful old library. The inside says, *I love you more than books.*

Charlotte blinks. Damn it, she's going to cry again. The thing is—it makes her realize something she forgot. Something obvious. People should come before books. People should come before all art. A tear slides down Charlotte's nose.

"I don't know if I ever told you this," Carly says. "It's kind of, I don't know, personal? Embarrassing? But my grandma only learned to read a couple of years ago."

"Wow." It's hard to imagine a life that long without books in it. Charlotte thinks of Carly's grandma Baba, who came from Croatia, in her little housecoats with Kleenex and wrapped candies in the pockets. She never even thought to ask much about Baba before.

"One of the first adult books she read was *A Mile of Faces.* It took her *months.* When she got to the end, she kept saying, *Shh, shh, shh.* I'll never forget when she finished. The last page . . . She was crying. She had to wipe her eyes and blow her nose. And then she stared up at me and didn't say anything. It was just . . . She saw the magic."

Carly, beautiful, strong Carly, incredible athlete, who can throw a javelin like it's a matchstick—she looks helpless. Charlotte can't speak. Ella is silent too. Adele has appeared in the doorway, but she just stands there, and even Marvin is sitting like a quiet gentleman, just watching.

"He's broken my heart," Carly says. "He's broken so many hearts, Char. You should have seen Baba when she heard about this. She wasn't just disappointed. She was *crushed*."

And now, here's the funny thing: Carly isn't comforting Charlotte. Charlotte is comforting *her*. Charlotte's fears of blame slink away to the dungeon they belong in. She wraps her arms around her friend. "Thank you for speaking out," Carly says softly.

Ella—well, it's probably partly her anxiety, but she gets carried away in the emotion, and she charges at Charlotte and Carly and wraps her arms around them too, group hug, a wobbly group, which gets off-balance and stumbles backward toward the couch. Then Marvin gets carried away, probably *his* anxiety, and he starts barking and jumping like a wild guy.

"Oh my God!" Carly says, laughing. Her butt is half off the couch.

"Get off! Get off!" Charlotte cries, because Ella has fallen on top of her.

"Ow, your toenails, Marv!" Ella shrieks as the dog hops up on their legs.

"You guys!" Adele says. "Someone's going to get hurt!"

Which is ridiculous, of course. They've been hurt already. All of them have. Even Baba, a once-illiterate old lady from Croatia, who Luca Bruni doesn't even know exists.

And then things take an even darker turn. The comments and name-calling go up by a jillion when bestselling author Jocelyn

K. Sullivan retweets Charlotte's photo, with the comment *WOW. L.B. is my longtime friend, and he's never been anything but kind and funny and full of RESPECT FOR WOMEN. #CON.*

Or rather, the comments and name-calling go up by 285,000, the number of followers Jocelyn K. Sullivan (*author, rebel grrl, lover of pancakes*) has, multiplied by *their* followers. Jocelyn K. Sullivan's book of stories was a finalist for the *LA Times* Book Prize, and the adaptation of her book *Stop Time* just came out in theaters. *Hasn't he gone through enough in his life? I NEVER saw him flirt.*

What a spoiled bitch, replied Daniela Reynaldo (*novelist and grammar snob, de rigueur 4 evah*), 325,000 followers.

People forgot to do the math. If this were an ancient Roman stadium (and honestly, that's what it feels like), there were 285,000 plus 325,000 lions and one her. Power times a half million, and she still lives at home and can't even afford to buy her own car yet. *Lots* of people could forget about the power they had. Lots and lots and lots, and not always the ones you'd expect, either.

Avni gets packages in the mail that scare her. Threats, pornography. Someone puts a pile of shit on Katerina's step. Someone keeps taping condoms to Sarah's windshield. Charlotte gets a tiny bottle of mouthwash in her mailbox: *Use this next time.* Avni gets in a car accident, she's so distracted. Avni's writing means everything to her, but why open herself up to what will happen if she's ever even able to get published? she tells Charlotte. Katerina's so anxious she can barely do normal life stuff, let alone write. She changed majors. Creative writing doesn't mean what it used to. When Avni can't stand one more comment about her breasts or *fuckability* or the color of her skin, she shuts down her social media accounts. Kat's roommates force her to go to her university's counseling center when she won't get out of bed. She's having nightmares about him and that orphanage, the babies thrown into the water. Charlotte's arms have broken out in a nervous rash. She feels angry and short-tempered one minute, and teary and filled with regret the next. The words people have used—they circle her mind like wolves. Her mouth does feel dirty.

None of these people, *none* of them, know Avni, or Katerina, or Charlotte. They don't know what they love or what their dreams are or what haunts them. They don't know how talented Avni is, and how afraid she can be, down deep. They don't know about Katerina, how she lives that moment again and again, when her mother walked away forever. They don't know Shaye, either. Shaye, who has been silent. Shaye, who no one has heard from. Shaye, with her hard-drinking dad. Shaye, who pretends to be tough but really isn't, who writes with this strange fierceness that makes you want to cry. Who must feel terrified and wrecked now too, even if whatever they did was something she wanted. Even if she maybe loved him. Especially if she did. She must have really gotten a knife to her heart, Shaye with her tattoo, *Deeds not words.* And her other tattoo—*I refuse to sink.* Charlotte hopes it's true, that Shaye still refuses to sink, though they may never find out what happens to her.

And those people don't know Charlotte, who tries her best, and still gets a little nervous when she drives on the freeway, who gets those stupid migraines, and has a favorite dinner choice, chicken parmigiana, when her family goes to Olive Garden. Those people don't know them at all.

But they don't know Luca Bruni, either.

The one thing that's maybe hardest for Charlotte to understand: How many women's lives are equal to one man's?

Chapter Thirty-Seven

Laura Beatrice Cappello, poet.

From a noble family in Venice, she entered the convent most likely as a teen. She was tutored by poet Filippo Binaschi, and male poets addressed poetry to her, even love poems. Though she was a nun, her work appeared in a 1559 anthology of female poets, since she was already well known at nineteen.

(1540–1617)

For the last few weeks, Charlotte has mostly stayed inside. She doesn't want to go out. Not to get coffee, not to see friends, not anywhere, for any reason. She definitely can't imagine starting college, so she decides to wait until winter quarter to start at Seattle U, which upsets her dad. Honestly, she wants everyone and everything to just stay away, as if she's under her own quarantine from the plague. Yasmin, though—she's as determined about Charlotte's mental health as she is with everything else. Yas got that internship at NASA, and she got into Stanford on scholarship, and now, home again for a visit, she's going to bring Charlotte back into the world. It's one of the biggest jobs of friends, Charlotte knows, to bring each other back into the world, but she doesn't want to be someone's job. *Halloween party. You're coming,* Yasmin says. *You don't even have to wear a costume, okay?*

The party is at a house in the University District, fifteen minutes or so from Fremont, where Charlotte lives. She borrows her mom's car. From the second she drives up and sees all the people standing out on the front porch, and hears the thump of music, she begins to feel anxious. This was a wrong move. There are zombies, and horrible creatures with open wounds, and too many girls dressed like sexy cats in fishnet stockings. And she's uncovered, no costume, no mask to hide behind. It's fall, and the air is damp, nothing like the warmth of those summer nights, but it whooshes back, the dinners on La Calamita, the sky strung with stars and white lights. She hears the music, a record spinning on a record player, the sound of longing and mystery, so very different from the opinionated thump coming from that house, and she hears the clink of glasses and laughter around the table. It's weird, but here at this party, it's like she's outgrown something she hasn't even experienced yet.

The house is in a dangerous neighborhood, where there are frequent robberies, and assaults, mostly young women walking along with their iPhones out and purses swinging. After she locks her car, Charlotte wears her handbag across her chest and keeps her valuables concealed, except, you know, the most valuable thing, her actual self, is hard to hide. And now that private things about her are so very public, Luca Bruni and his tongue in her mouth is practically written on her skin, like a tattoo for every passerby to gawk at.

Glowing pumpkins flicker on the porch, jack-o'-lanterns with grimacing mouths. A guy and a girl talk on the lawn. He's a medieval knight, and she's a witch in a tight black dress. He leans in and kisses her. There's loud laughter that sounds like people are already drunk. On La Calamita, she gets in a speeding boat and drives away from that villa, the hospital for the doomed, and away from Bruni, the mad doctor coming out of the doors of the tower, asking what haunts them. She heads to the ancient, tilting Venice, with its wavery reflections in the canals, and the smell of the water, old, and deep, and full of secrets. Her own kiss waits for her, because there is Dante with his dark curls and eyes so soulful, you'd be tempted to call them pools, because who wouldn't want to jump in.

Inside the Seattle house, she walks sideways between the jammed-in people and the Goodwill couches and tries to find Yasmin. Yasmin knows the party-giver's girlfriend. She thinks she hears Yasmin's voice in the kitchen, and yeah, there she is, dressed as a unicorn, talking to her friend, whose pink hair, nose ring, and flannel shirt are just life as usual in Seattle, and to a guy who looks like someone she knew in middle school, who's wearing a T-shirt that says *Error 404, Costume not found.* He's scraping pita chips around the side of a plastic container of hummus, mostly gone.

"Char!" Yasmin hugs her hard and long, so hard and long

that anyone looking on can tell that it's a Hug of Meaning. A hug that says she's recently experienced something of great difficulty, a hug that says too much.

"Hey. You look adorable."

"I am so hot in this thing, I'm dying." Yas waves her unicorn hoof in front of her face. "This is my friend Peyton. Peyton, Charlotte."

"I'm going as the person who only has plaid in her closet," Peyton says.

"Hey, we have the same costume," Charlotte says, sticking her arm next to Peyton's. Peyton laughs. Just being in this room with people doing ordinary things makes pieces of her body ache. Yasmin hands her a Diet Coke, because Yas hates when people drink when they're not allowed to yet.

"You go to UW?" Peyton asks.

"Seattle U, but not yet? I'm starting late—winter quarter."

"I want to take a quarter off. Maybe ski season," the guy in the *Error 404* shirt says.

"Nice," Charlotte says. *He's* nice, too. It gives her a little courage, remembering that there are nice people in the world, lots of them. Someone turns the music way up, and someone else yells, "Turn it down! The neighbors are dicks!"

"Hey, you could catch up on your Hawthorne." Peyton pokes his shoulder. And then to Charlotte: "Logan and I met in contemporary fiction. Aka, Famous White Dudes of Lit."

Charlotte's face flushes. It's really, really hot in there. Her courage is gone just like that. This was a mistake.

"Wait . . . ," Peyton says. "You. Oh my God! Yasmin's friend *Charlotte*? I know who you are! Let me just say, *thank you*, you know. On behalf of everyone who's been there." She raises a fist, as if they're all in this together, but anxiety is filling Charlotte, because they aren't all in this together. She's learned that. There isn't an all. There isn't a together. There should be, but there isn't.

"*Luca Bruni?*" Peyton says to Logan. It's explanation enough. His eyes go wide.

"No shit?" he says. "Charlotte of *the tongue*?" The pita chip stops halfway to his mouth. Then he actually sets it down. Straight on the counter, no napkin, no nothing, because he can put that thing wherever he wants.

"Hey, watch it," Yasmin scowls, an angry unicorn.

He holds a hand up. "Hey—we're fine. I don't mean it in a bad way. I get it."

But Charlotte has frozen. She knows whenever someone says, "I get it," that they don't get it. They'll never in a million years get it.

Logan folds his arms. "I'm not gonna stop reading the guy, though. Hey, I'm sorry, but if we cut out all the creative assholes who did shit like that, we wouldn't have Salinger. We wouldn't have *Dickens*."

"Hey, Yas?" Charlotte says. "I think I'm going to . . ." She's backing away. Already, she's almost to the kitchen door.

Yasmin reaches for her arm. "I'm sorry, I'm sorry! Don't go."

"What did Dickens do?" Charlotte hears Peyton say.

"Eighteen-year-old mistress. The wife found out, and then he made the wife look mentally disturbed in his writing."

"What an asshole."

"Yeah, but what about *Great Expectations*, *David Copperfield*, *A Christmas Carol* . . . ?" He's counting on his fingers, but now Charlotte is in the living room, scooting herself through the crowd, bumping a guy's elbow, causing him to spill his beer.

"Fuck! Be careful!" the guy says.

"Char." Yasmin grabs her arm. "He doesn't know what he's talking about. He's a creep."

Who knows if that's even true. He didn't look like a zombie or a monster, just a regular guy in a T-shirt.

"I gotta go."

Yasmin takes her fingers. "Please try again," she shouts over the noise.

"Next time," Charlotte lies.

It's a cool fall night, and she rolls down all the windows in the car so she can smell it better—the delicious mix of moss and rotting leaves plus clouds full of rain. There's the big glowing moon again, reminding her that stuff is old, old, old. It's the kind of night that makes the words come, words that she wants to write down, but won't. *Swirl*, and *stars*, and *light* and *dark* and all the words in between those words.

She pulls up into their driveway. A few lights are on inside. She's relieved to get home. It hasn't been all that safe of a place lately, with her mom's temper, and her parents fighting, and her dad, silent with judgment. But it's the safest she's got.

Marvin hops up around her knees, and she pets his head and drops her bag onto a kitchen chair. She looks in the fridge for something to solve all her problems. Milk and eggs, ketchup and yogurt. Nearly empty salad dressings, something covered in Saran Wrap—it's not enough. The fridge door slaps shut.

Upstairs, she can hear the soft murmur of her mother on the phone. Ella's already asleep. Charlotte gets into bed. Sleep has been a problem. When she lies down, it's like she's been on a boat for a long time. Her head spins. Her body is a buoy, sloshing around at the whim of the waves, bashing into docks. Washed ashore, mostly. Picked at by gross seagulls and kicked by strangers.

Tonight, the moon is so bright. It's been there longer than five hundred years, and it's hard to believe, but it's the same one Isabella di Angelo once gazed at. That moon knows more than the sorry humans it shines its light on. Charlotte doesn't ask it for magic, though. She just gets out of bed.

She opens her laptop. This is the laptop that she worked her butt off to buy, two jobs after school her junior year (waitress at George's Café, and tutoring little Aiden Harlo in fifth-grade math). This is the laptop that she wrote "The Blue Night" on, the story that got her into Bruni's program. And it's the one she brought with her on that astonishing, incredible, *no way!* trip to Italy that summer. It was a Laptop of Hope. Now all of the stories she's written on it are hidden in a blue icon on the desktop named *Untitled Folder.*

She types *Luca Bruni* into the search engine bar. She narrows the results to the past week. To her horror, the results pour in. Interviews, blog reviews of his book releasing in just a few weeks. Announcements of upcoming appearances. *Volumes Books, Denver, Luca Bruni, beloved author of* A Mile of Faces *and more, 7 p.m.* Worse: love, love, love for him. Endless love. Everyone's favorite. The guy on every syllabus, in every lesson plan, the guy that everyone recommends, because he's so awesome. Forever and abundant love, and she knows that will never be enough for him.

Her stomach aches, or maybe that's her heart. It's the whole middle part of her body, so it's hard to tell.

He goes on; she doesn't.

Now she looks up a word: *quarantine*. Based on *quarantino*, Italian for *forty*, the number of days you were required to stay in isolation during the Black Death, the plague. First use: Venice. Of course. She's been in that house longer than forty days now, though.

The phone startles her. It's after midnight. Dante never usually calls this late. He worries about her, with everything she's going through, and always tries not to wake her. When she answers, his face is so sweet, and such a wonderful sight, she almost wishes she were back there. She can't go back there, but for a second she wants to.

"Charlotta!" His eyes are lit with electricity, and he almost sounds alarmed.

"What? Are you okay?"

"I hope you are not sleeping, but you won't believe it! Dottoressa Ricci just phoned me."

When he says this . . . she feels the smallest sliver of light inside. Dim as old moonlight, but there.

"But it's Saturday morning."

"Saturday, Sunday, Monday. It doesn't matter! I tell you, she has a nail on the head! She can only think of Isabella, Isabella, same as when she studied Veronica Franco. But, Charlotta, she found something. In the baptismal records of San Zaccaria."

"Baptismal records? We already know about Isabella's birth."

"But we didn't realize she had *a child*."

Chills shoot up her arms. Charlotte's heart speeds. She's suddenly full of nervous energy. She picks up her laptop and paces her room as Dante speaks.

"It's obvious, *sì*? But not to us! *Ai nostri occhi sono foderati di prosciutto*, Charlotta! Our eyes were covered with ham! Matteo was the only child of the doge. And Isabella was the only child of Matteo. If there are descendants, *she* had to have had a child herself."

"Oh my God. Of course. Why didn't we even think of that?"

"Dottoressa Ricci *did*. From the first day! She has been searching for Isabella's name in the baptismal records of San Zaccaria, and now she has found her! This was maybe the event, you see, that changed her writing from book one to book two? Because the first book, well, she writes about love of God, and love of Venice, but Dottoressa Ricci believes this is not the true meaning. 'He is a lamp at my feet.' 'He will always be praised in my thoughts and soul.' 'Him, distant, I have sent my silent note.' *He*, and him, so many times! And when she talks of her city, she mentions 'the warm desire that rises in the breast of those who love in absence,' and 'the ardent fire of her love.' That is passionate, yes, for a city?"

"I like Seattle, but there is no warm desire that rises in the breast."

"*Love*, Charlotta. She's writing about love for a man."

"A man."

"Yes. But then, in the second book . . . she is angry, and outspoken. Dottoressa Ricci thinks she has been unjustly punished. A man, men, have used their power against her. This is *logico*, yes? Think of what happened to Sister Antonia. Jailed. Perhaps killed. We don't know what they might have done to Isabella. But a baby was born. A daughter, Marina Cara."

"Marina Cara?"

"The baby."

It's crazy, but this name fills Charlotte's heart with some delicate, exquisite *hope*. Maybe even *love*. "Did they list a father?"

"No father. But we can guess maybe who? It is right there, in his biographies."

"Antonio Tasso," Charlotte says.

"Antonio Tasso." On the screen, Dante beams. "We will look for proof. Charlotta, you must come back. You'll bring the book. I'm not asking for the moon. Dottoressa will pay."

"Dante . . ."

"All right, all right. I know, I know. But when can you send more pages from *The Verses*? In the last ones you sent, there were two poems written for a person. *Mia Laura. Cara Laura.* Who is this Laura?"

"*Cara*, the baby's name, too," Charlotte says.

"It means *beloved*, *dear one*. We don't know if there is a connection! Now we are trying many combinations—Laura and *Il Toro*. Laura and Isabella and *Il Toro*. In the *banca dati*, but also, I am searching one by one, the letters from the flood. 'This is where we will find the story,' Dottoressa Ricci says. 'In letters, where people speak freely to each other.' This was the truth when she studied Veronica Franco. Can you send more pages soon? *Dai!* Dottoressa Ricci is *un osso duro*."

"The minute I wake up," Charlotte says. "I promise."

"*Grazie a Dio! Mille grazie.*"

After they hang up, Charlotte's spirit feels . . . lifted. Overcome, with the brief, bright beauty of a sunrise. A baby. A baby! *Marina Cara*.

How could she not have realized it before? There *had* to have been a child, if she herself is a descendant. It seems astonishing. It seems like a miracle, that someone survived. That they kept on surviving for five hundred years.

Chapter Thirty-Eight

Modesta Pozzo
(wrote under the pseudonym Moderata Fonte), feminist writer, poet, and playwright.

Mostly unknown until 1980, she was an important writer of her time, influencing other female writers like Arcangela Tarabotti and Lucrezia Marinella. She herself was inspired by teen writer Issicratea Monte. Her best-known work is The Worth of Women: Wherein Is Clearly Revealed Their Nobility and Superiority to Men, *a debate on sex roles, but she also championed equal access of education to women and wrote both romance and religious works. She was considered a child prodigy and died at thirty-seven.*

(1555–1592)

Charlotte crouches on her knees in the basement, *The Verses* carefully opened in front of her. She aims her phone camera down. *Snap.* Next page. *Snap.* Her long dark hair is pulled back into a ponytail, which swings down over one shoulder. She's wearing the same old sweatpants and T-shirt she keeps putting on day after day, because, aside from her brave attempt at that party the night before, she's barely left the house. In middle school, she used to be embarrassed when she'd have a blemish on her face, but now her whole self feels like a blemish. Her decisions, the parts of her body, the mouth he put his tongue in.

Snap. Turn page. *Snap.* Her eyebrows scrunch together as she peers down, trying to get a clear image for Dr. Ricci. This feels urgent. Dr. Ricci's determination, her obsession, her skill, matched with Charlotte's despair and need, all heading toward Isabella's pain and passion from another time—it has a strange alchemy. It is all happening at the dot, Charlotte can feel it. It's possible, isn't it, that a book can save you? Books have always saved her, ever since *In Max's room a forest grew.* But of course, books can ruin you too, because, well, look what's happened. *The Glass Ship* transported her from her own bedroom to a haunted island.

Snap. Turn page. *Snap!* Turn page! She's sick and tired of despair, of her self-quarantine from a different sort of plague. Sick of heartbreak, and shame, and hiding. She's restless, but it's the insistent kind of restless. Do you know that agitation you feel when you're searching and searching for a good book? It's that times a million. The kind of agitation where you don't even know the particulars of what you need. Just *something.* Rescue, answers, comfort, a place to disappear. It's a lot to ask from any book, even *The Verses.*

Rain patters on garbage can lids and drips off the long, bare finger-branches of fall. She's been at this for hours. She sits up from her slouch, stretches. Cranes her neck left and then right to urge the kinks out. She tilts her chin down and then up. Up—her eyes land on the bookshelf in front of her. Lately, she can't read, let alone write. The way she loves, *loved*, books—it feels gone. Maybe gone forever. The thing about *after* is that it's permanent.

And then, shit. Shit! What the hell! God, what is that doing here? The big blocky font shouts. The shiny red cover waves its arms. She stands up and grabs the novel and flings it like something slimy and dead. How had she missed it before? How had any of them not noticed? No idea, but ugh! *The Forever King* has been sitting on their shelf all this time. Gross, gross, gross.

It thunks on the floor, lands over by the wicker rocker. But down there on the carpet, the book just asserts its presence. It's loud, the way objects can sometimes be, the way kings can be, and so Charlotte sticks a pillow on it, and then another one, and she can still hear that book under there, so she sticks some more books on it to drown it out. The pile of stuff looks a little unhinged, so she covers it with an afghan some old relative made. It's still loud. And magnetic, insisting that she *see* him.

She puts her head into her hands. She puts her head into her hands. She presses her palms to her eyes with a surge of grief. Tears spill and then roll down her nose. She's mad at herself for crying. She doesn't want to cry anymore, but too bad. Crying decides when it's done, not you.

But *when* will it be done, how? Her chest aches with sadness. Her heart feels like a knotted ball of loss. And the thought is unwelcome, but it's there anyway: she misses him. She misses Luca Bruni. She misses the glass ship enchantment of him—the grand, the glittering, the impossible and dreamlike *fiction* of him.

She misses her *belief* in that. Her *love* of that.

And she misses the magic of his words. She is heartbroken with longing for that moment when *The Glass Ship* rested on her knees as she sat alone in her room at night, when that magic was something pure and powerful to her, and nothing else. When those words filled her and understood her and changed her.

She wipes her eyes with her sleeve. She clears her throat. And she looks down at what else is on the floor. There's the book that can't be silenced even with all the stuff on top of it, and there's the one sitting right there out in the open that she doesn't even listen to right then.

That ancient vellum book, that voice. Those words.

And damn it, she realizes it. It hits her so hard, like a wave, like a flood, like a sudden swell finally strong enough to sink any untouchable glass ship riding any imaginary sea: he's not the only one with the magic. There were lots of people with the magic—women like Isabella di Angelo and Arcangela Tarabotti and Veronica Franco and even the sisters sneaking their voices into art, their signatures. Them, along with hundreds of others who have vanished, who have been unseen, or overlooked, or ignored, or forgotten, five hundred years ago or today.

Snap. Turn page. *Snap*, goddamn it. Books might fill you or change you, but that change was *yours.*

"Char?" her mother yells.

"I'm here!"

"Are you still down there? You've been there forever."

She has. She's been taking photos for hours, only getting up to eat a snack or pee, and then she goes back to *The Verses.* Dante interrupts with texts. *Mille grazie, bella. Mille grazie, polpetta. Mille grazie, amore mio.* A thousand thanks, beautiful, little meatball, my love. Her body feels like a gnarled old tree, but she keeps going.

Her mother pops her head into the basement. "Char, you need to stop. That book has been here for years. This isn't exactly urgent."

But it is. How can she explain? *It's time.*

"She wrote that poem. She did. And she had a baby, and then something happened to her."

"Honey, I know. But you can't *do* this to yourself."

"She became *a mother*, mom. Isabella is *yours*, too. And Ella's! The answers are *somewhere.*"

Charlotte looks up. She and Adele . . . They meet eyes.

Adele knows where that *somewhere* is. Charlotte never thought she'd ever, ever, ever have a desire to go back there, but right then she feels the tiniest flicker of want. It seems astonishing and horrible, that flicker. It's the relentlessness of unfinished business, past and present.

Adele spots that look in her eyes. "Forget it," she says. "No way. What if he's there?"

"He won't be. He's been promoting his book, and he lives in Boston during the winter anyway."

It's a lie. She saw Luca Bruni's tour schedule online, for the novel that used to be called *Moment before the Fall* but is now titled *The Lion*. It's his last stop: *Libreria Toletta, Venice*, in just a few days. Libreria Toletta, the large bookstore near Ca' Foscari University, where Dante goes. Who knows how long Luca will be staying, but he's probably there, in Venice, right now. She imagines him strutting around the narrow streets, people calling out to him, commanding attention just by the way he walks. She imagines, what? Bumping into him, maybe. Some big, final confrontation, where she gives him what he deserves and puts this ugly mess to rest forever. But this is a lie too. This flash of fury-revenge is the kind you have when you're safe in your own basement, because, in truth, the idea of seeing him makes her anxious to the point of nausea.

"No, Charlotte. Just no, okay?"

"I have to keep sending these, then," Charlotte says.

Her mother sighs. "Let me bring you some dinner."

Charlotte's eyes are so dry, it hurts when she blinks. She sends the last pages, the final poem. She lies on her back right there on the carpet. It's dark outside the windows, and the only sounds are the patter of rain and the *ticktick* of the wall clock. It's so late. You'd think she'd be falling asleep right there, but she's weirdly jazzed. As she stares at the ceiling, she remembers the beautiful dome of San Zaccaria painted with the white puffy clouds and cupid angels.

Her phone buzzes right by her head, startling her. She has the ringer off so it won't wake anyone.

"I can't move," she says to Dante. "I seriously can't believe I finished."

"Tesoro! Bella tesoro!"

God, hearing him makes her so happy. He does. "You are the sweetest and the cutest, and I adore you," she says. You can say stuff like that in the vulnerable folds of no sleep.

"Sono pazzo di te."

"I'm crazy about *you*."

His voice turns serious. "You have to come now."

"Dante . . ."

"No, I mean it, Charlotta. You do. Dottoressa Ricci . . . She found . . . At first, she found one letter. When she searched 'Laura,' plus '*Il Toro*,' plus 'San Zaccaria' . . . A letter, Charlotta, from your Isabella di Matteo Angelo, signed I. M. A. It was addressed to Laura Carafa. And when she looked up Laura Carafa . . . she found a flood of letters, Charlotta, and documents, mentions in a book, even. Laura Carafa was an important nun, a sister with Isabella at San Zaccaria. They were close. They wrote to each other often. There is so much—you must come."

"So much?"

"So much."

"Do we know what happened to Isabella? The baby?"

"There are many letters, Charlotta! So many! We don't even know yet. It will take months! But something important. Very important. Be ready for this news."

"I'm ready."

"A few of the letters have the smallest bit of broken wax. A bit of broken floss."

Her heart nearly stops. "Floss."

"Yes. Like the letter with the poem in the Marciana."

"Oh my God. Are there any more like that one? To the Phoebus guy?"

"No, no. None are to anyone named Phoebus. It is her correspondence, Sister Laura Carafa's. Or *Mia Laura*. *Cara Laura* of the poems! Letters from Isabella, and other people too. But Charlotta. There is another shock."

"Tell me."

"In the first letter she found, your Isabella mentions *Il Ladro*. The Thief. A man she calls *The Thief*! Charlotta, do you know what this means?"

She can barely breathe. "Yes."

"We almost have him. Antonio Tasso. We are so close. The poem! The Thief. The red thread and wax. We just need a bridge, from one to the other. Just a bridge! There is so much here to look through, though. It will take time. Dottoressa says you *must* come."

"I want to. I do. But, God, Dante . . ."

"What? Tell me, and we can fix it."

"He's there. Luca Bruni. Probably right now. For a signing at Libreria Toletta."

"He's here?"

"Maybe he'll just fly in and out, but maybe not. I have no idea."

"Charlotta. I know this will be difficult for you. But this is bigger than him. This is *why* you must come. We cannot fix him being here, but we can fix something that is . . . *al di là di*! Beyond. Dottoressa is right. She says you must find the Thief, not for her, but for *you*."

Al di là di. It sounds so beautiful, beyond.

When she looks back at that moment, Charlotte will always think about the way stories begin so, so much earlier than you realize, long before the first chapter. And she'll think about the way stories continue, too, the way that words carry meaning, over the ages and every circumstance, through plagues and floods and wars, through falling and rising again. She'll think about the way books can save you, and lead you through fog and deep lagoons, down twisting streets and dead ends, and away again, in a speedboat under the moon, white pages riding waves.

But she will also think about the missing books. The books that never were. The voices that fought to be heard but were never heard, or heard and then forgotten. Because there are all the books written by men, but there are all the books *about* those men too. Heavy anthologies, biographies fat with importance, details of those men's birthplaces, and influences, and themes, and deaths. Books filled with extensive notes and careful study. Books thick with power and permission and force. She will imagine a ghost library of all the other books that aren't there, and will never be there. All the voices and stories of women behind one kind of wall or another. Voices and stories stolen by thieves.

And she will remember the thought she has right then, as she looks at that single vellum book, open in front of her. A book written five hundred years ago. The thought is directed at Antonio Tasso, but not just Antonio Tasso. It's a beautiful thought. A shining one:

You're finished, asshole.

Chapter Thirty-Nine

Barbara Salutati, writer, poet, singer, and celebrated courtesan.

She helped write several of Machiavelli's works, though she never received credit. Now, she's primarily known as his lover.

(1520 or so, dates unknown)

The long plane ride is familiar, and the airport is familiar, and standing there at the platform with her bag in the night is familiar. But after what happened, none of it will be magical like the first time, she tells herself.

She's wrong, though. Some things will always be magical—ancient cities, the written word, love. She's riding in a boat once more, but there is no Aldo. There's no opera blasting. No Vivaldi with his young girls in the orphanage. The driver is bored with her, another American tourist. It's a regular taxi, if you can call a beautiful wood-paneled speedboat bumping along in the shimmery darkness *regular*.

And now there it is—that weird, enchanted place, that shabby, spectacular, flickering stage set, that unreal and impossible city on a sinking island in a lagoon. It shouts its stories to her as the boat gets closer. Old stories, of plagues, of doges, of young women locked away, of convents and cruelty and rulers and poets. Art against impossible odds. Newer stories, of different sicknesses, and power and cruelty, and art against impossible odds.

It's late, but of course Dante is there. He wouldn't miss her arrival for anything. His hands are in his pockets. It's a different season, cold now, and he's wearing a coat. It's the first time she's seen him in a coat.

"Dante!" the boat driver calls. She forgot how everyone seems to know each other here.

"Giorgio," Dante calls back, and waves. And then, when he spots her, "Charlotta! Charlotta!"

He practically lifts her out of the boat. Who knows how it happens, but somehow, Giorgio is paid, and her luggage is out, and they're almost at Dante and Maria's house above Alta Acqua Libreria. This takes longer than it should, because they keep stopping to kiss, and stare at each other, and say things like *Can you believe it? You're here*, and *I can't believe I'm here*, and more things involving those important words: *you*, *here*.

Maria is up late too. She hugs Charlotte and kisses both of her cheeks. Charlotte will stay in that perfect, charming, book-filled alcove. There are two quilts on the bed now.

"You have been through so much. You must be so tired," Maria says.

It feels like the most truthful thing anyone has ever said.

She is so, so tired. But in that alcove, in the small circle of Dante and his mother and those books, she can hardly sleep. Too much is waiting. Too much, for too long.

The next morning, when they walk to Biblioteca Marciana, Charlotte swears she can feel him everywhere, Luca Bruni. She expects to see him coming out of doorways, expects to hear his voice suddenly booming from an alley. He's on every corner where they all once stood, and she's sure she sees his particular shoulders on a man on a bridge, but no. He's probably not even there. He's probably on airplane, heading home, since his signing at Libreria Toletta was happening as she herself was buckling her seat belt for takeoff.

When they get to Conservation and Restoration, though, Luca Bruni's shadows vanish. There are several letters on delicate yellowed paper spread across a large table, and shivers run up Charlotte's arms when she sees them. She understands why this all takes so much time now. How anyone can read those letters is a mystery. The handwriting is ornate and smushed onto the page. The way they talked back then was so flowery that it's head-spinning.

"What a remarkable find!" Dr. Ricci has said this, like, twenty times. She's beaming at the letters like they're a newborn baby. Her hair is pinned up as usual, but some strands have escaped, and the green, jeweled bird clip has slipped to an angle. Her cheeks are flushed, and her brown eyes flash. This is what passion looks like, Charlotte can tell.

"This is Laura Carafa's correspondence, you see? A nun at San Zaccaria—letters written to her, which she saved." Dr. Ricci points to a document in a dark, bold hand. "This is one from a Gaetana Ferrazzi. Laura has a *special friend*. It seems they write to each other a lot. He describes her youthful beauty, but also criticizes Laura for her 'sprightliness.'"

"Nice guy," Charlotte says.

"And this one is from Laura's own father. The Carafa family was very influential, and it seems Laura has asked him to use his power to help a friend. A beloved friend, now pregnant, so she is not prosecuted."

"You think this is Isabella?"

"We don't know. There are no names mentioned. He is only writing to Laura to deny her request. 'I say that each and every time a public sin and scandal has been committed, the great leader must oppose the sin publicly.' He refuses help. He thinks she *should* be punished," Dr. Ricci says. "'She is a lascivious girl, in spite of her divine gifts.'"

"He's calling her a slut," Charlotte says.

"He also says that in spite of 'two witnesses,' the father of the baby has denied wrongdoing," Dante says. His eyes are lit with excitement too. "'Secret sins will harm others, but not him.'"

"So basically, even though he was caught, the guy says he didn't do it, and that she sleeps around," Charlotte says. Hey, Blake Trevor tried that trick with Bree Nevars during their junior year.

"But now. *Now.* Do you see *these* two?" Dr. Ricci taps her manicured finger near two letters set apart from the others. "These are to Laura Carafa from your Isabella. Written in her own hand."

It was one thing, imagining Isabella walking those same streets, or living behind the walls of that convent, or saying prayers behind those grates, but these are pieces of parchment she *held.* Those are her words in ink. That small curve of red wax Charlotte sees—Isabella melted it with her own *hands.*

"Can I touch it?"

Dr. Ricci gives a *hmm*, which isn't a yes or a no. Still, Charlotte reaches her finger out to the hardened wax. There's only the lip of the red seal left, nothing else.

"Do you see it?" Dante points. "I. M. A. Her initials. This is why we didn't find them by her name in the *banca dati*. And look. *Mia Laura. Cara Laura.*"

"What do they say?" she asks. *Mia Laura*—it's all Charlotte can make out.

"'I am very glad to hear from you that you are well. It is one of the greatest comforts I have in this world to hear of your welfare,'" Dr. Ricci reads. "Isabella's letter is full of sadness. Of separation. But she tells Laura that her friendship has been a *meraviglia*—a wonder. 'My sister's love may not be forgotten.' Isabella has been sent away somewhere. She uses the word *fuga*—flight, or maybe escape from a prison. She says she is like a deer with an arrow clinging to its side. It is heartbreaking!

This is October 1575. And here is where we see it, the words *Il Ladro*. The Thief."

She taps the words.

"Wow. *Wow.*" It's so crazy. There it is, *Il Ladro*, in Isabella's beautiful script.

"We don't have proof that The Thief is Tasso," Dr. Ricci says. "But she tells Laura that he has taken so much. She speaks of sharing her work with him, of his 'unexpected betrayal' and turning on her with lies."

"It's got to be Tasso," Charlotte says. She can't take her eyes off those words: *Il Ladro*. The Thief.

"Tell her about *Il Toro*," Dante says.

"She is maybe *afraid* to use their names. And if she is angry at The Thief, she is even more angry with The Bull. *He* is the one responsible for her being taken away. Locked up. He is the more cruel and vicious one. He is the one on whom she 'meditates her revenge.' But we don't know who he is! Ugh!"

"We will, we will," Dante assures Dr. Ricci.

"At the end of this, she speaks of 'defending females against the attack and hatred and mockery of men.' Protecting them from the 'social practice' of committing young girls to convents. The same language of her second book! It is signed 'Your truly loving friend while I breathe, I. M. A.' Beautiful. So beautiful."

Charlotte just shakes her head in awe. "What about the other letters?"

"We don't know yet. These have taken *days*. And there are

likely more, and more still when you and Dante search again with this new information. We must check the documents from the flood one by one. You are not here for vacation, you see?" Dr. Ricci presses her lips into a firm line, but her eyes are happy.

"What about the best part?" Dante asks. "We found it yesterday, while you were traveling. Tell her."

"I am saving it for last, Dante." Dr. Ricci beams with the surprise. "Here." She points. "This line in Isabella's letter to Laura Carafa. Do you know what this is?"

It's impossible to read, let alone in Italian. "No idea."

"Be ready for the shock!" Dante says.

Dr. Ricci holds Charlotte's eyes for one long beat, and then reads: "'It is a truth that each soldier carries a quiver of arrows and a well try'd Spear.'" She leans back, folds her arms.

Charlotte's struck. That phrase. Of course she recognizes it: it's one of the lines in Tasso's poem. "Oh my God. She said the same thing in 'In Guerra.' She *did* write it, didn't she? She did." It's incredible. The women who'd been whispering to each other for centuries were telling *the truth*.

"We don't have proof yet," Dr. Ricci says. "This is a phrase in a letter. Scholars will all say, '*She* is quoting *him*.' We need more. But there is one certain thing. "In Guerra"—At War. The soldiers she talks to Laura about here? She is not speaking of armies from different countries. She is speaking of *men* and *women*."

"No," Charlotte says. "No way."

"Yes." Dr. Ricci is so pleased with herself. You've never seen anyone so pleased in all your life.

"All of those term papers, all of those tests, all of those students writing about Tasso and Alexander the Great? All those stupid essays about battles and soldiers and weapons?" Charlotte can't believe it. She just cannot believe this.

"She was writing about a different war. The war between the sexes."

Chapter Forty

Isotta Nogarola, Venetian feminist writer and poet.

Famous by the age of eighteen, she wrote about gender and the nature of women, arguing about the idea that Eve was seen as more sinful than Adam. Her work was met with hostility and false accusations by both men and women, who claimed that "an eloquent women is never chaste." She worried that her fame was because of the novelty of her gender and not her talent, but she inspired generations of others.

(1418–1466)

Dante has gotten a special leave from classes. The research they're doing is more important for his degree in conservation science for the cultural heritage than any class. A discovery like this—a lost poet, the true author of "In Guerra"—it could be one of the most important literary discoveries in decades. Dr. Ricci's already talking about *the book*. The one she'll write, with their help, same as she wrote about Veronica Franco. *Better, even!* she says. A book to replace a missing volume on the shelf of the ghost library.

That week, after work, after typing endless variations of words into the *banca dati*, sifting through the meaningless results, and searching the flood documents until her eyes blur, Charlotte and Dante have dinner with Maria at home. Or they go to a *bacaro* and eat *cicchetti*—small plates of fried meatballs or shrimp or hot crostini with *lardo* or Parmesan. There's no sign of Luca Bruni. He probably did go home. Maria hasn't heard anything, and no one they know has seen him. Charlotte begins to relax and feel safe. She lets the city become hers, and hers and Dante's, even more.

They kiss in alleys and up against walls, but it's cold and drizzly outside. Their coats get sopping wet, and drops of rain dampen Dante's curls and drip from Charlotte's nose. It's romantic the first few times, but then just soggy. Love is easier in the summer. It's hard to find anywhere private, and Dante has those hips and those jeans, and those soulful eyes. A few times, they stay late at the Biblioteca Marciana, when the lights are dim, and, surrounded by history and books, and right across from the Doge's Palace, the palace of her very own ancestor, they have sex. It's not especially comfortable, but who cares. This imperfect is perfect. *Sei la mia vita*, he whispers in her ear. She doesn't need to know what it means exactly. She can feel what it means.

By the third day of working on the second letter, they have a good sense of what it says. Laura and Isabella had been discussing an altarpiece. It's almost finished. Isabella congratulates Laura on her years of work and dedication. Dr. Ricci explains how the nuns would commission the art for churches, raise money to pay the artists, influence what was in the art itself. Charlotte knew this already, but she listens again carefully. It all feels different when it's right here in front of her. Isabella's friend Laura Carafa is one of those nuns who wields her artistic power behind walls.

There's more to the letter, though. Isabella hears that The Thief has gotten married. There's talk of the procession through the city, and the *cassa*.

"A house?" Charlotte guesses.

"No, no, no!" Dr. Ricci scowls. She can be a little impatient. "In other regions, they call it a *cassone*, but in Venice, *cassa*. Do you know it?"

"Not really. A caisson? I know what *that* is. It's a watertight box. We made one for our physics project."

Dr. Ricci shakes her head. "Before the *nozze*—the legal ceremony of marriage—there was a procession through the city, following the bride as she moved from her childhood home to the home of her groom. She would often travel on a white horse, with a belt that her father had put around her waist to tell everyone she was chaste. Often the bride was a child, fourteen or younger, to make certain she was a virgin. The groom, well, he would be in his thirties, a match decided years before."

"Gross," Charlotte says. She imagines Ella on that horse, heading toward some old dude—ugh. She forces away the thought.

"The *cassa*—it was carried in the procession. It was a very large wooden chest, highly decorated, and the bride's dowry went into it. Clothing, jewelry, money, deeds to property sometimes, gathered for *years*. To pay him, for taking her. Girls had to have one for the convent, too, but they were small and plain, not much inside. So the convent was a cheap option, yes, for families? That's why many of those girls were there."

"It didn't leave them a lot of choices. Get married, or go to the convent."

"Or become a prostitute," Dante reminds.

"Choices? There were no *choices*," Dr. Ricci says. "Here. Let me show you the *cassa*."

She types on her computer, and Charlotte moves to her side to see. "They look like fancy caskets, but bigger," Charlotte says. Some are even on platforms, rising high like the tombs she's seen in the churches here.

"Here's a nice one for you, Charlotta, with the wedding scene," Dante jokes, and she socks him.

"So, in the letter, Isabella talks about the *cassa* and The Thief getting married. But she also tells Laura that *Il Toro*, The Bull, has written to her. He has been cruel. He is *del mio mal superbo*, 'heedless of my pain,' she says. She is awaiting her fate somewhere. And she is scared. 'How bereft and deprived I am of all hope,' she says."

"That's awful," Charlotte says. "I'm worried."

"I am too," Dr. Ricci says. "This is very bad. At the end, though, she seems to be sharing a joke with Laura. Laura has made her some kind of *pignus*. A pledge or a promise. It's a secret that pleases them very much."

"What promise?"

"Listen." Dr. Ricci reads. "'If you do so, I will be always

immovable! If you scorn the cruel *Il Toro*, and that vulgar throng, my desired yearnings will aspire to the heavens for eternity! Oh, who could tell what we speak of? With you, my very self is concealed!'"

"What does she mean?"

"I don't know!" Dr. Ricci throws her hands up. "This promise Laura is making her—Isabella also says it will be like her own *anellamento*. The part of the wedding ceremony where the ring is placed on her finger. *L'anellamento. L'anello.* The ringing, the ring."

Charlotte's been back in Venice for eight days now. Eight days of waking up in that book-filled alcove, eight days of tiny cups of espresso in the morning before they head to Biblioteca Marciana. Every now and then when Charlotte's alone, taking a walk to call home or to text Yas or Carly, say, or going out to get lunch, she's looked across the canal at the small island of La Calamita. She can't see it very well from there. She's not even sure she wants to. That whole island is a struggle, a solid piece of unfinished business she has to contend with before she goes on to whatever comes next.

On that eighth day, her neck is knotted and her shoulders feel like they've become permanently hunched. They haven't found any more letters. The original "In Guerra," in a slender glass case, now sits on one of the tables, removed from its usual room for further study. Dr. Ricci wants them to hunt for both *Il Ladro* and *Il Toro* again too, in all of Laura

Carafa's papers, in any document in the *banca dati*, in all of the recent convent documents not yet cataloged. She is sure, *sure*, that *Il Toro* is also a critical piece of this puzzle.

Charlotte's spent hours searching the *banca dati*, finding every form of "bull" and "thief" in every document and manuscript and letter in the collection, to pass on to Dante for reading. No luck. She's spent hours looking through a magnifier at ancient, delicate parchment. This is like being an archaeologist at a dig site, knowing that bones had been found there once but having no idea if there are others. Sifting through dirt with the hope that you might find a fragment of bone.

Il Toro, Il Ladro. Her head is beginning to ache, the throb of a frustration migraine. Each document is a story of some sort, one she can't even read, even if she did know the language. But she might spot those two words, that large swoop of a *T* or an *L. Il Toro, Il Ladro, Il Toro, Il Ladro.* Two mysterious, nameless men. One who is likely the horrible Antonio Tasso, if only they could prove it.

Her eyes scroll and blur. She blinks them clear. *Il Toro, Il Ladro. Il Toro, Il Ladro . . .*

Il Ladro? No. Wait.

Is it?

In front of her—a letter from the flood. Loops squashed between other loops, but it's an *L*, and there's an *O*. She's pretty sure, anyway. And when she looks at the manuscript as a whole, she becomes more sure. It's almost impossible to identify anything by the handwriting, but there's something about the beauty of these particular loops and swirls. Her heart begins to thud with possibility. There's no signature. There are no names. But the letter begins with an endearment, as the others did. *Cara Mio*.

"Dante," she says.

"Hmm?"

"Dr. Ricci!" she shouts.

It's the tiniest fragment—a piece of a jawbone, the smallest curved bit of a skull. *Il Ladro* again. The Thief is back.

"Let me see, let me see," Dr. Ricci says. "Move, please." She's impatient and greedy. You can tell she really wants to be alone with this letter. To pore over it and study it without the inconvenience of their presence. "I'm sure it's her. Another letter from Isabella. Can you go get us some coffee? *Andiamo*."

Now that Charlotte has dug and sifted, she's the errand girl, but she doesn't really mind. The faster it's translated, the more quickly she'll find out what happened to Isabella. It's beginning to haunt her, truly haunt her now, what happened to her and the baby. Besides, they *do* need coffee. Dante has dark rings under his eyes, and Charlotte can't stop yawning. It's a miracle she spotted the words at all. She and Dante stayed up late last night. Way too late. He thought to bring a blanket this time, and it was so good to lie there together, his body on hers and under hers and then next to hers, just looking up at cracked volumes of vellum.

"I'll be quick," she says.

Chapter Forty-One

Irene di Spilimbergo, painter.

While not a writer herself, after her death in Venice at age nineteen, she became the subject of nearly four hundred poems from esteemed poets, including Torquato Tasso, Girolamo Muzio, and Stefano Guazzo, among many others. For them, she was the equivalent of Laura to Petrarch—ever innocent, feminine, their idea of perfection, her true self essentially unknown.

(1540–1559)

There's only one place to go nearby: Zaini. Coffee in Venice isn't taken outside in paper cups; coffee is sipped at leisure in little glass ones. Enjoyed, lingered over. But Zaini has the paper cups with plastic lids. Amazing pastries, too. Dr. Ricci had shoved a lump of money at Charlotte, and whenever she does this, Charlotte knows Dr. Ricci wants something sweet and beautiful along with her coffee.

Charlotte is staring into the glass case at all the little possibilities—desserts that look like tiny hats, and miniature wedding cakes. She thinks she'll get those lovely elegant domes, with—

She feels his presence before she sees him. It's that energy that comes off him in waves. She looks over, and—there he is. Luca Bruni. She's shocked. Stunned. She made him disappear, but of course, he was never gone. Oh, God, he's been there the whole time.

He looks . . . well, he looks like himself. Tall, with that geeky awkwardness that makes him so endearing, and his hair all a curly mess. Handsome-but-not; confident, definitely. Her stomach flips. She feels a rush of memories, and, weird, because the good memories come first, before the bad ones. She wants to cry. She wants to hug him, or maybe smack him. She wants him to tell her everything—the whole rest of his story, what's happened since, and she hopes he doesn't say a single word to her. Back at home, she had imagined some great big confrontation where she put him in his place forever, but that's not what happens. No, what happens is a flood of feeling—longing, horror, disgust, sorrow, and the worst thing is, he is still more powerful, and larger, and older, so she just stands there, mouth gaping.

He sees her now too. His eyes widen in surprise. But she gets one of her wishes. He doesn't say a word. He doesn't speak to her at all. He just gives her a little two-fingered salute that seems maybe sarcastic, maybe dismissive, maybe the least sort of acknowledgment you could give a person. And then he orders. Six of the beautiful domes she admired. Every single one left in the case. He takes all of them, neatly tied up in a box, and then he leaves.

They were the ones she wanted, so now she has to order something else. Nothing seems as good, but it's hard to tell just by looking at them. Either way, if she was hungry before, she isn't now.

She feels a creeping embarrassment as she walks back. An uncomfortable unease. The feeling is familiar, actually. It's shame. It doesn't have an exact target; it's in all of her. She needs one of those paper ponchos to cover herself, like when she visited the church with her shoulders exposed. His power made her feel ashamed, the way she just stood there, silent, in front of it. She feels like she let all of them down. Avni, Katerina, Shaye, herself.

The humiliation fades when she carries the coffee back into the research room, though, because the minute she walks in, Dante urges her over. He motions madly with one arm as she sets the cardboard tray on a far desk and takes off her coat.

"Charlotta! Hurry. Come see." Man, he's cute. She wishes she could climb onto his lap right there, with his eyes all lit up with happiness.

"*Basta!* Shh," Dr. Ricci snaps. It's as if they're looking at something fragile, something that might be broken, even by sound. Dr. Ricci is very possessive of anything Isabella. Careful, too. *Respectful.* But now she hands Charlotte her small black magnifier. And instead of *Il Ladro*, she points to a different word. "Look. Can you read it?"

Charlotte peers through the magnifier. "I'm not sure." There's a *P* maybe. An *S* at the end. The middle—no way.

"Phoebus," Dante whispers.

"Phoebus?" Charlotte looks up. It can't be. "Really?" She looks into the magnifier again. Yes, yes. *Phoebus*, the very same word sitting in that glass case, on the poem that Tasso supposedly sent to his elder cousin.

"Isabella is writing to Laura about The Thief again. But she is *also* calling him Phoebus," Dr. Ricci says.

Charlotte is too struck to speak.

"Charlotte, do you know what this means?" Dr. Ricci stares at her hard. "'In Guerra'—Tasso did not send this poem to his elder cousin Febo di Goldini, like the scholars say. *Isabella* sent that letter in the case to *Tasso*, for his critique, for his praise. This was what she called him—*Phoebus*. A nickname. In mythology, Phoebus was *the god of poetry*."

The god of poetry. It feels like a slap. A slap, because it's Luca Bruni she thinks of now, not Antonio Tasso. And Katerina, and Shaye, and herself, and their whole group. The way they complimented him and kissed his ass. It makes all the sense in the world, because nothing has changed, that much is clear. The god of poetry—wow, that egomaniac Antonio Tasso must have *loved* that.

"But if *she* sent *him* that poem, what about the *T* in the wax?" Because there's still that, his signature in that wax. "How did that get there? It's definitely a *T*." She stares down at it in the case next to them. It's unmistakable, the long center, the cross at the top, the sides filled in with decorative wisps.

"I don't understand it," Dr. Ricci says. "And this *Phoebus*, it is *still* not enough, not with his *T* there. That *T*, ugh! Telling everyone, 'Tasso, Tasso!' But we are getting closer to her."

"Her handwriting looks different in this one too," Charlotte notices as she looks at the letter in the case. "From the letters we just found, I mean."

"All of you is different before and after heartbreak. All of you is different before and after betrayal," Dr. Ricci says.

It's too wet to even go out. Dante cooks dinner at home. It's a simple meal—gnocchi, bread, wine. Warmth and carbs, as the rain pours down. Maria keeps looking out the window. "I hope the rain doesn't ruin the Festa della Madonna," she says, and then says again.

The Festa della Madonna—another festival to celebrate the end of another plague, this time the one in 1630, but it's a much more personal and heartfelt tradition, Dante tells her, than the Redeemer Festival. It's not a big party like before. This one is both joyful and solemn. The doge prayed to the Virgin Mary for help, promising he'd build a church in her honor if she intervened, and almost immediately the deaths reduced, and a year later stopped completely. Way to go, Mary! Every year since, the Venetians travel across another temporary bridge set up from one side of the Grand Canal to the other, where the Church of the Madonna della Salute stands. The festa is in two days.

"What she really means is that she's worried about the shop now that the *acqua alta* is coming," Dante whispers in the kitchen. "She is too superstitious to say it." Superstition is big here, Charlotte knows now—the number seventeen is unlucky, and if you spill olive oil, that's unlucky, and feathers in a house are unlucky, and so is a hat on a bed. And don't even get anyone started on the evil eye. "Last year, it was code orange. Very high level. One and a quarter meters. Other years, the rain stops."

"When will it happen?"

Dante shrugs. "Certain events collide. High tide, and then low pressures, and our wind friend sirocco, and our other friend the moon. And then the water rises and floods the city."

"It sounds so scary."

"Big puddles, they are not scary. Glistening streets, no. But with serious *acqua alta*, one-point-eight meters, code red, ninety-nine percent of the city is underwater." He makes his eyes large. "Not good for books."

"Books, or *people*." God, no wonder Maria is nervous. Charlotte feels the wing flap of anxiety too. "Is there any warning? Or does it just whoosh in?"

"Sometimes we know, four or five days before. Sometimes it changes quickly. By the hour. But there are different sirens. In an emergency. One long sound at one-point-one meters. At one-point-two, it is one long sound and then rises to another.

One-point-three, it rises again, higher sound. Beep, beep, BEEP. Four crescendos, that's the highest."

"I hope the rains don't ruin the festa," Maria says again from the other room.

"Let's pour the Cynar," he says. This time, it's Maria who needs it. Charlotte, too, now, after this information.

When the warming liquid calms her, Maria stops looking out the window. Dante tells his mom about finding the word *Phoebus* in the new letter. *The god of poetry.* How they still need more proof that Isabella wrote the poem. Something definite, since Tasso's signature is stamped right on it. How Dr. Ricci is like a possessed woman.

And then Charlotte tells them. It's like a confession: "I saw him today. Luca Bruni. In the coffee shop."

"You didn't say before!" Dante says.

She makes a face. "I was . . . I don't know. Embarrassed."

"Stronzo! Bastardo! Pezzo di merda!" Maria spits. When they get angry or upset or impatient, the Italian flies, and Charlotte can't keep up. But she knows what these words mean. *Asshole, bastard, piece of shit.* "I just heard this, too, that he was maybe still here after Art Night at Libreria Toletta. Art Night, where you can hear a lecture or meet an artist?" Charlotte nods. "I heard from Camilla, who knows Donna Gia, who is Anete's sister. Anete, married to Aldo?"

"We never met Aldo's wife," Charlotte says. "Only his son."

"He also has a daughter, Marisa. Luca Bruni was always *provarci con lei*. How do you say it?"

"Hitting on her," Dante says as he brings out a plate of almond cookies and sets them on the coffee table.

"No wonder Aldo seems to hate him."

"Camilla says there is trouble with the seawall. That's why he has maybe stayed. They are too late to fix it."

"What do you mean, too late?" Charlotte asks.

"Nothing has been done, and nothing has been done, and now, the rains—La Calamita could flood." Maria makes a scoffing sound in her throat. "Bruni, *baciami il culo*!" Okay, Charlotte can translate this one: *Bruni, kiss my ass*. "*I* don't invite him to the *Art Night*. *I* don't fill my window with his books."

"In America, lots of people say that's censorship. They say things like, if we got rid of any male artists who behaved badly, we wouldn't have anyone left. We wouldn't have Picasso. We wouldn't have Hemingway," Charlotte says.

"Picasso can't go to the Art Night, can he?" Maria reaches for a cookie, sets it on a napkin. "The dead ones, they don't get the fancy invitation in the mail, we don't hand them money, we don't sit in the audience clapping, while they strut on a stage, like . . . *cascamorti*." Maria applauds, looks upward at an imaginary stage, and pretends to swoon dramatically.

Dante snorts.

"If someone wants a copy of Luca Bruni, they can go to the library," Maria says. "They can go to *Libreria Toletta*. We all make our own choices about this. For me? No. We must stop the myth of the virtuoso genius, the big important man with the *grosso cazzo*." She pretends to swagger while holding a large, swaying penis.

"Mamma!" Dante says. But he loves it. His eyes are all mischievous in agreement.

"Here, it is *always* about the big important man. Writers, artists. The Petrarchs and Tassos and Vivaldis and Michelangelos and Caravaggios. Always, since the beginning of time, and it is still the same. *Still!* But tell me," she says, boring her eyes into Charlotte's, just like Dr. Ricci, passionate and insistent. "Tell me. *Why* is Picasso Picasso? *Why* is Hemingway Hemingway? Vivaldi Vivaldi? They had great talent, but Marie Vorobieff, she had great talent. Suzanne Valadon had great talent. Nella Larsen had great talent. Frances Burney. Settimia Caccini."

"I don't know them," Charlotte says.

"Exactly! You see? And what about your own influences, Charlotte? Who has inspired *you*?"

When Maria looks at her like that, Charlotte feels skewered. And guilty. Bad, because, yeah. She's thinking of the books she read and loved in Ms. Perlman's and Mr. McNulty's classes, AP Lit and creative writing, her favorite classes. *The Great Gatsby*, *Of Mice and Men*, *Romeo and Juliet*, *The Scarlett Letter*, *Fahrenheit 451*, *A Mile of Faces*. She loved all of those books. Her top three favorite authors are there.

"You're right," Charlotte says. "I mean, I'm here because *he* inspired me. Luca Bruni."

"Since you are this tall, they teach you that in school." Maria levels her hand toward the ground. "*He* is the one to admire.

He has talent, she has talent, there is lots of talent! But who gets to be the genius? Who is *brilliant*? *He* is brilliant. You cannot shine if you are put behind walls, can you? You cannot shine if you are forgotten. Our own history has been left in the darkness, and how can there be a true history when half of it is missing? The light shines on *him* as genius, the light has shined on *he* and *him* for centuries, on the great man with the power that we give him. *Why?* Why, and what happens when we do—ah! Those are the real issues."

"I know what happens when we do. You get Luca Bruni. You get Antonio Tasso," Dante says, and wipes cookie crumbs from his shirt.

"Well, the light shines so, so bright on him that he feels he can do no wrong! All of that praise and attention and study of his great works—he thinks he is the *source* of the light. He's a god in his own mind, a lawless god. But it is one great lie. We chose him, we *made* him, as we have for centuries. All these arguments, about how we cannot do without his great art—it is still us choosing him. Light should be spread around. A great light focused in one place . . . It can cause a fire."

Chapter Forty-Two

Bianca Angaran Nievo, Venetian poet.

She wrote in a regional dialect known to be comic and sometimes vulgar. She was accused of heresy in the 1560s, and again in 1570, when she was confined to a convent. On orders of the inquisition, she was executed the following year.

(1531–1588)

It has been raining so hard that Charlotte has to borrow a pair of Maria's rubber boots. Water slaps up over their toes as she and Dante head into the library. Everyone in the city walks with their shoulders hunched and their heads down. There's a slew of umbrellas, which suddenly whip inside out during a gust of wind. Little old ladies wear clear plastic hats knotted under their chins. A few unlucky tourists wear plastic bags tied around their ankles in makeshift galoshes. The boats continue to chug along.

"And I thought it rained a lot in Seattle," Charlotte says.

"I am anticipating the siren at any time." Dante's not the only one. You can feel the edginess in the air.

But it's not only rain that spills down on this gray day. When they reach Conservation and Restoration, they find something awful. Shocking. Dr. Ricci is sitting at her desk with tears streaming down her face. She doesn't bother to hide them.

"Dottoressa!" Dante says.

"Are you all right?" Charlotte's heart clutches. She has no idea what might be wrong—her child, maybe. A sick relative, a bad diagnosis. It's funny—they've spent hours together in these rooms, poring over letters of intimate correspondence, yet she knows very little about Dr. Ricci's own life. Dante mentioned a maybe-husband, and a maybe-brother, but that's all. Today, her desk is a mess, as well—books and papers, and more letters, and this is alarming. She's so orderly and careful.

"Il Toro," Dr. Ricci says. She can hardly speak.

"Il Toro?" It wasn't what Charlotte was expecting, not at all. But now she feels dread.

"I found him! The Bull. The Bull, Charlotte. He was *the doge*. Tasso was the thief, but *The Bull*—he was Isabella's own *grandfather. He* sent her to prison. Her father, too. Nicolo Zorzi Angelo *and* Matteo Angelo. It's here. Right here!" She swoops her hand over her desk. "She might be killed. For the shame her affair brought them. For her pregnancy. For her outspoken words in that book. *They* put her there."

Oh, God. Charlotte's chest fills with horror and grief. Her own eyes fill with tears.

"She is talking again of the *pignus*. The promise. A vow Laura has made to her. Something again about being risen up above the men who wronged her, the doge in particular. On a marriage chest? Or a box of some kind. Like a monument to her sufferings. A promise of immortality. But Isabella—she is *presso il fine amaro*, at the bitter end."

Dr. Ricci presses her palms to her eyes.

"Dottoressa," Dante says quietly.

Charlotte can't speak. Tears slip down her cheeks. It's awful. It's so awful. Isabella's own grandfather. Her own father.

When Dr. Ricci lifts her face again, she looks devastated. "Isabella is writing about *naturalis*. A child born when the mother is not married. She is asking if Laura will protect the baby. She refers again to her ring. Her only remaining possession. She wants the ring to be Laura's. The letter is . . . a *testamento*."

"A will?" Charlotte whispers.

Dr. Ricci nods. "Charlotte. Charlotte! Isabella was only twenty years old."

There are still more documents to search. All the convent papers from the flood—there may be more about those men, *Il Toro* or *Il Ladro*. But something else feels more urgent to all of them right now, more important even than proving Tasso had stolen that famous poem from her. They want to know what happened to Isabella at the end.

Dr. Ricci is desperate. So they're searching through the *banca dati* again. Charlotte squints at images of the *necrologi*, the death registers of Venice during that time. These are long, thin volumes, and from 1537 to 1578, there aren't many that have survived. Dr. Ricci has narrowed down the ones to hunt through. It's nearly impossible to read them, and it may be a hopeless task. Women and children are sometimes not even identified by name at all, only by flat, impersonal words, *widow* or *child*, and by the profession of their father. Next to that—the reasons for death, and where they were buried. There are small drawings in the margins too, so the record keepers could find things easier—little daggers to indicate stabbings, pistols for shootings, crosses to indicate a religious occupation.

But there is no *Isabella* written next to a cross. No answers at all, not yet.

"Laura Carafa—she was influential. A powerful sister through her work with the art commissions. This promise, it is possible that Isabella's likeness has been placed in an artwork," Dr. Ricci says. She looks up from the *necrologi*, rubs her forehead as if to make the answer appear. "Isabella keeps talking about the ring, the ring, the ring. Her signet ring? She was from an influential family. She would have had one. This is what I am guessing. A signet ring is normally destroyed after a person's death, though, so it is hard to understand why she would give it to Sister Laura. And do you know, if they killed her, her father, her grandfather—a crime like that would have barely been noticed. If only I could understand the ring. Ah, *magari*. I don't know what happened to her," Dr. Ricci says. "I wish I could save her."

• • •

Charlotte wishes she could save her too. Or at least, redeem her.

Twenty years old.

Charlotte and Dante are somber when they walk home. It's hard to want to stop and kiss and be happy. By the time Isabella was Charlotte's age, she would have been locked behind convent walls for years already. She would have published her first book of poetry when she was only eighteen. Tasso, already famous himself, would have snuck into the convent like Casanova, arriving by gondola maybe, to the back door. There would be no long nights under a blanket with books all around, walking down the streets of Venice holding hands, stopping to kiss while jammed up against alley walls. Maybe Tasso was there to teach her, his young student, same as Vivaldi. Same as Luca Bruni. Maybe she was awed by his talent. *God of poetry.* Maybe she thought it meant something. *She* meant something. And when she learned she didn't, she went on. She published her second book of poetry after that, bold, outspoken, after he betrayed her. Somehow, she did.

And now, Charlotte remembers that day in Luca's village, when he told them how he escaped that place. *Remembering, every fucking day, who came before me. Learning from them, honoring them.*

Well, *this* is who she'll remember every fucking day. *This* is who she'll learn from and honor: Isabella, writing behind bars, Arcangela Tarabotti, Veronica Franco, all of them. She will look for more of them, write down their names, so they're not forgotten. They've shown her what she can be. They've shown her how to *persevere*, how to still make art in spite of the odds against it. *That* is what brilliance is to her now.

The water is up to their ankles. They're nearly to the bookstore, to Dante's home above, when a sound erupts. It's so loud and shocking that Charlotte gives a little scream.

It's high-pitched. One long tone, like an air raid siren in those movies about World War II.

"What do we do?" She looks at Dante, and she's been with him so much over the last few days that she's almost forgotten to really *see* him. But there he is, like a surprise. And he's so beloved to her right then. It is an old-fashioned word, but look where they are. He's standing on ancient streets in an ancient city, with water up to his ankles, and an iPhone in his pocket.

"Oh, Charlotta!" He's looking at her the same way, as if she's a sudden surprise. "Look at you, *bella*. Don't be afraid. It is a disaster, but it is the same disaster that it's been for years."

They don't go home. They expect high water, but there's no telling how high. Maria has closed the shop, but there's a glow of lights in the windows of the Alta Acqua Libreria bookstore, named for this very event. Maria, Dante, and Charlotte spend the evening moving books up off the ground, or putting them into plastic tubs or boats, if they aren't there already. There are so many books.

"Which ones especially?" Charlotte asks.

"The ones you have never heard of."

Maria stares at her hard, and Charlotte understands. "The old, rare copies. The women."

"Yes. When those are gone, they'll be gone forever. We have to make certain they're not lost."

They work into the night. They slosh around in their boots from one part of the store to the other. A stray cat has found refuge, sitting on a high stack of books. There's that tense, on-edge feeling again. It's unnerving. Another siren wail might come at any time. Maybe with a crescendo of notes. Two, or three, or even four.

"I hope it doesn't ruin the festa," Maria keeps saying.

Chapter Forty-Three

Barbara Bentivoglio Strozzi Torelli, poet.

Married at sixteen, she and her daughter entered the Corpus Domini convent for protection after her cruel husband imprisoned and threatened her. After her husband's death, she remarried, but her second husband was murdered shortly thereafter, likely by her first husband's family. Her poem about the murder has been called the best sonnet in the Italian language.

(1475–1533)

But it doesn't ruin the festa. By some amazing good luck, the level of flooding stays low enough that the tradition, which has been going on since 1631, goes on once again. In spite of the way it rains and rains, there's a magic trick in the weather. Maybe the Madonna really is where it's at, miracle-wise, because the sky is still gray, but that morning, there's a peek of blue, a pause in the showers.

Well, it's her day anyway. After twelve years of the plague, she, they believe, began to stop the dying within hours. It reminds Charlotte of the framed quote her mother hung in their kitchen at home. *If you want something said, ask a man. If you want something done, ask a woman.*

Maria is bustling around with nerves and excitement. The store won't be open today, and there will be no researching Isabella or anyone else at the Marciana. It is all *happening at the dot*, again. They take the winding route from the store that leads right past San Zaccaria, down to Saint Mark's church, next to the Biblioteca Marciana and the Doge's Palace. And then they walk along the bank of the Grand Canal until they reach the Gritti Palace, once the private home of a doge, now a hotel.

It's getting crowded. There's a throng of people packing together, but they're mostly women, Charlotte notices. Women of all ages—gray-haired and dark, stooped and youthful, mothers and daughters and daughter of daughters.

"Can you see the bridge?" Dante asks.

It's hard to, with all the people there. But in a brief break of the crowd, she can spot the high platform that stretches across the canal to the church of the Madonna della Salute. Maria leans close to Charlotte, though it's not difficult, since they're nearly smushed together. "The raised platform," she says. "Every year it reminds me of the tall sandals the *cortigiane* would wear, to keep their skirts off the wet ground."

"Courtesans?" Dante says. "The prostitutes."

"Tall sandals?" Charlotte has never heard of this.

"Sandals, *chopines*, tall as stilts. This is what they would wear. Up to twenty inches high! So she could be identified, yes? By the men? They were early *zoccoli*, you know. High heels."

"Wow," Charlotte says. She doesn't know if she'll ever look at high heels the same way again.

The crowd moves forward like one body toward the bridge. "She won't see anything like this," Dante says to his mother. "Her first time. We should take a *traghetto*."

"Yes. Good, good."

Maria takes Charlotte's elbow and veers her out of the crowd. They head toward a dock, also crowded but less so, where several oversize gondolas wait. The boats rock and slosh in the water as people step in. Now the gondolier holds out his hand, and in she goes, too. Charlotte loses track of Dante and Maria, but yes, they are behind her. The women, because that's who she mostly sees around her, link arms to steady themselves. An old woman in a black coat slips her arm into the crook of Charlotte's, and the younger woman in a puffy red jacket on her other side does the same.

When the boat is full, the gondoliers, one at the front, one at the back, push the boat away from the dock. Charlotte watches the gondolier nearest to her; he wears the traditional black-and-white shirt, and an untraditional baseball cap, and he digs his long, long oar into the water again and again as they bob and sluice through the waves, their arms still linked to keep their balance. And she can see that bridge. The bridge is filled with women, women clutching purses and holding candles, mothers grasping the hands of small children, old ladies in furs, women in camel-hair coats and parkas, woolen hats, scarves wrapped around their necks, the platform shifting and swaying as they make their way from one side to the other. And in that boat, with the old woman in the black coat on one side, and the young woman in the puffy jacket on the other, Charlotte is making that crossing too, and her throat gets tight with tears, because this has been happening for centuries, this crossing. Throughout every kind of weather, no matter how deep the water, they have done this. Her arms are looped with the arms of two women whose stories she doesn't know, though she's sure they have them. She can see it in the way that the old woman stares at the waves with fixed certainty, and the way that the younger woman looks at the waves with questions in her eyes.

The high, many-sided, white jewel box of the Church of the Madonna della Salute gets closer and closer. It has a white dome, and on that dome, there's a tiny figure. At least, it looks tiny from there. The gondola slides into the pier, and they step out, and the women who were linked with Charlotte ever so briefly are gone, vanished in the crowd. Outside the church, the steps are filled with people. A man covered in a long black cloak, wearing a white mask with the long, curved nose of a bird, and a wide-brimmed black hat, waves incense at the crowd.

"The plague doctor," Dante says.

"So creepy," Charlotte says.

"They stuffed the beak with herbs back then, so he wouldn't catch it."

That man in the bird mask is eerie, but set against that eeriness are the stalls all around the church, selling food and candles. Maria hands over some money, and now Charlotte is holding a long white candle, and so is Dante, because, of course, while there are mostly women everywhere, there are men, too. Good ones, with sweet eyes like Dante's, and old eyes like Aldo's. Eyes that remember to see others and to give respect.

When they reach the steps, Charlotte looks up. The tiny figure up on the dome is a Madonna. Her head is slightly tilted down, and she has a serene expression. One bronze hand is out, and the other is holding something, maybe a scroll, or a scepter, it's hard to tell. Her head is ringed with stars. Wouldn't it be incredible if *this* was Isabella? The statue up high she talked about in her letters? Made in her likeness? Well, it isn't possible. This is a statue from a hundred years later, and even Laura Carafa would've been gone by then. Charlotte likes the thought, though.

The crowd pushes inside, carrying their candles. They move to the altar, where there's a large rectangular table with holders to set them in, and it's glowing, brilliant. There are long, new candles just set in place, and short ones that have been burning for a long while, wax dripping, so many candles. They edge until they get close enough to light theirs. A woman next to Maria lights Maria's with her own, flame to wick, until two flames touch. It's quiet, aside from the rustling of coats and children's voices. In spite of the number of people, Charlotte's chest fills with emotion. The moment is solemn, and heartfelt.

The women all around her briefly close their eyes. *Thank you,* Charlotte says to Isabella, as she lights her candle. *Thank you.*

Candles go out, more are lit. It doesn't matter how long yours lasted, or how large or bright it was; what mattered is that it was there. The candles are a bank of light. Lit, gone, lit again. Charlotte looks up at the inside of the dome. A balcony with curved windows circles it, but the top of it is plain. It's not like the dome at San Zaccaria, where beautiful winged angels fly in the clouds.

Maria tugs Charlotte's sleeve. They walk out like children on a field trip, Maria holding Charlotte's arm, Charlotte holding Dante's hand, edging their way outside again. And outside, the mood changes. Celebration. Food. Little toys for the children, bought at the stalls. Of course, they eat. Candied fruit and chestnuts and fried pastries. And then, this time, they walk the length of the bridge back again.

Charlotte feels different. If she were to write it—well, she wouldn't have words. It's just a change in the weather, a certain wind, the sirocco, the tide, the moon, creating an alliance. But something feels finished. Something feels new.

On the other side of the bridge, the rain starts again. Starts—no. It's a deluge. She feels sorry for the people still outside the church, who are likely running and screeching, old ladies in fur coats taking cover under any possible roof, children tilting their chins up, because it's also magical. There's a real alliance now, the sirocco, the moon, the tide. The rising water.

Chapter Forty-Four

Veronica Franco, Venetian poet and writer.

Married off at age fifteen and separated shortly after, she became a courtesan at nineteen to provide for her family. Her first book of poetry, which was published in 1575, challenged male poets like Petrarch, who praised the silent, unattainable woman. It was also openly sexual, and, in it, she defended herself against humiliating poems written about her by poet Maffio Venier, defending, too, all women who were verbally or physically attacked by men. She was brought to trial at the inquisition by men who despised her for her actions. Although she was freed, her reputation never recovered, and she died, impoverished, at forty-five.

(1546–1591)

Everything is closed because of the holiday. Now it is so cold and damp out, they tuck themselves inside. Maria makes *castradina*, a special soup made of cabbage and mutton and rosemary, eaten during the week of the festival. If Charlotte were at home in Seattle, this is the sort of night they'd make a fire in the fireplace. But Venice has always feared fires. The buildings are made of wood and sit very close together.

The glassblowers were even moved to Murano to keep the city safe, she recalls. The Doge's Palace was destroyed by fire four hundred years ago, Charlotte once read. And nearly four hundred years before that, four hundred years before Isabella was there herself, the monastery at San Zaccaria burned, destroying the original church and killing a hundred nuns who had taken refuge in the cellar. While each glowing candle was a gift, fire had always been dangerous to them. More than any rising water.

Maria eyes the rain, rain, rain.

"Is there anything we can do?" Charlotte asks. Maybe they should go back to the store, make sure that everything that could be saved is saved.

"We've done what we can. It's not always up to us," she says. "We will survive, *tocca ferro*."

"Touch iron," Dante says.

It's the most terrifying sound she's ever heard. That same sound as the night before, but worse. One long, piercing tone. And then a rising tone. Another rising tone. Another rising tone. Another rising tone. Four crescendos. She remembers what it means. At least one-point-four meters of water. Four and a half feet.

Charlotte sits up in the curved nook surrounded by books. She looks at her phone. Four thirty a.m. She hears footsteps coming down the crooked, tilted hall. Dante, dressed like a grandpa in his old T-shirt and boxers, but somehow adorably sexy, if anything like that was on her mind. It isn't. She's terrified.

He whispers. "There is nothing to do, *cara*. You're safe. We're here up high in a building that has lasted. There is nothing to do," he says again. "Go back to sleep." He kisses her forehead and tiptoes back down the hall.

That siren—it didn't sound safe, but Dante has been through this many times before. She edges back under the covers. Her mind swirls with images and anxiety. Women with linked arms, the feel of the black coat and the puffy jacket. Women with full stories of their own, instead of a single sentence in relation to a man. Women, not bodies used for sex, or married off, or locked away.

The candles, the bridge, the wax. *What haunts you?* It's like those moments your mind is trying to work out a problem, when even the problem itself is unclear. Like something is lost. Like something is nearby, but lost.

She can't go back to sleep. She tosses, turns, flips her pillow to one side and back again. The candles, the wax. The Madonna high up on the dome. She kicks off the covers, lies there awhile, covers herself back up again. A promise, a vow. High up, but on a box of some kind. The dome. Inside the dome. A plain dome, a decorated dome. A dome decorated with—

Angels.

Beautiful angels, with outstretched wings.

Wings, like a *T*.

Like a T.

But not a *T.* Not a *T* in red wax at all.

An angel with outstretched wings. Little curved wisps.

How had they not seen it before? How, how?

They only saw the *T*! They only saw Tasso, him, he, when Isabella di Angelo, *of angels*, was there all along. There, with her voice, saying, *I was here. I was the one. Me, me, me.*

Isabella's ring. It was *her* ring pressed into that red wax on that poem she gave him. It was her signature.

The Madonna on a box, one that resembles a *cassa*, the box that held a girl's dowry before marriage . . .

A caisson. A large watertight chamber.

A chamber.

A crypt.

For eternity. My very self concealed. Charlotte is pulling on clothes. She's pulling on boots. If what she thinks is there is truly there—it will be proof. It will be proof without a doubt. Proof that it is Isabella's signature on that poem, proof that Laura Carafa fulfilled her promise. *Sometimes they put themselves in the art. Their rings, their signatures. To say, You will see me, yes? Even though you have locked me away, I am here.* She's scared to go out there, in that rising water, but not scared enough. No. She is brave to go out there in that water. Brave enough.

What fills her—the same passion that flames in Dr. Ricci's eyes, and in Maria's eyes, but it's also the fixed certainty she saw on the face of the old woman with the black coat, and the questions on the face of the young woman in the puffy jacket. It's Avni's fierceness, and Katerina's survival, and Shaye's raging talent. She feels all of that. She feels all of them.

She makes her way downstairs. Turns the doorknob as quietly as possible. Outside, on their street, the water is up to her shins. The sky is filled with the pink tint of morning.

She wades. She is hurrying, but it is difficult, with this force of water against her legs. She doesn't have to go far, though. San Zaccaria is only a few streets away. She crosses the bridge at Calle de Mezzo, and the water in the canal is high and dark, but tinged with pink light. Now she crosses another bridge, the Ponte del Diavolo. The walls of the old convent are up ahead, and beyond that, San Zaccaria. She sees its beautiful white face in the morning light. She wades toward it.

She hasn't thought this through. The church will be closed, for sure. She walks up the steps. She pulls on the handle. It isn't closed. It's open, unbelievably and miraculously open.

There's no one inside. It's dry in there, at least so far. There's that smell again, melted wax and ancient prayers. And the plain door, marked with the words *Please close door behind you.*

Her heart is beating hard. It's creepy as she descends. There's only one dim yellow light in the curved stone stairwell. She has a moment where she feels outside of her own body. A girl walking down to a crypt. A girl who is sure that someone waits for her there.

The bottom three steps have also filled with water now. It's so deep down there. It's up to her knees. The ancient tombs of the doges set into the brick walls are so, so silent.

Everything has a dim yellow glow, golden, and the pillars reflect in the water. Under the brick arcs of the crypt, the box sitting in its very center reflects in the water too, and so does that statue on that box. That statue of the Madonna, set high.

The water sloshes as she wades through it. It's cold and deep, but not so cold and not so deep that Charlotte can't reach her. The Madonna looks upward. One hand reaches out. The other hand is tucked beneath layers of stone skirts. And even though she wears a look of gentle suffering, she is the only visible figure there, the only figure still standing. She has outlasted the others in that room, the doges, the powerful men, now only ash.

Charlotte's pants are drenched. Her sleeves are soaked. The water splashes upward, dirty and old. She doesn't notice any of that. It doesn't matter. The water presses against her legs and she presses back, and when she reaches the box—the one that resembles a dowry *cassa*, everything of value to a girl, but the one that is a caisson, too, a watertight tomb—she climbs onto its bottom edge. It's not quite a prayer to the Madonna, but Charlotte says it, "Please, please, please." Her voice echoes in that eerie place. If she looked down, she would see that *she* is also reflected in that pool, but she doesn't look down. She reaches. She feels for that stone hand underneath the skirts, and she touches the cold stone fingers, and even though she can't see what's there, she can feel it. It's unmistakable. There's a stone ring, crafted in the likeness of the original, and on that ring, she can make out the edges of what seems like a *T.*

But it's not a *T.*

Not at all. Her fingers make their way along the straight backbone.

And then her fingers edge along the outstretched wings of an angel.

Chapter Forty-Five

Isabella di Morra, poet.

Born in a noble family, she was unknown in her lifetime. She was gifted in poetry and literature, but her brothers forced young Isabella to live in severe isolation and virtual imprisonment in a castle by the sea, perhaps because they were jealous of her talent. While there, she dedicated herself to her poetry, her only solace. After beginning a secret correspondence and then an affair with the married poet Diego Sandoval de Castro, her brothers murdered Diego, the tutor who carried the letters, and then Isabella herself, who was only twenty-five. Her work is considered to be among the most powerful and original poetic expressions of Italian literature from the sixteenth century, a forerunner to all romantic poetry.

(1520–1545)

So many things happen after this. First, the moment where Charlotte begins to sob there in the drowned crypt, at Isabella's feet. There are those seconds when her *Please, please, please* turns into a *Thank you.*

And then there's the flight back up those steps, her pants

heavy with the weight of water, so heavy she can barely lift her legs as she drips puddles onto every step, as she makes her way back outside again, wading back home, trying to run, breathless, in that surreal and magical, flooded and ancient place.

There's her return home, her home here, anyway, where Dante is awake because he felt her absence. He's been trying to call, but her phone only rings and rings in the alcove of books, where she's left it behind. He's worried sick. Maria is worried sick.

And then there's the trip the three of them make. Back to San Zaccaria, but when they get there this time, someone has arrived. They've closed the church. Maria speaks forcefully to the man by the door. There are many insistent hand gestures, and raised voices, but then he finally lets them in.

Maria opens the unremarkable door off to the right, and Dante rushes through the cold spiral, ignoring Charlotte's cries to be careful going down the wet stairs. He wades to the statue, with Charlotte beside him. When he reaches up and feels Isabella's hand, he cries out, and tears roll down his face.

Charlotte takes a moment to notice it—the way the pillars shimmer in the water. And the stone caisson, and the weeping boy, and the girl reaching out to him. The couple embracing in the knee-high water. She takes it in, deeply, deeply enough that one day, she'll know just how to write it.

And of course, more stuff happens. Because they must all come again, with Dr. Ricci and Fabio Mendizzi, the head of the Ministry of Culture, so that there will be no more arguing with the guards at San Zaccaria. Venice is so flooded that people are staying inside. She sees a man riding down a canal in a kayak. Maria has lost hundreds of books written by long-dead men. No rubber boots are tall enough for this. There's destruction, but not fire. The last time it flooded like this, a bunch of drowned letters and papers surfaced, truth and stories, from the old convent of San Zaccaria.

And of course, still more stuff will happen. Later. Charlotte will call Avni and Katerina, Yas and Carly, and tell them about Tasso and Isabella, and a tenacious redemption spanning five hundred years. Dr. Ricci will head back to her office, to research and study and eventually write the book that will tell the world about Isabella's "In Guerra," and about her secret triumph, hidden in a statue, commissioned by her beloved friend Sister Laura Carafa.

Right then, right at that moment, though, there is much that Charlotte does not yet know—like how Isabella died, in prison, or during the plague, or killed by her own father or grandfather. The only thing that's certain is that she did not live until age eighty-three, like Antonio Tasso, lauded and remembered forever.

And there are other things that Charlotte does not yet know, like whether she will stay there with Dante for a while, or return home, or never return home. She doesn't have those answers, and any story that ends with answers is a lie anyway. She only has pieces—bits of red thread and wax, lines and paragraphs of the story so far. Love, his skin on hers, sweet eyes, an unlikely connection, necessary reminders of goodness, that's what she's sure of.

This is what's happening right now, though, this late afternoon after finding Isabella. Charlotte has walked to the dock near Saint Mark's, the spot where she would always wait for Aldo and his boat. *Walked* is not the right word. *Waded* is still the right word. The water is high. The Venetians are going about their lives, regardless. She feels like a Venetian. She is one, going back and back and back. She has to talk to her mother and sister, to tell them the story of where they came from. She wants to do it alone. So she wades to the pier, and she climbs on top of a box near the dock, so she's up out of the water. Her cheeks are rosy from the cold, and her dark ponytail falls over one shoulder. She calls Adele and Ella, and they talk for a long time, until her mother worries if this is costing too much.

Honestly, it has all cost too much—the young women behind convent walls, the forgotten ones, the shamed ones, from five hundred years ago and now.

After Charlotte says goodbye, she stays up there where's its dry. She looks across the lagoon, to the other side. She sees La Calamita, that island of half ash. A few hours ago, they heard the news about the seawall there, about the fracture and a break, how the flooding was like nothing the island had ever seen before. Skulls are rising, junk is stuck in muck, the ash is wet and thick as cement. The damage is impossible to measure yet, after this *acqua alta*, the worst since 1966. Charlotte doesn't feel glad about this. She's not filled with some revenge-thrill of glee. She's not filled with sharp grief, or pangs of love, either. There's only the sludge and sediment and mud of sadness, similar to what will settle over La Calamita and even over the island of Venice, too, once the water is gone. The mess that will have to be cleaned up.

That's when she realizes it. She is standing on a box. You know, so she doesn't stand right in the water when she talks. It is not a tomb or a wedding chest. It's just a box of life preservers, out by the dock. A beat-up old box filled with the kind of orange vests you pop over your head so you don't drown.

Her hands are freezing. They are not the hands of a young woman who held a pen, who wrapped letters in floss, who pressed her ring, her signature, into warm wax. Hers are today hands, belonging to a young woman who sometimes paints her fingernails all different colors, who scrolls to see the stuff on her phone, who holds a cardboard cup of coffee, but who *also* holds a pen. Now she stuffs her hands into her coat pockets, just like the statue of Isabella di Angelo, with her hands under her robes.

Do you see? It is all happening at the dot. Mirror images, reflections in a pool. The statue in the crypt of San Zaccaria, the statue of Isabella of angels, looking heavenward, and her long-into-the-future descendant standing on the box of life preservers. She looks heavenward, too. Or at least, she looks up into the sky. She realizes that it doesn't really look like those skies that are painted on the domes in the churches. There are no puffy white clouds and perfect blue hues. This one is murkier, with many shades of gray, much less clear. If she were to write it, *when* she writes it, this is how she'll describe it. No gods, no angels.

What she'd really like to see, though, is what's beyond that island. But she can't see past it. Even on her toes, she can't. She's trying. Her chin is stuck out, and it's pretty precarious, the way she wobbles there. A gondolier passes, but so does a speedboat. The ancient buildings tilt and sway. But look, *look*. She is doing the thing that Veronica Franco and Isabella and Laura Carafa and Avni and Shaye and Kat and so many others have done for years and years—trying to glimpse a far-off place she can't yet see, keeping herself above water, in a world that has changed, but not enough.

Acknowledgments

Biggest thanks, as always, to my invaluable, treasured agent and friend, Michael Bourret, and to my fierce, passionate editor, Liesa Abrams, who brought this book into existence with her full, shining heart. Huge appreciation, as well, to Reka Simonsen, my kind and thoughtful editor who carefully brought it over the finish line. A shoutout of love and deep, deep gratitude also goes to all the members of my former Simon Pulse team, most especially Mara Anastas: forever family. And enormous thanks, too, to both my new team at Atheneum, and to all those at S&S who continue to give their talent and energy and generosity to my books: Jon Anderson, Justin Chanda, Anna Jarzab, Caitlin Sweeney, Cassie Malmo, Beth Parker, Michelle Leo and the whole fantastic education and library team, Jeannie Ng, Rebecca Vitkus, Sara Berko, Laura Eckes, Alissa Nigro, Elizabeth Mims, Christina Pecorale, Christine Foye, Emily Hutton, Victor Iannone, and Leah Hays.

And to my dear family: you, you, you. Boundless love and daily gratitude to my extended family, and to my life's joy: Sam and Nick and Erin and Pat and Myla and Charlie. And to my husband, John, one word: *Beloveds.*